I've travelled the world twice over,
Met the famous: saints and sinners,
Poets and artists, kings and queens,
Old stars and hopeful beginners,
I've been where no-one's been before,
Learned secrets from writers and cooks
All with one library ticket
To the wonderful world of books.

© Janice James.

The wisdom of the ages
Is there for you and me,
The wisdom of the ages,
In your local library

There's large print books
And talking books,
For those who cannot see,
The wisdom of the ages,
It's fantastic, and it's free.

Written by Sam Wood, aged 92

THE SHADOW OF THE MARY CELESTE

On November 4, 1872, the sailing ship *Mary Celeste* left New York. Exactly one month later, she was found abandoned — but completely seaworthy — some 600 miles off the west coast of Spain, with no sign of captain or crew. The disappearance is the most celebrated enigma in maritime history, but after years of exhaustive research Richard Rees has unravelled the mystery. Written in 'factional' form through the eyes of detective/journalist Michael Callaghan and his estranged wife Colleen, the book tells of a fascinating web of intrigue and deceit.

RICHARD REES

THE SHADOW OF THE MARY CELESTE

Complete and Unabridged

ULVERSCROFT
Leicester

First published in Great Britain in 1995 by
Robert Hale Limited
London

First Large Print Edition
published 1997
by arrangement with
Robert Hale Limited
London

British Library CIP Data

Rees, Richard, *1935 –*
The shadow of the Mary Celeste.
—Large print ed.—
Ulverscroft large print series: adventure & suspense
1. English fiction—20th century
2. Large type books
I. Title
823.9′14 [F]

ISBN 0–7089–3726–8

Published by
F. A. Thorpe (Publishing) Ltd.
Anstey, Leicestershire

Set by Words & Graphics Ltd.
Anstey, Leicestershire
Printed and bound in Great Britain by
T. J. Press (Padstow) Ltd., Padstow, Cornwall

This book is printed on acid-free paper

To my dear son and daughter,
Huw & Elisabeth
and their equally dear families
Claire, Lowri & Adam
Mark & Georgina

Acknowledgements

For their invaluable research, editorial and structural help and advice without which this book would never have been completed let alone published, I would like to thank: John Bright-Holmes, Alexandra Hine, James Hale, Derrick Langford, Elizabeth Murray. Also, John Hale and Gillian Jackson of Robert Hale, Publishers.

On a personal level, 'thank you' to: Willie and Sheila Waddell, Bill Fedrick, Menna Eveson, Mark Brittain, Jan Tavinor.

Drs Desmond McCabe and Alison Harvey; Mr Nigel Bickerton, and the nurses of Wards 19, Paddington, and Brenig, Glan Clwyd Hospital, Bodelwyddan, North Wales.

My heartfelt gratitude to you all.

The New-York Times.

NEW-YORK, TUESDAY, NOVEMBER 5, 1872.

MARINE INTELLIGENCE.

NEW-YORK......MONDAY, Nov. 4.

Cleared.

Steam-ship: Minnesota, Morgan, Liverpool.
Bark: Odin, (Ger,) Olts, Cork or Falmouth.
Brigs: Osprey, (Br.) Taylor, Buenos Ayres,
Mary Celeste, Briggs, Genoa.

ONE month later, on Wednesday December 4, 1872, some 600 miles off the west coast of Spain, Second Mate John Wright of the brigantine *Dei Gratia*, nineteen days out of New York, spotted an approaching vessel on the grey horizon, about four miles off the port bow.

Training his telescope on the ship, and seeing her tattered sails, he immediately drew her to the attention of his captain, David Reed Morehouse. From the port-rail, and swiftly joined by First Mate Oliver Deveau and the rest of

1

the *Dei Gratia*'s crew, the nine men watched the obviously stricken vessel draw nearer. Her deck, silent and empty, exuded the eerie feeling of a ghost-ship. The name on her bows read *Mary Celeste*. Her unmanned wheel was turning sluggishly and aimlessly from port to starboard, then back to port, as her rudder obeyed only the movement of the sea. For some reason, the forehatch cover was off, lying alongside the foremast, allowing the recent high seas to have poured into her hold. Her foretopsail hung by its four corners. The main stay-sail lay loose across the top of the forrard deck house. Only the lower topsail jib and foretop-staysail were set. The rest were still furled. Her standing rigging looked to be good. But most of her running rigging had been carried away.

Slowly, the unmanned vessel drifted ever closer, until she was no more than a hundred yards away.

Captain Morehouse raised his hailer. "Brig ahoy! Brig ahoy!"

There was no answer from the *Mary Celeste*.

Morehouse tried again. "Brig ahoy! Brig ahoy!"

Still no reply. Just a strange deathly silence, broken only by the creaking of the *Celeste*'s rigging, the dull flapping of her torn sails, and the wind whistling across her empty decks.

Prologue

Jesus asked his disciples: 'Whom say ye that I am?'

Simon Bar-jona replied: 'Thou art the Christ, Son of the living God.'

Then Jesus said unto him: *'Blessed are thou, Simon Bar-jona. From henceforth thou art Peter. Upon this rock I will build my Church. And the gates of Hell shall not prevail against it. And I will give unto thee the keys of the kingdom of Heaven. Whatsoever thou shalt bind on earth, shall be bound in Heaven. And whatsoever thou shalt loose on earth, shall be loosed in Heaven.'*

(Matthew 16: 15 – 19)

Rome, Monday, 8 July 1872

NEARING midday, on Monday, the 8th of July, in the Year of Our Lord, 1872, Pope Pius IX — the two hundred and fifty-fourth inheritor of the covenant made by the Christ to Simon Peter — stood

5

at a first-floor window in the 'Room of the Popes', one of five Tuscan-styled halls in the once magnificent Appartamenti Borgia, looking down on the Piazzo Pontifico, and the Vatican gardens beyond.

Wearing his white cassock, Pius was waiting for a certain man to join him, hence his only reason for forcing his shaky, 86–year-old legs down two flights of stairs from his private rooms, holding on to the walls all the way. Because, only via the Appartamenti — and greatly in need of restoration, thought Pius, gazing around at the frescoed walls and ceilings, painted by da Udine and del Vaga — could this visitor, who was under banishment from Rome, now gain access into the Vatican, despite Pius being Supreme Pontiff of the Church Universal.

The Church Universal! Pius thought bitterly. Throughout the rest of the world, maybe, but no longer in Italy, or even Holy City itself. Not since 20th of September 1870, twenty-one months ago.

It was a day vividly imprinted into

6

Pio Nono's memory: Victor Emmanuel's guns bombarding the Aurelian Gate, creating two breaches on either side of the Porto Pia, then his soldiers pouring through, violating Rome by their presence, leaving him with no alternative but to order his papal forces to lay down their arms and surrender.

The Papal State had been the last to succumb to Victor Emmanuel's ambition to unite all the separate Italian provinces into one kingdom, with himself on the throne. Ever since that evil day, Pius, God's appointed Bishop of Rome, The Vicar of Jesus Christ, Successor to the Prince of Apostles, Supreme Pontiff of the Universal Church, Patriarch of the West, Primate of Italy, Archbishop and Metropolitan of the Province of Rome, Sovereign of the Vatican City, and Servant of the Servants of God, had been forced to suffer the indignity of being held prisoner under house-arrest in the Vatican. And worse was to follow, if his secret informant inside the Italian Assembly was to be believed. For Victor Emmanuel's latest intent was to pass an Act through parliament, which would impose even greater indignity upon both Holy City and Holy Church.

No sooner had Pius learned the details, than he'd decided to end his strategy of silent protest against his treatment at the hands of this evil, atheist usurper. His role as the martyred 'Prisoner in the Vatican' was over. It had failed in its objective to stir up the passions of the Church outside Italy, and inundate Victor Emmanuel with a flood of worldwide governmental protests.

It was time to act. Such action meant only one Order. The Society of Jesus.

The fourth vow sworn by each member of the Society, a vow peculiar only to the Jesuits, was one of special obedience to the pope. But their main instructions came from one man alone. And only one man — their Father-General: Pierre Jean Beckx.

For over twenty years, since being appointed head of the Order, Beckx' great wisdom and spiritual insight had proved invaluable to Pius. This was why he had now sent for him from Fiesole, where, ever since the Society's banishment from Rome, twenty-one months ago, the Father-General had taken refuge in the secluded villa of his Jesuit friend, the Count de Ricasole.

The pope glanced at his delicate gold pocket-watch. It was exactly twelve. After a lifetime of the strictest discipline, it was certain that, despite the personal danger of returning to Rome, not only would the 77–year-old Jesuit-General obey his pontiff's call, but he would also be on time. Pius turned expectantly to the inset panel of winged cherubs, painted by Michelangelo.

He heard the click. The panel slid open, and Pierre Jean Beckx, head of the Society of Jesus, stepped out of the centuries-old, cobwebbed passageway, and into the Borgia Room of the Popes.

He was wearing a dark suit instead of a black cassock. Pio Nono moved to greet him, struck by Beckx' decline of body in the two years since they'd last met.

With obvious stiffening of bones, the Jesuit Father-General slowly lowered his frail body on to his knees, then leant forward and kissed the pontifical ring.

"Your Holiness."

Looking down at Beckx' snowy-white

9

head, seeing it for the first time without his habitual black calotte, Pius thought: we are both of us getting older and frailer in God's service. If He will but give us the time to resolve this present crisis, and enable me to bequeath my successor a Church restored.

"My friend. My very good friend." Pius helped the Father-General to his feet, feeling, as he did so, the absence of flesh on his bones.

"I thank you, Holiness." Beckx' voice had lost much of its deep timbre, further evidence of bodily ill-health. "As you see, my aged frame has become beset with aches and pains. However, the mind is fortunately still vigorous and, as such, at your Holiness's command."

Hearing the familiar steel in Beckx' voice, Pius looked deep into the Jesuit's eyes. Seeing the ardent fire still burning within them, and the familiar lean face still inflexible, despite the added lines, the Pontiff relaxed.

"That is good to hear, my friend. Not since the days of your own founder, the Blessed Saint Ignatius Loyola, has the Church been so in need of the Society's

10

direction. And not even in those evil days, was it subjected to such open and violent attack. See for yourself . . . " Pius indicated to the window.

Reaching it, the two men looked down at the off-duty soldiers ambling along the carefully laid-out pathways as though the grounds were there for their sole pleasure.

"There are guards on all the gates," Pius stated, sombrely. "No one is allowed in or out without an authorized permit. This applies to each and every person resident or working within the Vatican. Even then they all have to satisfy the captain of each checkpoint as to their credentials, and also fully explain their reasons for wishing to pass through their impertinent barriers."

"A violation of Holy Church's supreme authority," Beckx declared. Despite a Jesuit ruling that every emotion other than spiritual should be kept under control, Pius nevertheless detected a note of anger in the Father-General's voice, and was quietly uplifted by it.

Realizing he was remiss in not having asked whether the journey from Fiesole

11

had passed without incident, Pius rectified his omission.

"None, Holiness," Beckx replied, explaining how he had travelled openly by train from Florence to Rome, mingling with the people in an ordinary-class compartment, then by cabriolet to the corner of Borgo Santo Spirito.

With his mind's eye, Pius pictured the dark narrow street with its entrance facing the far south-east corner of the Piazza di San Pietro, and the dark grey building, numbered 5, which, until their expulsion from Rome, had housed the headquarters of the Society of Jesus.

"Nor any problem entering the premises?" he questioned.

"Again, none, Holiness. It was unguarded. And the locks unchanged."

The Pontiff gave silent thanks for the life of Alexander VI, the Borgia Pope who had linked the property to the Vatican.

Not that he in any way approved of either of Alexander's reasons for doing so, Pius quickly tempered his gratitude, thinking of how the lesson of Chapters 6 and 7 of the Book of Romans — the conflict of good and evil within the soul of man — had so manifested itself in Rodrigo de Borja, the Spanish soldier-cardinal, commander-in-chief of the papal armies, who, in 1492, had emulated his uncle Calixtus III, by becoming pope.

Being also somewhat of a historian, Rodrigo possessed a centuries-old parchment telling how the early Roman Christians had been allowed by Emperor Nero to remove and bury the dead from his Circus. According to the record, they had chosen a small green hill on the west bank of the Tiber, known in those days as Mons Vaticanus. Within days of his election as pope, taking the name, Alexander VI, Rodrigo had put his servants to dig under the Vatican's vaults. Paid to secrecy, then rewarded with the loss of their lives, the men soon discovered an opening leading to an ancient necropolis, which, when extended, had revealed a hidden city of the dead: a maze of crooked, narrow, subterranean passages with uneven floors and walls of brown brickwork inscribed with Christian symbols, stretching under the ground from beneath St Peter's Basilica all the way to the east side of St Peter's Square. It had been a small matter for Rodrigo — with his considerable Borgia family wealth — to have a staircase built into the wall of his papal apartments, connecting it to a tunnel running under the square, and then extend it to emerge inside the inner wall of one of his many privately owned properties: number 5 Borgo Santo Spirito.

One of Alexander's reasons for having it built was as a secret access for his many mistresses into his bedchamber. The other was to enable Lucrezia, his illegitimate daughter, to entice men Alexander wanted eliminated into the Appartamenti with certain unholy promises, and dispose of them by pouring poison into their solid-gold goblets from a cavity inside one of her many jewelled finger-rings, then having their bodies taken back into the tunnel and left to rot with the ancient dead.

This had taken place almost sixty years before the creation of the Society of Jesus by its first Father-General, Blessed Saint Ignatius Loyola, and the tunnel's existence had therefore remained

14

a Borgia secret. But when Alexander's great-grandson, Francisco de Borja, chose to become a member of the society, and was then elected General, making 5 Borgo Santo Spirito his headquarters, he had used his knowledge of it to gain private access to the then pope, thus enabling him to act as papal advisor in secret, without inciting the jealousies of cardinals of other Orders living within the Vatican, and all anxious to be granted that particular privilege.

From then on, the tunnel had stayed a Jesuit/Papal secret, used by each succeeding Father-General to gain covert access into the Vatican, and the incumbent pontiff's ear.

Including today, when it was needed most.

"Holiness, may I have your permission to be seated? My old limbs no longer have the strength they once had."

"But of course, my good friend; forgive me."

Pius indicated a magnificently tapestried high-backed chair, sadly covered in dust from neglect. Then, resting his own stiffening frame on a similar chair, he began: "There is no need for me to remind you of the considerable — and but for the Grace of God, one might almost say, irreparable — damage which has already been perpetrated by this usurper on the Church throughout Italy: the suppression of all our religious orders. And his forcing through the Assembly four sacrilegious Acts, illegally transferring some forty thousand of our properties into the ownership of the State. Unfortunately — "

Pius paused to give effect to his next words. Beckx waited, his eyes fixed on his pontiff.

" . . . still he is not satisfied. Only three days ago, I was informed that this blasphemer, this anti-Christ, has appointed a commission to compose the wording of yet another Act, which he intends to present to the Assembly before the end of the year, the purpose of which . . . the purpose of which . . . "

Righteous anger caused Pius to choke on his words.

"The purpose of which," Beckx took over, his face impassive, "is to apply the provisions of all previous Acts to every last one of our properties here in Rome, including the Vatican."

Beckx humbly met the pope's surprised gaze. "Like your goodself, Holiness, besides sharing the confidences of the Count de Ricasole, I too have my sources within the Assembly. When I received your command to come to Rome, I immediately knew the reason. The question is: what action are we able to take? We have already allowed a year and nine months to pass, making only passive protest. Now, with barely six months or so before this new Act is passed, I fear we may already have left it too late."

Pius heard the tone of condemnation in the Father-General's voice. Despite knowing the unspoken criticism was valid, he felt constrained to justify his reasons for choosing the path of peaceful resistance.

"My friend," he replied, defensively, "when confronted with crisis, we all react in different ways, each according to his own temperament. In my case, with you no longer in Rome to kneel with me and pray to God for guidance, I was forced to seek the advice of others, none of them, unfortunately, with your spiritual insight. Many suggestions were made, including my leaving Rome for good and establishing an alternative Vatican in another country, in particular the United States of America, where freedom of religion under its Constitution, seemed to offer a certain permanence. I gave it serious consideration, but then realized that the American Church and I would soon find ourselves in disagreement. It is still a young Church, full of new ideas, which do not coincide with our own — as you, my good friend, witnessed for yourself at the Vatican Council, just two years ago. Whereas you and I are of the old school, traditionalists, who see Rome, and only Rome, as the Holy City. After much solitary prayer, I therefore came to the conclusion that, as the Church's figure-head, it was my sacred duty to remain in the Vatican, to be seen by the rest of the world as refusing to succumb to worldly authority. Thus, the only way I shall leave here, my friend, will be either by death or by force."

Pius looked at the Father-General, awaiting his response.

Beckx stroked his chin thoughtfully with long claw-like fingers. Finally, he gave voice. "Even so, your Holiness, I fear that when the new Act is passed, and the Vatican becomes state property, force is what this arrogator will use."

"Which is why I sent for you." Rising to his feet the Pontiff slowly paced the room, hands clasped together across the front of his long white cassock. "Having decided to make my stand, I must now abide by it, especially now that Bismarck has decided to emulate Emmanuel by stepping-up his *Kulturkampf* policy of persecuting the Church in Germany."

Pius paused and faced Beckx. "With regard to this, I am afraid I have grave news for you, my friend. Four days ago, Bismarck committed his worst atrocity yet. It pains me to tell you, but . . . "

"He banished the Society from Germany," Beckx interrupted, his voice evidencing no emotion. "Forgive my presumption, Holiness, but as I have already mentioned, despite the seclusion of de Ricasole's villa, I still retain my sources."

"As I see," Pius commented. "You will

therefore understand why it is becoming increasingly necessary for me to remain here in the Vatican. As Supreme Pontiff of the Church Universal, there is no other course of action open to me. Whereas you, my good friend . . . " Stopping in mid-sentence, the pope looked straight at the Jesuit General.

"Whereas I have other means at my disposal," Beckx responded in a low but brooding tone.

"Precisely."

Beckx looked up. In his eyes, Pope Pius IX saw the cold steel of resoluteness. Total commitment.

"My friend," he prompted, sudden hope rising within his breast, "you have already formulated a strategy?"

"Three days ago, Holiness; immediately I heard what this second anti-Christ, von Bismarck, had done. A message recalling a certain priest is already on its way to Berlin."

Fiesole. Monday, 15 July 1872
One week later, safely back in de Ricasole's hilltop villa, looking down the Arno valley to the distant domes

and rooftops of Florence, Father-General Beckx was sitting behind his desk, facing a young German priest by the name of Karl Heinrich Becker, who, until two years ago, when every Jesuit in Rome was banished from the city, had been employed by Beckx in the Congretatio de Propaganda. From its inception in 1622 by Gregory XV — the pope who canonized both Saint Ignatius Loyola and Saint Francis Xavier, the two founders of the Jesuit movement — the College of Propaganda had been housed in a large building on the Piazza di Spagna. Its primary task had been to send missionaries, mostly Jesuits, to the four corners of the globe to recover — extremely successfully — all territories lost by the Apostolic Church of Saint Peter to the Protestant Reformation.

"They are both Anti-Christs," Beckx was declaring. "The mark of Satan is upon them. It is evidenced by their evil actions, and their persecution of Holy Church."

Still in his black travelling suit — he had been ushered into the Father-General's presence within minutes of his arrival — Becker kept respectfully silent, awaiting his superior's invitation to speak.

"In the twenty-one months since I arrived here — thanks be to Saint Ignatius for his protection on my journey from Rome . . . " Now wearing his black cassock and calotte, a crucifix hung from Beckx' neck. He raised it to his lips and kissed it.

"Amen," whispered the German priest, crossing his breast.

"Amen," the Father-General responded. "During this time, Satan's attacks upon the Church have greatly increased."

Becker heard the restrained anger in Beckx' voice, and saw the flash in his eyes. The spirit still burned within him, he thought, despite the drastic decline of his body, so broken and bent since their last brief meeting, the day Victor Emmanuel had entered Rome.

The General was sitting hunched in a throne-like, carved wooden chair in a dark, shadowy corner of the large, sparsely furnished room. The vaulted ceiling gave it a monastic feeling. The latticed window-screens were closed, shutting out the mid-morning sun, intensifying the sombre effect of the umber-coloured walls. The wall behind Beckx was shelved from floor to ceiling and crammed with brown, leather-bound books. The other three were bare of decoration, save for the chimney breast above a cheerless braziered fireplace, on which was a dark wooden cross, bearing the sagging body and bloodied, thorn-crowned head of the crucified Christ.

With a reverential pride in the similarity of their surnames — a vanity kept under the due subjugation of a Jesuit priest — Karl Becker silently assessed the Belgian who ruled the Society of Jesus; the man who had followed his trail all the way from Berlin to the deserted castle outside Genoa, where he had taken refuge to avoid arrest, then brought him — travelling night and day without rest — to Fiesole.

Despite his advanced years, Beckx' pale, deeply-lined face still evidenced the sharpness of intellect which had made him Pio Nono, Pope Pius the Ninth's secret confessor and spiritual advisor. There were some inside the

Vatican — and still resident there today — who'd been so jealous of Beckx' special relationship with the Holy Father, they'd maliciously whispered he was the real power behind the papal throne, calling him 'The Black Pope' behind his back, knowing their innuendoes would carry back to Pius, forcing him to dispense with Beckx' services.

But their attempts had created the very opposite effect to that intended. Not only had Pio Nono remained faithful to his good friend, he had also leaned more on him for spiritual guidance, thus enabling the Jesuit-General to counsel him to declare as part of the Church's dogma, the long accepted doctrine of The Immaculate Conception of the Blessed Virgin Mary. And almost exactly two years ago, on 18 July 1870, Pio Nono had taken Father Beckx' advice when he placed before the First Vatican Council the matter of his Papal Infallibility, requesting the conclave of cardinals gathered in Rome from around the world, to confirm that when speaking *ex cathedra* from the throne of Saint Peter, he did so under the divine authority of

God, and as such his ruling could not be challenged.

As though reading Becker's mind, the Father-General suddenly stated, "The Evil One is on the rampage, constantly warring against Holy Church's supreme authority."

Because Satan is never off the offensive, Becker thought to himself. The invasion of Rome, happening just nine weeks after Pius was declared Infallible, had been no coincidence. It was Lucifer's immediate response to the decree. And then, adding evil on to evil, daring to challenge God's rule by having Victor Emmanuel incarcerate the Vicar of Christ as a prisoner inside the Vatican.

Blessed Pius — Pio Nono — who, only nine weeks before the invasion, had stood up, arms outstretched, identifying himself with the crucified Saviour, as 533 voices, minus only those few misguided American cardinals who had walked out in protest, loudly declared in unison: "*Placet! Placet!*" — 'It pleases! It pleases!' — confirming that Papal Infallibility was now added to the Immaculate Conception as part of the dogma of Holy Church. A decision sealed, in that same instant, by the Almighty Himself with an accompanying clap of thunder, followed by a bolt of lightning which flashed about the *baldacchino* and into the conciliar hall, bathing the white-robed figure of Pio Nono in a holy glow.

Beckx leant forward. "And now that the Adversary has persuaded Bismarck to emulate Victor Emmanuel in attacking the Church, others will seek to follow. It is time for the Society to act."

Karl Becker agreed, heart, and mind, and soul. Had he himself not suffered greatly at the hands of both men? When Victor Emmanuel's army had entered Rome, he had been forced to flee the Congregation, leaving behind the results of three years' work. Travelling rough across Italy, he had finally crossed into Germany, then journeyed on to Berlin, eventually reaching the seminary where he had spent ten years as a novitiate and given a post as a tutor. But Germany had changed greatly in the seven years he'd been away. Renamed 'The Second Reich' by its new Protestant military leader, Prince Otto von Bismarck, it was now the supreme martial power in Europe, and at war with France. Within months of his arrival in Berlin, the people were glorying in Bismarck's victory over the armies of Napoleon III, the occupation of Paris, and the Reich's annexation of the rich provinces of Alsace-Lorraine.

The one exception to the mood of patriotism sweeping the country was that of German Catholics, who were steadfastly refusing to obey Bismarck's recent diktat that Germans owed their first allegiance to the State. Loyal to Holy Church, they were being persecuted for their faith by Bismarck's *Kulturkampf* policy of systematically closing Roman churches and seminaries, forbidding Catholic teaching, and throwing dissident bishops and priests into prison.

When the Jesuit seminary in Berlin was closed, Becker assumed command of its ejected priests and novices, and formed an underground resistance, printing and distributing tracts encouraging German Catholics to stand fast, even unto the ultimate punishment, death, in the certain knowledge that Heaven would be their eternal reward.

But eleven days ago, Bismarck had retaliated by expelling the Society from the Fatherland, blaming them for inciting unrest. For the second time in two years, Becker was forced to flee a country, eventually finding refuge for himself and his band of fellow priests and novices in a remote deserted castle outside Genoa.

Beckx continued, his eyes piercing Becker's, "As I wrestled in prayer, our founder, the Blessed Saint Ignatius, appeared to me in a vision. His face shone with the glow of one who sits at the right hand of the Saviour in Glory, but his expression was stern. 'For twenty-one months you have allowed the Prince of Darkness to rule over the affairs of men without retaliation', he accused. 'During this time, all you have done is to kneel and pray. Prayer has its place', he confirmed, 'but I formed the Society to be active, to be in the forefront of repelling and reversing the attacks of the Evil One. Must I remind you of how we combated the attacks of the Anti-Christs Luther and Calvin, reversing the spread of their evil blasphemies against Holy Church? Did you not absorb my teachings? In my

Spiritual Exercises I continually stress the necessity for zeal. Therefore I come to you now, as a special messenger from our militant Lord, bearing His order for you to commence battle against these evil allies of Satan'."

The Father-General leant back in his chair, his gaze holding the German priest to his every word. "I was then emboldened to reply that any such counter-revolution would need to be financed, and all that we owned had been taken from us. 'Find one among you to sail to the New World', our holy founder replied, as his image faded, and the sound of his voice grew fainter. 'There, in our Church of Saint Francis Xavier in New York, he will find a man whose first loyalty is to Holy Church. In his hand he holds the key to the wealth which will ensure the downfall of these Satanic usurpers'.

"With this," Beckx continued, "the vision of Saint Ignatius ascended above me and passed through the ceiling back to Heaven. In that very same moment, Father Becker, you came into my mind. I remembered your excellent work at our missionary college in Rome, the reports of your organized resistance in Berlin, and I knew, without any doubt, that you were the one whom our blessed Saint had already chosen to undertake this most holy of missions."

Clasping his hands across his breast, Beckx waited for Becker's reaction, taking in his pale face with its fine ascetic features, especially the slate-blue eyes which, at their first meeting, had gripped Beckx' own with their strange, contradictory mixture of icy coldness, and sudden flashes of intense fire.

Becker bowed his head in silent prayer.

With the introductory letter from Peter Barr Sweeny — plus the New Yorker's request for a personal audience with Beckx to discuss his proposals in more detail — safely locked away in his desk, the Jesuit Father-General continued to appraise the flaxen-haired German priest; aware of his fervency for the true faith, his intense loyalty to the Society of Jesus, and also his implacable possession of a Jesuit's special commitment and zeal.

Becker's head remained bowed.

"The very fate of the Church rests in

30

your hands," the Jesuit Father-General prompted, knowing his order could not be refused. Becker met his gaze and Beckx saw the intensity he was looking for.

"The Celestial Mary be praised," Beckz declared. "I leave you to decide your exact course of action. Should you think it necessary, choose someone you can trust to accompany you. Join the church either as a member of the congregation, or you may feel it better to offer your services as a priest. But be cautious. Keep your mission veiled, as did our Lord Himself, when He attended the Feast of Tabernacles in Galilee, 'not openly'," Beckx quoted, "'but as it were in secret'. Apply deliberation to your every thought. Discretion to your spoken words. And strategy to your every move. In so doing, our Heavenly Father will surely bless your endeavour. Ensure that all telegraphed messages conclude with the code-word: *Opus Dei* — the Work of God. And finally . . . " Beckx emphasized his final instruction, "never forget, my son, that in the furtherance of God's work, the end justifies the

31

means." To emphasize the maxim even more, Beckx changed from Italian, and repeated it in Becker's own tongue: "*Der Zweck heiligt die Mittel.*"

Rising swiftly from his chair, Becker knelt before his superior. Under his black hair-shirt, his jagged crucifix of unsmoothed iron pressed hard against the Father-General's knee, piercing his breast. The sharp pain sent a surge of religious ecstasy through Becker as he experienced — with a Jesuit's ingrained sense of the imagination — the agony which his militant Lord must have felt as His hands and feet were pierced, nailing Him to the Cross of Golgotha.

Beckz placed both his hands on the German's head, and gave his blessing: "*Benedictus qui veni in nomine domine.*"

Book One

Book One

1

New York. Three and a half months later.

Wednesday, 30 October 1872

AFTER two years in Europe, Colleen had forgotten how small it was. Sandwiched in the middle of a row of four-storeyed brownstone houses, the Church of Saint Francis Xavier on West 16th Street — with its simple wooden cross on the roof apex starkly silhouetted against the overcast sky — looked crushed and decidedly plain, compared to the ornate grandeur of the Roman churches she'd attended while abroad.

Descending from her cab, Colleen glanced towards Fifth Avenue, surprised to find it was even busier and noisier than she remembered, with endless crowds of people crossing at the intersection, and beyond them continuous lines of wagons, coaches, hansom-cabs, and the familiar 'Yellow Bird' and 'Red Bird' omnibuses; all rushing past in both directions, as if there were not enough hours in the day.

Sixteenth Street, by comparison, was reasonably calm, with only a few horse-drawn vehicles, and a couple of men pushing handcarts, using it as a means of getting to, or from, Sixth Avenue.

After paying the cab-driver Colleen walked through the open gate in the surrounding black iron railings, and entered the left porch finding the church's hushed, hallowed atmosphere a soothing relief after the noise of the hectic world outside. It looked exactly the same; nothing had changed. She paused and gazed down the two aisles, separated by rows of plain wooden pews, remembering standing there in her white lace wedding gown before the high altar, below the large white-marble statue of the Madonna and Child, and the life-sized statues of Saint Ignatius and Saint Francis Xavier, with Michael alongside her, looking into each other's eyes, and both promising to love and obey until death did them part. She quickly turned her face away, noticing as she did so that the frescoes

36

depicting the stations of the Cross lining the chapel's walls, were still richly coloured, showing no signs of fading. No, Colleen sighed inwardly, nothing had altered here, while her own life had been irrevocably changed.

The church was almost empty; just four people — a dark-coated man and three black-veiled women — kneeling apart in prayer, and a solitary priest in the far corner of the left transept, standing before a smaller statue of Mary holding the Christ Child, below which was a side altar.

The priest was a stranger to her, but after being away for so long, this was no surprise. Young Jesuit priests had always been sent to St Francis Xavier for the kind of pastoral training only to be found in a city like New York. Within months they were gone, called away to the missionary fields, oftentimes as far away as South America, or China, following in the steps of Saint Francis Xavier himself.

The priest lit a candle, then placed it in a holder in front of the altar, and prepared to kneel as Colleen started down the aisle. At the hollow echo of her footsteps, he turned, and stood waiting for her to reach him.

Despite the gloom, Colleen was immediately struck by the priest's paleness of face, and the fairness of his hair, both accentuated by his black robe. He was about the same height as Michael — five feet eleven — and slim, with a lean face. Yes, she thought, very handsome. And in his early thirties. Despite his priestly vocation, he was sure to flutter a few young hearts.

"May I be of help?" The voice was whispered, and most definitely foreign.

Apart from a faintly raised brow, his pale-blue eyes regarded her with complete detachment. There was no reaction to her femininity, no trace of the response which she all too often saw in the eyes of most men she was introduced to, despite never seeking it.

"I'm hoping so," she replied. "I'm sorry, Father, but having been abroad for the last two years, I'm afraid I don't know your name?"

"Becker."

"Becker. German?"

"Yes."

Handsome on the outside, she found herself assessing him, but very few people, even his fellow priests, would ever get to know this man inside. Already, having exchanged only a few words, Colleen could feel the unseen barrier with which he surrounded himself. It was his eyes. There was a detachment about them, as though he was looking at something far beyond his immediate vision, something which only he could see. The young maidens of Saint Francis Xavier need not waste their dreams on this particular priest, Colleen thought. The man was irrevocably wedded to the Church.

"What part of Germany?"

"Berlin."

"Berlin! I spent a month there. A beautiful city. But not the best place for Catholics at the moment, I'm afraid," she commented, remembering the refugees crowding the station before her train journey out of Germany, and the way a number of them wearing crucifixes had hastily removed them and stuffed them in their clothes when off-duty soldiers sauntered amongst them on the platforms.

"The Lord will restore the vine," the priest replied, a steely edge to his voice. "In the meantime, Miss . . . Mrs . . . ?"

"Lowell," Colleen stated. She no longer used her married name, it belonged to the past. "Colleen Lowell. Miss." She extended her hand. Used to the limp handshake of clerics, she was surprised by the muscular strength of his grasp.

"You wish confession?" the priest asked, eyes boring into hers.

For some reason his gaze made Colleen uneasy. This, plus her anxiety for her father's health, the way he was reacting to being drawn ever deeper into the Tweed Ring investigation, caused her to rush her words. "Not today, thank you. It's to do with my uncle. He was . . . maybe still is . . . a member of Saint Francis Xavier's. I need to contact him urgently. All I know is that he's somewhere in Europe. I called on my aunt, but the house is closed. Before exploring other sources, I thought I'd try here first, since he was so devoted to this church. He might still be sending

40

contributions . . . " Her voice tailed off.

The priest was silent for a long moment, looking deep into her eyes. As though he was trying to reach into her soul, Colleen thought, a sudden cold shiver running down her spine.

"Somewhere in Europe?"

Colleen was certain the whispered question contained a sinister tone.

"Yes."

Again a lengthy pause. "And the name of your uncle?"

"Sweeny. Peter Barr Sweeny," she replied. "How long have you been at Saint Xavier's, Father?"

"This is my eleventh week."

"Then you won't have met him personally. Nevertheless, I'm sure you must know all about him."

"Very little," the priest replied. "But I do know we do not have his address."

"Are you sure?" Colleen demanded, beginning to feel agitated and increasingly impatient — and strangely uneasy in this man's presence. His cold gaze, his whispered voice, were peculiarly disturbing. "Is Father Hudson still Rector?"

41

"He is."

"Then if I could please see him, maybe he . . ."

"Miss Lowell! Forgive me, but to repeat, we have no knowledge of where your uncle is. During only my second week here, Father Hudson's secretary was taken ill and I filled his place. One of the letters was from the city's detective squad asking this very same question. Father Hudson told me this was a routine monthly request from Police Headquarters and directed me to reply in the usual manner: that we have not heard from Mr Sweeny since the day he left New York, but should we do so, we would immediately inform them."

"Thank you, Father. I'm sorry to have troubled you." Giving the priest a polite smile, Colleen abruptly turned to go.

Father Becker watched her walk quickly out of the church, feeling no guilt for his lies. He not only knew Sweeny's present whereabouts but also his complete itinerary. He and Jacob Kaufmann had discussed it so many times in the secrecy of the confessional it was imprinted into his mind.

But that knowledge must remain sacrosanct between himself and the German diamond-merchant. And Becker's shadowy Black knight protector.

★ ★ ★

Jacob Kaufmann was worried. Worried sick something might yet go wrong, even at this late stage.

Usually when he felt this way, just the very sight of Gerda — who today was sitting at her wood-inlaid desk, writing letters to their relatives back home in Germany — was enough to reassure him that the risk was well worth it.

Gerda was a solid, large-bosomed woman and, being portly himself, this was exactly how Jacob liked her. Tonight, she was wearing his favourite outfit: a maroon silk blouse with a high collar, and a voluminous maroon silk skirt. She was certainly handsome, with her hair pulled back tight and fastened in a bun. But it was obvious that the strain of the last weeks was getting her down also. This made the reality of his situation even more acute to Jacob. He did not want to lose her. Nor their beautiful mansion.

From his high-backed chair by the fire, Jacob surveyed the drawing-room, feeling a sudden surge of pride at the outward display of his success. The room was as big as a ballroom and featured large oil paintings in heavy-moulded gold frames; the walls were half-panelled in walnut, surmounted by a pale-blue brocaded wallpaper. A thick carpet matching the blue velvet curtains spread from wall to wall. Two massive crystal chandeliers hung from the embossed ceiling; with a heavy gold-framed French mirror above the white-marble fireplace. The furniture was the absolute proof of his social standing: red, green, and blue sofas, *chaise-longues* and chairs, some in velvet, others in silk, some plain, the rest striped, interspaced with carved, solid display tables, on which rested large china ornaments and figures, mostly Dresden or Meissen.

Reassured, Kaufmann stared back into the fire. There was no way he was going to lose either Gerda or home. All the arrangements had been made with the utmost care.

Nothing could go wrong.

"Gerda."

His wife stopped writing and looked up. "Yes, Jacob?"

Kaufmann loved her guttural accent — the same as his own, both of them having arrived in New York as children.

"I shall be staying at the Astor House for the next five days. My paperwork has been piling up. I must complete it before Tuesday."

"Is that when the *Mary Celeste* sails?" Gerda asked with a slight frown.

"Yes, *mein schatz*."

"And it will then be all over?"

"Almost. It would be now, had the *Venango* not gone up in flames." Kaufmann sighed. "But I give you my word after her replacement has sailed a fortnight on Friday, all our fears will finally be at an end."

"And then you will retire, Jacob? As promised?" she prodded, holding his gaze.

"Completely, Gerda. After this, there will be no more buying or selling of diamonds, not even for my ordinary clients." Kaufmann felt an inner relief at the thought.

"You have been very careful, Jacob?" Gerda asked, her brow furrowed with worry. "You are sure there is nothing to connect you to Mr Sweeny?"

"Nothing, my love. My books show no record of our transactions. The purchases were spread evenly over the last twelve months, all in small amounts, using Exchanges in ten different cities right across America, and never once in my name."

"*Gut!*" Gerda Kaufmann gave a sigh of relief. "And Father Becker?"

"Today was his last day in St Xavier. He will also be sailing on Tuesday."

"*Gut!*" his wife repeated. "And the *Mary Celeste*'s crew? Did he find the men he was looking for?"

"Yes, eventually. They are joining the vessel tomorrow morning, just before she commences loading. And now, *mein schatz*, continue with your letters. The way Count Bismarck is persecuting the church, our relatives will need all the moral support you can give them."

Visibly happier Gerda returned to her correspondence.

Kaufmann settled back into his thoughts, remembering last evening's final meeting with Father Becker, the priest's face so pale and ardent as he rechecked every detail. Kaufmann reviewed them once more in his mind, making sure he had left nothing out.

Check one: both vessels bound for Genoa with legitimately cleared cargoes.

Check two: both vessels with one extra barrel on board.

Check three: send the telegraphs to Sweeny.

Check four: Genoa. Unload only the legitimate barrels, retaining both extra barrels in the holds.

Check five: finally, sail from Genoa to Palermo — unless Sweeny's offer was refused. In which case, the instructions would revert back to Marseilles, as originally planned.

Becker might think he was in control, but he was not, far from it. Well might he quote his maxim of 'the end justifies the means'.

Kaufmann himself much preferred the

47

one he had learnt from Sweeny: never let the right hand know what the left is doing.

★ ★ ★

Paris, 8.40 p.m. Sweeny sat back in his armchair and relaxed as the Paris-Naples train pulled out of the Gare de Lyons. Pulling a leather cigar-case from his inside pocket, he carefully chose a corona, smelt it, then showed it to the young, slim, black-cassocked Jesuit priest, sharing his luxury saloon and anterooms.

"You don't mind, Father?" he asked, raising his bushy eyebrows.

The Sicilian priest smiled, the whiteness of his teeth accentuated by his dark skin and black hair. He was a handsome devil, Sweeny conceded, but looks weren't everything. It was money that got you places.

"Not at all, Mr Sweeny."

He couldn't really object, not after I'd already selected it; it was, as the French said, a *fait accompli*, Sweeny smirked to himself, rather proud of the few phrases he'd picked up since being in Paris.

Lighting up, he slowly drew on the cigar, then contentedly exhaled a thin stream of smoke. "Next stop, Florence."

"With God's grace," Father Guiliamo Cottone replied.

"Sure," Sweeny agreed, pulling the Paris-Mediterranean Company's timetable from his pocket. "We'll be stopping at Dijon for something to eat at three-fifteen in the morning, after that, the next stop is Macon at six, then it's straight through to the border post at Modanne . . . " Sweeny looked up. "Seven and a half hours! Say, that's a hell of a . . . sorry Father . . . that sure is a long time to go without a break. I guess we'd better stretch our legs at Macon first, what do you say?"

Father Cottone smiled. "That seems sensible, Mr Sweeny. I will wake you up. I shall be rising at exactly five for prayers."

"Sure, Father, thanks." Sweeny returned to his schedule. "According to this, the border-check takes forty-seven minutes." He looked up. "That's a strange time.

49

You'd think they'd make it an even hour."

The priest smiled again. "Italian time is forty-seven minutes ahead of French time, Mr Sweeny. Modanne is only a brief pause for the customs-men to come on board."

"You mean, no stopping?"

"I'm afraid not."

"That means . . ." — Sweeny studied the timetable — "that the first stop after Macon isn't until Turin. That's twelve and a half hours! I'm sure glad you thought of bringing a luncheon basket, Father."

"I journeyed on this train from Naples to Paris," Father Cottone explained. "I can still feel the hunger-pangs."

"Lucky for me," Sweeny remarked. "Still, I'll be glad when we finally arrive in Florence. I wired the top hotel and booked their best rooms. The Hotel De La Ville on the Piazza Manin. Hope you like it. According to Baedeker, it's nob class."

Father Guiliamo Cottone acknowledged his host's generosity with a slight incline of his head. "I must confess I am looking forward to it. Luxury such as this is far beyond my province."

"Yes?" Sweeny questioned, sounding surprised. "I thought you said your uncle was rich? And that he owned the biggest villa in Palermo?"

"He does," the young Sicilian confirmed in a subdued voice, with no trace of boast. "But before Victor Emmanuel, I rarely stayed with him. I lived in a small house attached to my church in Bagheria. It had only two rooms and a kitchen."

"That must have been rough," Sweeny sympathized, thinking of his mansion back in New York. "But speaking of this King Victor Emmanuel, it sure is a crime what he's doing to the Church. It's funny that God ain't struck him dead for all the evil he's doing."

"God moves in a mysterious way," Father Cottone replied gravely.

"And that's a fact. Look at the way He brought us together, sitting next to each other in Notre Dame." The East-Sider pronounced the 'Dame' as he would back home. "It just goes to prove that what the Bible says is true. The Almighty really does take care of

His most generous givers." Shaking his head with the wonder of it all, Sweeny continued, "If it wasn't for my writing to Father Beckx, to suggest a meeting to put a stop to this Victor Emmanuel guy, I wouldn't be on this train to meet him. I've been hearing about the Father-General for nearly twenty years now, but I never thought I'd ever get to see him face to face." Sweeny sighed contentedly, taking another puff of his cigar.

The young priest glanced into the darkness on the other side of the window, then looked back into the saloon. "God's predestination, Mr Sweeny," he stated, sitting forward earnestly. "We are both part of His great plan. This is why He brought us together. Why He ensured our meeting in the cathedral. When God so intervenes, then we have a duty to respond by openly demonstrating our willingness to follow His divine guidance. Before your meeting with Father Beckx, kneel and ask God to direct your path. Bring the question of Victor Emmanuel before Him in prayer. Seek His answer. And He will reply in such a way that His purpose for you will be so clear, there will be no doubt in your mind as to the course you must take."

A silence filled the carriage, as both men dwelt on their own private thoughts.

Predestination! Father Guiliamo Cottone thought wryly. More like preparation! Within hours of their hearing that Peter Barr Sweeny had arrived safely in Paris, he'd been sent there for the sole purpose of gaining the confidence of the mastermind behind 'The Tweed Ring', the man who had been instrumental in swindling $200,000,000 from the city of New York. His next brief — the preliminary discussions of their proposal — had been even simpler. All he'd had to do was to convince Sweeny that his invested money would be repaid four-fold, and from that moment on, the man had been impatient to commence the Journey.

Human strategy plus clinical planning, rather than divine guidance, was the secret taught in Saint Ignatius's *Spiritual Exercises*. During his ten-year training as a novitiate, Guiliamo had mastered this lesson well.

Predestination! thought Peter Barr

Sweeny. It made one feel good inside to know that one was part of some great eternal plan. Not that predestination was enough. When the Almighty sent the main chance your way, you had to grab it with both hands. OK, so, maybe Cottone's scheme was revolutionary, but provided they could agree terms, it would make New York's haul seem like chicken-feed.

And if they were unable to agree, then what the hell! Nothing was lost. From what he'd heard about Florence, it would be well worth the journey just to see the sights.

Besides, the vessels weren't leaving New York until Tuesday, the day before his meeting with Father-General Beckx. Allow thirty days to cross the Atlantic — twenty-five, to be on the safe side — that still gave him plenty of time to wire Gibraltar with instructions to revert back to Marseilles, as originally planned.

Slowly exhaling, Sweeny watched the cigar-smoke drift gently up to the carriage ceiling.

2

Thursday, 31 October 1872

"WATCH that barrel!" The warning shout came from Winchester, Captain Benjamin Briggs's shipping-agent. Briggs swivelled around. Winchester was standing over the open main-hatch, looking down into the hold. Alongside him was the large, portly, bearded man with a German accent, who had accompanied him on board the *Mary Celeste*. Winchester had not introduced him, but Briggs had overheard his agent address him as 'Jacob'. He was wealthy, judging from his clothes: black overcoat with a black velvet collar, finely creased dark-grey and black striped trousers, shining black leather boots, black silk top hat, and a grey silk cravat, fastened with a jewelled gold pin.

"Watch *that* barrel!" Winchester repeated his instruction, seeming to emphasize the 'that'.

Briggs crossed to the hatch and peered

down. One of the new all-German crew raised his hand acknowledging the warning. He and one of his compatriots took hold of the barrel and began rolling it towards the corner of the empty hold.

"Anything wrong, Mr Winchester?"

"Nothing, Benjamin," his agent replied, straightening up. James Henry Winchester was of average height and build, neatly dressed without being dapper, with medium-length hair below the rim of his top hat, long trimmed sideburns attached to a tidy goatee beard, and a moustache that refused to grow thick.

"It was just that he was handling it on his own, nothing more," Winchester explained. "We don't want any breakages, not with alcohol. The smell would fill the ship and give the men ideas, especially with you not allowing any liquor on board."

Very true, Briggs thought, and sensible of Winchester to warn the crew to be extra careful, right from the start.

His own refusal to allow drink on his vessels had been instilled in him by his father, Captain Nathan Briggs, a strict disciplinarian, under whom he had served his apprenticeship, and whose Articles of Agreement always contained the clause: 'No grog will be allowed on board'.

He glanced back into the hold. This was only the first load, and under the eye of the new second mate, Andrew Gilling, a 25–year-old Dane whom Briggs had met for the first time only an hour ago, when he and the new crew, all chosen by Winchester, had reported to him on deck. The four Germans were working in pairs: the two Lorenzen brothers stacking in one corner, and Goodschaad and Martens in the other. All four were from two islands, Fohr and Amrum, off the coast of Northern Prussia. And typical of the people from that part of the globe, were extremely fair-haired, with piercing blue eyes. As was Gilling, the Dane.

The five men had all given the same lodging-house as their New York address: 19 Thames Street. A bit coincidental, Briggs thought, but probably they always worked together as a team.

Turning away from the hold, his gaze followed the second net-load of barrels as it swung across the deck, stopping over the open hatch. On a command from the first mate, Albert Richardson, the gantry operator down on the pier coaxed his dray-horse slowly backwards, allowing the net to descend gradually into the hold. Despite the keen wind blowing up the East River, the grey was already sweating, steam rising from his powerful muscles, and the snorts from his nostrils clearly visible in the thin air.

He was a good man was Richardson, Briggs said to himself, pleased at having been allowed to choose his first mate. Hailing from Stockton Springs, Maine, Albert had served as his first mate on board his last brig, the *Sea Foam*. Wiry but tough, clean-shaven, and only twenty-eight, he was an excellent sailor and, equally important, had a steady nerve. With a rough forty-day voyage in front of them, his first on board the *Celeste*, it would be good to have someone he could depend on alongside him, Briggs thought, especially as they'd be surrounded by so many foreigners.

Unusual for a sailor to be beardless, Briggs mused, still watching Richardson. He himself was rather proud of his own dark bushy beard and moustache, but

58

being tall and broad he could carry it; maybe Albert, a much smaller man, felt that a beard would not suit him.

A sudden gust of cold air swept over the deck. Briggs swung his arms across his chest to warm himself up, and looked towards the galley where the only other American member of the crew, Edward Head, the young 23–year-old, newly married steward and cook from Brooklyn — was making a hot brew.

Concerned about his wife and small daughter being out in this cold wind, Briggs crossed to the ship's rail, where they were supervising the unloading of some items from home. With little Sophia wrapped up warm in her arms, Sarah hadn't noticed the cold. She was more concerned about the safety of her melodeon, carefully watching its transfer from the cart on to the gang-plank. Whenever she sailed with him, the organ always came along. Briggs smiled fondly, doubly grateful she was joining him on the voyage. Not only would he have her company, but there was also the evenings to look forward to: singing hymns together in the privacy of their cabin, after his day's work had been done. When not at sea, Benjamin was a regular member of his father-in-law's Congregational church back in Marion, Massachusetts, and a firm believer in giving proper praise to God for all His many blessings before turning in for the night.

Dark-haired, pretty and petite, yet resilient, Sarah was his cousin and childhood sweetheart. Married over ten years ago by her father, the Reverend Leander Cobb, when Briggs was twenty-seven and Sarah only twenty, she'd made him a good wife, often sailing with him on his voyages, mostly to Mediterranean ports. Even their honeymoon was at sea — on board his first command, a schooner, *Forest King*.

She was also a wonderful mother. Fondly, Briggs looked down at them both. Today was Sophia's second birthday. Sarah had used Head's stove to bake her a small cake with two candles. And this afternoon, Sarah's brother, Willie — the Reverend William Cobb — was coming specially from Boston (where he was the librarian at Congregational House) and the three of them were taking Sophia for a coach ride in Central Park before returning to the *Celeste* for a birthday tea. It was a pity Arthur couldn't be with them, Briggs mused, thinking about their son back home in Marion, but as he was now seven it was time he started his education, and Grandma Briggs would take good care of him.

Still leaning on the rail, Benjamin looked past Sarah at the teeming activity of South Street.

New York was only 250 years old, yet it was already second to London as the busiest seaport in the world. And South Street's bumpy cobbled surface stretching from Battery Park to where the East River turned at the great bulge of Manhattan at Corlears Hook, was the city's most maritime street — its counting-houses, warehouses, rum-holes and grog-shops all fronting on to the river.

Sloops, schooners, square-riggers and brigs from every part of the globe were crammed side by side in both directions, as far as the eye could see; row after row of two-masted, three-masted vessels, their bowsprits and jib-booms jutting out over the two-mile-long quayside, moored alongside pine-planked slips which — supported by open piling and projecting some 200 to 300 yards out into the river — were themselves extensions of the many side-streets and alleys leading into South Street.

Turning his gaze left, Briggs looked up in wonderment at the steel girders of the new Brooklyn Bridge towering high above him into the sky, right alongside the *Mary Celeste*'s pier 50 mooring, between Roosevelt and James Streets. It was a stupendous feat of engineering, Briggs thought. All work had halted some twelve months ago, because of the city's lack of funds after the débâcle of The Tweed Ring, but construction had soon resumed. The noise was deafening.

Briggs continued to gaze across the grey waters of the East River towards the Upper Bay, from where, in five days' time, they would take their last look at New York. Giving only a passing glance at the grand mansions of the wealthy on Brooklyn Heights on the other side of the river, Briggs's thoughts returned to his new command, which, in his opinion, was even further evidence of God's blessing upon their lives.

Just two months ago, when he'd been seeking a new command, Winchester had immediately offered him the *Mary Celeste*, a brig which he'd recently purchased. Her previous name was *Amazon*. Why it had been changed, Winchester hadn't bothered to explain. To Briggs's mind, her new name: *Mary Celeste* — 'Celestial Mary' — offended his Protestant ear.

However, Briggs had kept his opinion to himself because, not only had Winchester offered him the command, but also a one-third share of the vessel, even advancing him the loan of the $3,600 required to buy it. Briggs still wasn't sure why. The only explanation he could think of was that Winchester must feel that, by being part-owner, it would give him greater incentive to safeguard both the vessel and cargoes.

Winchester had taken him to the shipyard, where the *Celeste* was being reconstructed. Briggs was delighted with the improvements. An extra deck was being added increasing her depth from 11' 6" to 16' 2"; her length from 98' 5" to 103'; her breadth from 25' to 25' 7", and her displacement 206 tons to an estimated 282 tons. Although her two masts were retained, the topsail had been divided into an upper and lower topsail for the sake of easier handling, thus allowing a reduction in the number of men required to sail her. She had also undergone extensive repairs: three-quarter poop extended, several new timbers, new transoms, part new knightheads, stern and stem; new bends and topsides and stern; and patched with yellow metal. The total cost was known: $11,500, and already reflected in the $3,600 value of the one-third partnership.

Looking back on it all, Briggs could still hardly believe his luck . . . correction, he thought: blessing.

He had immediately wired Sarah to join him, and last Sunday, she and Sophia arrived in New York.

Briggs glanced towards the main hatch, where another net full of barrels was descending into the hold. At the pace everyone was working, loading should be completed by early tomorrow afternoon at the latest.

That would leave Sarah and him free to enjoy the next three days. More sightseeing on Saturday. Church on Sunday. And then, on Monday evening, the eve of their departure, they'd been invited to a farewell dinner at the Astor House, by their good friend David Morehouse, of the *Dei Gratia* . . .

Dei Gratia! Briggs thought. Another Romish name, meaning 'God's Grace'. David was also carrying a cargo for Winchester. And he too was destined for the same ports as the *Celeste*: first, Genoa; then Palermo.

Strange coincidence, he thought. But no more than that. Especially as it was he who had got David the contract in the first place . . .

"I'll be off, Benjamin!"

Briggs looked towards the raised voice. Winchester was standing at the top of the gang-plank. 'Jacob' was already on the pier waiting.

"Going so soon?" Briggs returned, slightly puzzled by the brevity of

Winchester's stay.

"Yes. Everything seems to be in good hands. See you in the office at ten o'clock Monday morning. I'll have the Articles of Agreement and crew-list ready for you to take to the commissioner."

As Briggs leant on the ship's-rail, watching the two men merge into the bustle of South Street, the incident of the barrel flashed through his mind's eye, and suddenly he felt uneasy.

3

Five Days Later,
Tuesday, 5 November 1872

IT was obscene. Michael Callaghan looked down at the corpse. All right, so life was cheap on the East Side, and after two years on the Detective Squad he should be immune to violent killings. But this one was different. The dead man's fat, naked, middle-aged body, already turned grey, was sickening enough, but what made it so gruesome was the way he had died. His attacker must have crept up behind him and in one sudden movement, placed his hands on the man's shoulders, his knee in the base of the spine, and snapped it in two. What other explanation was there for the body being as it was, doubled up the wrong way, the buttocks bent back almost to the shoulder-blades, and the legs taking the feet past the top of the victim's head?

Turning away, he instructed Patrolman

Hagan to remain with the corpse, and climbed up the stone basement steps. It was a typical East-Side alley, grey and narrow, a dark forbidding slit between two five-storey warehouses. He crossed to the second officer — in this part of the city, cops always went about in twos.

"Name?" he asked. "Just for the record."

"Murphy," the man replied, not turning his bull-neck but staying as he was, legs astride, facing the growing crowd, and twirling his long night-stick as a threat to the more curious not to come too near.

"Who found it?"

The stick stopped in mid-spin and pointed to a ragged male wretch sitting hunched against the warehouse wall at the edge of the crowd. Seeing the empty bottle held upside down in his hand, Callaghan knew what to expect.

"Fetch him here."

"He can't stand," Murphy declared. "Someone slipped him a bottle and he ain't stopped drinking since."

As if to confirm this opinion, the man slipped slowly sideways, releasing

68

the empty bottle which clattered across the grey cobbles.

"What d'I say?" said Murphy, his chest swelling, and retwirling his night-stick with an added flourish.

"Couldn't you have stopped him?" Callaghan asked.

"T'was me duty to protect the corpse, Murphy retorted, belligerently, "not take care of drunks."

Callaghan sighed. "Did you question him?"

"Just t'ask how he found the body."

"And?"

"Went t'sleep there after the Shamrock." Callaghan knew it: a nearby grog-shop on South Street. "T'body was there when he woke up. Underneath him. Hadn't even noticed it. He came out of t'alley like a banshee out of hell. Me and Pat was passing at t'time. I stayed with the deceased, while Pat ran back to the First as fast as he could, minding the weight of him, to tell Sergeant Kelly."

"Was the body naked when he found it?"

"Like a new born baby, he said, but not as pretty, says I. Tis the work of a madman, so it is," Murphy added knowingly, walking purposefully towards the advancing crowd, slashing the air with his night-stick.

Callaghan agreed. No sane man could have committed so vicious a crime.

A cold gust of wind blew in from the river. Callaghan shivered, pulled his overcoat collar up over his ears, and returned his thoughts to the 'John Doe'.

At first glance, the motive seemed to be robbery. His brief examination of the body — the smooth skin, corpulent stomach, soft hands, manicured nails — indicated the victim was obviously wealthy.

But why remove every stitch of clothing?

Assuming that the man had been wearing expensive items — gold watch and chain, diamond fob, gold rings, and maybe jewelled — and assuming that his top clothes — overcoat, suit, shoes, even his shirt, necktie, and tiepin — had all been worth stealing, why take his underclothes and socks? Never. No East-Side thug would bother. Quick escapes were their pattern, ensuring that very few of them were ever caught.

Maybe it was all just a cover-up, to conceal the victim's identity? But some relative or friend was bound to report the man's disappearance to their local precinct station, who, in turn would forward the details to the Bureau of Inquiry for Missing People at headquarters; the Bureau would check with the city morgue, and within days the body was bound to be identified.

Within days! Callaghan thought. Maybe that was the aim? To delay identification.

If so, then once the victim's name was known, someone would stand out as the prime suspect. The lover of the dead man's wife perhaps? Or a business associate whom he'd discovered to be defrauding him?

Whatever the reason, Callaghan reflected, he needn't have killed the poor bastard in this way. The murderer had either hated his victim, or, as Murphy had suggested, he was insane.

Still, the best place to start was Missing Persons.

"Murphy!"

The patrolman only half-turned his

head. Callaghan had met similar insubordination during the War. It was time to be firm.

"Find a sack or something. Cover the body — straighten the legs first — then see if you can find someone amongst this crowd who can identify the guy. While you're doing that, Hagan can check the nearby shipping-offices and warehouses."

Without waiting for a reply Callaghan started down the alleyway. Passing through the crowd, he rumpled the hair of one of a number of bare-footed urchins, pausing to give him a handful of pennies.

"Gee, thanks, mister!" The others crowded around their pal.

"And where d'hell are you going?" Murphy yelled after him.

"Back to the First to arrange for the corpse to be taken to the morgue," Callaghan shouted back over his shoulder.

He entered the noisy, hectic activity of South Street, where vessels were being loaded and unloaded, with boxes, barrels and lumber cluttering up the wharfs, forcing sailors, longshoremen and passengers alike to pick their way between them and the horses hoisting cargoes in and out of the holds.

The crime had been committed in an alley between Wall Street and Old Slip. Alongside pier 12, a glossy horse-drawn cart from Stewarts — New York's most fashionable department store, six-storeys of white marble built by Alexander Stewart, a poor immigrant lad from Ireland who'd worked hard and struck it rich — was being loaded. The foreign symbols on the crates showed that this particular cargo had come from the Orient. The pungent aroma of spices carried across the street to Callaghan, and no doubt the rest of the cargo would appeal equally well to the city's pampered society ladies.

It symbolized the disparity between New York's rich and poor.

Behind South Street lay the city's overcrowded tenement district with street names like Murderer's Alley, Rag Picker's Row, Cat Alley, Rotten Row and Cockroach Row, which until twelve months ago had been known as Tweed's Town, where 'Boss' Tweed and 'Brains' Sweeny had terrorized the polling-stations to ensure their re-election to office.

Tightly packed rows of ancient buildings and clapboard houses, all in varying states of decay, it was home to New York's rapidly expanding immigrant population.

So what the hell had the War against the South been all about? Callaghan asked himself. The North had said it was to free slaves; yet all the time they had their own form of slavery: poverty, affecting whites just as much as blacks, with the avarice and corruption of the wealthy keeping the underprivileged shackled to their over-crowded hovels. Still, Callaghan thought, now that The Tweed Ring had been exposed, maybe the election of some honest politicians would repair the damage.

There were only a few vessels out on the East River; but one, a brig with furled sails being towed to the Upper Bay, caught his attention. Near the prow stood a woman with a small child in her arms; she was encouraging the little one to wave goodbye as the brig made for the open sea.

"Want a better look?"

A gnarled old ex-seafaring type standing alongside Callaghan was offering him a brass telescope. Training it on the vessel, Callaghan focused on the woman.

Of medium height, with a round, pretty face, and dark hair escaping from under her bonnet, she was wearing a heavy overcoat, as was the child, a little girl about two years old, also bonneted and shawled against the wind blowing in from the Atlantic. They continued to wave and seemed to look right at Callaghan. On a sudden impulse, he gave them a brief acknowledgement, then returned his hand to the telescope.

The vessel was freshly painted and extremely trim, fit for anything the Atlantic had to offer. A fine brig, Callaghan thought, as he read her name on the bows: *Mary Celeste*.

★ ★ ★

It was polling-day in the presidential election between the present Republican holder of that office, General Ulysses S. Grant, and the Democrat nomination, New York's own Horace Greeley, owner of the *New Yorker* magazine and the *Tribune* newspaper, and, as a consequence, the streets were crowded.

Callaghan entered New Street. The First Precinct's offices were on the first floor of No. 54, above the fire station known locally as 'The Eighteen Hose'.

Except for Police Headquarters, the First was the busiest station in New York. With a huge tenement population, half of whom were Irish, it took a force of one captain, three sergeants, two detectives, and between eighty to a hundred men — depending on injuries sustained in the course of duty — to control it. Its triangular boundary — from the Battery up Broadway to Fulton Street, then along Fulton to the East River, and down the river-front back to the Battery — contained not only the immigration clearing-house at Castle Garden, but also the consulates of most other countries, and a major part of the representative wealth of the USA: the Sub-Treasury, the Assay Office, the Stock Exchange, money brokers, bullion dealers, diamond merchants, shipping offices, and national and foreign banks.

Today, in an effort to prevent the vote-rigging of recent years, most of the municipal police were out protecting the polling stations. When the First had asked for cover, Callaghan had been seconded to them from headquarters.

He reached No. 54, stone steps and iron railings leading up to the front door, with dark blue lamps on either side. The hallway was brown and peeling. Taking the wooden stairs two at a time, he entered the grimy office where only the desk-sergeant was on duty. A big man with an impressive moustache and beard, Sergeant John W. Kelly's copper badge was so highly polished that the poised bald-eagle on top of the shield had been almost rubbed away. "Was it like Hagan said, or was he exaggerating as usual?"

"Worse." Callaghan described the method of killing.

Kelly whistled through his teeth. "Bejabers! Sure, and that was no way to go, not even if he'd stood up in Harry Hill's and said he was a Republican and a Protestant. Any clues to the body's identity?"

"None. Anyone reported a missing person?"

Kelly shook his head. "Not unless

Greeley's read the *Times* and decided to disappear." He brought a folded copy of the newspaper from under the counter and opened it at page 8, for Callaghan to see the main block-letter headline:

NIGHT BEFORE ELECTION
Politicians were busy at the various Assembly headquarters as bees in a hive. Ballots were being folded, and all the artful dodges and tricks to be practised at the election were being perfected at the Greeley headquarters. But all interest in the national election seems to have faded as all the parties agree that Grant will surely be elected.

"With the front-page declaring Republican gains in most of the places that voted yesterday," declared Kelly, "tis enough to make the poor man go into hiding. That's all he needed, right on top of his wife."

Greeley's wife, Molly, had died only five days ago, after a long illness, leaving the Democrat to face the election grief-stricken. It was thought he might gain a sympathy vote as a result, but that was not to be, according to the *Times* prediction.

"How are you voting?" Callaghan asked.

"Me? Wouldn't waste me shoe-leather," Sergeant Kelly replied disdainfully. "Democrat. Republican. 'Boss' Tweed. 'Brains' Sweeny. President Grant. Senator Colfax. What's the difference? They're all in it only for themselves."

Callaghan agreed. In retaliation after the *Times'* exposure of the Ring, their Democrat rival, New York's *Sun*, had uncovered a fraud which they called 'The Credit Mobilier Scandal', by which a leading Republican senator had pocketed huge bribes from the construction of a Union Pacific railway line. In an effort to influence voters in the race for the White House, the *Sun* had brought it all to the nation's attention and demanded Grant's resignation. But to no avail, it seemed, Horace Greeley's appearance: tall, plump, bald, wispy beard, round pink face, and small eyes framed by exceedingly large spectacles had been exploited to the full by Republican newspaper cartoonists, especially the *Times*, and it looked as though Grant's 'war hero' tag was going to carry the day.

Kelly was right, Callaghan thought. Tweed's Democrats? Grant's Republicans? Was no one clean in politics anymore? It all made him want to sail away again, on one of his brother-in-law's ships.

The thought made him remember the brig sailing down the East River, with the woman and child waving goodbye to New York. Where were they bound? he wondered, glancing at the shipping news, and checking the list of brigantines amongst the cleared vessels:

Osprey (Br). Taylor. Buenos Ayres.
Mary Celeste. Briggs. Genoa.

That was the one. So, the captain's name was Briggs. And the woman and little girl were no doubt his wife and daughter. Bound for Genoa, were they? On days like this, it made him feel like going after them. Maybe after he'd solved this murder case?

Callaghan made for the door. "I'm

off to headquarters. To check missing persons."

★ ★ ★

Callaghan turned down Exchange Place, into the deafening bustle of Broadway, crowded with people taking advantage of the day off because of the election. With the horses back on the streets after the distemper outbreak, the avenue was resounding to the rumble of densely packed omnibuses, wagons, carts, the clatter of hackney-carriages, and people everywhere, all of them, it seemed, in a hurry; their mixed appearances making New York's fast increasing immigrant population immediately apparent: Irish, Germans, Jews, Italians, come to the USA to escape either famine or persecution in Europe. Even during his own thirty-year lifetime, the city's population had grown from 400,000 to 1,000,000. Soon there'd be no damned room to breathe.

Callaghan reached Trinity Presbyterian Church, on the corner of Rectory. Surrounded by three-, four-, five-, and a few six-storeyed buildings, Trinity's towering spire easily made it New York's tallest edifice. Reaching out towards a God who wasn't there, Callaghan thought.

A Yellow Bird omnibus drew up. He got on, squeezing between a large, fur-wrapped woman, and a stern-looking man in a black overcoat and stovepipe hat, as they headed up Broadway.

The avenue epitomized New York's rapid transformation. Only a few years ago it had been mostly residential but now, stretching all the way to Bleeker Street, there were nothing but top-class hotels, like the Astor House, and fashionable shops like Stewarts, with its lines of waiting carriages and uniformed footmen contrasting with young girls in ragged dresses plying the pavements, trying to earn the price of a loaf of bread by vending hot corn, with their cries of: 'Here's your nice hot corn, smoking hot, smoking hot, just for the pot'.

"Bleeker Street!"

The shout brought him back. He descended from the omnibus. This far uptown the traffic was not so frenetic, and he walked the two blocks east to

No. 300 Mulberry Street, the city's new five-storeyed Police Headquarters.

The Detective Squad occupied Rooms 5 and 6 on the ground floor, with The Bureau of Enquiry for Missing Persons — a mouthful of a title, Callaghan always thought — in the adjoining room.

He checked the bureau first, but none of the John Does fitted his murder victim. His next call was the telegraph office in Room 1 in the basement, where he asked Superintendent Crowley to let him know if and when a Missing Persons came in, corresponding to the description of the body. After five days in the city morgue, unidentified corpses were taken to Hart's Island and buried without ceremony in Potter's Field. The least the poor guy deserved was a proper funeral, Callaghan thought, as he headed upstairs to discuss the case with his chief.

Captain James Irving had replaced Captain James Kelso — a personal friend of 'Boss' Tweed's — when Kelso was promoted superintendent two years ago. There were rumours that Irving had paid a bribe of $15,000 for the appointment, Tweed's rate for a police captaincy. He was a burly man with a ruddy complexion, the lower half of his face hidden behind a large moustache and beard.

Today, his mind seemed to be elsewhere. Callaghan concluded his report and waited, the large wooden clock on the wall loudly ticking away the seconds, as the captain continued to look past him into the distance. Finally, Callaghan coughed and Irving's eyes returned to the room, focusing on him.

"The post-mortem?" Callaghan repeated.

"What the hell d'you want a post-mortem for?" Irving demanded irritably.

"To determine how long he's been dead. And confirm the cause."

"Damn it, man! We've got enough confounded work to do without going through unnecessary procedures and form-filling. Besides, what does it matter how or when he was killed, it was obviously for the money? We don't need any blasted sawbones to be telling us that."

Despite his apparent detachment, Irving had obviously heard the gist of the report.

"I think there's more to it."

"And what gives you that idea?"

"A sixth sense. And the fact he was completely naked."

"Sixth sense nothing! It's a typical assault by thugs from East Side, and we haven't got a cat-in-hell's chance of catching them."

"What about identifying the body?"

"What about it?"

"How much time do I give it?"

"You don't. Just file your report and forget it."

Callaghan gave it one last try. "But what if he's got relatives: a wife, or children, worried about him?"

Irving spoke slowly and finally. "Then they'll report to their nearest precinct, and that's Missing Persons' responsibility. Now, if you've finished, I've got more important work to do, helping the District Attorney prove the case against Tweed."

Two weeks ago, the grand jury had again dismissed all charges against Mayor 'Elegant Oakey' Hall, one of the four leading Tweed Ring players. With Sweeny and 'Slippery Dick' Connolly both having escaped to Europe, there was only 'Boss' left. City officialdom was thought to be divided over Tweed's fate. Half wanted him locked up, while the other half was rumoured to be praying for him to make a run for it.

Suspecting that Irving's true motive in assisting the DA was to cover up any evidence of his own bribe, Callaghan got to his feet.

"Ten gets you one that Boss gets off. If Oakey can, then Tweed's a sure-fired certainty."

"Get out," Irving growled.

4

A MILE out, in the sheltered confines of Upper Bay, the *Mary Celeste* rode at anchor, her sails furled, on a shallow flat off Staten Island. Because of the gale-force head wind hurtling in through the six-mile gap between Sandy Hook and Coney Island, Briggs had decided to wait until the wind dropped before venturing out into the open sea.

At his desk, Briggs glanced towards Sarah, who was sitting on the bed, darning a tear in one of Sophia's play-dresses. Their small daughter was standing by her side, cuddling her doll, Sarah Jane, and turning over the pages of a photograph album placed on the bed.

With deliberate casualness, Briggs took a key from his waistcoat pocket, unlocked his desk drawer and, for the umpteenth time, began reading the letter spread open inside.

Sarah sighed and looked up. Briggs swiftly closed the drawer and locked it, replacing the key. Seeing the sadness in her brown eyes, he rose and sat down beside her, placing an arm around her shoulders.

"What is it?" he asked gently. "Is it Arthur?"

"Yes," Sarah replied, tears welling in her eyes. "I do hope he will be all right."

Drawing her head on to his shoulder, Briggs caressed it. "Don't worry," he reassured her, "Grandma Briggs will enjoy looking after him. And we'll be back home before you know it."

At the mention of Grandma Briggs, Sophia looked up sharply, pointing a stubby finger at the photograph of a stately lady sitting on a studio chair, wearing a dark voluminous dress and staring fixedly into the camera. "Gamma Bis, Gamma Bis," she lisped, searching her mother's face for confirmation.

Sarah Briggs gave a half-smile and stroked her daughter's hair. "Yes, darling. Grandma Briggs." Then brushing the tears from her eyes, she gave her husband a brave smile. "You are right, Benjamin. I'm sorry to be so maudlin. I realize he needs the schooling, nevertheless I miss him." She straightened her shoulders. "Still, I'm looking forward to seeing Genoa, and meeting up with David and Desiah again. How lucky you were able to get them an alternative cargo, and to the same ports as ourselves. Desiah would have hated Curaçao."

Briggs removed his arm. "Yes, it was fortunate." He stood up, restless. "I'd best check the crew."

"Benjamin! What is worrying you? Is it that letter? You've been on tenterhooks ever since it came on board."

Briggs forced a smile. "Letter? You mean the one from Winchester wishing us God's-speed? No, Sarah, it's not that. It's simply the frustration of being stuck here, especially with so much resting on this voyage."

Despite his unconvincing tone, Sarah knew that Benjamin's ability to repay Winchester's loan of $3,600 depended on the success of the trip.

"Then be of good faith, Ben," she reassured him, "and God will bless your endeavours. The weather will lift, and we will soon be on our way." She smiled.

"And now, if you must, go check your crew."

But as her husband left, Sarah's smile faded. Picking up little Sophia, she held her tight for comfort. Sarah had known Benjamin far too long not to realize when he was lying.

5

IT was eight that evening before Callaghan signed off duty.

It had been a long, hard, gruelling day, quelling clashes between rival gangs of Republican and Democrat supporters. The real trouble had erupted about four in the afternoon, when telegraphs of Grant's successes began pouring in from around the country, confirming the *Times'* predictions of a Republican landslide. Realizing that they'd lost, a mob of Democrat voters, who'd been gathering outside the *Sun* since midday, looted the surrounding buildings, then set them on fire, and finally, with a cry of 'Let's gut it', had set off for the *New York Times*.

The succeeding battle left the First with a number of injured, but the fight took the steam out of the rioters, and as darkness now descended, they were licking their wounds inside grog-shops and gin-palaces.

Callaghan reached Broadway to find a solid mass of horse-drawn traffic with myriad coach-lamps dotting the length of the avenue, and fusing into a massed blur in the far distance.

There was no point taking an omnibus, Callaghan decided. It would take hours. The only way to move was through the side-streets. Seeing a cab unloading a male passenger, he ran across to it. "Greenwich. Carmine."

Falling into the seat, he felt a wave of exhaustion sweep over him. What a hell of a way to make a living! he thought, and in that same moment, decided to resign from the force.

Face it, Callaghan. There's no damned point hanging on any longer. Either Sweeny, the blasted shyster!, has already managed to get the $200,000,000 abroad, or it's so well hidden, it will never be found.

He shrugged off a slight, guilty feeling about the John Doe. But what did it matter if the stiff ended up in Potter's Field? Mausoleumed cemetery or lime pit? The dead didn't know where they were buried. Good or bad, believer or atheist, it was the same end for all — oblivion. Total and absolute.

He studied his reflection in the cab's darkened window.

Had he changed that much since Colleen walked out on him? Hardly at all in physique: five-eleven in bare feet, broad shouldered, 150 pounds. His waist may have thickened, but no more than a couple of inches since the war, when to be hard and fast decided whether one lived or died. The fine sabre scar across his right cheek that Colleen used to trace with her finger was now almost invisible. Yet the face mirrored in the window was that of a stranger, without feeling, and so prone to smile it was difficult to recognize. He studied his eyes — it was said they were the mirror of one's soul. If that were so, then heaven help him, because the eyes gazing back at him out of the darkness were emotionless, devoid of joy; they were the eyes of a man who saw the world for what it was, harsh, uncaring, uncompromising, where only the tough survived.

A feeling of barrenness swept over him. His thoughts went back in time to the war and the destruction of the Shenandoah. This was how the people of the valley must have felt seeing all their lands and the fruits of their labour so completely wiped out.

Pressing back into his seat, and for about the thousandth time, Callaghan relived the events of seven years ago . . .

* * *

Two years after enrolling, Callaghan was a war veteran, a major; yet only a couple of years younger than his commander, General George Armstrong Custer, as the 8th New York Cavalry moved out of its winter headquarters in Winchester, to begin the journey south to clear the Shenandoah of its last pocket of Southern resistance.

For two days they rode, through torrential rain, men and horses dripping in mud. The valley that had once seemed like paradise to Callaghan, its fields rich with golden grain, and orchards thick with fruit, was no more. 'Destroy it', General Ulysses S. Grant had ordered. Now the landscape looked like Hell, a

Yankee-created Hell; farmhouses, barns, corncribs, gristmills, bridges, and fields all burnt to the ground.

What was the sense of it? Callaghan asked himself, as they rode on. How could any righteous cause justify such wanton destruction? The people of the Shenandoah had been hard-working, God-fearing. Where was the hand of their Heavenly Father in all this?

Damp, cold and miserable, the cavalrymen eventually reached Waynesboro, where a small Southern force led by Jubal Early was holed-up on a knoll at the western approach to Rockfish Gap.

Charge! Custer ordered, leading from the front. In galloping columns of four they rode straight for the lines, shells bursting around them, blowing men and horses to smithereens, then over the breast-works, sabering fleeing 'Johnny Rebs' to left and right.

American against American. Brother against brother. Friend against friend.

Suddenly a bullet hit Callaghan in the chest, lifting him out of the saddle and leaving him face down in the mud. He felt a violent explosion of pain, then blacked out.

He woke in a wagon-train crowded with wounded. A young boy, no more than sixteen, wearing light-grey, was lying across his lap. The kid's stomach had been cut wide open with a sabre. Could it have been his? Callaghan wondered, as the boy clutched the awful wound closed, looking up with unseeing eyes and calling for his father. Callaghan embraced his enemy to his chest, giving him whatever comfort he could. But as the rooftops of Fredericksburg appeared in the distance, the boy gave a gurgling sound and died, his hands sprawling loose, and his guts spilling out over the wagon.

Holding him tight, Callaghan ceased believing in God.

Regardless of the colour of their uniforms, the survivors were divided into three classes by Northern army surgeons: minor cases, amputees, and those with little or no hope of survival. Because his wound had suppurated, and the bullet was so close to his lung, Callaghan was placed with the hopeless on the hard planks of a commandeered molasses warehouse, which stank of death.

Exhausted and resigned to dying, he fell asleep.

When he woke feeling feverish, a green-eyed, auburn-haired nurse was kneeling beside him.

"Would you like a blanket?" she whispered. "Or some water?"

Despite his pain, Callaghan forced a grin. "Champagne and two glasses."

"We've no champagne, I'm afraid. But I can find some whiskey. What are we celebrating?"

"Our engagement."

"Goodness!" she responded, going along with the joke. "When did that happen?"

"A moment ago. Didn't you feel something pass between us?"

"Was that what it was?" The nurse cooled his forehead with a damp cloth. "Well, shouldn't we go out to celebrate?"

"How about Delmonico's?" Callaghan longed to caress her face, the high cheekbones, the stray lock of tawny hair.

"That's an invitation I shall hold you to," she replied. "But first, I'd like to take a look at your wound."

As she eased the blood-dried cloth from his chest, Callaghan tried not to grimace. Nor could the nurse prevent herself pulling a face. "Don't start for Delmonico's without me." She stood to her feet. "I'll be back in five minutes."

"I promise to wait, if it takes to eternity."

When the nurse returned, she was accompanied by an elderly surgeon. After examining the patient, they huddled in consultation. At last, in answer to her pleas, he agreed to operate.

Callaghan remembered being moved into the operating tent. When he came to, it was five days later. For four of those days, the surgeon told him, he'd hovered between life and death. Had it not been for the nurse's full-time care, day and night, he would not have pulled through.

"May I see her to thank her?" he whispered.

The surgeon apologized. "I'm sorry, son, but she's catching up on some much needed sleep."

"When will she be back?"

"Tomorrow morning. Now get some rest."

Later that day, Callaghan, despite his protests, was loaded on to a wagon with other wounded, and driven fifteen miles to Aquia Creek on the Potomac, where a steamer was waiting to take them to an army hospital in Washington. Watching Fredericksburg fade into the distance, an aching void in his heart told him he had found, and now lost, that once-in-a-lifetime love that young men often dream of, but rarely discover, without even knowing her name.

On the journey he suffered a relapse. But determining to go back to Fredericksburg and find her, gave him the will to pull through. A month later the war ended, and he was transferred to a civilian hospital in New York to recover. By the time he was well, all field hospitals had been closed, and the military were in such confusion none of his letters to the army's nursing authorities were answered.

Returning to the family newspaper, his father, some twelve months later, had asked Callaghan to interview a new, young novelist. The daughter of an

Edward Lowell — a wealthy business man from Greenwich, who was related by marriage to Alderman Peter Sweeny, of the powerful 20th District — her first book was being launched later that week.

"Do I have to?" he groaned.

"Someone has to," his father replied. "It may as well be you."

"OK. What's the novel about anyway?"

"According to the publisher, it's 'a romantic love-story set in the turbulent days of the Civil War'."

"Romantic! What the hell would a young society girl know about it, closeted away in New York?"

"Michael, you're a newspaper man. Just go to the house, write the article, and forget about it. For all you know, she may turn out to be another Elizabeth Stoddard or a Kate Field."

Callaghan conceded. Recent years had seen a number of independent women in the headlines. The two his father had mentioned were the current talk of New York. Elizabeth Stoddard — wife of Richard Stoddard, the poet — already had two novels published: *The Morgensons*, and *Two Men*. As for Kate Field, journalist, lecturer, actress, friend of the Brownings, George Eliot, and Anthony Trollope, she was now working on her *Pen Photographs of Charles Dickens*, which she had already sold to a Boston publisher.

An hour later, Callaghan was standing in the Lowell's drawing-room, his back to the fire, looking across into the hall, and watching a dark blue skirt come into view down the curving stairs, then a small waist, a tight bodice with cream lace which accentuated the young novelist's bust-line, and finally her face with its high cheekbones, green eyes, and profusion of auburn hair . . . .

Entering the room, she saw him and stood still. Swiftly crossing over to her, Callaghan opened his arms, and Colleen threw herself into them.

Later, much later, when he finally remembered about the interview, she reminded him of his invitation in the Fredericksburg warehouse.

"You mentioned something about Delmonico's?"

"What about this evening?"

"Perfect."

"Consider the table booked."

"And the champagne?"

"The best. With two glasses . . . "

★ ★ ★

Callaghan remembered the evening as though it were yesterday. The clinking of goblets. His proposal. Colleen's acceptance. One month later, they were married in Colleen's church: Saint Francis Xavier's on 16th Street.

At the reception he had met Peter Barr Sweeny for the first time. Only forty-two, short, solidly built, not yet running to fat, his large head covered with a mass of thick-black hair, and sporting a jet-black walrus moustache, Colleen's uncle had sauntered over, puffing his cigar, and introduced himself.

"I'm Alderman Sweeny of the Twentieth District. You've probably heard of me?" His accent, his whole manner of speech, was a strange mixture of his original East-Side dialect, and an obvious attempt to refine it.

102

"Of course, Mr Sweeny. Who in New York hasn't?"

Peter Barr Sweeny was one of the four leading members of The Tweed Ring, four Democrat aldermen currently under investigation by the *New York Times*, of fraudulently diverting city funds into their own pockets.

Their leader was William Marcy 'Boss' Tweed. A bearded, powerful hunk of a man, alderman for the 7th Ward. And Grand Sachem of Tammany Hall.

Two more named by the *Times* were: Abraham 'Elegant Oakey' Hall — the current Mayor of New York, slim, agile, wavy-haired with a short, stylish beard, always faultlessly dressed. Also, the city's Financial Comptroller — Richard 'Slippery Dick' Connolly, a tall, slimy, beanstalk of a man, with a long narrow face, who always wore a black, stove-pipe hat, which made him look even taller.

But the Ring's mastermind was undoubtedly Peter Barr Sweeny. Physically squat and ugly, he was a devious attorney with a dark, brooding, Machiavellian nature, and a sinister, dual personality. On his corrupt side, inventor and manipulator of The Tweed Ring's fraudulent empire; on the other, one of the Jesuit Church of Saint Francis Xavier's most faithful and ardent worshippers. Religiosity and evil combined, that was Sweeny, with evil predominating, as Callaghan now knew only too well.

Already described as 'The Man in Black' by the *New York Times* because of his permanent black attire, Sweeny had been born in New York of poor Irish parents, both of whom ran saloons. Thanks to the large number of priests in his family, he'd been educated at St Peter's Catholic School. After his graduation, his uncle, Senator Thomas Barr, realizing his nephew's razor-sharp mind, had arranged for him to read law in the offices of James T. Brady, a colourful leading New York attorney. Later, when Sweeny was admitted to the bar, his uncle helped him enter politics, and to become, at thirty-one years old, ward boss of the powerful 20th District.

"When my uncle, Senator Barr, decides to retire, I'm gonna take over from him."

"If all goes well, Mr Sweeny."

"It will, son, I'll make damn sure of that. Now that you're family — my wife, Sara Augusta, is a first cousin of Colleen's father by the way — I hope you're gonna write some good things about me in your father's paper." Sweeny stroked his thick, walrus moustache. "The *Times* is starting to get a bit personal lately, accusing us of diverting city funds. All lies, of course. Nevertheless, we — that's Alderman Tweed, and myself — could do with someone telling our side of the story."

"We pride ourselves on telling the truth, sir."

Nicknamed 'Brains' by the *Times*, Sweeny was no one's fool. He realized Callaghan was discreetly telling him that no favours would be granted just because of their new family connection.

"The truth," he repeated, his tone suddenly hardening, "is that a fact?" He paused. "Did you know that Colleen's father is chairman of a number of companies who've recently won some big city contracts?" Callaghan detected an underlying threat in his question.

"Yes, sir. He's told me about them.

They were won on best tenders, as I understand."

"So I believe," Sweeny replied, removing his cigar and studying the smoke. "So I believe. Still, it's good to keep things in the family, don't you think, son? And now you're one of us, it might help you to bear that in mind." He paused. "Congratulations on your sudden marriage by the way. Only known each other a month, too?" He jammed the cigar back in the corner of his mouth. "Colleen's not expecting a happy event, by any chance?" Before Callaghan could reply, Sweeny had wandered off, furiously chewing his cheroot.

As her mother had died when Colleen was only fourteen, there was a very close bond between her and her father. And Callaghan had also got on well with him, right from the start.

From the moment he carried his bride over the threshold of their newly purchased mews house in Greenwich, their next four years had been blissful . . .

Then, like a dark bolt out of the blue, had come Sweeny's slick theft of their newspaper, leaving Callaghan's

106

father and mother homeless and broke. As for himself and Colleen . . .

But, again — what the hell! He had to accept it. He and Colleen were now of the past.

Revenge was what dominated his mind. One day, even if it meant selling his soul to the Devil, the opportunity to get even with Sweeny would surely arise.

And when it did!

The cab drew to a halt. Callaghan descended, paid the driver, and began walking the two blocks to his mews house off Bedford.

6

COLLEEN was sitting at her writing desk in her bedroom, trying to decide on the ending of her second novel, based on her experiences in Europe, and written during her travels.

But worry about her father kept breaking her concentration. The more he was being dragged into The Tweed Ring investigation, and the ever increasing likelihood he would be indicted like Tweed and Mayor Hall, the more he was taking to drink. This was why Mr Phelps, their family attorney, had contacted her in London, advising her to return home. And this was why she was determined to find Sweeny, and get his sworn affidavit, clearing her father of being knowingly involved in any fraud.

Colleen forced her mind back to her manuscript, but, after re-reading the penultimate chapter four times, she turned to a copy of her first book,

Blown by the Winds of War, hoping for inspiration.

Flicking through the pages, she glanced over how the heroine — the independent-minded daughter of a New York society family, who, despite her parents' protests, had registered for a basic course in nursing run by the city's physicians, and was then posted straight to the battlefront — had met the hero as one of a wagon-train of wounded. He was a Northern cavalry captain, dark and handsome, a man obviously used to seeing death, yet there'd been tears in his eyes as she'd had to prise a dead, Southern boy-soldier from his grasp.

The memory of his tears had remained with her throughout the long, hard day of helping the surgeons, and mopping-up after each operation. Coming off duty, she'd eventually found him in a warehouse left to die.

Sensing her presence, he'd opened his eyes. They were deep blue. Despite his obvious pain, he'd grinned up at her, and she'd felt her heart miss a beat.

Having assisted at the operation to remove the bullet, she'd then nursed him four days and nights without sleep. When, on the fifth morning, his fever subsided, she had finally retired exhausted to her own bed, and slept twenty-four hours without waking.

But then, on returning to the medical tent, there was another soldier lying in her officer's place. Fearing he'd died while she was asleep, she turned anxiously to the nearest nurse, only to be told he'd been transferred to an army hospital in Washington.

A month later, the war ended. But, by the time the heroine got to the capital, the hospital was closed and its files mislaid.

In the resulting chaos of peace, her letters to the authorities went unanswered. Not even knowing his first name, the heroine was forced to resign herself to the heartbreaking fact she had lost him — but then she'd thought up the idea of writing a novel, and leaving the ending in the air, hoping against hope that the officer would read it, find her, and they would live happily ever after.

Colleen threw the book down. Happily ever after! How remote was fiction from reality. To think she'd once believed that love . . .

"Colleen!"

Her father was calling from his study. By the sound of his slurred voice, he'd been at the whiskey again.

She rose to her feet and headed downstairs.

* * *

Although Colleen was no longer there to greet him, Callaghan was usually glad to get back to Greenwich.

Its slow, backwater, village atmosphere, the way it refused to succumb to New York's insatiable growth, normally lifted his spirits. This was why he had chosen to walk the last few blocks home, hoping the tree-lined cobbled streets dimly lit by gaslights, the pavement restaurants, and the rich variety of houses, from Dutch-farm period to early American would diffuse his feeling of emptiness.

But tonight, the neighbourhood had no effect on his mood.

Entering his mews house, he first poured himself a large whiskey, neat,

111

and knocked it straight back, feeling the spirits burning away at the ache in his stomach. He then put a match to the fire. In no time, the flames were roaring up the chimney, warming the room. Too tired to cook, he cut a hunk of bread and some cheese, carried them into the drawing-room, poured himself another whiskey, and without lighting the oil-lamps, flopped into the high-backed chair by the now blazing hearth.

Eating his snack, he glanced at the portrait of Colleen in its ornate gold frame on the far wall. Painted on their wedding anniversary, just two and a half years ago, her happiness at the time still seemed to radiate out of it. Two and a half years ago. Only weeks before everything had suddenly gone wrong . . .

★ ★ ★

It was strange how one always remembered the small things first; the rays of the afternoon sun slanting in through the windows of his father's newspaper office, lighting up hundreds of tiny dust specks floating about the room. And then the expression of horror in his father's voice, and the shock in his eyes, as he reacted to Sweeny's ultimatum.

"Redeem the loans by midnight, or I foreclose!"

Foreclosure. What broken dreams were in that one word. So many years of ambitious toil, hopes, dreams, aspirations, two homes, plans for the future, all suddenly under threat because of one man's evil machinations.

His father stood to his feet, the desk between him and Sweeny.

"But my loans aren't with the Bowling Green Bank."

The Bowling Green was one of two banks owned by The Tweed Ring. The other was The Guardian Bank for Savings.

"They are now." Sweeny's deep gravelly voice betrayed gloating satisfaction. "Purchased this morning from your bankers, together with the deeds."

"Deeds! Both sets?"

"Yes. Business and house. Paid top price for them." Brains wore his high-crowned black silk top-hat, making no effort to remove it.

As his father collapsed into his chair, cupping his face in his hands, Callaghan strode purposefully around the desk. Sweeny retreated towards the door.

"Midnight!" Callaghan protested. "That's impossible. You've got to give us more time. If you don't, then by all that's holy, Sweeny, you'll pay for it."

Sweeny grabbed the door-handle. "Michael, forget the threats. I'm acting within the law. Lay a finger on me, and I'll have you inside so fast you'll be behind bars before you know it. And next time your father signs a loan agreement — if his credit holds good for there to be a next time — I suggest he gets a good attorney to help him read the small print first."

Brains opened the door. "If only you'd listened to me at your wedding, Michael, none of this need ever have happened. Still, you've got until midnight. That's a whole six hours . . .

★ ★ ★

The Callaghans had failed to redeem either loan. The newspaper was taken.

114

And his parents were evicted from their home, their furniture repossessed under a clause in Sweeny's 'small print'.

In shock, they left New York that very same day for Savanah, to stay with Michael's sister, Francesca, and her ship-owner husband, Jonathan.

Meanwhile, in New York, Michael was on the receiving end of yet another shock, when Sweeny's carriage pulled up outside his front door. Callaghan looked down at the man, making no attempt to disguise his loathing, but determined not to sink to Sweeny's level and obey his instincts to beat him black and blue until the man could no longer stand.

"Are't you going to ask me in?" Sweeny said, with deliberate sarcasm.

"Over my dead body."

"Anytime." Sweeny drew on his cigar and blew out the smoke. "Just say the word."

"OK, Sweeny, that's the pleasantries over. I take it you're here for some purpose? Some writ you want to serve, maybe?"

"Say, we are in a bitter mood today! All's fair in business, and don't you ever forget it, Michael. Pity you had to learn it the hard way. Like I said earlier, you ought to have agreed to my proposition four years ago. Anyway, how are your parents? I hear they've moved to Savannah to live? The climate should suit them. I probably did your old man a favour. You gotta admit it, Michael, the paper's style was somewhat stale. By the time we've revamped it, and got some decent articles written, you won't recognize it."

Callaghan fought to control his anger. Sweeny's reason for stealing the paper was obvious. Now under sustained attack from the *New York Times'* campaign, The Tweed Ring needed a reputable daily to enable them to fight back, requiring its pages to refute the *Times'* allegations, which so far had lacked hard evidence. His father's newspaper had been tailor-made for them.

But one thing was still puzzling Callaghan: from where had Sweeny found out about the loans?

He'd explored all the possibilities, and kept coming back to either Patrick Oates, his father's trusted bookkeeper, or their banker, William Samson? One of them must have fallen to a bribe. There was no other explanation. The mortgages had been a closely guarded family secret.

"You wouldn't believe the plans our new chairman has got for the paper." Sweeny interrupted his thoughts. "But then, I'm forgetting, he's probably already told you about them?"

Callaghan remained silent, all at once realizing Sweeny's reason for being here. This was his one weakness: a sadistic enjoyment to gloat over his victims and watch them suffer.

"You mean he's not told you yet?" Sweeny queried in mock surprise. "I guess he's been too busy. He's probably waiting until you and Colleen go around there, so he can tell you about it over dinner?"

Callaghan felt himself go cold, but betrayed no emotion.

"Say, I'm sorry, Michael," Sweeny feigned self-reproach. "Me and my big mouth. Now I've gone and spoilt it for him. Listen, when you see your father-in-law next, give him my apologies. And thank him for the information. Sorry,

I can't stop. I've got other matters to see to."

Too stunned to move, and his mind spinning, Callaghan watched Sweeny clamber into his carriage, and settle into his seat. Having satisfied his peculiar pleasure, Brains tapped the driver's window with his silver-topped cane and, as the coach moved off, peered at Callaghan through the rear window, and mockingly raised his top-hat.

The rumbling of the iron-rimmed wheels on the cobblestones jerked Callaghan into action. He slammed the door shut. Colleen was standing motionless in the middle of the drawing-room, her face white. For the first time ever he was oblivious to her beauty — did not even see her.

"Did you know?" he demanded.

"No, Michael, I swear," she replied, with some concern.

"I don't believe you," he angrily rejected her denial. "It explains everything."

"Explains! Michael, please!" Colleen protested.

He brushed her plea aside. "You heard what Sweeny said. I'm to thank your

118

damned father for what's happened. And he could only have found out about the mortgages from you . . . "

"Michael!" Her green eyes flashed.

"I'm not saying you told him deliberately. It probably slipped out in conversation, but one thing's for certain: your creeping father went running to Sweeny with the information — on all fours, with his tail between his legs, ready to lick his boots. And why not? As chairman of most of Sweeny's other companies, he's been his lapdog for years, getting kickbacks for signing pieces of paper pushed under his nose, and never bothering to read the print . . . "

"Michael!" Colleen's passion was visibly rising, her cheeks were becoming flushed. "Knowing how you feel after all Uncle Peter has done, I'm going to ignore what you've just said. What's more, I deny saying anything to Father about the loans, either intentionally or accidentally. As I've told you before, Father never involves himself in the daily running of the companies; his appointments are merely honorary. All he does is sign minutes of monthly meetings . . . "

"Knowing they've been prepared by a crook like Sweeny!" Callaghan scorned. "He must shut his eyes every time he picks up a pen!"

"Michael!" Colleen's voice was now dangerously tense. "So far, nothing's been proved against Uncle Peter. The *Times'* allegations are no more than hearsay. I'll admit he's ruthless, and for myself, I've no time for the man, but Father says he has no reason to doubt him, especially as he and Mr Tweed seem to be running the city so efficiently . . . "

"What else can he say?" Callaghan demanded, still steaming over the betrayal. "It damn well pays him to turn a blind eye. He gets his income from city contracts awarded by the Ring. It's no wonder he's able to live in such luxury, surrounded by staff, not caring what happens to my mother and father . . . " Callaghan choked on his words.

"You've just gone too far, Michael!" Colleen's face was suddenly drained of all colour, her tone cold. "Either you apologize, and accept my word that I said nothing to Father, or . . . "

120

"Or what?"

"Or I'm leaving."

"That's fine by me."

Colleen had stood there for a long moment searching his face. He deliberately avoided her gaze. When finally she spoke, her voice was distant. "If it's fine with you, Michael, it's certainly fine by me. I'll send Mary around for my clothes . . ."

Those mundane words had been the last to pass between them.

After a restless night he'd awoken to an empty bed, his heart still full of bitterness. Staring up at the ceiling, wondering what to do with the rest of his life, his thoughts had shifted to his parents, finally prompting him to rise.

Stuffing a few items into a case, Callaghan had taken the first train to Savannah. He arrived to find his mother already responding to the tightly knit family atmosphere — which so suited her Italian nature — looking after her three grandchildren, for Jonathan and Francesca to rebuild their shipping business, which had been ravaged by the Northern blockade of Southern ports during the war.

But his father was brooding by the fire, locked into a shell, his only conversation to blame his own 'selfish ambitions' for placing Callaghan's mother in such a vulnerable position. "Everything lost," he kept repeating, "all because of me. Home, furniture, paintings, china, ornaments, even some sentimental things your mother brought over with her from Italy, all gone because of my signature on a piece of paper." Regardless of her constant reassurances that all that mattered was himself, nothing she said could lessen his guilt.

Meanwhile, Callaghan was feeling his own pain over Colleen, and fast turning to drink in a vain attempt to forget her. Realizing he must find another way, he turned to his brother-in-law one evening when they were sitting on the verandah.

"I'd like to spend some time at sea."

"No problem," his brother-in-law replied. "I'll give you a week's tuition, then you can head the yacht south, hugging the coast . . . "

"No, Jonathan." Callaghan hadn't a

vacation in mind. "On one of your brigs."

"They've no berths for passengers, Michael."

"I meant as one of the crew."

"A seaman! Are you out of your mind?" Jonathan asked. "Have you any idea just how tough the life is?"

"No. But it can't be any worse than the war."

"But why, for pity's sake? Is it to do with Colleen?"

Callaghan didn't wish to discuss her. "Let's just say I need to get away. See new places. People. Countries."

"Michael, listen . . ."

"Jonathan, I've made up my mind. If you won't take me, then I'll sign on with someone else."

And with this, his brother-in-law had reluctantly given in. The brig, *Elisabeth Bellis*, had taken Callaghan around the Atlantic, from Savannah to Havana, then south to Caracas, Rio de Janeiro, across the southern ocean to Capetown, and finally, six months later, back to Savannah, a hardened seaman, but with his mind cleared, realizing how much he'd wronged Colleen, and anxious to return home to ask her forgiveness.

This decision had collapsed the day after his return, when his father suffered a massive heart attack and died in his arms. His last words were to warn him, "Michael, don't bear grudges. It eats away at your soul. Forget Sweeny. Make it up with Colleen. Start a new life together before it's too late. Learn from me, before it's too . . . "

Even as his father's last breath rasped out, Callaghan dismissed his words, and had once more blamed Colleen.

But he charged Sweeny even more. What he'd done was tantamount to murder, and even before the funeral, Callaghan began plotting his revenge.

★ ★ ★

Meanwhile, in New York, the *Times* campaign had reached the stage where public pressure had finally forced Mayor Hall into agreeing to the appointment of a Committee of Investigation to examine the city's books, kept by Dick Connolly.

Five of New York's most respectable

men were chosen to sit on it: Moses Taylor, Marshall O. Roberts, Edward Schell, George K. Sistaire, and Edward D. Brown. Their chairman was John Jacob Astor III, a friend and Fifth-Avenue neighbour of Tweed's.

On the very eve of the November 1870 city elections — still two months before the death of Callaghan's father — and with the odds very much stacked against any of the Ring being re-elected, the six men — immediately branded by the *Times* as 'The Astor Whitewashing Committee' — published their findings, clearing The Tweed Ring of all allegations; declaring: 'We have personally examined the securities of the Department and Sinking Funds, and found them to be correct'.

The Ring and some 50,000 red-shirted Democrat supporters immediately celebrated with a torchlit parade on City Hall. The next day, all four ringleaders: Boss Tweed, Brains Sweeny, Slippery Dick Connolly, and Mayor Elegant Oakey Hall were returned to office . . .

* * *

After the funeral, with a plan formulating in his mind, Callaghan returned to New York and went straight to the *Times*, to sound it out on his old acquaintance, Louis Jennings, its Chief Editor.

In his mid-thirties, slim, with a trim moustache, pointed beard, and always well dressed, Jennings was English. Previously United States correspondent for the London *Times*, he was an acerbic writer and a trenchant investigator, who'd needed little persuasion from George Jones, owner of the *New York Times* — a first-generation Welsh immigrant from Poultney, Vermont — to lead the campaign against the Ring.

After receiving Jennings's condolences about the death of his father, Callaghan began the conversation with the comment, "I hear that James Watson, the County Auditor, has recently been killed in a sleighing accident."

"True," Jenning replied. His pronounced English accent and affectations were all deliberate, intended to hide a penetrating mind. "Can't say I shed any tears. He was a Ring man through and through."

"So I understand. Has his position been filled yet?"

"Hardly. He's not due to be planted out of harm's way under the sod until tomorrow."

"Good. So how about O'Rourke applying for the position?"

"Matthew?" Jennings thoughtfully stroked his beard. O'Rourke was the *New York Times*' best undercover freelancer, who'd wormed his way into the Tammany Hall crowd by pretending to be an ardent Democrat. "Why, Michael, that's an excellent idea. With his experience as a bookkeeper before becoming a newsman, he's absolutely ideal for the role. A few months in the Treasury Department, and we should have all the evidence we need."

"That's what I thought. At the same time I can get myself into the Detective Squad at Headquarters. It will give me the opportunity to probe into places where a reporter can't get into, and also pick up on any inside gossip."

"Even better. But how can you ensure you'll be sent to Mulberry Street, and not one of the precincts?"

"General William 'Baldy' Smith. He was a friend of my father's."

"The old Northern warhorse?"

"Now Police Commissioner Smith."

Opening a desk drawer, Jennings pulled out a whiskey bottle and two tumblers. "Michael, old chap, you've just made my day." Half-filling both glasses, he handed one across, then raised his own and proposed: "Here's to the demise of the Ring!"

★ ★ ★

A week later, at Companies Registration Office, Detective Callaghan was checking through the files of firms which had been awarded city contracts, searching for a familiar name which he could link to one of the Ring, a person on whom he could apply pressure to talk, when suddenly one leapt up at him off the page.

Patrick Oates!

His father's ex-bookkeeper!

Realizing its terrible significance, Callaghan spent the rest of the morning desperately flicking through the rest of the files, feeling a mixture of remorse and joy. Oates's name appeared on the lists of nine other companies.

Callaghan sat there for a long while, collecting his thoughts, rehearsing the words he must use to beg for Colleen's forgiveness. Finally, he walked out of the office and headed for Greenwich, his legs feeling like lead.

* * *

The new butler closed the study door behind him.

Edward Lowell was sitting behind his brown leather-topped desk. He was a burly man with thinning hair, a large moustache and a beard. Coming from a wealthy family, he was unused to hard work, but prior to the newspaper fiasco, Callaghan had genuinely liked the man. He had always been genial, fully approving of his daughter's choice of husband.

Now, however, he remained seated, and did not extend a welcoming hand.

"Well, Michael? What can I do for you?" His tone was gruff.

Callaghan hesitated. His prepared speech was for Colleen.

"Well?" Edward Lowell snapped.

"I've found out about Patrick Oates, sir. I've come to apologize."

"Apologize!" Lowell shot to his feet. "I should damn well think so! Do you realize I could have had you for defamation of character. In fact, I seriously considered it, except Colleen persuaded me otherwise."

"I wouldn't have blamed you, sir. My behaviour was inexcusable. My frustration and anger got the better of me, and I spoke out without thinking. I'd like to see Colleen, if I may, sir, to try to explain . . ."

"Explain!" Edward Lowell cut across him. "Do you think for one moment that she'd see you, after all your accusations?"

"I was hoping she might, sir. Perhaps if you would tell her I'm here, then . . ."

"I can't."

"Can't, sir? Or won't?"

"Can't. She heard you were back in Greenwich, and took off three days ago on an extended tour of Europe. Said she never wanted to see you again, and

I can't say I blame her. So I'm afraid your visit has all been in vain."

Callaghan went suddenly numb. Europe! That was a hell of a way to go, just to avoid him. And even further proof — had he needed it — of how much she must hate him.

"Sir, if I wrote her a letter, would you send . . . "

"Don't waste your time, Michael. She gave everyone instructions that on no account were you to be told any of her destinations."

Callaghan glanced towards the connecting door to the drawing-room as he heard the sound of china breaking.

"One of the maids being clumsy clearing away my mid-morning tray," Edward Lowell explained. "And now if you'll excuse me, we have nothing more to discuss."

Still in shock, Callaghan turned to go, then paused, feeling he was under an obligation to warn his father-in-law.

"Sir, please don't think I'm speaking out of turn, but I happened to hear that the *Times* is planning a second campaign, which may this time succeed.

I trust you won't take offence at what I'm about to suggest, sir, but I think you should seriously consider resigning your various chairmanships . . ."

Edward Lowell's face darkened with anger. "Michael, I think you'd best leave. But before you go, let *me* tell *you* a couple of things. First, I never even knew that Peter had made me chairman of your father's newspaper, not until Colleen told me. In the circumstances, I immediately refused it. Second, let me remind you that Mr Tweed and his associates, including my cousin-in-law, have just been given a clean bill of health, clearing them of all suspicion, and leaving their conduct of the city's affairs beyond any reproach."

Colleen's father crossed the study and opened the door. "Please let yourself out, and don't return."

★ ★ ★

From that day, Callaghan's determination to see Sweeny behind bars had fuelled his appetite for work. Continuing his investigations between his routine detective work, he'd spent every waking hour pursuing clues.

But the vital breakthrough came from O'Rourke. With the accuracy of a practised bookkeeper, he was copying every ledger he could lay his hands on and handing the false accounts over to the *Times*. Louis Jennings was now in possession of such explosive facts and figures, that the case against the Ring could finally be proven.

With the dexterity of a financial juggler, Sweeny had created a litter of stocks and bonds for just about every project under the sun: City Improvement Bonds, Brooklyn Bridge Revenue Bonds, Central Park Improvement Stocks, Streets Improvement Bonds, Fire Department Stocks, Croton Aqueduct Bonds, Accumulated Debt Bonds, Tax Relief Bonds, and so on — the list was endless. Furthermore, there was no money in any of these funds — the Ring had syphoned it all off, to the tune of at least $200,000,000, according to O'Rourke's estimates — nor was there any money in the treasury; and the city was at least $100,000,000 in debt.

On July 22, 1871, the first issue of the *Times'* new campaign hit the streets. The headline read:

THE SECRET ACCOUNTS.
PROOF OF UNDOUBTED FRAUD
BROUGHT TO LIGHT

The following day, Comptroller Slippery Dick arrived at the *Times* offering Jennings and George Jones a bribe of $500,000 to drop the exposé. Realizing he had the Ring on the run, Jennings published Connolly's offer in the next issue of the *Times*, adding an open refusal, and continued printing the facts until public opinion rose to such a fever pitch, that Mayor Hall reluctantly agreed to the appointment of a second committee to re-examine the books.

Known as The Committee of Seventy — and composed of men such as Judge James Emott, William F. Havemeyer, and Robert Roosevelt — it immediately secured an injunction against all four members of the Ring, preventing them from acting further on behalf of the city. By the 24th October, the new committee had fully endorsed the extent of the fraud, and the District Attorney was instructed to commence criminal proceedings.

But, by then, Slippery Dick had already flown, leaving Boss Tweed, Mayor Hall, and Brains Sweeny to face the music.

Papers were served on all three, with Callaghan volunteering to be the one empowered to call on Sweeny . . .

★ ★ ★

West 34th Street. Sweeny's mansion was in darkness. No glimmer of gaslights or oil-lamps shining between curtains which had been drawn tight across every window. All the way up from ground floor to dormer attics, the building exuded an air of silent emptiness, of sudden desertion.

Too damned late! Callaghan swore to himself, crumpling the warrant into a tight ball and stuffing it in his pocket. Removing his hip-flask, he took a long swig of whiskey, then slouched away towards the gates.

From behind the mansion came a sudden clatter of hooves and rumble of wheels. Spinning about, Callaghan saw two black horses and a carriage hurtling down the drive towards him, the coachman flicking his whip across the backs of the thoroughbreds, urging them on.

Eyes rolling, nostrils flared, the horses bore down on Callaghan. Diving for safety behind the wall-pillar, he saw Sweeny's unmistakable short, squat shape sitting inside the coach. For a brief moment, their eyes met. The attorney's dark evil gaze bore into Callaghan's, then he grinned.

Brains Sweeny smirked triumphantly at his adversary through his black walrus moustache, showing brown, tobacco-stained teeth. Lowering his window, he raised his habitual high-crowned black hat and doffed it at Callaghan with an exaggerated flourish.

Images of Colleen, his father, and his mother, flashed through Callaghan's mind, resurrecting all the pain and rage of the last two years.

He exploded into action. The coach was slowing down, forced into executing a ninety-degree right turn before making for Fifth Avenue, and Callaghan sprinted after it. He drew level with the right-side window, to find Sweeny glaring at him through the closed glass, his ugly face now showing alarm.

The coach straightened and began to increase speed. Bolted on to its frame between window and door was a metal pull-up grip. Grabbing it with his left hand, Callaghan allowed the carriage's momentum to increase his stride, at the same time wrestling the door handle open with his right. His feet slipped from under him. Holding on with both hands, his arms and body stretching at an angle towards the rear wheel, and shoes scraping along the floor, he fought to recover his running pattern.

Hearing the window drop, he twisted to see Sweeny leering down at him, a silver-topped cane raised high in his hand. Brains paused, visibly relishing the moment, then whipped the stick across the back of Callaghan's left hand. Despite the searing pain, Callaghan held on. Sweeny struck again. Fearing his fingers being broken, Callaghan let go.

Still clinging to the door-handle with

his right hand, Callaghan flipped over, his legs trailing, banging against the spinning spokes of the rear wheel. The strain of holding on was agonizing, He could feel his fingers being forced apart. A few seconds more and he'd be drawn under the coach and crushed.

Using his last strength, Callaghan pushed himself off the door-handle, rolling away from the carriage, and missing the wheel by inches.

Coming to a stop, he got to his knees and watched the coach moving away from him. Reaching the end of the street, it turned left into Fifth Avenue, heading north out of the city.

The last he saw of Sweeny was the shyster leering at him through the rear window, his top-hat raised in mocking salute.

★ ★ ★

That was eight and half months ago. During that time, with the help of the Canadian and Irish police, they had managed to trace his escape route. He had crossed the Canadian line at

Champlain, then on to the small village of Pont Neuf, near Quebec, and the house of an Irish Jesuit priest, where he'd remained hidden for two months until passage was arranged for Ireland. Arriving in Dublin roughly six weeks later, it was believed he'd been given sanctuary in some isolated monastery deep in the Irish countryside. Nothing further was heard for over four months, until two weeks ago, when the Irish Garda heard a whisper that he'd been smuggled out of the country on a fishing-boat. That very same week, the *New York Times'* correspondent in Paris had —

The rat-tat of the knocker broke Callaghan's thoughts.

He crossed to the door and opened it.

7

CALLAGHAN stood still with shock, unable to move.

"Hello, Michael."

A moment passed before he was able to reply.

"Colleen!"

His voice sounded far away, as though it was not his.

"Well? Aren't you going to ask me in?"

He stepped aside as she brushed past him, the familiar scent of her perfume enveloping him and intoxicating him with her physical nearness. It was as though time had rolled back, and past sorrows were no more than a dream.

Colleen stood at the fire warming her hands, and looking around the room.

"I like the way you've rearranged it, especially the dresser, it looks well in the alcove."

"I tried to imagine how you would have done it," he replied, with quiet candour.

"Oh, come, Michael. You always had taste."

"Mostly learnt from you."

"Did it work?" Her green eyes were probing and serious.

"Did what work?"

"The changeabout. Did it erase the memories?" Colleen asked.

He didn't answer, his pulse racing, his mind teeming with questions.

She gazed at her portrait in its ornate gold frame on the wall.

"You kept it?"

"Yes." Callaghan's pulse was beginning to slow down. "When did you arrive home?"

"Last week. Father is unwell."

"I'm sorry to hear that. What's the matter?" Their dialogue sounded so polite in his ears, so unreal, more like two strangers than ex-lovers.

"His heart. He's being dragged into this dreadful Tweed affair."

"Yes, I heard."

"There's a rumour he's to be indicted. But he's innocent, I swear it," Colleen vehemently protested. "After you called to see him, he took your advice and

141

looked more deeply into the contracts. When he saw what was happening he resigned every one of his chairmanships. Until then, he truly believed in Uncle Peter's integrity, despite what you . . . "

"Colleen! How did you know I called on your father?"

"He wrote to me," Colleen lied. She'd been in the next room, heard every word, and hadn't left for Europe until a week later. But now was not the time for confession. Her father had begged her to ask Michael for help. Otherwise nothing on earth would have brought her back to him.

"Did he also tell you about my finding out it was Oates who . . . "

"Yes. But that's all water under the bridge."

"Colleen, I'm sorry I reacted the way I did." His words, pent up for over two years, came out in a rush. "After Sweeny left, I lashed out without thinking. I shouldn't have let him get to me. Nor been so stupid as to accuse you of . . . "

"I don't want to talk about it, Michael." Her voice was firm, her gaze unwavering. "It all happened too long ago."

Callaghan was unwilling to give up "But, Colleen! I want to . . ."

"Michael! For the last time. It's over."

He saw how set her face was, the determination in her green eyes, and his heart sank.

"The fact that you could suspect me, never mind accuse me, was enough. It's still enough." The words were out before Colleen could stop herself, and Callaghan stepped back as if he'd been slapped.

I'll have to say something placating, she thought, otherwise he'll never agree to help. "Now that I'm back, maybe we can become friends again. But please understand, I want nothing more. The sooner we make our separation legal, the better; we both need to get on with our lives."

OK, Callaghan thought, feeling his neck stiffen, if that's how you want it.

"Fine," he replied, trying to make his voice sound indifferent. "I take it you mean divorce?"

"Yes. But amicable. I want nothing from you."

Callaghan's amusement was genuine. "Don't worry. I've nothing to give." He sighed. "Is that what you came for?"

"No. I'm afraid I got sidetracked." Her phraseology was still from the war years, Callaghan noticed, not that of accepted society. It was part of her individual charm and he still loved it. He still loved *her*. But he was damned if he was going to show it.

Colleen indicated to her old fireside chair. "May I sit down?"

"Please. Would you like something to drink?"

"Nothing, thank you."

She waited for Callaghan to take the chair opposite. "Very simply, Father tells me you're now with the Detective Squad at Police Headquarters. I also heard from another source that your department is still chasing Uncle Peter, or rather — Sweeny. The *uncle* part is over, with what he's done to my father."

"So now you know how I felt."

"Yes, I do," Colleen replied, meeting his gaze. "I also did at the time."

"Yes, I since realized. So, why do you want Sweeny?"

"To sign an affidavit clearing Father of what was going on."

144

Callaghan gave a scornful laugh. "Sweeny! Signing an affidavit! You're not serious, surely?"

"Perfectly. It seems all your attempts to find him have so far failed. And should you succeed, then knowing Sweeny, you've no chance of extraditing him back to face trial, so he's got nothing to lose."

"Maybe, but if you're hoping to get him to put his monicker on a piece of paper, then you don't know what makes Peter Sweeny tick. He actually enjoys watching people suffer. Ask him to sign, and he'll laugh in your face."

Colleen's eyes flashed. "I can try! It's better than sitting in New York watching Father kill himself."

"Colleen, I'm sorry, but I'm afraid I can't help," Callaghan explained. "The *Times'* Paris correspondent recently sent in a report that Sweeny'd been seen there — some New York tourist thought he saw him in Notre-Dame Cathedral. But after a week of ferreting, all the *Times'* man came up with was a possible postal address in Montmartre, but nothing more. We asked the French police for help, but they said he's our problem. And our Embassy's got more to do than spend time trying to find him, especially as there's no proof the sighting was genuine."

Colleen looked back at him, her eyes steadfast, determined.

"Paris. Do you have the address?"

"No. I can get it from the *Times*, but it won't do you any good. As I said, it's only postal, and not confirmed. As for Sweeny, he could be anywhere in Europe. Or England. Or even back-tracked to Ireland."

"Nevertheless, it's a starting-point," Colleen stated, with stubborn determination. A sudden thought struck her. It meant they would be together for weeks, no, months on end. Something she would never have contemplated less than an hour ago. Even so . . .

She looked at him, intently studying his face. "Michael? How much would you give to find him?"

"You know the answer to that," he replied, meeting her gaze. Attempting to read her questioning eyes, his heart gave a sudden leap. "What's more," he added, hardly daring to hope he was right, "I think I know what you're about to suggest."

Colleen gave him her first smile. It lit up the room for him.

"Are you willing? Father will gladly pay," she offered.

Callaghan felt like springing out of his chair. Just a short while ago his life had been at a crossroads. And now this. It was also a wild-goose chase, but at least they would be together. Besides, who knew, the postal address might lead to something? It certainly couldn't achieve less than he had so far, sitting behind a desk in New York. "Funnily enough," he said slowly, trying hard not to show his exhilaration, "I'm thinking of resigning. If we do find him," he added, anxious to give weight to her idea, "I'll make sure he signs your affidavit first, before getting him to the American Embassy, and leave the legalities to them."

"That sounds OK to me."

The army phraseology again, Callaghan thought. Unladylike, unique, and absolutely charming.

"When we reach Paris," she continued,

"we'll write him a letter. Then keep watch on the address and follow whoever comes to collect it. Meanwhile, on Sundays, we can attend Notre-Dame, and during the evenings frequent the best restaurants and casinos. With all that money, he must emerge occasionally to enjoy it. If we're patient, and assuming he's still there, our paths are bound to cross."

Callaghan grinned and Colleen's heart missed a beat, just as it had when he'd smiled at her that first time, in the Fredericksburg warehouse.

"Miss Lowell, welcome home," he said. "I think it's a wonderful plan. I'm especially looking forward to the Parisian-evenings part."

"On a purely business-like basis," she warned, with a firmness she did not feel.

"Absolutely platonic," Callaghan agreed, crossing his fingers behind his back.

8

ENCOMPASSED by the lights of New York, Brooklyn, Jersey City and Staten Island shining across the waters of the Upper Bay, the *Mary Celeste* rode at anchor, her mooring lights gleaming, surrounded by other vessels waiting for the Atlantic storms to abate.

In their cabin, Sarah Briggs, aware of Sophia sleeping soundly beside her, snuggled closer to Benjamin for warmth, and saw her husband's eyes were open, staring at the dimmed oil-lamp swinging from the ceiling.

"What *is* troubling you, Ben?" she whispered. "It can't be the loan. You've borrowed before and it has never caused you this much concern." Raising her face and resting it on her palm, she voiced her innate suspicion. "Be honest with me, Ben. It's the unnecessary fuss Mr Winchester made over that extra barrel. That's it, isn't it? You suspect him of something nefarious, like smuggling contraband, perhaps?"

Even in the dim light she could see his reassuring smile was forced. "Of course not. Mr Winchester is an honourable man. He'd never become involved in crime. No, it's just the frustration of being stuck here when we should be twelve hours into the Atlantic." Pulling Sarah back on to the pillow, Briggs kissed her on the brow. "Now try to get some sleep. Who knows, by tomorrow the wind may have dropped and we can be on our way?"

★ ★ ★

In the galley, the steward, 23–year-old Edward Head of Brooklyn, put away the final supper plate, and knelt in front of his sea-chest, from which he took a glistening new leather-bound book, inkpot and pen. Placing them on the table, he sat on the bench, and, in the light of the oil-lamp overhead, carefully wrote on the flyleaf:

The Diary of Edward Head,
of 145 Newell Street,
Greenpoint, Brooklyn.
Steward on board the
brigantine 'Mary Celeste'

150

After allowing a moment for the ink to dry, Head turned the page, and began:

To my dear wife of two weeks; Emma. Tuesday, 5 November 1872. After leaving East River this morning bound for Genoa, and then Palermo, we were forced to anchor off Staten Island, because of the storms out in the Atlantic. I have been out on deck looking at the lights of Brooklyn, imagining which is yours, and wishing I could fly across the water to be in your precious arms for just one more night before we hopefully set sail tomorrow.

As I cannot, I therefore feel nearer to you, Emma, my love, by dedicating this diary to you.

First, let me tell you about my shipmates. The captain, Benjamin Briggs, is a strict, but fair man, and according to the first mate, is an excellent seaman. His wife is also on board, her name is Sarah Elizabeth, and she's the kindest natured of women. They have their daughter, Sophia Matilda, with them, a pretty little thing who calls me 'Edad'. One day, Emma, you and I may be fortunate enough to have a little one just like her.

The first mate, Albert Richardson, is twenty-eight. His wife's name is Frances, but he calls her Fanny. During the recent war, when he was only eighteen, he served with the Maine Volunteers.

The second mate's name is Andrew Gilling. He is twenty-five. I have not spoken to him much, so know little about him, except that he comes from Denmark.

Head paused to consider whether to include the fact that Gilling and the rest of the crew had been lodging in the same house. Then, deciding it was irrelevant, he continued writing:

All four seamen are German. Their names are Volkert Lorenzen, who's twenty-nine and married with a daughter. His brother, Boz, twenty-five, who's engaged, and Gottlieb Goodschaad, twenty-three, who come from the same village, called Utersum, on the island of Fohr, off Northern Prussia. They're all friendly fellows, unlike the fourth German, who's a strange, silent man, with hair so fair it's almost white, like an albino, and cold blue eyes which normally show no emotion, but can suddenly pierce right through you. He's always on his own, seeming to prefer his own company. His name is Arian Martens; he is thirty-five, and comes from the island of Amrum, also off Northern Prussia.

Head paused, and thought uneasily about Martens. There was no doubt about it. The man quite definitely gave him the shivers.

Fiesole, Italy
Straining his eyes in the flickering candlelight, Father-General Beckx read the telegraph from New York just delivered by messenger from Florence. It was dated November 4 1872:

153

'Cargo valued $10,000, sailing to-morrow. Arriving 5 – 6 weeks. Similar cargo following 10 days later.

Opus Dei.'

Beckx noted the figure down on paper, missing out the comma, then added the agreed four noughts, and drank-in the resulting sum: $100,000,000. With a further $100 million to follow, it confirmed all the rumours of Peter Sweeny's immense wealth.

By his success in organizing the shipments, Father Becker had fully justified Beckx' decision in appointing him for the mission.

The Father-General brooded. With Sweeny arriving tomorrow, the news could not have come at a more critical time for the Church. Only yesterday, Count de Ricasole had informed him that the wording of the evil new Act was almost complete. Unless they acted quickly, Holy Church would be legally — *evilly*! — robbed of all her remaining properties, even the Vatican: The Holy See of Saint Peter.

If this was allowed to happen, not only would it leave them virtually powerless in Europe, but it would also have a devastating effect on their missionary programme for the rest of the world.

But with Sweeny's millions at his disposal, Beckx knew votes could be purchased. The Act would be vetoed. And Victor Emmanuel's downfall — and Count Bismarck's — could then be engineered.

Unable to remain seated with rare excitement, Beckx slowly prised himself out of his chair, then, leaning on his stick, he dragged his feet across the floor to the long shuttered windows. Opening them with shaking fingers, he stepped out on to the patio into the cool of the late evening, and gazed down the Arno valley at the distant lights of Florence. Cradle of the Italian Renaissance, its churches were still full of religious paintings by Michelangelo, Leonardo da Vinci, Raphael, Donatello and others; works belonging to the Church, but which — through armed might — were now the property of the State.

Beckx permitted himself a rare smile.

155

How true was Blessed Saint Ignatius's saying: that while The Society of Jesus lives, the Church of Rome will never die.

Florence

In the dining-room of the *Hotel De La Ville*, Sweeny dropped his knife and fork on to the empty plate. Pushing it aside with a loud satisfied sigh, he selected a toothpick, leant back in the ornate armchair, unfastened his two bottom waistcoat buttons, and looked across at Father Cottone.

The Sicilian was wearing the same dark suit he'd exchanged for his cassock just before approaching the Italian border at Modanne.

"That was some meal, Father." Picking between his teeth and swallowing the findings, Sweeny went on, "I doubt Delmonico's could have done better."

"It was excellent, Mr Sweeny," Father Cottone agreed. "I am grateful to you for your generous hospitality."

"The pleasure's all mine, Father." Sweeny dismissed the young priest's gratitude with a casual flick of his

156

hand. "And my thanks to *you* for showing me Florence. All the paintings and sculptures! Those guys really had talent. Especially Michelangelo. That *David* statue must have taken some carving." Sweeny's face hardened. "But it's back to business tomorrow, and our meeting with Father Beckx. I've booked the carriage for three. That give us enough time?"

"Ample, Mr Sweeny."

"I'm looking forward to getting down to detail," Sweeny stated. "After seeing what this Emmanuel guy's doing, it's time he was sorted out. It's sacrilege that all the churches we visited are now owned by the State, and not only did we have to pay to get inside them, but we also had to apply for permits. Churches are for the faithful, for them to make confession and ask forgiveness, not money-making attractions. Don't you agree, Father?"

"I rather think you are addressing the converted, Mr Sweeny."

Brains gave a low growling chuckle. "Yes, sorry, Father." He took his cigar-case out of his pocket, selected one, and

157

lit up. "But come tomorrow, whatever the General's got planned, I've got some ideas of my own to contribute. Just leave it to me, Father, Peter Barr Sweeny will soon sort out this King Victor Emmanuel."

9

"**M**ESSAGE for Callaghan!"

Callaghan looked up from drafting his resignation. Framed in the doorway, Sean Haggerty, telegraph's messenger-boy, was a thickset youth, and pimply, with extraordinary long arms and a permanent smirk.

"Here!" Callaghan called out.

Haggerty crossed the room. "S'from Brennan," he slurred. Richard Brennan was one of the telegraph operators.

Callaghan sighed, "Haggerty, if Darwin had only known of your existence, he could have saved himself twelve years of controversy." He picked up his bone paper-knife and pointed it at the boy's middle. "Now," he threatened. "You've got two seconds."

"Two wires just come in, both for Missing Persons. One's from the Fifteenth. Some priest from Saint Xavier's gone

159

missing on East Side. The other's from the Eighteenth. Some woman's reported her old man missing. Brennan says the description fits your John Doe."

"Name?"

"Becker," Haggerty replied, "Father Karl Becker."

"The other one, Haggerty."

The youth consulted a crumpled note in his hand. "Coughman," he pronounced slowly.

Callaghan took the paper. "Kaufmann, Haggerty. It's German, not asthmatic. What's the address?"

"Twenty-fifth Street, east of Madison."

"What number?" Callaghan persevered.

Haggerty's smirk returned. "I forgot. Ask Brennan."

Callaghan sat pondering, then decided: what the hell. Might as well see it through. It was no more than a slight diversion on his way to the *Times* to get Sweeny's address. He could finish the letter in Jennings's office, and drop it off before going on to Colleen's.

★ ★ ★

It was a sunny but piercingly raw day. Callaghan got off the omnibus at the corner of 25th Street, raising his collar against the harsh east wind. He walked one block east to Lexington, past solid brownstone mansions built on land which, only twenty years ago, had been vacant lots and fields, on to the north-west corner of 25th and Lexington. Reaching the double doors of the Kaufmann's pillared front entrance, Callaghan rang the ornate bell.

After a long pause one of the doors slowly opened, revealing a dark-suited butler. His look of disdain remained unaltered as Callaghan introduced himself. He glanced at the detective shield, then, in an aloof Boston accent, pronounced, "If you'll please wait a moment," and closed the door.

Callaghan took out his watch, noting that two minutes passed before the butler returned.

"If you'll come this way, Mrs Kaufmann will see you." With slow dignity, the butler led the way through a massive hall with a carved sweeping staircase of marble, past exotic plants in large gilt vases, statuettes on pedestalled columns, into the vast drawing-room.

Callaghan almost closed his eyes at the clash of colours, the vivid blue carpet and curtains, and chairs of almost every hue. The Rainbow Room, he thought to himself.

A large, heavy-bosomed woman, with her hair tied back in a bun, and wearing a grey blouse and skirt, was sitting at a writing desk in the far corner. Although she must have been aware of their entrance, she continued writing for at least a minute before looking up.

"The policeman, ma'am."

"Thank you, Robert." Her voice had a definite German accent. First-generation, Callaghan decided. Born in Europe.

"You have news?" Her question was imperious. But Callaghan sensed it was all an act.

"Possibly, Mrs Kaufmann."

"What do you mean, *possibly*?"

A number of silver-framed photographs were arranged on the table by her side. Callaghan's gaze fized on the largest picture — a big man with a walrus moustache and a beard.

162

"Mrs Kaufmann, is that a photograph of your husband?"

"Naturally."

Callaghan crossed the room and studied the picture. The face staring back at him was unquestionably that of the dead John Doe.

Callaghan turned to Mrs Kaufmann who was watching him with her eyes full of fear.

"Mrs Kaufmann, I'm afraid I have grave news."

★ ★ ★

Some ten minutes later, she stopped shaking and sat by the fire, sipping the glass of the brandy that Callaghan had poured for her.

"I'm afraid I must ask you some questions, Mrs Kaufmann," Callaghan apologized. "You didn't report your husband missing until eleven, Tuesday night, at least thirty-six hours after he met his unfortunate end. Why the delay?"

"There was no delay, whatsoever." He voice was subdued. "Mr Kaufmann had urgent matters to attend to which

163

necessitated him remaining in town for a number of days. He stayed at the Astor House and wasn't due to return until six on Tuesday evening. Jacob was most punctilious. Therefore, when he had not arrived home at eleven, I sent my maid to the nearest precinct to make enquiries."

"I see. May I ask what was Mr Kaufman's occupation?"

Callaghan noticed the slight hesitation before she answered. "He was a diamond merchant."

"Did he have an office?"

"Certainly. But I do not have a key," Mrs Kaufmann added hastily.

Too hastily, Callaghan thought. "May I have the address?"

"A building near the corner of Front and Wall Street. I'm afraid I don't know exactly where."

Highly unlikely, Callaghan decided. So, why was she holding out? Whatever her reason, the corner of Front and Wall Street was only a stone's throw from where Kaufman's body was discovered. Having discarded the 'wife's-lover' theory, he was on the point of asking about a possible business partner, when Mrs

Kaufmann questioned: "When can my husband's body be released from the morgue?"

"Whenever you can arrange it, Mrs Kaufmann."

"*Gut.* I'm sure Father Hudson will attend to everything for me."

"The Rector of Saint Francis Xavier's?" Callaghan queried, with increased interest.

"Yes."

"The same church as Brains Sweeny?"

Again Mrs Kaufmann hesitated. "Yes. Mr Sweeny unfortunately chose to attend Saint Xavier's." She began rushing her words. "A terrible witness to those outside the faith. But I'm glad to say we never knew him. He occupied a pew on the other side of the church."

Callaghan noticed her hands trembling, and realized it was from fear, not shock over her husband's death. Remembering Haggerty's other missing person's report, Callaghan decided to pursue this coincidental connection. "Do you know Father Karl Becker, Mrs Kaufmann? He's one of your priests."

The woman's panic was now unmistakable, showing clearly in her eyes, and the wringing of her hands as she tried to control their shaking.

"Father Becker?" Her voice sounded strangulated inside her throat.

"Yes. I believe that's his name. Karl Becker. He sounds to be of German descent, like you and your husband. If so, then you would have had things in common."

Mrs Kaufmann took a long time to reply. When she did, it was so whispered, Callaghan was hardly able to make out the words.

"Yes. We knew him. But very slightly. He only arrived in New York some three months ago. But he was a wonderful priest. Within only a week of joining Saint Francis Xavier he had opened a soup kitchen for the needy on East Side."

"Mrs Kaufmann, forgive me, but you're referring to him in the past tense. Almost as though he's left, or he's dead. By some chance, you don't happen to know something about him that we don't?"

She was slowly recovering her composure. "Only that he seems to have gone missing.

166

It was announced in church on Sunday morning, when prayers were made for his safekeeping."

"I see." Callaghan decided to alter his line of enquiry.

"Mrs Kaufmann. Was your husband born in America?"

"No. In Germany."

"When did he arrive in this country?"

"At the age of five, with his parents."

"Was his father a diamond merchant?"

"No; an official with a German bank."

"Then Mr Kaufmann built his business up from nothing."

"Jacob was always very industrious."

"And very successful, judging by your home."

"It was purchased from the proceeds of some excellent Stock Market investments." Mrs Kaufmann's tone was suddenly very wary, defensive even. "Mr Kaufmann was an extremely astute man."

Carefully watching for her reaction, Callaghan paused before asking his final question. "Mrs Kaufmann. Did your husband have any dealings with The Tweed Ring?"

"Certainly not," she refuted indignantly.

167

But Callaghan again saw fear in her eyes.

* * *

Callaghan followed the black-robed priest into the library. The last time he was in Saint Xavier was for his wedding, but this was his first into the inner sanctorum. Replacing his copper detective badge in his overcoat pocket, he glanced around.

It was a dark room, one wall shelved with leather-bound books, the others coloured brown and spaced with black and white engravings depicting Jesuit representations of Heaven and Hell, with Hell predominating: stark, visual reminders, in accordance with the teachings of Saint Ignatius Loyola, the Society's founder, of the dreadful eternal punishment awaiting those who choose not to side with God. Callaghan gave them a cursory glance, then looked away.

In the centre of the room was a long wooden table, plain and bare, surrounded by a number of Spartan chairs.

The priest turned to face him. He was in his mid-thirties, lean, thin-faced, grey eyes, clean-shaven and bald, with narrow strips of grey hair along the sides of his head.

"Do you have news of Father Becker?" the Jesuit asked, in a refined New York accent.

"I'm afraid not, Father," Callaghan apologized. Then, omitting the gory details, he told him of Jacob Kaufmann's murder. At the conclusion, Father Murray closed his eyes, and his lips moved in silent prayer. "What a sad reflection of today's violent society," the priest said at last. He shook his head, despairingly. "Mr Kaufmann worshipped here every Sunday — he rarely missed — and also attended our monthly Alumni Sodality meetings. I know that Father Hudson is extremely committed, but I'm sure he will find time to call on Mrs Kaufmann to pray with her, and render his consolation. And in the event that Mr Kaufmann committed any venial act since his last confession, special mass will be said for his sin to be purged, and his soul delivered from purgatory."

"That should console her," Callaghan replied dutifully. "Father, to your knowledge did Kaufmann know Sweeny?"

The Jesuit was momentarily silent, obviously disturbed. Small wonder, Callaghan thought. After the publicity of the last twelve months, Brains had to be Saint Xavier's least favourite son.

"Mr Sweeny?" Father Murray repeated, cautiously.

"Yes. Peter Barr Sweeny. Also known as Brains. Alderman for the Twentieth District, and a personal friend of Boss Tweed."

Murray recovered his composure. "Yes, they knew each other well. The Kaufmanns sat in the pew behind the Sweenys, and Mr Sweeny also belonged to the Xavier Alumni Sodality. But what relevance does this have on Mr Kaufmann's death? As you're aware, Mr Sweeny left New York some twelve months ago, in unfortunate circumstances. I fail to see any . . . "

"Please bear with me, Father. Just a couple more questions. This priest who's gone missing on East Side . . . "

"Father Becker."

"Yes. Father Becker. I gather he's not been in New York long?"

"Barely three months."

170

"When did he go missing?"

"Last Wednesday. A week ago, exactly. When he did not arrive back for prayers, we . . . "

"Arrive back? From where?"

Murray's expression became cross. "Detective Callaghan. I gave all this information to the station captain of Fifteenth Precinct on Thursday morning."

"I'm sorry, Father," Callaghan apologized, "but what with the presidential election and a shortage of men, I'm afraid it's taking a couple of days for things to filter through to headquarters. So, if you would bear with me, I'd be grateful."

"Very well." Father Murray continued to frown. "But now that it *is* with your department, please do whatever you can. As time passes, we are becoming more and more concerned about him. This isn't at all like Father Becker. He is the most punctual of men, attentive to his duties. I fear something terrible must have happened to him. He would never . . . "

"We'll do everything possible to find him," Callaghan reassured. "Now, if we

171

can get back to last Wednesday. From where did Becker fail to arrive?"

"His soup kitchen on East Side which he started the first week he arrived from Germany. He was a most godly and caring priest." Murray shook his head. His look inferred he'd already assumed the worst.

"Yes, Mrs Kaufmann mentioned something about a kitchen. He was obviously a very compassionate man. Hopefully, still is," Callaghan added. "Tell me, during the time he's been at Saint Xavier, did he ever get to meet Mr Kaufmann?"

"Certainly," the Jesuit affirmed. "It was at a Sodality meeting. As they were both German, there was an immediate affinity between them. So much so, that Father Becker became Mr Kaufmann's regular confessor."

"Did he indeed? That's very interesting," said Callaghan, aware he was on to something. "Thank you, Father, I won't take up any more of your time."

"And Father Becker?"

"I'll get on to it right away, Father. You have my word."

172

10

"BUT I've met him!" Colleen exclaimed. "In Saint Xavier's, a week ago today."

They were sitting on opposite sides of the drawing-room hearth of her father's home, as dusk closed in around them. Callaghan was for a moment lost in the pleasure of Colleen's company. With her green skirt spread about her, and the dancing flames of the fire playing shadows on her face, highlighting the copper flecks in her green eyes and accentuating her high cheekbones, she was looking adorable.

He forced his mind back to Becker. "You're sure? According to Father Murray that's the day he went missing."

"I'm positive. He's about your height. Extremely fair hair, blue eyes, slim. There was something strange about him."

"Strange? In what way?"

"It's difficult to explain. It was more a sort of force exuding out of him; almost elemental." She lowered her voice. "I hesitate to say this about a priest, but the only word to describe him is sinister. My spine went quite cold."

Knowing Colleen's ability to read people, and that she was not given to exaggeration, Callaghan was puzzled. "But that doesn't agree with Murray's 'godly and caring' description of the man who opened a soup kitchen for the poor."

Colleen shrugged. "I'm sorry, Michael, that's the way he affected *me*. There again, maybe I over-reacted. Perhaps it's just that he has, or had, an antipathy for women?"

"Possibly," Callaghan said, not wholly convinced. "But whatever his true nature, he was Kaufmann's confessor. That, and the fact that Kaufmann and Sweeny sat next to each other at church, proves Mrs Kaufmann was lying. I saw it in her eyes when she said her husband had never acted for the Ring." Callaghan gave a wry smile. "It's always a case of being wise after the event. When you think about it, diamonds are the perfect commodity. Small, easily hidden, and a ready market of Diamond Exchanges available throughout the world. While I've been running round in circles serving warrants on every damned bank I could find, Kaufmann's the man I should have been looking for. He was holding the two hundred million all the time."

"So who killed him?" Colleen asked. "And why?"

"The order definitely came from Tweed." Callaghan was in no doubt. "There's a rumour circulating headquarters that the district attorney has found someone to testify against him, which will not only ensure his conviction, but also allow Oakey to be reindicted. Assuming Kaufmann was that witness, and he'd made a deal with the DA — immunity from prosecution — Tweed would have heard about it from his cronies on the force . . . "

"Surely not even Tweed would be desperate enough to resort to murder?" said Colleen, her eyebrows frowning in disbelief.

Oh, no? Callaghan thought, reviewing the facts of the case. A fourth-generation American from a most respectable Scottish family, William Marcy Tweed was elected Alderman for the 7th Ward at the age of 28. He began by selling favours to local businessmen: saloon licences, ferry and streetcar franchises, building contracts and the like. Such practices rapidly elevated Tweed to Grand Sachem of Tammany Hall. Systematically diverting city funds over the years, he was now New York's third largest estate holder, with a huge mansion on the corner of Fifth Avenue and 43rd Street, and a magnificent steam yacht.

But did Boss risk losing enough to resort to murder?

"He wouldn't think twice," Callaghan stated. "If he's found guilty, all his assets will be sold, and the proceeds returned to the city. He'd not only be ruined, but also imprisoned. If it was a choice between that and Kaufmann's life, then it would be 'goodbye Jacob, thanks for all your help'."

"I'm not so sure," said Colleen, still in some doubt. "But I think we can rule out Mayor Hall. Murder doesn't seem his style."

Callaghan nodded thoughtfully. Despite

176

all the bad publicity, Abraham Oakey Hall was still Mayor of New York. Always elegantly dressed, he was English on his father's side, aristocratic French on his mother's. He got his BA from New York University, then trained at Harvard Law School before marrying the daughter of one of New York's best families. A familiar figure at all the best clubs, including the prestigious Union, Oakey had already survived two trials, one with a hung jury, the second in which all charges were dismissed. Hardly conditions warranting his involvement in murder to prevent a third trial.

"You're right," Callaghan agreed. "Murder and Elegant Oakey don't go together. Besides, he's got the best firm of attorneys in New York. He'll keep brazening it out in court."

"What about Connolly?" Colleen asked, wondering how involved the missing City Comptroller could be.

"We can definitely strike him off," Callaghan said. "According to Louis Jennings, he's still on his world tour, currently sailing down the Nile on a riverboat. It's thought he managed to smuggle out some five million dollars, and he seems perfectly content with his present lifestyle."

Colleen looked searchingly at her ex-partner. "And Sweeny?"

Callaghan had already given this much thought. "Yes, and no," he equivocated. "We can assume he's up to his eyeballs in the scheme to convert the money into diamonds; it was probably his brainchild. But as for Kaufmann's murder, I doubt it. Even if he is hiding in Paris, telegraphs take too long for him to be constantly involved. Much as I'd like to think he was party to it, this was probably a snap decision by Tweed and Tweed alone."

"You don't think he did it himself?" Colleen queried.

"Well, he's certainly big enough, and strong enough, to break someone's back in two. But I don't think he'd actually commit murder. He'd hire a professional."

Colleen pursed her lips. "But what if the killer's not from New York? Finding him will be like looking for the proverbial needle in a haystack."

"Not necessarily," Callaghan replied.

"In the first place I doubt that Tweed had time to bring in someone from outside. But, if he did, someone will have heard a whisper. Most of our arrests result from tip-offs. Pillow-talk in Greene Street's brothels, loose tongues after one too many in places like Harry Hill's. Especially Harry's. Tweed might live in a Fifth Avenue mansion, but he still did his drinking there, mixing with every known criminal and hooker in New York. If he wanted to hire a killer, that's where he'd start looking. And Harry'll know all about it."

"But will Hill tell you?"

"Fifty per cent of our information comes from Harry. We have a sort of reciprocal arrangement with him. He keeps us informed, and in return we approve his annual application for the renewal of his saloon licence."

Colleen was silent, absorbed with her thoughts. Finally, she looked across at him, her green eyes clear and challenging. "*If* Tweed is behind it, then why strip the body? Surely he must have realized it wouldn't take long for Kaufmann to be identified?"

179

"That's still puzzling me as well," Callaghan admitted. "There has to be a reason, but so far I can't think of one."

Colleen became thoughtful again. "What about Father Becker? Seven days is a long time for him to be missing?"

"He's probably suffered the same fate as Kaufmann," Callaghan replied, sombrely.

"Surely not!" Colleen protested. "A priest! No, Michael! Not even Tweed could sink that low!"

"I'm sorry, Colleen, but there's no other explanation I can see. Becker was Kaufmann's confessor. Kaufmann told him everything about the Ring. Becker advised him to turn state's evidence. From that moment on, Becker was as much a threat to Tweed as Kaufmann."

"But whatever Kaufmann revealed to Becker during confessional would have been sacrosanct."

"Sacrosanct!" Callaghan scorned. "Tweed wouldn't know the meaning of the word."

Colleen shivered. "I only hope there's a simpler explanation for his absence — a

180

temporary loss of memory, perhaps?"

"Wandering the streets for seven days in a priest's cassock? I'm sorry, Colleen, but that's highly unlikely."

She gave a resigned sigh. "You're probably right, but I'll pray for him, nevertheless. Meanwhile, if we could only *prove* that Tweed is behind Kaufmann's death, he'd be tried and convicted for murder. Maybe with nothing to lose, he'd confess to the fraud charges, and not only implicate Sweeny, but also betray his address. Not even Sweeny could get out of that. He'd be extradited for sure."

"It's worth a try," Callaghan agreed. "Much as I hate saying goodbye to those long Parisian evenings, it makes better sense, and probably offers more chance of success."

"Paris was always a business trip," Colleen said, giving him an enigmatic glance. "But what if we give ourselves a deadline? Say to the end of the year? If we haven't achieved anything with Tweed by then, we revert to our original idea."

Callaghan nodded. "By the way, getting

back for a moment to your father. You're sure there's nothing I can do?"

A look of worry returned to Colleen's face. "I only wish there was," she sighed, "but I don't see what. As I told you, when he heard this morning from Mr Phelps that he's to be indicted, he took the whisky decanter up to his room and is refusing to open the door. There's no date set for the court hearing as yet, but it won't be before March of next year. That's why I suggest we give ourselves until the thirty-first of December before giving-up on Tweed. If proceedings develop while we're abroad, Mr Phelps can always ask for an adjournment on the grounds of father's ill-health, and wire us in Paris to let us know the situation . . ."

"If Sweeny's there," Callaghan remarked. "Don't worry," he added hurriedly as he caught her sudden frown of concern, "if he's not, then however long it takes, we won't give up until we find him."

Reassured, Colleen gave him a brief smile, then leaning across the butler's-table for the silver coffee-pot, she topped-up his cup.

"So, Michael, getting back to Tweed, what's your next step?"

Sitting back in his chair, and sipping his hot drink, Callaghan started explaining.

★ ★ ★

Benjamin Briggs was leaning over the *Celeste*'s rail, staring disconsolately out to sea, as he listened to the wind howling in through The Narrows. Far beyond the channel he could see the Atlantic rollers crashing against the east side of Sandy Hook, then funnelling in, the anger partially sucked out of them as they swept across the sandbanks, then finally expending themselves in the deeper waters of the Lower Bay.

A steamship — *Calabria*, Liverpool — swept past, violently rocking the anchored *Celeste* in its wake. There were only a few passengers, immigrants by their appearances, leaning over the port rail and waving. Most would be on the starboard side, getting their first glimpse of New York.

Briggs raised his hand in brief acknowledgement, then half turned as

Sarah crossed the deck and joined him. He put an arm around her shoulders. "Where's Sophia?"

"Taking a nap."

In silence they watched the ship heading across the bay, turning slightly to starboard as it approached its berth on the Hudson.

"Benjamin?"

"Yes, dear?"

"Who was that man with Mr Winchester on the first day of loading?"

Not fully concentrating, Briggs asked, "What man, Sarah?"

"The portly one with a German accent, expensively dressed."

"Oh, yes. His name was Kaufmann. Jacob Kaufmann. He's a friend of Mr Winchester's. Apparently, he came out of curiosity. He'd never seen a vessel being loaded before."

"Benjamin," Sarah Briggs looked worriedly into her husband's eyes. "What you told me about the barrel incident, don't you think it was a little peculiar, the two of them leaving so soon after? As though they attended merely to ensure that the barrel was safely loaded." She reached for his hand. "Ben, what if it *does* contain contraband? Shouldn't we put financial considerations aside, and turn back to inform Customs? If it turns out they're involved in some felony, Mr Winchester can hardly demand repayment of his loan."

Briggs stared out to sea, unable to meet her gaze. "As I said before, I made too much of the whole thing. I have no doubts about Mr Winchester's integrity. Please, Sarah, accept my judgement and let us not speak of the matter again. Rather, we must pray for a break in the weather so we can get under way."

"Of course," Sarah murmured, but looking down, she saw how tightly Benjamin was gripping the *Celeste*'s rail.

Fiesole
Beckx watched Sweeny's carriage receding down the long dusty drive into the gathering dusk. Then, leaning on his stick, he limped back inside.

Thanks be to Saint Ignatius, the meeting had gone excellently. Greatly due, it had to be admitted, to Father

Cottone, who had cleverly gauged the American's mood. Prevailing upon Sweeny's desire to be regarded as a 'Defender of the Faith', the young Sicilian priest had deferentially supported Beckx' every word, adding to them whenever necessary, until everything had been agreed — including an honorary papal title for Sweeny: Knight of the Golden Spur.

Beckx lowered himself into his chair, his mind racing ahead.

Now he could approach those politicians already earmarked as potential sellers of votes, without waiting for Father Becker's arrival.

Thus, with God's Grace, and the intercession of the Celestial Mary, the Father-General continued to brood, they had achieved the first phase of the plan: vetoing Victor Emmanuel's evil Act. The next phase, the removal of both satanic dictators, Victor Emmanual and Bismarck, could begin as soon as the first vessel had docked.

Leaning across his desk, Beckx opened Becker's draft treatise on the current situation facing the Church. They'd discussed it in great detail at their final meeting.

Beckx concentrated on the passages he'd scored as most relevant, commencing with the introductory quote from Saint Ignatius himself: *Preserve always your liberty of mind. See that you lose it not by anyone's authority, nor by any event whatsoever.*

The second highlighted section related to the Bull of Canonization of Saint Ignatius, formulated by Pope Gregory XV, in which the services rendered by the Society of Jesus to the Church of Rome, were clearly listed. Becker had heavily underlined one of them.

The strenuous defence of the Holy See.

The treatise went on to probe into the various theological differences existing within Holy Church, between those who followed the teachings of the Dominican, Thomas Aquinas (1225 – 1274), and those who adhered to the views of the Franciscan, Duns Scotus (1265 – 1308). Although Jesuit theology was principally in agreement with Scotus, nevertheless, Father Becker had studied the doctrines of both men with eclectical discernment, and had included one of Aquinas's most quoted instructions: *The morality of every action is determined by the end in view.* In brackets behind it, Father Becker had added: (*The end justifies the means*).

The German priest had concluded his treatise by citing from the works of Francisco de Suarez (1584 – 1617), the Spanish-Jewish Jesuit, on what action should be taken against despotic rulers:

The tyrant may be either a usurper, or a legitimate ruler, but whose rule has become an intolerable oppression, and a permanent menace to the well-being of the State.

Because of this, he has declared war, thus allowing the just waging of a war of self-defence against him. Any citizen who takes his life, is acting in the name of the State, and in the cause of its just warfare. It is lawful to kill him for the defence of the State cannot be achieved in any other way.

188

Beckx thoroughly concurred. Closing his eyes, he began thinking of the second phase of the plan. With the funding assured, it soon would be in operation.

★ ★ ★

In the time he'd known Sweeny, Father Cottone had never seen him in this mood. Previously so expansive and friendly, he was sitting glowering in the corner of the carriage, bushy eyebrows knitted together, black eyes narrowed into two thin slits as he chewed an unlit cigar. His dark mood so filled the carriage it felt almost difficult to breathe. It was such a sharp contrast to his fawning attitude of two hours ago, when he'd fallen to his knees on meeting the Father-General, reverently kissing Beckx' finger-ring of office.

Cottone stayed silent, realizing he was seeing the true nature of the man, sitting there squat and motionless like some slimy, poisonous toad.

Rolling his cigar to the side of his mouth, Sweeny snarled viciously, "Buying votes ain't gonna be enough. I'm speaking as someone who knows.

Back in New York, I used to buy people's souls, but it still wasn't enough to keep me there. The Father-General's plan will only get this new Act killed off. It won't get the Church restored, or the Pope released. Beckx is gonna have to come up with something much bigger."

"Which he is doing," said Father Cottone. "As he explained in great detail."

"Sure, it's an ambitious plan, right enough, but it's only got a fifty-fifty chance of succeeding," Sweeny grated. "I'm talking one hundred percent. But don't worry, by the time we reach Palermo, I'll have given my ideas more thought and worked them all out. When are we meeting the General again?"

"In five weeks. Sunday the fifteenth of next month."

Brains rolled his cigar to the other side of his mouth. "Five weeks. That'll give me plenty of time."

11

"MESSAGE for Callaghan!" Haggerty screamed, as if sheer volume might give his words import.

Callaghan winced, looking up from his notes.

"Brennan says there's another stiff on its way to the morgue. He was done-in the same way as the first one."

Half an hour later, Callaghan was standing on the wooden pier at the foot of Twenty-sixth Street, shivering despite his thick overcoat and upturned collar. Thrusting his hands deep inside his pockets, he watched as the *Seneca* — pride of the Harbour Police — approached the jetty, smoke pouring out of her long black funnel.

A low overcast sky was creeping in from the Atlantic. The buildings on the other side of the East River, all the way from Williamsburg to Long Island City, were covered by a thin blanket of mist. Away to the left, the narrow shape of Blackwells Island — home of the city's workhouse, lunatic asylum, almshouses, and penitentiary — rose forlornly out of the grey waters.

Her paddles in reverse, churning the water, the *Seneca* slowly slid in sideways, bumping gently against the pier.

Callaghan leapt on board and approached the police captain standing at the rail. "Captain Smith?"

"Yes. Mr . . . ?" the captain requested, in a slow drawl.

"Callaghan, sir. Detective Squad, Central Office."

"What's your hurry, man?" the captain asked, reaching for his pipe.

"With your permission, sir, I'd like to see the body," Callaghan replied, cautioning himself to remember his rank.

"Hell, he's in no shape to run away. Why the urgency?"

"The manner of death, sir," Callaghan said, respectfully, though he chafed to be done. "I understand his spine was snapped?"

"Certainly was. By a madman, I'd

say." The captain paused for a puff. "When we picked him up he folded in two, just like a rag doll."

"I'm investigating a similar killing," Callaghan stated, and explained about Kaufmann.

Captain Smith turned and led Callaghan to an oilcloth-covered mound in the middle of the deck. "He's no oil painting," he warned, pulling back the covering. "The rats found him before we did."

Callaghan looked down at the grisly sight. From the chest downwards the body had been almost entirely eaten away. But the face was mostly untouched. Add the distinctive fair hair, and identification should be no problem. Feeling suddenly nauseated, he turned away.

"I felt the same way when I first saw him," Smith sympathized, letting the cover drop.

Callaghan felt the deck rising and falling on the swell of the river. Swallowing, he asked, "Were there any clothes?"

"Not a stitch."

"Any watches, rings, personal effects?"

"Only this. Found it under the body."

Smith dug in his pocket and handed Callaghan a metal crucifix.

It was made of crude iron, roughly fashioned, with jagged sides. Worn next to the skin it would cause laceration, and tear holes in clothes. Obviously made for hanging on a wall, Callaghan decided.

"You said *under* the body, sir. Then it wasn't in the water?"

"No. A workman found it, lodged against the pilings of the new Brooklyn Bridge."

"Could you tell whether he was killed there?"

"Possibly," Smith stated. "Could also have been dumped in the river, and got carried there."

"Downtown, sir? Or higher up?"

"Couldn't say. This stretch has got as many underlying currents as a temperamental woman. He could have been thrown in anywhere between The Battery and Corlear's Hook."

"Thanks for your help, sir." Callaghan turned to go.

"Tell you one thing that puzzles me," said Smith. "When we found him, he was lying on his back, and the rats hadn't got to that part of the body. There's no bruising at the base of the spine. A mite peculiar, don't you think, considering the way he was killed?"

Callaghan stopped in his tracks. There'd been no bruises on Kaufmann's back either.

★ ★ ★

As the carriage rattled its way up Fifth Avenue to the city morgue, Callaghan tried offering Father Murray some hope.

"There's always the chance it may not be Father Becker."

Murray looked down at the crucifix in his hand. "Thank you, Mr O'Callaghan, but this is definitely his. I fear we must prepare for the worst."

"With respect, Father," said Callaghan, trying to make conversation, "it's Callaghan, not O'Callaghan. Blame my great-grandfather. He fell for a Scottish Presbyterian who was visiting Ireland, and dropped the 'O' into the Irish Sea when he moved to Scotland."

Murray responded with a flitting smile. "Callaghan. O'Callaghan. Your roots are

195

still Irish. Are you in the faith?"

Scenes of battle, with pieces of human bodies being blown high into the air, flashed through Callaghan's mind.

"Father, if you'd been in the war, and seen all the senseless suffering, you would have lost faith in religion. Take your own Church. You preach of a loving heavenly Father, yet at the same time subscribe to the doctrine of a God who sends little children to Purgatory. You're asking people to believe in a contradiction!"

"Come, Mr Callaghan," Murray objected, "you are being rather harsh. Let me . . . "

"Father, admit it," Callaghan interrupted. "Your faith and beliefs — especially that of the New Testament Saviour who so loved the world that He died on the Cross in order to save it — are founded on nothing more than a figment of Pauline theology."

Unable to ignore this verbal gauntlet, the Jesuit replied, "Don't forget the writings of such secular historians as Josephus, Suetonius and Tacitus, Mr Callaghan. You can't dismiss them lightly." Father Murray leaned forward, his steely gaze belying his soft voice. "When our Lord Himself was subjected to similar scepticism, He would reply by asking a question. I will therefore emulate His example by asking you: if the Church's doctrines are based on falsehood, what then, do you think, is the reality?"

Callaghan replied, without hesitation, "The way that man, supposedly created in God's image, treats his fellow man. I've seen men blow each other into bits over a battlefield — scenes that defy the imagination." He sighed, then continued with feeling, "As far as I'm concerned, you can turn the other cheek and keep your New Testament. It was written by a bunch of pious con-men. If the Almighty exists at all, He has remained in the Old, still feeding on blood sacrifices."

"No longer, Mr Callaghan," the Jesuit responded with calm dignity. "The ultimate sacrifice was made nearly nineteen hundred years ago, when Christ gave His life for the salvation of . . ."

Callaghan cut across him. "Father, can we get on to Father Becker?"

But Murray persisted. "For the sake of

your eternal soul, I would rather continue our conversation. Callaghan looked away out the carriage window, and saw they were approaching Fifth-Avenue Hotel, facing Madison Square. Six storeys of gleaming white marble, and said to be the most magnificent hotel in the world, its public rooms were a popular meeting-place for Wall Street brokers, while its private rooms were often a trysting-place for the high-class prostitutes, pretty young things dressed in the latest fashions, parading outside the gilded entrance-doors, hoping to 'hook' a rich client.

As Broadway's traffic merged with Fifth Avenue's in a densely packed sea of vehicles crawling past the square, the noise of iron-rimmed wheels and horses' hooves on cobbles, and drivers shouting and honking horns became ear-shattering, precluding further conversation.

A bulletin-wagon plastered with adverts drew up alongside them. Callaghan pretended to read them: 'Pear's Soap', 'Barnum's Museum', 'Brandreth's Pills' — the latest cure-every-known-ailment fad, small brown things and very bitter.

Their coach pulled away, and turned into East 26th Street. As the traffic and noise slowly lessened, Father Murray turned away from the window, but Callaghan got in first. "We're not far from the morgue, Father, so if you don't mind I'd like to get back to the investigation." Not waiting for a reply, he continued, "Assuming the murder victim *is* Father Becker, you said he'd been in New York about three months?"

"Plus a few weeks. He sailed from Genoa, to escape the wave of anti-Christian persecution currently sweeping across Europe . . . "

"Anti-Christian?" Callaghan challenged. "I thought it was only anti-Rome?"

"That in itself proves we are dealing with Antichrist," the Jesuit remonstrated, the colour suddenly rising in his pale cheeks. "It is the Holy Catholic Church — not some apostate breakaway — which was ordained of God to be the Church Militant, and carry His message to the four corners of the globe. *We* are Christ's army, the sole Defenders of His faith. This is why the Devil never ceases to attack us, deploying his minions to do his evil work. Victor Emmanuel in Italy, Bismarck in Germany. The proof is there for all to see, with the Holy Father imprisoned in the Vatican, and the Society of Jesus under constant Satanic attack."

Not strictly true, Callaghan thought. Pius was not a prisoner in the real sense of the word; his incarceration was self-inflicted. A Law of Guarantees, passed by the Italian Assembly over twelve months ago, had promised to respect the Pope's inviolability, guaranteeing him full liberty to exercise his religious practices and allowing him access to Catholics throughout the world by special postal and telegraphic facilities, plus an annual income of three million lire a year out of State revenues. Except for the postal communication, Pius had refused the Assembly's sanctions, preferring the law to retain the character of a hostile edict imposed by a treacherous conqueror, thus allowing him to pose, in the eyes of Catholics worldwide, as a 'prisoner in the Vatican'.

However, Murray *was* correct in

claiming that his own Order was always under attack — except that 'Satanic' was a somewhat colourful description. Besides, the Jesuits had been a source of controversy ever since their beginnings, expelled from many countries over the centuries. They should be used to it by now.

Callaghan returned to the murder. "Getting back to Father Becker, what can you tell me about him?"

"Having known him only three months, there's very little I can say," Murray apologized. "At the time that Rome was invaded and so flagrantly violated, he was employed by our Missionary Society in the Piazza di Spagna. He escaped to Berlin, where he was teaching in our seminary there, when Bismarck banished our Society from Germany also. As a consequence, Father Becker decided to leave Europe altogether. As soon as he arrived in New York, he sought refuge in Saint Francis Xavier's. Within his very first week he opened his mission on East Side. Why anyone should want to kill such a godly man, I simply cannot imagine."

Callaghan was puzzled. "You said that he was once employed by your Missionary Society?"

"Yes. It was a high office, appointed by Father Beckx himself."

In researching an article for his father's newspaper on the influence European religions had on America's fast growing immigrant population, Callaghan had learned quite a bit about the Church's Missionary Society. Or, to give it its proper title, which Murray had so interestingly avoided, *Congretatio de Propaganda*, the Congregation of Propaganda. For a priest as young as Becker to be personally recommended to a position there by the Father-General of the Jesuits, suggested that he was being groomed for high office.

"Then why the demotion when he arrived in America?" Callaghan asked.

Father Murray gave a thin smile. "When a Jesuit priest is given a position of authority, it lasts only for the duration of the appointment. There is no permanent standing within our Society. When the term of office comes to an end, then, regardless of reason — even if it's

202

persecution — a Jesuit loses all status attached to his old position. No matter how humble his new position, he takes a vow of absolute obedience to the one who appoints him. When Father Becker sought refuge at Saint Xavier, Father Hudson, after praying to Saint Francis for guidance, offered him a position as priest, which Father Becker naturally accepted."

"What made him choose America?" asked Callaghan, musing out loud.

"Probably our Constitution," Murray suggested, a sudden note of pride in his voice. "After his experiences in Italy and Germany, our freedom of worship must have been particularly appealing."

The Jesuit hesitated, as though unsure whether to continue.

"Speaking personally," he finally declared, "I am of the opinion that Holy Church would be best served if the Holy See was transferred from Rome to Washington. Europe is of the past; a Byzantium with no future other than a parallelism of the old Roman Empire. There's nothing but war, rumours of war, and revolutions to look forward to. America, on the other hand, faces an exciting and challenging future. By the year two thousand, the population of the United States will be over five hundred million, and it is inevitable that the seat of world power will one day rest in the United States. This *must* be recognized by the Church and the Holy Father. Rome's days are numbered. It is a provincial city slowly dying in an out-of-the-way corner of a small inland sea. If the Holy Church is to continue its task of world evangelization, we should be sending representatives to Victor Emanuel, requesting that he allow the Pope to leave Rome and establish a new Vatican in Washington.

Callaghan concealed a smile. Alone of all the Catholic Orders, Jesuits were bound by a vow of 'blind obedience' to their General and to the Pope. Yet here was Father Murray, betraying himself to be a staunch American at heart.

"Do other American Catholics take this view?" Callaghan asked.

"Almost all," Murray replied.

"Would the Pope consider it?"

"No," the Jesuit stated emphaticaly. "On this matter, the Holy Father's position is extreme ultramontane. He sees Rome, and only Rome, as the centre of the Church's authority, claiming its tradition and its history, as proof of divine election, and publicly declaring that he will remain in the Vatican until the See of Saint Peter has been fully restored to Holy Church."

The coach was approaching the city morgue, a low gloomy-looking building at the rear of Bellevue Hospital.

"Well, the Pope must be right," Callaghan commented. "Didn't he declare himself to be infallible two years ago?"

★ ★ ★

Getting down from the coach, Callaghan waited for Murray to follow. A biting wind from the adjacent East River, and the sight of its swirling grey waters flowing past at the end of the street, made him huddle into his overcoat. Winter wasn't far off.

Clutching the hem of his cassock, Murray descended the coach steps and followed Callaghan through the entrance lobby, into the morgue's 'exhibition hall'.

Roughly twenty feet square, it was a depressing room, with a cold brick floor and damp mouldy walls, divided by a full partition with a long window, behind which were five marble slabs, tilted to display the bodies.

Today, there were four on view: three men and a young woman, all naked, apart from narrow strips of oilcloth covering their genitals. To delay decomposition, they were being sprayed with cold water from hydrants suspended over each slab. Wall-hooks held their clothes and personal items. If bodies were not identified within five days, they were taken to the lime-pit on Hart's Island; but clothing and effects were stored for six months to be compared against future 'Missing Persons' reports, then they too were destroyed.

The body from the East River was laid out on the fifth slab. Unlike the others, it was covered by tarpaulin up to the neck. The spray from the hydrant was bouncing off the tarp, creating a misty curtain, though still allowing a clear view of the face and fair hair.

Father Murray took one look, then crossed himself and knelt on the cold brick floor to pray. Callaghan tactfully withdrew, going outside to the coach to wait.

It was ten minutes before Murray appeared, his face deathly pale.

"Back to Saint Xavier's?" Callaghan queried, with solicitude.

The Jesuit shook his head. "The Willett Street Mission. Father Becker's helpers must be given the sad news."

"Sure," Callaghan said, his thoughts racing ahead with his own plans. First, Harry Hill's. Then the Astor. Kaufmann's office. And finally, the *New York Times*.

The carriage rumbled down Bellevue, then along First Avenue. Suddenly, Murray broke his silence. Looking across at Callaghan, he asked, "Who could possibly have committed these evil deeds? First, Mr Kaufmann. And now Father Becker."

"Becker was killed before Kaufmann," Callaghan pointed out. "At a guess, a couple of days earlier. As to who killed them, I have an idea. But at the moment it's only a theory."

"Only someone deranged could deliberately break someone's back in two." Father Murray shuddered.

The Jesuit placed his hand on the door-handle as the carriage slowed to a halt outside a tumbledown, clapboarded house. "Whoever this killer is, I pray you find him for Father Becker's sake. Just look at the result of his labour."

Callaghan watched the long line of down-and-outs, male and female, slowly filing through the door of the house to claim their bowls of soup. In the garden a group of ragged children were shrieking with laughter over a game of baseball, using a broken branch of wood as a bat, and a ball made from bits of material tied together with string. "It was in obedience to Christ's instruction, 'Suffer little children to come unto me, and forbid them not'," Murray observed, "that Father Becker opened his heart to these poor unfortunates of the East Side, showing them God's love in a practical way, by providing them with food . . . "

Callaghan gave a sigh of exasperation. "If God was so loving, He would have ensured they never went hungry in the first place." He drew a ten-dollar bill out of his pocket. "Here, buy them some food from me."

Murray opened the door. "Your bitterness has become a self-erected barrier, Mr Callaghan. While it remains you will never come to know God. May He have mercy on your soul and bring you into His fellowship. I will remember you in my prayers."

Leaving Callaghan holding the bill, Father Murray descended from the coach. Exchanging brief words with the needy as he walked up the path, he disappeared inside the house.

★ ★ ★

Callaghan climbed the wooden stairs to the verandah of Harry Hill's large, shabby, two-storeyed timber-framed dive.

Paying his twenty-cents admittance fee at the blue-lanterned door for men — the red-lamped was for women, who got in free — he entered the raucous, smoky atmosphere of the large ground-floor bar. Its long counter stretching the whole length of the room, Harry's was a second home to pimps, prostitutes, pick-pockets, drug-dealers, counterfeiters and every other kind of New York criminal. Callaghan recognized a number of faces: Dutch Heinrich, Sheeny Mike, Big Nose Bunker, Dublin George, all well-known thieves. Among the prostitutes he spotted Gallus Mag, armed as always with her pistol and club, Sadie the Goat, and Hell-Cat Maggie, her teeth filed to sharp fangs, and long pointed thimbles on her fingers, to dissuade clients from trying to get away without paying.

Harry was standing behind the bar. Short, stocky and muscular, of indeterminable age, he looked every inch the ex-prizefighter that he was. Callaghan pushed his way through the crush.

"Harry! Can I have a word?"

Hill looked up, bottle in one hand, glass in the other, his thick moustache nearly concealing his grim frown. Filling the glass and placing it on the counter, he dropped the bottle to the thickly sawdusted floor and sauntered over, wiping his hands on his dirty apron. Trading information for his tavern licence was a reluctant necessity for Harry and, as a consequence, his manner was never too friendly.

"Hope it won't take long, Callaghan. We're busy."

"A couple of seconds, Harry. Tweed been in lately?"

"Nah," Hill replied, dismissively. "Ain't seen him for months."

Dead-end number one, thought Callaghan. One thing about Harry, his information could be relied upon one hundred percent.

"That it?" Hill queried.

"Yes," Callaghan confirmed. "That's it."

Hill reached under the counter, and brought out a glass and a full bottle of his best whiskey. "You want your usual?"

Callaghan thought about it for a brief moment. "No thanks, Harry. The case I'm on needs a clear head."

"Wonders will never cease," said Harry, sarcastically.

★ ★ ★

Between Barclay and Vesey, the Astor
House Hotel was an impressive blue-granite
building, with an imposing four-columned
entrance, and eighteen top-class shops
occupying the ground floor.

Callaghan entered the crowded lobby
and approached the front desk. The male
clerk, a man in his thirties, dark-suited,
with spectacles and receding hairline,
greeted him politely.

"May I help you, sir?"

When Callaghan showed his badge,
the clerk's response was immediate.
"Just follow me," he whispered, hurrying
Callaghan into a back office.

"I'm enquiring into the movements of
a Jacob Kaufmann, Callaghan explained.
"According to his wife, he checked in
here on Thursday, the first of November.
I'd like to see his luggage."

"I'm afraid I can't help. Mr Kaufmann
checked out Monday evening, a day
early. I was on duty at the time. There
was another gentleman with him."

"Can you describe him?"

The clerk took a moment to recollect.

"He was about your age and height. Extremely fair hair. And wearing a black suit."

Thanking the clerk, Callaghan made for the main door, puzzled as to who this stranger could be. Had he just been given the description of Kaufmann's and Becker's killer?

★ ★ ★

Captain Briggs and First Mate Richardson stood on the bow of the *Celeste*, facing into the Atlantic wind.

"Well," Briggs asked, "what do you think?"

"It's dropped some," Richardson conceded. "But not enough."

Briggs reluctantly agreed. The message from his friend David Morehouse of the *Dei Gratia* was extremely specific: leave New York as instructed. Briggs was still unhappy at having lied to Sarah, saying the letter was from Winchester. But what else could he do? And from the urgent tone of the letter, the sooner they were out to sea the better.

"What about this man Martens?" he

asked, remembering another worry. "Is he shaping up?"

"Some," Richardson replied. "I don't think he's sailed before, but he's resilient enough. His not speaking English is the biggest problem."

"You don't think we should change him?" Briggs queried. "Being stuck here gives us the ideal opportunity."

"No," Richardson dismissed the idea. "Just give me a couple of days with him at sea. I'll quickly make a seaman of him."

★ ★ ★

Kaufmann's office block was not what Callaghan had expected. Unlike the hectic bustle of most commercial blocks — with several floors of offices filled with male clerks, scratching away at account books, this was almost silent, the only noise being the muffled sound of traffic from outside.

Kaufmann's office was on the second floor with only his name J. Kaufmann, in gold lettering on the door. Since it would be another twenty-four hours before a search warrant was granted, Callaghan opened the door with his pick-lock.

The room was carpeted in dark green, complementing the rosewood furnishings. There were three oil paintings in matching gold frames along the wall, depicting hunting scenes: a fox hunt, a stag at bay, and a boar chase. Behind the desk, the only window was draped with green velvet curtains, matching the carpet. Callaghan saw at a glance that the large black safe in the corner would need an expert to open it.

He crossed to the cupboard and picked its flimsy locks instead. The five shelves were divided alphabetically, each containing a number of files fastened with black ribbon. Kneeling down, Callaghan searched the S and T slots on the bottom shelf, but there was nothing on Sweeny or Tweed.

Crossing to the desk, he checked the leather valise on the floor, but it contained nothing more than crumpled shirts, a couple of stained, starched collars, a woollen nightgown, shaving tackle, and a discarded longjohn and vest.

The desk drawers were locked, but

Callaghan soon picked them open. The top left held Kaufmann's letter-headed stationery. The one below contained a two-column cashbook, written-up to Monday, 4 November, the day he was murdered; and three ledgers: the first indexed A – J, the second K – R, and the third S – XYZ. Quickly flicking through them, Callaghan was disappointed to find nothing in the names of Connolly, Hall, Sweeny or Tweed.

The deep right drawer seemed to contain only blank working pads, but as Callaghan removed them, he found Kaufmann's calendars.

There were five, the most current on the top, and last year's underneath it. He opened the 1872 book to Monday, the 4th, the day of Kaufmann's death. It was blank, but the facing page, for Tuesday, had two elliptic entries, one with the crossed-out letter V, and the other with the letters MC. Callaghan flicked back through the pages. Nothing for Sunday, Saturday, Friday, but then on Thursday, 31 October, both sets of initials were repeated, again with the V crossed out. There were two entries for Tuesday,

29 October, but this time, full names had been noted in copperplate handwriting: Harold Gould and Kenneth Maddocks. Searching back to January 1, Callaghan found at least one entry for every day but Sunday, giving the full name of each client. Interspersed among these were a few personal memoranda, such as 'Wedding Anniversary', and 'Gerda's Birthday'. But there were no more entries with initials only.

Returning to the cupboard, Callaghan began checking the names against the files, starting with Gould and Maddocks. They all seemed to be legitimate clients, but he could find no files for anyone with a surname starting with V, and although there were four Cs and three Ms, none had the two initials together.

Callaghan picked up the 1871 calendar, thumbing back through its pages. December. November. Still detailed names in the same sloping style. 31st October. 29th. 28th. 27th. 26th. 25th. He stopped abruptly at the 24th as he saw the initials: PBS. The proof he was looking for! Peter Barr Sweeny. And the date was significant, because it was on the 24th that criminal proceedings were instigated against the Ring. That same evening, Sweeny had skipped the country . . . almost crushing him under his coach wheels in the process.

Still turning back the pages, Callaghan saw that PBS recurred on the last Friday of every month. There were no initials for Tweed, Hall or Connolly, but as Sweeny was the architect of the Ring's many schemes, this was hardly surprising.

As Sweeny was the only client entered as initials, it followed that the two most recent appointments — V and MC — had something to do with the Ring. Reopening the current calendar to Tuesday, 5th November, Callaghan again puzzled over the initials, then turned the page to Wednesday, the 6th. The memo leapt up at him: 'Telegraph PBS'.

He smiled, hardly able to believe his luck. So Sweeny was *still* involved, all the way from Paris. Kaufmann was to have wired him the day after his meeting with MC, except that he'd been murdered that same evening . . .

The same evening! Maybe MC was the killer? The same man who had accompanied Kaufmann to the Astor House? If so, then Callaghan already had his description, and now his initials.

MC — and V — were most likely agents being used by Kaufmann to buy diamonds for the Ring. The Tuesday meeting could have been for MC to hand over his consignment . . . but perhaps Tweed had paid him to dispose of Kaufmann instead?

Maybe Sweeny was also party to the decision? Callaghan thought, filled with sudden elation. That would make him an accessory to murder. If the case could be proven against Tweed, then maybe he'd blab and implicate the conniving bastard?

Callaghan returned to the calendar. Turning to the following week, on the top of the page for Tuesday, 12th November, was a third set of initials: DG, written in pencil. The same pencilled initials were entered for Friday, then on Saturday there was again proof of Sweeny's involvement: 'Telegraph PBS', also noted in pencil. As Kaufmann did not seem the kind of person to do anything without reason, the obvious conclusion was that ink stood for confirmed matters and pencil meant provisional. Then next Wednesday, Callaghan thought to himself, when DG walks into his office, he'll find me waiting.

Taking a sheet of plain paper from Kaufmann's drawer, Callaghan quickly copied the initialled entries:

Thursday	31 October	V (crossed out) MC (ink)
Tuesday	5 November	V (crossed out) MC (ink)
Wednesday	6 November	Telegraph PBS (ink)
Tuesday	12 November	DG (pencil)
Friday	15 November	DG (pencil)
Saturday	16 November	Telegraph PBS (pencil)

Stopping in at Sloppy Louie's, a seaman's restaurant forming part of the Fulton Ferry Hotel, for a bowl of its famous bouillabaisse, Callaghan then made his way to the *New York Times* building on the corner of Park Row and Spruce Street.

As Callaghan approached Jennings' office, he could hear the busy raised voices from the newsroom next door, and the distant clanking of the presses. One could almost smell the print. He shrugged off a sharp pang of nostalgia and hurried on.

Louis Jennings was writing, desk and floor covered in papers.

"Michael! Talk about coincidences." The Englishman got to his feet and extended his hand. "I was intending to call at your home tomorrow, now you've saved me the journey. Delighted to see you. Have you found out anything more? Tweed's trial will be commencing shortly, and I'd like to present the district attorney with as much ammunition as I can muster."

"Possibly, Louis, but first I'd like to study your files?"

"But of course." Jennings gestured to the only other chair. "Brush the papers off and sit down. What's happened?"

"I may be on to something. I'm not promising, but if I'm right, and I can prove it," — Callaghan knew he was being precipitate, but was too excited to keep quiet — "it will not only guarantee Tweed's conviction, but

221

Sweeny's as well."

"You're beginning to intrigue me." Jennings stroked his goatee. "Would you care to expand?"

"I'd rather not, Louis, not until I'm certain," Callaghan replied in more sober vein. "But in case something should happen to me, I'll leave my findings in a sealed envelope with Sam Phelps, the attorney."

"Sounds very ominous, but right-ho, if that's the way you prefer it." Jennings reached for his brass-knobbed walking stick and English bowler hat. "Actually, I'm due at a meeting, so you may have the use of my desk. That's on one condition," he added, pausing at the door.

Callaghan grinned. "Provided the exclusive belongs to the *Times*?"

Jennings smiled. "Precisely."

It took Callaghan a couple of hours to check the Ring's files, but nowhere in the mass of papers did he find anyone with the initials V, MC, or DG. He did, however, make a note of Sweeny's postal address in Paris, then decided to call it a day.

12

"SO, Sweeny *is* involved," Colleen mused. "At least this tells us he's not yet received his share of the two hundred million."

Tonight she was wearing a russet-brown frock with pale yellow lace, the autumnal shades of a New England fall, complementing her auburn hair and soft green eyes.

"The calendar only confirms his involvement in converting the money into diamonds," said Callaghan. "It's not sufficient proof he knew of the killings."

"It's enough for me," Colleen stated. "He and Tweed could have agreed a code for sending messages. And, as far as Kaufmann's death is concerned, it was probably decided weeks ago, immediately he'd completed his part in the transactions."

"Possibly," Callaghan agreed. "But not Becker's. Sweeny would see his own grandmother rot in Hell if he thought he could make money out of it, but the Catholic side of his nature would never sanction the killing of a priest. Sweeny would also know that the confessional is sacrosanct, and that Becker would never reveal what Kaufmann had told him. As far as Becker's death's concerned, our suspect is Tweed, and Tweed alone."

"Yes, you're probably right." Colleen became thoughtful, then gave a brief shudder. "I know he was no holier in God's eyes than any of us, but it makes my blood run cold to think of someone deliberately murdering a priest." She shivered again. "What about Kaufmann, do you think he was killed by the man who accompanied him to the Astor?"

"Most certainly. The fact that the last calendar entries were still in pencil shows he never had the chance to ink them in. The decision to kill him must therefore have been made earlier that afternoon, after he told Tweed that everything had been completed. Whoever this mystery man is, everything points to him being the killer. Tweed sent him with Kaufmann to the hotel to pick up his luggage, after that it was *kaput*-time for Jacob. The killer then stripped the body, but before he could dump it in the East River, he was disturbed, and had to leave it in the alley."

"But again, why remove his clothing?" Colleen demanded. She paused as a thought struck her. "What about your original theory: to delay identification? In Kaufmann's case, not so much as a person, but because he was a diamond merchant."

Callaghan sat up. "You mean . . . ?"

"Exactly. To buy time to get the diamonds out of New York."

"Of course!" he exclaimed. "It had nothing to do with Kaufmann or Becker as individuals. It's the stones. With Sweeny in Europe, that means by ship . . . " Callaghan stopped, suddenly recalling the brig he saw sailing down the East River on the morning Kaufmann's body was found, and how he'd focused the telescope on the name on her prow: *Mary Celeste*. MC!

"Miss Lowell, take a bow," he congratulated Colleen, taking the folded note out of his pocket, and handing it to her to read. "Those are the initials I found in Kaufmann's calendar. I think MC refers to a brig named *Mary Celeste*. As I was leaving the scene of Kaufmann's murder, I actually saw her being towed to Upper Bay. I later read her destination in the *Times*. She's bound for Genoa."

Colleen studied the paper. "What's the significance of Thursday, thirty-first of October?"

"That would be the day she was loaded."

"In that case," she reflected, "assuming that DG also refers to a ship, she isn't due to be loaded for another five days." She looked up, her green eyes bright with excitement. "That should give us plenty of time."

"The Shipmasters Association, first thing tomorrow morning," Callaghan promised. "They'll have her name and details on file."

"What will you do when you find her?"

"Impound her. Find the diamonds, then present Tweed with the evidence and trust to him confessing and involving Sweeny. That will ensure Sweeny's extradition. Then if neither Sweeny or Tweed will sign an affidavit clearing your father's name, Oakey will. Especially if I promise not to include him in my report. He'll cooperate, rather than have his neck stretched."

"Let's just pray it will work out that way," Colleen smiled approvingly, then grew thoughtful again. "I wonder why Kaufmann crossed out the V, especially as she was due to sail the same day as the *Celeste*?"

Callaghan shrugged. "The Shipmasters will tell me. Unless the *Times* has something on her? Do you keep old editions?"

"Sometimes. In Father's study."

Callaghan stood up, and crossed to the communicating door.

"Forgive the mess," Colleen apologized. "Father's still reacting badly to the thought of losing this place, and the fear of imprisonment." She sighed. "Mother had more resilience, it was the Irish in her. She'd have told the District Attorney to go to hell, and then fought him all the way through the courts, just like Mayor Hall."

"So that's where you get it from," Callaghan commented, drily. "I'd like to have met her."

The study was in a shambles, files and documents everywhere. In the corner was a pile of unopened *Times*. Gathering them up, Callaghan returned to drawing-room, handed half to Colleen, and dropped back into his chair.

"It's certainly stormy out on the Atlantic," Colleen remarked. "Listen to these 'Arrivals': Steamship *Minia*, Cardiff, strong gales; Italian bark *Magdalena*, hurricane carried away foremast head, and fore-top-mast with yards and sails."

"Same here," said Callaghan. "Dutch steamship *Rotterdam*, strong westerly gales; Brig *George Latimer*, strong gales, lost sails." He looked up. "I hope Mrs Briggs and the little girl are OK."

"Mrs Briggs? Little girl?" asked Colleen.

"The wife and daughter of the *Celeste*'s captain," he explained. "I assume that's who they were. I saw them on deck. The child's no more than two. Pretty little thing. Her mother was cuddling her in her arms, getting her to wave goodbye to New York, probably trying to distract

228

her from heading out to sea."

"Poor mite," murmured Colleen.

She quickly thumbed through the rest of her papers. "There's nothing here."

"Nor here," said Callaghan, discarding his and sitting back. "No matter. I'll find out tomorrow." He paused. "In the meantime, there's one thing that keeps puzzling me."

"What's that?"

"The *Celeste*'s destination: Genoa."

"What about it?"

"Well, why Genoa? Sweeny's still using the Paris postal address. And there's the report from the *Times* correspondent that he was seen at the Opera House. So, if he's in hiding in France, why hasn't he chosen a French port? Brest? Or Le Havre? Or even Marseilles?"

"He must be on the move again," said Colleen. "To Italy?"

"Yes. It's the only explanation, which suggests another reason why Tweed wanted to delay Kaufmann's identification."

Colleen waited for him to expand.

"To allow him to skip New York and join up with Sweeny."

Colleen's eyes flashed. "Yes! That makes sense! Michael! We must stop him! Tell Headquarters."

"No way!" Callaghan replied. "Tweed would know about it within the hour. I'll ask Louis to post a couple of his newsmen on him. I've promised him the exclusive . . ."

"Jackson!"

The voice was Edward Lowell's. The cry came from the hall. Both Callaghan and Colleen sprang to their feet and hurried to the door.

"*Jackson!*"

The yell grew louder with irritation at the butler's delay.

Callaghan threw open the door and saw Colleen's father standing unsteadily at the top of the curving stairs, one hand grasping the handrail. He was wearing a red smoking-jacket, its belt hanging untied, his shirt collar was also unfastened and lacking a tie. He was swaying, obviously drunk. Losing patience, Lowell leant over the rail to look under the staircase to the passage door leading into the kitchen. "*Jackson! The blasted decanter's empty!*"

Overbalancing, Lowell lost his grip, and fell headlong down the long stairway. Bouncing from wall to oaken banisters, arms and legs flaying, his heavy frame accelerated his fall until he crashed down on to the marble floor, and lay silent, unmoving.

Callaghan heard Colleen's frightened gasp as he hurried to Lowell. He immediately saw from the twisted head that Edward Lowell's neck was broken. The open, unseeing eyes staring up at him, confirmed he was dead.

"Father!" Colleen cried.

Callaghan spun around to shield her from this death. Her face drained of colour, Colleen tried getting around him, but he held her shoulders fast. She struggled against him, silently.

"Darling, I'm sorry," Callaghan murmured. "There's nothing you can do."

Colleen looked up at him, her eyes pleading to have misunderstood, then she sagged against him. Callaghan lifted her up in his arms and carried her back into the drawing-room.

Hearing the passage door open, Callaghan saw Jackson and the maid,

Mary, standing there, staring aghast at Lowell's inert body. Raising her hands to her mouth, Mary stifled a scream.

"Jackson, send for a doctor. There's no urgency."

"You mean, sir . . . ?"

"I'm afraid so."

The butler headed back for the kitchen.

"Mary. Get me a blanket."

The rounded middle-aged maid, who'd been with the family since Colleen was born, made for the stairs, carefully skirting the body.

Callaghan faced back into the drawing-room where he'd left Colleen in a chair by the fire. Still mute with shock, she was staring glassy-eyed into the flames, her body trembling uncontrollably.

Callaghan poured a large brandy, and knelt at her side. "Here, drink this."

When Colleen remained unmoving, he held the glass to her lips. She took a sip, oblivious, then coughed as the spirit burnt her throat.

Turning to him with tears of grief welling in her eyes, she grabbed his arm, her hold tightening. "Michael, are you certain? Maybe he's only unconscious?"

"No, Colleen. I'm sorry. He's gone."

Suddenly her grief erupted as if his words had broken through the barrier of her shock. She fell against him and wept, so heart-broken she was hardly able to catch her breath, her frail shoulders shuddering beneath his strong arms as the sobs racked her body.

As Mary entered the room, and gently wrapped the blanket around Colleen, she was followed by Jackson. "I've sent the coachman for the doctor, sir."

Callaghan left Colleen with Mary while he and Jackson carried Edward Lowell upstairs to his room.

When he returned, Colleen was wiping the tears from her eyes. She looked up at him, her face pale and drawn. "Sweeny did this." Her voice was flat, emotionless. "As sure as putting a pistol to father's head."

"Colleen, believe me, I know how you feel," Callaghan said, remembering too well the day his father had died in his arms.

"I know you do," she said softly. "And I now understand why you reacted as you

233

did." Colleen placed her hand on his arm. "It's Sweeny. He destroys everyone he comes near." She tightened her grip on his arm. "Oh, Michael, let's make a vow that we won't rest until we've found him. Not only found him, but proved that he's involved in the deaths of both Kaufmann and Father Becker. Yes," she insisted, as Callaghan started to protest, "Becker as well. If he stands to profit, then Sweeny's evil enough to murder even a priest. We must find the evidence and get him extradited. And if they hang him, well, he deserves it." Her hold was so tight it was hurting. "Promise me, Michael."

"I promise."

Colleen looked long into the fire. Then, she suddenly broke the silence, gazing up at him with forlorn entreaty.

"Michael?"

"Yes?"

"Will you stay here with me tonight?"

"Of course. I'll make up a bed on the settee."

"No, I mean, *with* me. I need to feel the warmth of your arms around me, holding me tight."

Leghorn, Italy

Brains Sweeny and Father Cottone were sitting on the verandah which connected their lavish suite of rooms in The Victoria and Washington, the port's finest hotel. The setting sun was casting its final rays over the Porto Vecchio — the inner harbour — highlighting the yellows, reds, greens, of the brigs and fishing-boats tied up alongside the quays. Beyond its walls, larger boats with deeper draughts, ferries and ocean-going steamships, lay at anchor in the Porto Nuovo, inside the protection of its semicircular mole.

The sky was pale blue and clear, not a cloud in sight; the evening meal had been excellent; and his cigar was superb. Sweeny was at peace with the world. Exhaling a cloud of smoke with a sigh of contentment, he commented. "The diamonds should be well on their way by now. Have all our travelling arrangements been made?"

"Everything is in order," Father Cottone confirmed. "We arrive in Palermo midnight, Tuesday. My uncle's carriage will be waiting on the quayside. By one o'clock in the morning you will be installed in his villa in Monreale. It's also the seat of the Bishop. Should you wish to attend church, or confessional, during your stay, you have only to say."

Sweeny narrowed his eyebrows and looked across at the Sicilian priest. "I thought Victor Emmanuel had closed all the churches." He spoke in his deep, grating voice.

"In the rest of Italy, yes," Father Cottone replied. "In Palermo, we organize things very differently. As you will soon discover when you arrive there." He gave Sweeny a thin smile.

New York

The Church of Saint Francis Xavier: in the reflected light from the candles lighting up the body of the church, Father Murray entered the confessional, and pulled the curtain closed.

Kneeling down, he crossed his breast and addressed the meshed grille. "Pray, Father, bless me, for I have sinned."

There came the answering blessing: "The Lord be in thy heart and on thy lips, that thou mayest truly and humbly confess thy sins, in the Name of The

Father, and of the Son, and of the Holy Ghost."

Dutifully reciting the first part of the confiteor, Murray then proceeded to detail the first of his sins. "Today, I lied when I told someone I was not of the Holy Father's ultramontane persuasion that Rome and only Rome is the Holy City chosen of God to be the . . ."

★ ★ ★

Briggs entered the cabin as Sarah was tucking the blankets around Sophia. Briggs sat down in a chair and waited as she gently stroked the little girl's head, crooning softly to soothe her to sleep. Several moments later, Sarah joined him, sitting on the other chair by the desk. "Sophia's been restless," she explained. "She woke up asking for Arthur and Grandma Briggs and Grandma Cobb."

"It's understandable, cooped up in this small cabin," Briggs replied. "She'll be better when we get under way."

"But when, Benjamin?" Sarah asked. "Poor baby, I'm beginning to think I should have left her at home with my mother. Arthur could have called in and played with her on his way from school. This wait is becoming frustrating, even for me."

"Maybe daybreak," Briggs ventured as he began to undress for bed. "The wind is beginning to lessen."

"I'm too awake to sleep," Sarah declared, somewhat cheered. "As there may not be enough time in the morning, I'll write a final letter to Mother Briggs, and give it to the Sandy Hook pilot for posting."

As her husband wearily settled into bed, Sarah picked up a leaded pencil and began to write:

Brig Mary Celeste
Off Staten Island,
Nov 7th 1872

Dear Mother Briggs
Probably you will be a little surprised to receive a letter with this date, but instead of proceeding out to sea when we came out Tuesday morning, we anchored about a mile or so from the city as it was a strong head wind,

238

*and B said it looked so thick and nasty
ahead we shouldn't gain much if we
were beating and banging about.*

She paused, thinking ahead to the
dawn and hoping Benjamin was right.

*Accordingly we took fresh departure
this morning with wind iight and
favourable, so we hope to get outside
without being obliged to anchor.*

Again she paused. Benjamin's brother,
Oliver, who was also the captain of a
brig, had been due to arrive back in
New York before they sailed, and Mother
Briggs had told Benjamin to make every
effort to see him. Better say something
about him:

*Have kept a sharp look out for Oliver,
but so far have seen nothing of him.
It was rather trying to lie in sight of
the city for so long and think that
most likely we had letters waiting for
us there, and be unable to get them.
However, we hope no great change
has occurred since we did hear and*

shall look for a goodly supply when we reach Genoa.

Sophia thinks the figure 3 and the letter G on her blocks is the same thing, so I saw her whispering to herself yesterday with the 3 block in her hand — Gam-gam-gamma.

Wondering what next to say, Sarah realized Mother Briggs would be concerned to hear about the new crew:

Benj thinks we have a pretty peaceable set this time all around if they continue as they have begun. Can't tell yet how smart they are . . .

In the galley, Edward Head sat down to his diary and entered his thoughts for the day:

Thursday, 7 November 1 a.m. At last it seems the waiting is over. The first mate reckons the wind is dropping and come the morning we should be on our way. By this time tomorrow I shall have taken my leave of you, my dearest Emma. I trust the voyage will be uneventful, and that before March is out I'll be holding you in my arms once more. If the crew is anything to go by this is assured. They seem an extremely capable lot, with the possible exception of Martens, that is. Yesterday I heard First Mate Richardson tell Second Mate Gilling that he doubted Martens had been to sea before, because he seems to know so little about sailing terms, but I think the first mate might be judging him too hasty, as Martens can only speak German.

13

Friday, 8 November 1872

THE American Shipmasters Association was above the Atlantic Mutual Insurance offices at 47 Wall Street. Formed in 1860 by John Divine Jones, the President of the Atlantic Mutual, the Association collated information on ships sailing in and out of American ports, concentrating especially on New York.

As Callaghan approached the counter, a middle-aged clerk looked up, peering through his horn-rimmed glasses. "Can I help you?" he asked in a clipped, precise voice.

"I hope so," Callaghan replied, showing the man his badge. "I'm investigating a murder case and I've come across some initials which I think may represent the names of three vessels. They've either recently left — or are due to leave — New York bound for Europe. Would you mind checking for me?"

"Always pleased to assist the police," the clerk replied. Taking Callaghan's notations he disappeared into the next room, returning in less than five minutes with three files.

"Your assumption was quite correct," he said, opening one of the folders. "The V stands for *Venango*. She was a brigantine, owned by the Venango Oil Works, Venango Yard, Weehawken . . . "

"Was?" Callaghan interrupted.

"Yes. She was destroyed by fire on the twenty-seventh of October."

"Accidental?"

The clerk referred to a document. "There's some dispute. The company is claiming smouldering pipe tobacco as the probable cause. But the insurers aren't satisfied, and the investigators are looking into it."

"Where was she bound?"

"Originally for Marseilles, but then the orders were changed to Palermo, calling into Gibraltar first."

"Why call into Gibraltar, if she was bound for Palermo?"

"Orders sometimes get changed," the man explained. "The New York agents wire new instructions to agents in Gibraltar, who then pass them on to the captains."

"I see. There's no mention of Genoa on the *Venango*'s file?"

The clerk shook his head. "No."

"What was her cargo?"

"One thousand, seven hundred and thirty-five barrels of petroleum. The contract has since been awarded to . . . " — he looked up at Callaghan — "the brigantine *Dei Gratia*, which corresponds with your second set of initials DG." Putting the *Venango*'s file to one side, he opened the next one.

"The *Dei Gratia* is a British registered brig, owned jointly by Messrs Heney and Parker, Shipping Agents, of 25 Coenties Slip, South Street, and the *Gratia*'s captain, David Reed Morehouse, from Sandy Cove, Bear Island, Nova Scotia. She was previously moored at Erie Basin, preparing to sail for Curaçao, but this new contract must've seemed more profitable. The owners relinquished the Curaçao run and sailed the *Dei Gratia* down to the Venango Yard three days ago to be loaded." The man peered owlishly through his glasses. "The ship's brokers are Funch Edye and Co, of 48 Beaver Street. No crew details have been registered yet," he finished, closing the *De Gratia*'s file.

"The cargo's destination?" Callaghan halted him. "Has it been changed from Palermo to Genoa?"

"No. According to the file the *Dei Gratia* is instructed to sail only as far as Gibraltar, and remain there for further orders."

"Are you sure?" Callaghan queried.

The clerk raised his eyebrows, holding out the document for Callaghan to see. "Positive."

"Sorry. Please carry on."

The man opened the third folder. "The last initials stand for the *Mary Celeste*, a brig registered by four persons in a joint venture. James Henry Winchester, Shipping Agent, 52 South Street, has a half-share interest. The captain, Benjamin Spooner Briggs of Marion, Massachusetts owns a third. And Daniel Simpson and Sylvester Goodwin, of the same address as Winchester, have one-twelfth each. The ship left Pier Fifty on the East

River, last Tuesday, bound for Genoa, carrying one thousand, seven hundred barrels of alcohol, shipped by the New York branch of a German firm, Meissner Ackermann.

"Is she instructed to call into Gibraltar first, the same as the *Venango* and the *Gratia*?" Callaghan asked.

"It says nothing about Gibraltar on the Genoa instructions," said the clerk, studying the backlog of papers. "She was originally bound for Marseilles, like the *Venango*. Then her orders were also changed to Palermo, calling into Gibraltar first."

"But now she's bound straight for Genoa," Callaghan mused out loud, "without stopping at Gibraltar . . . "

"Not necessarily," said the clerk. "The captain could be under oral instructions to call there. It's not always written in black and white. Anyway, after unloading in Genoa, the *Celeste* is bound for Palermo to pick up a return cargo of fruit for New York."

Callaghan made some notes.

"Do you require the ship's complement?" the clerk asked somewhat eagerly, clearly enjoying his role in the investigation.

"Might as well."

"In addition to the captain, there's his wife and two-year-old daughter, plus a crew of seven." The clerk read out the full names, ages, and brief physical descriptions of the two mates, the cook, and four-man German crew.

As Callaghan wrote down the details he suddenly realized that another common denominator had entered the case: the German factor. Kaufmann and Becker were German. Also Meissner Ackermann. Funch of Funch Edye and Co sounded Germanic. And now the four seamen.

"An all German crew?" Callaghan remarked. "Isn't that unusual for an American ship?"

"Not especially," the clerk replied, noncommittally. "But if you want a closer look, the *Celeste* is still in the Bay, anchored off Staten Island. The Atlantic storms prevented her from sailing."

Thanking him, Callaghan left in a hurry, and hailed a cab to the Staten Island ferry terminal.

★ ★ ★

247

As the ferry tied up in New Brighton harbour, Callaghan noticed a tall, scrawny postman on the dock, with a large, half-empty sack over his shoulder. "Not a lot of mail today, skipper," he called up to the ferry's captain. "And only one from the pilot boat. Some silly coot — a brig — sailed out yesterday, without waiting for the wind to drop."

As the mailman came on board Callaghan flashed his police badge. "What was the name of the brig?"

"How in tarnation should I know?" the man replied, truculently.

Callaghan grabbed the sack.

"No one can interfere with the mail," the man protested. "Not even the police. Not without a warrant."

"Can you swim?" Callaghan asked.

"What kind of question is that?"

"You'll find out in ten seconds if you don't release the bag."

Seeing the look in Callaghan's eye, the man slipped the strap off his shoulder.

Among the letters was one written in a delicate female hand, addressed to 'Mrs Sophia Briggs, Rose Cottage, Sippican, Marion, Massachusetts'.

Callaghan hesitated, uncertain what to do. It was obviously personal, written by Sarah Briggs to a relative-in-law. But what if it held a clue? Undecided whether or not he should open it, Callaghan placed it in his pocket. "I'll make sure it gets posted," he said, returning the sack. The man did not argue, but quickly walked away.

Crossing the deck to the opposite rail, Callaghan stared at the angry, grey horizon. So, the *Mary Celeste* had sailed. That just left the *Dei Gratia*.

* * *

The name painted on the tall wooden gates read 'Venango Oil Works, New Jersey'. Ignoring the 'No Trespassing' sign, Callaghan squeezed through the narrow opening. A long wooden warehouse stretched towards the Hudson River where he could see the New York skyline emblazoned along the opposite bank. His eyes followed the wagon-rutted road extending alongside the shed, until it petered out into a stretch of wasteland, strewn with empty casks and rusting iron.

From the rear of the shed, a plankway, built on poles, extended across the wasteland to the water's edge, where it branched into two wooden jetties reaching out into the river. The nearest pier had been reduced to a few burnt pilings and hanging black timbers, alongside which the scorched roof of a forrard deck-house showed above the surface. Tied to the further pier was a brig, with sails furled, moving up and down on the flow of the river.

As he started toward the vessel, a shed window opened. "Looking for someone?" a voice called out.

"I'm a friend of Captain Morehouse of the *Dei Gratia*," Callaghan replied easily and the window closed.

Callaghan ploughed on, mud sticking to his shoes. There were sounds of activity from inside the shed, but on this bitter, grey day no one was venturing out. At the end of the building there was a wooden ladder leading up to the plankway. His footsteps echoing hollowly on the boards, Callaghan headed down the gangway to the jetty, and finally to the brig. *Dei Gratia* was painted in gold letters on her bow. Crossing her deck, Callaghan made his way to the main deck house and hammered on the closed hatchway, shouting, "Anyone on board?"

The hatch opened almost immediately to reveal the moustached and bearded face of a man in his middle to late thirties. He had narrow, piercingly blue eyes, and the healthy weather-tanned complexion of a sailor.

"David Morehouse?" Callaghan queried.

"That's me," the captain replied in a deep Nova Scotian drawl.

"My name's Callaghan. I'm with the New York Police, Detective Squad. I'd like to ask you some questions."

Morehouse hesitated. "What about?" he asked, apprehensively.

"I'd prefer talking inside," Callaghan stated.

Morehouse reluctantly nodded and withdrew. Ducking his head, Callaghan followed him down the stairs, across the saloon with its bare wooden table, into the captain's cabin. It was about fourteen feet by ten in size, the enclosed WC in the corner creating a recess for the double bed. A writing desk with two chairs stood against the opposite wall, with a small faded rug warming the polished planked floor. Two paintings of brigantines in full sail hung above the bureau.

Callaghan immediately noticed the half completed letter on the desk, which Morehouse quickly turned over as he sat down. "Take a seat," the captain invited, indicating to the other chair. Then, a shade too briskly, "What can I do for you?"

Certain that Morehouse had shown panic on hearing he was with the police, Callaghan decided to test him with a direct approach. "It's to do with Captain Briggs of the *Mary Celeste*."

This time there was no doubting the man's consternation. Though he forced himself to hold Callaghan's probing gaze, his strong hands clenched at the arms of his chair.

"The *Celeste* left yesterday for Genoa," Callaghan continued. "We believe she's carrying contraband. The Genoa police have been apprised of the situation and they will search her. If we're right, then Briggs will be sent back to New York to face charges. We also have reason to believe that you are involved," Callaghan pressed on deliberately to intimidate the man. "I've been instructed to remain on board until after you've loaded. The cargo will then be impounded and searched. If contraband is found, you will be arrested and charged, along with Captain Briggs."

Morehouse blanched, but did not speak.

"In addition," Callaghan piled it on, "there's the question of Briggs and yourself being implicated in the murders of . . ."

"Murder!" Morehouse half-rose to his feet, only to collapse back into the chair. "Murder!" he repeated, in shocked disbelief. "What murder?"

Callaghan produced morgue photographs of Kaufmann and Becker and tossed them on the desk.

Morehouse looked with revulsion at the twisted bodies lying naked on the tilted slabs, then turned and glared at Callaghan. "What the hell's going on? You can't involve me in the deaths of two men I've never even heard . . ."

"Murders," Callaghan corrected, "not deaths. Vicious, cold-blooded executions to ensure the silence of the two men who discovered what you and Briggs were up to. It makes no difference which of you carried them out, you're both guilty under the law, and the district attorney is bound to demand the death sentence. All we need to prove our case is the contraband. And a reliable source swears it's hidden in both your cargoes."

Morehouse half-opened his mouth to protest, but Callaghan wasn't finished.

"My captain is convinced of your guilt." He deliberately softened his tone. "But speaking personally, I don't think that either you or Briggs had anything to do with the killings. Your best chance is to tell me everything you know, now."

Morehouse covered his face in his hands. Finally, after a lengthy silence, he looked up, despairingly. "Yes! OK! I'll tell you." His voice tailed off.

Callaghan waited.

" . . . on one condition."

"Name it."

"Your promise that my wife and

children will be protected?"

"Protected?" This was unexpected. "From whom?"

"Is it agreed?" Morehouse persisted.

"You have my word on it." Callaghan produced his notepad. "Give me your wife's name and address."

"Desiah. She was to have sailed with me, leaving the children with her mother, but then this terrible nightmare happened." Morehouse went off on a tangent. "I was just writing to her, suggesting she and the children visit her cousin in British Columbia, in the hope they might be safer there. But maybe there's no need, now you've promised to protect . . . "

"Their address, Captain Morehouse."

"Oh, yes. Bear River, Digby County, Nova Scotia."

"I'll telegraph the Canadian Police as soon as I return to headquarters," Callaghan promised. "Now, tell me all you know."

Morehouse drew a deep breath. "You're correct in assuming that Briggs and I know one another. We sail the same routes, and often meet in various ports.

Our wives sometimes sail with us, and over the years, the four of us have become good friends. Anyway, we were both in New York — Benjamin as a part-owner in the ˙*Celeste*, which was at Hunter's Point undergoing a refit, while I was at Erie Basin getting ready to load for Curaçao — so we arranged to meet for an evening meal at the Astor House. That was a week last Monday, the twenty-eighth of October. Ben told me he was bound for Genoa with a cargo of alcohol, and after that, to Palermo, to pick up a return cargo of fruit for New York. The *Celeste* was moving down to Pier Fifty in two days' time, to start loading, and Sarah — that's Mrs Briggs — and little Sophia, were due to join him. When I told him what a lucky fellow he was to be sailing to Europe, rather than Curaçao, where there's nothing to do, Ben said if I could get out of the Curaçao contract he might be able to help me. Apparently, that morning he'd overheard his agent and a business associate, discussing the problem of finding a replacement for the *Venango*.

It seemed that her cargo — which was originally bound for Palermo — had been redirected to Genoa, and there was some urgency . . . "

"Genoa?" Callaghan interrupted. "You're sure about that? I was told your instructions were to sail only as far as Gibraltar, and wait there for orders?"

"Well that's what Ben heard them say," Morehouse insisted. "But you're correct about Gibraltar. However, if Ben heard right and the cargo is destined for Genoa, then I don't see the purpose of it."

"What about Briggs? Is he also calling into Gibraltar?"

"He made no mention of it," Morehouse replied. "But funnily enough, he did hear them say that, after Genoa, the replacement vessel was also to sail to Palermo, just like the *Celeste*, to pick up a cargo of fruit from the same firm, a company called Cottone. Ben remembered the name because it sounded like cotton."

Callaghan decided Palermo was a genuine pick-up, and Cottone one of Palermo's main fruit suppliers.

"Getting back to what Briggs over-heard," he prompted.

"Like I said, the agents were anxious to find another vessel to take-over the *Venango*'s cargo. Benjamin suggested I apply, so we could meet up both in Genoa and Palermo, then sail side by side back to New York. Anyway, the following day I mentioned the job to my partners, Heney and Parker, who thought it an excellent idea as the Curaçao run was not the most profitable, and I left them to arrange everything. Next day, I received orders to sail the *Gratia* down to Weehawken for loading. I wrote to tell Desiah the good news, then sent Benjamin a note inviting himself and Sarah to join me in a celebratory meal at the Astor House on Monday, that being their last evening in New York. Anyway, when I got there, Ben was on his own. He claimed Sarah was too tired to join us, but he seemed so jumpy, I guessed that was not the real reason."

Morehouse paused, raking his hands through his hair. "As soon as we'd ordered, he asked my advice over an incident that occurred during the loading of the *Celeste*. In fact, two things happened. First, Mr Winchester — that's Ben's agent and partner — went out of his way to instruct one of the German seamen to take more care of the barrel he was handling. Nothing peculiar in that, except that Winchester repeated the instruction several times and . . . oh, yes . . . there was a stranger with him, a big man, according to Ben, with a German accent. His name was . . . " Morehouse frowned, trying to remember.

"Kaufmann," Callaghan said. "Jacob Kaufmann."

Morehouse opened his eyes wide. "Kaufmann! That was it! How did you . . . " He paused. "Yes, I forgot, you're investigating . . . "

"Kaufmann's murder," finished Callaghan. "That's him in the top photograph. The one underneath, with only half his body left, is a Jesuit priest. Just so you know what you're involved in."

"Involved!" Morehouse protested. "I'm involved in nothing. I don't know what the hell's going on."

"Let's get back to what happened."

"Get back! After that, I can't even remember where I was!"

"You were saying that Winchester repeated the instruction."

"Yes. According to Benjamin, it was almost as if Winchester was drawing the seaman's attention to that particular barrel. Ben tried to forget the incident, but then, when loading was completed, the barrel count was found to be one thousand, seven hundred and one — one more than stated on the Bill of Lading."

"You're sure of that? The *Celeste*'s carrying an extra barrel?" asked Callaghan, wishing Colleen were with him to hear their conjectures verified as fact.

"Not just the *Celeste*," Morehouse growled. "But the *Gratia*'s getting one as well."

Callaghan looked sharply at the man. "How the hell do you know that?"

"It'll be easier to explain, if I come to it in proper order," said Morehouse.

"OK. Carry on."

"So," the Nova Scotian continued, "when Ben went to the office, he confronted Winchester about the extra barrel, but Winchester claimed it was only human error on the side of the shippers. Ben told him he wasn't satisfied, to which Winchester replied he was making a fuss over nothing, leaving Benjamin in a quandary as to what he should do."

"And it was on this that Briggs sought your advice?"

"Yes. He was in two minds whether to report it. We discussed it at some length, but by the end of the evening I'd convinced him it was not uncommon for such a mistake to be made. If his suspicions were right, and there *was* contraband on board, Customs would insist on opening every barrel. This could result in the entire cargo being ruined. I asked him if he could afford the financial risk? I told him, that as a partner in the *Celeste*, his over-riding interest surely lay in ensuring the cargo reached Genoa on time." Morehouse shook his head, obviously ruing his words.

"To which he agreed?"

"Only partially. Benjamin is a somewhat stubborn, rigid man. He agreed to sail, but as soon as he reaches Genoa, and gets the Bill of Lading signed, he's going to report the matter to the Italian authorities, and leave them to take whatever action they think necessary. We said goodbye, agreeing to meet either in Genoa or Palermo."

Morehouse paused before continuing, "But now comes the weird part. As I was making my way to the Hoboken ferry, I was waylaid."

Callaghan sat up.

"I didn't see my assailant's face, only that he had fair hair. He was wearing a black suit, and spoke with a foreign accent . . . "

"Accent? What kind?"

"I'm not sure. If I had to guess . . . German."

German! Callaghan's mind swirled. The German factor again. What the hell did it all mean?

"He came up behind me, held a knife to my throat, and forced me to tell him everything Benjamin had said. I repeated most of it, but left out that Ben intended telling the Genoese authorities. I was certain he was going to kill me . . . "

Morehouse stopped in mid-sentence, and gave a horrified glance at the morgue photographs. "Was it the same man did this?"

"Probably," Callaghan replied sombrely.

Morehouse rubbed his neck as though he felt the knife-point at his throat again. "Hell's bells! You mean if I hadn't mentioned that I was the captain of the *Dei Gratia*, I would have joined those two poor bastards . . . ?"

"More than likely. But you didn't, so what happened next?"

"I'd like to have you as one of my crew," Morehouse growled, a hint of threat in his voice. "You're an unfeeling son-of-a . . . "

"Wish on," replied Callaghan. "Now, again, what happened next?"

Still glowering, Morehouse cleared his throat. "He warned me that if I told anyone about Benjamin's suspicions regarding the extra barrel, or about the one coming on the *Gratia*, my family would be killed. Then he disappeared down some dark alley."

"Did you . . . ?"

"I haven't finished," Morehouse said,

irritably. "I was paralysed for a moment wondering what the hell to do. Ben was right. Something was going on, and it was obviously big. My first thought was for Desiah and the children's safety, and then I suddenly realized that the biggest threat was Ben himself. He was sailing the next morning, determined to tell the Genoa port authorities all about the barrel. Somehow I had to stop him. I couldn't go to him myself in case I was being watched, so I went back to the Astor and wrote him a letter — which I paid a boy to deliver — saying I had information about the barrel which, for his sake, and the lives of Desiah, and Ned and Harriet, we had to discuss before he reached Genoa. *But*, I warned him, their lives would be forfeit if he failed to sail as arranged. I asked him to make slow progress, and rendezvous with me at a point six hundred miles out of Gibraltar . . . "

"Is that possible?" Callaghan interrupted. "For two small brigs to meet at a prearranged point in the middle of an ocean?"

"I wouldn't have suggested it if it

wasn't. The only problem is these gales. The bearings I gave him are on the main shipping line between New York and Gibraltar. But in the event that these storms continue, I asked him to put in at Gibraltar and wait for me there instead."

"Will he?"

"I hope so," said Morehouse, his brow furrowed with worry.

"What do you intend doing when you meet him?"

"Tell him everything that happened, and ask him to tell no one about the barrel. It's our only choice."

"Do you think he'll agree?"

"He'd better!" Morehouse growled.

Callaghan glanced down at his pad, thinking it might help to have a summary of the instructions relating to both cargoes.

"May I use your desk?" he asked.

"Sure. Do you need me? There's a couple of things I'd like to check in the hold."

"As long as you're not thinking of doing a bunk!"

"What'd be the point?" shrugged Morehouse, leaving the cabin.

Already writing at the desk, Callaghan hardly noticed him go.

	Mary Celeste	*Venango Dei Gratia*
Original destination	Marseilles	Marseilles
First alteration	Palermo	Palermo
Calling at Gibraltar	Yes	Yes
Second alteration	Genoa	Genoa? (overheard)
Also bound for	Palermo	Palermo? (-ditto-)
Calling at Gibraltar	?	Yes: For orders

So where do I go from here? Callaghan asked himself, sitting back and studying the notes.

Once the brigs reached Genoa, the extra barrels would probably be diverted from the cargoes during unloading, and taken to wherever Sweeny had arranged. Almost certainly another diamond merchant, who would no doubt sell them off piecemeal, to avoid flooding the market and lowering the price.

Meanwhile, everything had almost certainly come to a dead end here in New York.

Firstly, whoever this mysterious killer was, his work was done, and the chances of now catching him were nil.

Secondly, even if the *Dei Gratia*'s cargo was searched and the diamonds found, everyone connected with the two vessels was certain to plead ignorance. And there was no hope of Tweed confessing, not without any hard evidence against him.

The spotlight had moved from New York to Genoa.

And he had no choice but to stay in it.

"Loading starts Tuesday?" Callaghan questioned, when Morehouse returned a few moments later.

"At daybreak," the other confirmed.

"Well, you've got your wish, Captain. I'll be sailing with you as one of the crew."

14

"IS there no other way?"

Colleen was looking at him with deep concern. Dressed in dark-grey mourning, she was sitting near to the roaring fire for warmth, her face pale, but outwardly composed, despite what she must be feeling inside.

"No," said Callaghan. "And it's not because Sweeny's waiting at the other end — although the thought of catching him red-handed is enough in itself. But there's nothing more I can do in New York. Even if we found diamonds on the *Gratia*, all the evidence to date, whether it's factual — like Kaufmann's calendar — or circumstantial — like the Saint Xavier's connection — implicates only Sweeny."

Colleen remained silent, her eyes still betraying her anxiety.

"I asked Morehouse where Pier Fifty is," Callaghan said. "It's right by the Brooklyn Bridge, next to where Becker's body was found."

Colleen frowned. "That suggests he was on his way to see Briggs, or . . . " She paused. "No. He obviously didn't get there, or Briggs would have told Morehouse about it."

"That's the way I see it," Callaghan agreed.

"But what would Father Becker want with Briggs?"

"To tell him about the hidden diamonds in his cargo, then get him to tell the police, and support Kaufmann's testimony. Briggs would have had nothing to lose, and everything to gain. A ten per cent reward of a hundred million dollars would have set him up for life, with plenty left over. Unfortunately for Briggs, Becker's killer got to him first."

Accepting the theory, Colleen gazed into the fire. A silence descended on the room. It was Colleen who broke it, still looking at the flames. "Mr Phelps says that Father Hudson is conducting both funeral services. But he then has a meeting which he cannot break. A Father Flynn is attending Father's burial. And a

Father Murray is performing the rites for Father Becker."

She turned to face Callaghan. "But let's change the subject. Monday will be here soon enough. Tell me what you plan doing after meeting up with the *Celeste*?"

Callaghan realized she needed to talk to engage her mind and banish sorrowful thoughts. "Get Briggs to sail on ahead to Genoa, while we wait in Gibraltar . . . "

"But I thought the plan was to sail together?"

"No. That was Morehouse's idea. But having the *Celeste* sail straight to Genoa, and the *Dei Gratia* only to Gibraltar to await orders, is obviously Sweeny's insurance in case something goes wrong with the unloading of the *Celeste*'s cargo. According to Morehouse, sailing time from Gibraltar to Genoa is about ten days. The *Dei Gratia*'s leaving New York eleven days behind the *Celeste*. Consequently, the *Celeste* should be entering Genoa at roughly the same time that the *Gratia* arrives in Gibraltar. That way, should there be any problems in Genoa, it allows Sweeny to wire

270

Morehouse and instruct him to sail the *Gratia* to another port. So, when we meet up with Briggs, I've got to persuade him to go on ahead . . . "

"And if nothing goes wrong in Genoa, then as soon as Morehouse receives his orders, the *Gratia* will follow on, sticking to Sweeny's original plan?"

"Exactly."

"Then what?"

"I'll follow the *Gratia*'s cargo to the warehouse, then wait for someone to turn up and take a barrel away. Hopefully, he'll lead me straight to Sweeny."

"But will he chance compromising himself by having the diamonds taken directly to him?"

"An odds-on certainty," said Callaghan. "The damned shyster won't risk the barrel being opened with him not there. And with four thousand miles between him and New York, he won't be feeling at risk."

"You're right," Colleen agreed, adding, "but there are still some questions unanswered."

"Such as?"

"The various changes of orders.

271

Marseilles is obvious enough. So is Genoa — assuming we're right in Sweeny being on the move again. But why did he redirect the cargoes to Palermo, then cancel the instructions, yet still make Palermo the second port of call?"

"Maybe Palermo was first chosen because it's easier to smuggle things into?"

"Then why change the orders to Genoa?"

"Because Palermo doesn't possess a Diamond Exchange?" Callaghan suggested. "And Sweeny didn't find out about it until a few weeks ago."

"Possibly." Colleen only half accepted his hypothesis. "But why hide the diamonds in other people's cargoes, when he could so easily arrange his own?"

"They probably are his. Knowing Sweeny, it's more than likely that the firms registered as the owners are no more than his paid nominees."

Colleen leant forward, temporarily distracted from her grief. "Which brings us to the German factor. It can't be a coincidence. Kaufmann. Becker. Funch is probably a derivation of Funck. Meissner Ackermann. The Hamburg insurers. The *Celeste*'s crew. And finally, the man who waylaid Morehouse — and almost certainly killed Father Becker and Kaufmann." She was perched on the edge of her chair. "What possible method could he have used, to leave no bruising on their bodies? And what about Desiah Morehouse?" Colleen's voice was strained with sudden panic. "Is his threat against her and the children real, or just a bluff?"

"We have to assume it's genuine. I'm delaying my resignation until the Canadian police reply. And the sooner they do the better. Because until I know the Morehouses are safe, I can't confront Sweeny, not without risking their lives."

"And Tweed?" Colleen asked, switching her line of questions.

"Louis's employing Pinkertons to watch him."

"So everything in New York's taken care of?" she stated, sounding suddenly and inexplicably casual.

"Just about."

273

"In that case, I'm coming with you. Just as we agreed." Though her voice was soft, it was filled with determination.

Momentarily robbed of speech, Callaghan swiftly gathered his defences and met her head on. "Coming with me! You're most certainly not! What on . . . "

"I most certainly am," replied Colleen, calmly.

Callaghan recognized her beguiling brand of resolve and knew he had little hope of winning.

"I'm too deeply involved to back out now," she said. "My father. Your parents. Our marriage. The newspaper. I want to be there when Sweeny's finally arrested."

"But the *Dei Gratia* doesn't . . . " he started objecting.

"I'll take a steamer." She picked up a copy of the *Times* from the mahogany canterbury. "I'm in luck," she exclaimed. "A British steamship, *Asia*, should be leaving for Gibraltar next week, maybe on the same day as you. Let's see. She took exactly three weeks to cross. Assuming she makes the same speed back, and the *Gratia* will take . . . ?"

274

She looked questioningly at him.

"About thirty days," Callaghan replied, giving in.

"Thirty days. Then I should be in Gibraltar a week before you. I'll wait there to ensure you arrive safely, and that the *Gratia* receives her orders to continue on to Genoa. I can then take a train to Genoa," she raced on, hardly aware of Callaghan as she made her plans. "That should take no more than two days, while the *Dei Gratia* will take at least ten. So I'll have ample time to discover where Sweeny is staying, and . . ."

"OK! OK! You're coming." Callaghan openly conceded defeat. "But only on condition you keep a low profile. For goodness sake, don't let Sweeny see you." Callaghan abruptly rose from his chair. "Which reminds me. There's still one thing left to do. The notes in Kaufmann's calendar. *Telegraph PBS*. Kaufmann was killed prior to sending the first wire."

"But surely Tweed will have sent it?"

"No. The calendar was locked inside the desk. If Tweed had seen it, and sent the wire, he'd have removed it."

275

"So what do you intend doing?"

"Send it myself, adding Kaufmann's name."

"But you don't know Sweeney's Genoa address."

"I'll use the Paris one. If he's already left for Genoa, he's bound to have made forwarding arrangements."

"How are you going to word it?"

"I'll keep it simple, saying the first vessel has sailed and the other's ready to leave — but, I'll omit their names. Always wise to hold something in reserve. And to prevent Sweeny wiring back, I'll add that Kaufmann's sailing on the second, inferring he's had to skip town, and that he'll wire the details of both vessels to Sweeny in Genoa, as soon as he arrives in Gibraltar."

"But to which hotel?" Colleen worried.

"With Sweeny! Genoa's finest, naturally. I'll get it from a Baedeker."

"Think twice, Michael!" she wasn't convinced. "What if Tweed *has* sent one, and added that Kaufmann's dead?"

"If he hasn't, and we don't either, then Sweeny's going to get twitchy. He'll telegraph Tweed, Tweed will wire him

276

back, and we'll be out there on the Atlantic, unaware of what's happening, while our chance of catching him is being destroyed."

"There could be trouble if Tweed's already sent one," Colleen persisted.

"With stakes this high, Colleen, that's a risk I'm willing to take," Callaghan said. "I'll draft it now, with my favourite author on hand."

Reaching into his pocket for his notepad, his hand closed on the letter. He showed it to Colleen. "Sarah Briggs's last letter before departure." He placed his thumb under the flap.

"You don't intend opening it?" asked Colleen.

"I've no choice. It may hold some clue."

"A *personal* letter?"

"You never know," said Callaghan, tearing along the crease. He quickly skimmed the words . . . how the weather had forced them to anchor 'about a mile or so from the city' . . . of Sarah's looking forward to 'a goodly supply' of letters in Genoa . . . noting Briggs's assessment of his crew as 'a pretty peaceable set this time, all around' . . . and finally, Sarah's chatty conclusion:

I should like to be present at Mr Kingsbury's ordination next week. Hope the people will be united in him, and wish we might hear of Mrs K's improved health on arrival. Tell Arthur I make great dependence on the letter I shall get from him and will try to remember anything that happens on the voyage which he will be pleased to hear.

We had some baked apples (sour) the other night about the size of a new-born infant's head. They tasted extremely well.

Please give our love to Mother and the girls, Aunt Hannah, Arthur, and other friends, reserving a share for yourself. As I have nothing more to say I will follow A Ward's advice and say it at once.

Farewell   Yours aff'ly   Sarah

Now feeling sorry he'd invaded Sarah Briggs's privacy, he handed it to Colleen. She hesitated over taking it, but curiosity won. She too only scanned the contents, then handed it back.

"She sounds a nice woman," Colleen remarked. "She certainly must love her husband, risking these Atlantic storms in a tiny brig, just to be with him. They'll be tossed about like a cork."

"You'll be braving the same seas and storms in a week's time," Callaghan pointed out.

"Yes. But on a large ship, not a brig." She gave him a knowing look. "And in case you're making comparisons, yes, I do want to be with you — at your side as your wife. But we have more bridges to cross before we can be as we were. Too many hurtful things were said and done to be repaired in a day. We're back to being friends, and that's a foundation on which we can build."

"OK," Callaghan said, feeling slightly disheartened. "I'll settle for that."

Colleen gave him a warm smile and his spirits lifted immediately.

"I'd be very grateful if you'd keep me company until after the funeral? I don't want to be here on my own."

"Of course. The *Gratia*'s not loading until Tuesday."

"Thank you, Michael. I'll get Mary to prepare you a room."

Monday, 11 November

The cemetery was cold and bleak. Dark, grey clouds hung low in the sky, a bitter wind whistled through the bare branches of the trees, swirling fallen leaves between the gloomy tombstones.

Veiled in black, and with the other mourners restricted to Mr Phelps, Jackson and Mary, Colleen held Callaghan's arm for support, as Father Flynn sprinkled the coffin with Holy water, praying the paternoster, and finally, concluding with: "*Dei requiescant in pace*" — 'May he rest in peace.'

"Amen," the mourners responded.

"Now let us pray," said Father Flynn, bowing his head for the final orison, the prayer for the living: "O Lord, we beseech Thee that whilst we lament the departure of Thy servant, we may remember that we are most certainly to follow him. Give us grace to prepare for that last hour by a good and holy life,

280

that we may not be taken unprepared by sudden death, but may be ever on the watch . . . "

I hope he's not being precipitate, Callaghan thought wryly, as they turned away from the graveside and headed back to the waiting carriages.

As Callaghan helped Colleen into their coach, a second hearse arrived with Father Becker's simple pine coffin. As the pallbearers raised it on to their shoulders, Father Murray and four young choirboys positioned themselves to enter the cemetery.

Callaghan hurried over to the Jesuit, anxious to offer some words of sympathy before the choirboys began. But Murray turned away the moment he recognized Callaghan, and immediately started the walk to the graveside, intoning: "*In paradisum deducant te angeli*" — 'May the angels lead thee into paradise. May the martyrs receive thee at thy coming . . . '

Returning to the coach, Callaghan climbed in. "That was strange," he commented, sitting beside Colleen, and tucking her arm under his.

"What?" she asked, continuing to look towards the grave.

"Father Murray. He deliberately ignored me. I wonder why?"

Colleen turned to him, her eyes wide with astonishment. "After your religious debate the other day, I'm hardly surprised."

Fiesole

Father-General Beckx was sitting at his desk, thinking about Father Becker.

Assuming he had been at sea for roughly a week, then in another five, he would be in Genoa with the first $100,000,000.

In the meantime, Beckx had not been idle. A Genoese diamond merchant who was Jesuit schooled, a true believer, was waiting in readiness. As soon as the diamonds arrived, each would be valued individually. Then the gems would be divided into small parcels to be exchanged for votes.

Simple. Neat. Efficient.

And also swift.

Time was of the essence and this was God's timing. The Act was being introduced to the Assembly by the Minister of Justice in only nine days' time, on the 20th November. But it would be another month before it was voted on. Close, with only days to spare, but enough.

It was all a matter of strategy. The path set out by The Blessed Saint Ignatius Loyola in his formulary, *Spiritual Exercises*, for the Society to follow until the end of time, when the Lord would come to gather up His true disciples for the Wedding Feast of the Redeemed.

Until then, Father Becker had ensured himself his earthly reward.

New York
The Church of Saint Francis Xavier was empty as Father Murray entered the confessional, and stiffly knelt, burdened with guilt.

"Pray, Father, bless me, for I have sinned."

"The Lord be in thy heart and on thy lips, that thou mayest truly and humbly confess thy sins, in the name of the Father, and of the Son, and of the Holy Ghost."

Father Murray closed his eyes, praying for divine strength.

"I last made confession four days ago. I had two sins to declare, but I was weak and only confessed one. The second concerns both Father Karl Becker and Jacob Kaufmann. I know who and what is behind these killings . . ."

15

New York.
Saturday, 16 November 1872

CALLAGHAN was standing on the prow of the *Dei Gratia* watching New York slip by on the port side, and searching the names on the tall sterns of the large steamships moored to their Hudson River berths.

Pier Forty-three, Colleen had said, close to Canal Street.

They must be nearing it. Training his telescope on the vessels, he swept it from one stern to the next, grey, blue, red, suddenly pausing as it focused on the name *Asia*, painted in large black letters on rounded white metal.

Angling the eyeglass upwards, he saw Colleen standing at the rails, dressed in chestnut-brown travelling clothes, trimmed with fur.

He closed in on her face, taking in every familiar feature. Then as the *Gratia* passed the *Asia*, he lowered the telescope

285

and waved. Colleen saw him and waved back enthusiastically. Walking along the port rail, Callaghan kept her in sight, then was forced to use the telescope again. As he readjusted the eyeglass, a low dark cloud passed overhead, casting a large shadow over the *Gratia* and the *Asia*.

Before he was able to focus on Colleen, the stern of another ship obliterated her from view. Still in the cloud's black shadow, Callaghan prayed it was not an omen of disasters to come.

Palermo, Sicily

"What the hell's Kaufmann playing at?" Sweeny snarled. Hurling his cigar into the bushes below the terrace of Salvatore Cottone's large villa, high on the slopes above Monreale, he stared disbelievingly at the telegraph forwarded from Paris.

"What has happened?" the ever attendant Father Cottone questioned.

"The goddamned fool's gone blasted crazy, that's what happened!" Sweeny glowered. "And I'm sure as hell not apologizing for my language. I'm justified!"

Only a few seconds ago he had been

286

relaxing, enjoying the warmth of the Sicilian winter sun as he looked down on the bay, and its surrounding city of Palermo. Content with his lot, he'd been congratulating himself on how well the meetings had gone in the three days he'd been here. All his plans accepted without question.

And then Kaufmann's wire had arrived! An infernal message out of the blue!

"Exactly what has he done?" the young priest asked.

Brains stood to his feet and began pacing the terrace. "He's damned well gone and changed my instructions again," he fumed. "Not only has he got both vessels sailing on different dates, but he's also gone and skipped New York on the second ship without including their names. And instead of both of them calling into Gibraltar to await my orders, only Kaufmann's vessel is stopping, and then solely for that stupid German to send me the details by wire, to some hotel in Genoa that I've never heard of. Genoa!" Sweeny's face was livid with anger. "What the hell do I want in Genoa? I've never been there, and I wasn't planning on going there either. What the hell's got into the stupid bastard? Unless I wired fresh orders to Gibraltar, the barrels were supposed to end up here in Palermo, not stinking Genoa!"

Father Cottone picked up the crumpled paper from the floor. Smoothing it out, he scanned the message. "Briefly worded," he agreed, "but there's no doubting its meaning. Why not wire some New York friend to trace the names of the vessels?"

"No point." Sweeny was bringing himself under control. "He's not given the dates of sailing. Nor whether he's using sloops, barks, or brigs. In any one week, there's hundreds leaving the East River. Plus, apart from your Father Becker, Kaufmann's the only one in New York who knows I'm here in Monreale. I don't want anyone else finding out, just in case they blab it to the police or the *Times*. You can't trust anybody these days."

"In that case, what do you intend?" Don Cottone's nephew queried. "Our next meeting with Father-General Beckx is four weeks tomorrow."

"Kaufmann's left us no choice," Sweeny grated. "We've got to postpone it. We'll have to go to Genoa and register into this Hotel de Genes to wait for Kaufmann's wire. But I tell you this, Father, and I don't mind saying it." Sweeny gave the priest a dark, confidential smile. "When he arrives, I'm sure as hell gonna make him pay for this. Maybe even borrow Nino from your uncle. He says he's the best ever with a stiletto. He can dig the wax out of Kaufmann's ear, see if that'll help him listen better in future. In the meantime, let's pray the good Lord keeps Kaufmann's vessel from sinking, because he's the only one who knows the name of the other. And I don't want anyone else opening that barrel, and getting their hands on my diamonds.

Book Two

Book Two

16

Wednesday, 4 December 1872

NINETEEN days out of New York, Callaghan was simply too tired to eat. He passed the galley, and went straight to the crew-quarters. Removing only his wet oilskins, he climbed wearily on to his top bunk, and stretched out.

It had been a rough passage, nothing like sailing on Jonathan's brig, especially the last eight days, when the gales had suddenly increased in ferocity, raging continuously day and night, howling across the deep and creating waves so mountainous that it seemed certain they must capsize. But each time, almost by a miracle, the *Dei Gratia* had somehow righted herself, and continued on towards her rendezvous-point with the *Mary Celeste*.

Not that there seemed any point in it, Callaghan brooded, for the unexpected drop in the wind just a few hours ago, when the storms had abated to squalls, had come too late. Briggs was too experienced a sailor to put family and crew at risk. By now he would be safely in Gibraltar . . .

"Sail ahoy!" The voice was John Wright's, the second mate.

"Where to?" Callaghan heard Morehouse call out.

"Off the starboard bow!"

Callaghan dropped off his bunk, donned his wet oilskins, and went back out on deck.

Morehouse was standing at the port rail, holding a telescope to his right eye. The Russian-born John 'Johnny' Johnson was still at the helm. Augustus 'Gus' Anderson was a few feet away. And Wright, a small compact man, in his late twenties, was standing by the mainmast, holding a spyglass and pointing out to sea.

Callaghan followed Wright's direction, narrowing his eyes as he looked across the mighty expanse of grey, rolling ocean, but he saw nothing. Then, as the *Gratia* crested a large wave, he just glimpsed a sail in the far distance before they plunged into another trough and a towering wall of water curled towards them, obliterating his view. The *Dei Gratia* rose again, the seas breaking across her deck. Again, Callaghan saw the sails. Even from this distance they looked torn. But the vessel was too far away to assess with a naked eye.

Was it the *Celeste*?

Keeping his balance against the roll of the deck, Callaghan made his way to David Morehouse's side. The captain removed his spyglass, but did not turn his head, as he muttered, "It's a brig. Sailing towards us."

Oliver Deveau, the first mate, emerged from the main deck house. A tall, lean, bearded man, in his early thirties, he spread his feet apart, steadying himself, then raised his 'glass and focused on the vessel.

"She's sailing very erratically," he eventually commented in a puzzled voice.

"I was thinking the same thing," Wright agreed. "She's yawing and falling off, pitching in and out of the wind. And only her lower topsail jib and foretop-staysail are set. The others are torn to rags."

Wiping food from their mouths, the two remaining seamen, George 'Jorjo' Orr, and James 'Jimmy' Higgins, appeared from the galley, followed by the 16–year-old cabin-boy, Willard 'Willie' Cleary. Remaining by the foremast, the three shaded their eyes with their hands and stared out to sea.

Refocusing his 'scope, Morehouse studied the vessel. "That's strange," he declared, a rising note of concern in his voice. "She's sailing on the port-tack, but her jib and foretopmast-staysail are on the starboard tack. With that setting, in this wind, she should be heading towards Gibraltar, not away from it."

The vessel drew nearer, her few remaining sails filling up, then sagging as she turned in and out of the wind.

"There's no one on deck!" Wright suddenly stated.

"Not even at the helm!" added Deveau, spyglass still trained on the vessel. "And from the way she's sailing, her wheel's not been lashed!"

"Maybe they're all sick?" Morehouse was attempting to respond normally to the situation, but Callaghan saw his hand trembling, trying to keep his telescope steady. "Food poisoning or something, and they're all inside, too ill to sail her?"

"They'd have lashed the wheel first," Deveau observed. "No, in my opinion, Captain, she's got the look of a deserted ship."

"Can you make out her name?"

The first mate adjusted his focus. "*Mary* something or other."

Lowering his telescope, Morehouse turned and looked silently at Callaghan, his face grey with worry.

"*Mary Celeste*," Deveau confirmed. "And her boat's missing!"

"Hell's bells!" exclaimed Wright. "Launching it in these storms would have been suicide, especially with her wheel unlashed."

Morehouse spun about. "Johnny! Get as close to her as you can! Gus! Fetch my trumpet!"

As Anderson — a stocky, fair-haired young man — made his way across the slippery deck, Johnson swung the wheel and headed straight for the *Celeste*. Covered in thick spray, the *Dei Gratia* ploughed her way through the heavy seas, rising then dropping as the huge Atlantic rollers crashed over her bows, swamping her decks.

At 300 yards, Deveau glanced anxiously at Morehouse. In such rough weather it would be risky getting too near, in case the unmanned vessel suddenly turned about and came into them.

Anderson returned with a speaking-trumpet. "Brace the yards and haul!" Morehouse yelled, taking the instrument from him.

Wright, Callaghan, Anderson, Orr and Higgins all instantly obeyed, running across the deck and pulling at the greased ropes, made even slipperier by the drenching spray.

The task accomplished, Callaghan turned to look at the *Celeste*. The gap was continuing to narrow as the two vessels slowly drifted towards each other. Her wet deck was silent and empty, the unmanned wheel was turning sluggishly and aimlessly from port to starboard, then back to port as her rudder obeyed only the movement of the sea. The forehatch cover was off, lying alongside the foremast, which meant that the recent high seas must have been pouring into the hold. Her foretopsail and upper foretopsail were mostly gone, torn from the yards by the storms. The lower foretopsail hung by its four corners. The main staysail lay loose across the roof of the forrard deck house. The lower topsail jib and foretop-staysail were set, but the remaining sails were furled. And although the standing rigging looked to be good, most of the running rigging had been carried away. The port rails, opposite the main hatch, were lying flat on the deck, indicating that the lifeboat had been launched from there.

Raising his hailer, Morehouse yelled, "Brig ahoy! Brig ahoy!"

There was no reply from the *Celeste*, now only a hundred yards away.

Morehouse tried again. "Brig ahoy! Brig ahoy!"

Still no answer. Just a strange eerie silence, broken only by the creaking of the *Celeste*'s rigging, the dull flapping of her torn sails, and the wind whistling across her empty decks.

"What the hell's happened?" Morehouse muttered from the corner of his mouth.

"Mystery," Callaghan replied, his voice equally low. "Get me on board her."

"Mr Deveau!" Morehouse called to the first mate. "Lower the boat!"

Deveau instantly moved forward, issuing instructions. "Gus, take over from Johnny." And to Wright: "John, we'll use the small boat. It'll be you, me and Johnny." The choice of Johnson as oarsman was obvious since the Russian was the best seaman on board.

"Mr Deveau!" Morehouse called, as the men converged on the smaller lifeboat lashed across the main hatch, rather than the larger boat suspended on the stern davits. "Take Lund with you."

Callaghan was using the alias 'Charles Lund' as a precaution in case Sweeny read the crew-list when they reached Genoa.

"No need, sir," Deveau replied. "Three's enough."

"That's an order, Mr Deveau!" Morehouse commanded.

The first mate hesitated, then gave a brief salute. The cursory glance he gave Callaghan was far from welcoming.

The lifeboat was swiftly untied and lowered into the water, young Willard helping Orr and Higgins at the ropes. Johnson went down first, taking his place at the oars, and Callaghan last. He sat opposite Deveau, who studied him openly, obviously puzzled at his inclusion.

Callaghan glanced up at the *Gratia*, where Morehouse was standing tensely at the ship's rail, suddenly looking ten years older. Callaghan nodded as the captain returned his gaze, then saw Deveau was watching, frowning with perplexity.

Johnson pushed an oar against the *Gratia*'s side, then rowed into the heaving waters. The rain had subsided, but the sea was still rough, raising the boat high on the crests of the rollers, then dropping it down into grey trenches that blotted both vessels from sight. But Deveau had chosen his man well. The Russian was a superb oarsman, and soon drew up alongside the *Mary Celeste*.

Plying his oars, he kept the boat

steady, as the others grabbed at the brig's trailing ropes, pulling themselves up the wet slippery lines and over the *Celeste*'s rails.

Callaghan stood there, chilled by the deathly stillness which hung over the vessel's water-soaked empty deck. The depth of the silence was only intensified by the melancholy sighing of the wind through the groaning rigging, and the flapping of loose sails. He felt as though there was something evil on board.

Deveau and Wright obviously sensed it as well. They stood quite still, as though fearful of moving forward. The second mate took a hasty look down at the lifeboat, as if reassuring himself that, if needed, the escape route was still there.

"Right," Deveau broke the silence. "Let's get started."

Pulling his knife from its sheath, he cut a length of rope, and crossing over to the wheel, lashed it tightly. Then, turning to the lazarette cover, lying on the deck alongside the open hatch, he shouted, "Lund, give me a hand."

Callaghan helped the first mate lift the cover and lower it back into place.

The task done, Deveau studied the brig. The binnacle had been torn from its cleats on the roof of the main deck house and lay, with its compass broken, on the deck. The main hatch cover was in place, but seeing the forehatch cover also loose on the deck, he summoned the others. "We'd best sound the pumps."

Reaching the main mast, Wright uncoiled the makeshift sounding-line lying on the deck and fed the bolt through the pump shaft, to the hold below. The cord became slack as the bolt reached the bottom of the hold. Wright pulled it up and examined the length of wet cord. "About three and a half feet."

"That's not much, not with the weather we've been having," said Deveau, surprised. "Obviously they didn't abandon ship because of leaking."

"No," Wright agreed. "And most of it will be from the sea coming in through the open hatches."

"Lund, you go check below, while Mr Wright and I test the pumps," said the first mate, already busily examining the machinery.

Callaghan crossed to the main deck house hatch. Descending the dark steps, he paused, overwhelmed with sudden uneasiness. But the saloon appeared to be reassuringly normal. One of the skylight panes had broken and seawater covered the floor, but there was no sign of panic. A paraffin-lamp swung slowly from the ceiling, the scrubbed wooden table and benches were bare, and the stove was stone cold.

Callaghan made straight for the captain's cabin and threw the door open. The room was in semi-darkness, its windows covered with strips of sail-canvas, but like the saloon everything was tidy and in place. There was no sign of hasty flight. Two sea-chests, with the name 'Briggs' painted on them, stood at the foot of the bed which was made up. A polished melodeon stood against a wall. In the middle of the room was a child's rocking-chair, occupied by a doll whose empty porcelain eyes were staring eerily into space. In the left corner stood a sewing-machine, beside it was a lady's work-bag. Alongside it was a third sea-chest, its back facing into the cabin.

Callaghan approached the captain's desk, disappointed to find its surface clear of papers. He tried the roll-drawer, convinced Briggs would have left a message, but it was locked.

He knelt and applied his pick-lock to the keyhole, intent on releasing the catch.

Suddenly, the lavatory door flew open, and a man holding a rapier stepped swiftly out. Before Callaghan could move, the weapon was at his throat.

17

THE man was completely dressed in black — suit, shirt, and high leather boots. He stood about five foot ten, but his slim build and vantage point made him seem taller. His skin was so pale, and hair so fair, that for a moment Callaghan thought he was an albino. But then he saw the slate-blue eyes regarding him with a frightening intensity. Was this man the fulfilment of his strange forebodings? He certainly looked the personification of evil, all in black, and holding his sword. It was a fine weapon, long and slim-bladed, with an ornate filigree hilt.

"Your ship? It is the *Dei Gratia*?" His voice was little more than a whisper, the German accent unmistakable.

"Yes."

"And your captain's name: David Morehouse?"

"Yes."

Callaghan saw a flash of triumph in

the German's grey-blue eyes.

"There were four in the boat. Where are the others?"

"One still in the boat. Two mates up on deck."

The man's eyes glanced towards the door. "On your feet. Slowly."

With the sword still at his throat, Callaghan was forced back into the saloon, and to the foot of the companion-way.

"Call your first mate down." The sword point pricked Callaghan's skin. "Make no attempt to warn him."

"Mr Deveau!" Callaghan shouted up the steps.

"Lund?" The mate's voice floated back through the open hatch.

"The captain's cabin! Rightaway!" he cried, then the German closed in, his sword still at Callaghan's throat, forcing him back to the cabin, and up against the corner wall.

Heavy footsteps descended the stairs, and seconds later Deveau entered. He halted as he took in the scene, his eyes wide with shock as he looked from the man in black to Callaghan with the sword at his throat.

"What in tarnation's going on?" he demanded in outrage, only his hoarse tone betraying his fear. "Who the hell are you?"

"I have a message for your captain." The German's voice was flat and emotionless.

"Message!" Deveau stepped forward. "I'm taking no . . . "

Callaghan felt a sharp stab of pain as the sword punctured his skin. It must have drawn blood because Deveau immediately froze, staring at him helplessly.

"You will give him these instructions," the German continued. "He is to transfer half his crew to this ship and sail both vessels to Genoa, ignoring his orders to call into Gibraltar. When we arrive in Genoa he is to say that he found this ship deserted in the Mediterranean, not the Atlantic . . . "

"Half-crews!" Deveau protested. "In this weather! You must be mad! We'd never make it. What's more — "

The German flicked the sword from Callaghan to Deveau, silencing his defiance.

"Should your captain refuse, remind him of the warning I gave him in New York." His sibilant whisper intensified the threat. "If I do not send word back, saying I have arrived safely, then his own wife and children will die, just as Captain Briggs's did."

Deveau's gaze flashed to the doll in the small rocking-chair, his face twisting in horror. He stared at the man with repugnance, ignoring the point at his neck. "You mean you've killed — killed a woman and child! What sort of animal are you?" He spat out the question.

The German's face remained impassive, impervious to Deveau's condemnation. Drawing his sword back, he directed his prisoners out the door.

Callaghan's mind was racing. With the threat against Desiah Morehouse now very real, the German held all the aces. They had no choice but to obey. But maybe . . . maybe they could alter the terms, and turn the tables on him.

Deliberately closing the cabin door, he waited until they were at the foot of the companionway, then showed Deveau his detective badge. "My name's Callaghan," he said in a low voice. "Michael Callaghan. I'm with the New York Police."

The first mate's eyes flashed with anger. Callaghan quickly clamped a hand over the man's mouth to stifle his reply.

"I'll explain everything back on the *Gratia*. Say nothing to Wright or Johnson. If anyone asks about my neck, I had an accident."

Deveau twisted his mouth free. "What the hell's happening," he hissed. "First a madman with a sword! Now a blasted gumshoe . . . "

"Shut up and get moving," said Callaghan, losing patience. "You heard the man. Refuse to co-operate, and you risk the lives of Mrs Morehouse and the children."

"OK, I'll make my report to the captain," replied Deveau, still angry and bewildered. "So this is why he sent you along? Meeting the *Celeste* was no accident?"

"You're wasting valuable time!" Callaghan prodded him forward.

"Maybe. But how d'you plan on dealing with Wright, Mr Copper-badge?

As second mate, he'll expect to be present when we report back to the captain."

"You'll just have to think of something."

"Such as?"

"Anything. Forget blasted protocol. Put him in charge of the *Gratia* while you see Morehouse. Then call me in. Wright can report after — if the Captain still feels up to it after hearing what's happened."

★ ★ ★

Morehouse was sitting collapsed over his desk, his face buried in his hands, when Callaghan entered his cabin. Hearing the door close, he looked up, his eyes bloodshot and filled with pain. "Benjamin murdered? And Sarah? And Sophia?" His uncertain tone sought denial, rather than the avowal of Callaghan's terse nod, but he quickly recovered himself. "What the hell are we going to do about my family. They'll be killed unless we do as he says."

He gave a despairing glance to the window. "But half-crews! In these conditions! It's near suicidal!"

Deveau nodded righteously, still looking

311

far from pleased. Helping himself to the medicine chest, Callaghan swabbed the wound at his throat. "Captain, first we owe Deveau an explanation."

Ten minutes later he was summing-up the situation, " . . . since the Canadian police failed to locate Mrs Morehouse before we sailed, we've no choice but to carry out the German's instructions, until we know she's safe."

"But where can she be?" the first mate demanded, in frustration. "Do you think . . . ?" His voice trailed off in uncertainty as he considered the possible answers.

"She left word with her neighbours that she was going to visit relatives," explained Callaghan, calmly. "But she didn't say which ones. And as she has cousins and aunts scattered all across Canada, as far as British Columbia; we won't know if the German's accomplices have got her until the police check every one of them out. It's possible the children had already been kidnapped when Desiah left her cryptic message with the people next door. But until we know where they are, we must do as the German says."

A silence descended over the cabin, each man consumed with his own thoughts: the captain grieving for his missing family, Deveau worrying about his men having to sail two vessels with half-crews, and Callaghan empathizing with both, at the same time wondering what could have happened on board the *Celeste* to cause this bloody scenario.

"Why kill them all?" Deveau suddenly asked. "And how? One man against so many? If he signed on as one of her crew, why only the *Celeste*? Why didn't they put someone on board the *Gratia* as well?"

"I can't begin to think how," said Callaghan. "But as to why the *Celeste* — it's because she was the first vessel to leave. And the ten days' difference in sailing time would have allowed the German to report to Sweeny in Genoa, the same time the *Gratia* was expected to enter Gibraltar for orders."

"So how did he find out about the rendezvous? And why keep it?" Deveau asked. "Why didn't he make the west coast of Spain instead? It's only six hundred miles away. He could have found

313

a quiet cove, unloaded the barrel with the diamonds, then travelled overland to Genoa in plenty of time for the *Gratia* to reach Gibraltar?"

"Because, according to what Briggs told Captain Morehouse, the barrel was the first to be loaded, and therefore impossible to get at without first discharging the entire cargo."

Deveau subsided into silence again, considering the options. "Then we've no choice. Our priority has to be Mrs Morehouse."

The captain sighed with agreement — and relief.

"It's not that simple," Callaghan interjected. "We *have* to stop in Gibraltar to find out if the Canadians have found Mrs Morehouse and children. If we sail straight to Genoa, then I won't be able to take on Sweeny without risking their lives."

"Sweeny no longer matters," Morehouse objected. "Desiah comes first. Wire your headquarters from Genoa."

"But that won't give me enough time. In the four or five days it will take for them to reply, the cargoes will be unloaded, and both Sweeny and his killer will have flown — "

"That's your problem," said Morehouse, dismissing the subject.

"No," argued Callaghan, attempting a different line. "It's *our* problem. Don't forget, the *Gratia*'s under orders to sail to Gibraltar. Until she does, we're not even supposed to know that Genoa is our port of destination. By making us say we found the *Celeste* deserted in the Mediterranean, rather than the Atlantic, the German is expecting us to register for salvage in Genoa, at the same time assuming that as both vessels have reached their destinations, there'll be no objection to the cargoes being unloaded."

"Yes. That's what he's got in mind all right," agreed Deveau.

"But, what will the Genoa authorities think when they discover the *Gratia* deliberately sailed past Gibraltar — the port to which she was ordered to report — yet somehow managed to arrive at the correct port, without any papers, accompanied by a derelict whose entire complement is missing, also bound for the same port?"

"We'll all be under arrest within an

hour of arriving," replied Morehouse despairingly, tapping nervous fingers against his desk.

"We — meaning everyone on board?" Callaghan pursued the point.

"The whole crew. Every Jack one."

"Including the German?"

"He'll be the biggest suspect as the *Celeste*'s only survivor!"

"And what about the cargoes? Especially when it's discovered that both hold an extra barrel," said Callaghan, hoping the German would listen to his case as peaceably.

"They'll be impounded and searched, for sure."

"And the diamonds discovered," added Deveau. "Making us all look as guilty as hell."

Callaghan paused, letting the scenario sink in. "But if we sail into Gibraltar as instructed, and claim salvage there, wouldn't it be agreed without awkward questions being asked?"

"I don't see why not. It should be a simple routine enquiry," Morehouse slowly nodded. "Especially if that bastard German's not on board. He'll have to be landed first on the Spanish coast. Then make his own way to Gibraltar and rejoin the *Celeste*, or travel ahead by train and meet her in Genoa."

"In that case, Captain, with your permission, we'd best proceed."

Callaghan included the first mate in his glance. They were now a team, and the circumstances they were facing together had removed any vestige of Deveau's earlier mistrust.

"Mr Deveau, I suggest you return to the *Celeste* and accept the man's terms. But you *must* convey to him that Genoa spells disaster; that his only hope is for the *Gratia* to sail to Gibraltar as ordered, and register for salvage there. It all rests with you," he stressed. "Somehow, you have to make him understand that unless he agrees, he is bound to fail. And so, then, will we all."

★ ★ ★

An hour later, the German having coldly accepted the logic of the case for Gibraltar, Callaghan and Deveau, along with Gus Anderson — chosen for

317

his strength — dropped over the *Gratia*'s side into the lifeboat, and headed for the *Celeste*.

Since no one else knew of the German's presence on the vessel, Callaghan had worked out a routine to keep it from Anderson. He and Gus were to bunk in the crew's quarters in the forrard deck house, while Deveau would occupy the first mate's cabin, next to the German's, in the main deck house. Callaghan was to do the cooking, thus enabling him to carry Deveau's meals — enough to feed two — over to the main deck house. As there would be so much work to do just sailing the brig, Gus wasn't going to have any leisure to realize there was a fourth man on board.

As they climbed aboard the *Celeste*, Callaghan gave an involuntary shiver, knowing he was boarding a death-ship. Again he wondered how this one man could have overpowered so many . . .

"Lund. Help me close the forehatch," Deveau ordered. "Gus. Secure the lifeboat to the stern rail, we'll hoist her up later. After that, we'll light the lamps, pump her dry, then get under way."

Five hours later, the ocean was in pitch darkness. They'd set the main staysail, lower topsail and foretopmast sail, and with Anderson at the wheel, were following the stern lights of the *Dei Gratia* — her canvas reduced to allow them to keep up — some 300 yards in front of them, off the port bow.

Callaghan was coiling rope when Deveau suddenly emerged from the main deck house, and summoned him to the crew's quarters.

Following Callaghan into the bunkhouse, Deveau closed the door. Placing his lamp on the table, he removed a bundle from under his thick jumper. "The *Celeste*'s log and log-slate, Michael. They were in the first mate's cabin."

Callaghan glanced at some of the entries, but they meant little to him. "I'm sorry, Oliver, you'll have to interpret."

"When we found the *Celeste* she was dead to rights on the northern route, above the Azores," Deveau explained. "But according to the log, as soon as Briggs left New York, he took the longer southern route, *below* the Azores, deliberately lengthening his voyage to

319

allow the *Dei Gratia* to catch up. Now, the real interesting fact is the final log entry." Deveau turned to the last page. "At eight o'clock, Sunday evening, the twenty-fourth of November, the *Celeste* was still south of the Azores. Briggs ordered the royal and topgallant sails taken in, shortening sail to two jibs, upper and lower topsails, foresail, and staysail — the exact setting we found on boarding her, eleven days later."

Deveau handed Callaghan the slate. "Now read that."

Knowing that the log-slate was used to record events of the day, before they were transferred into the log, Callaghan studied the chalked words:

Monday, 25th

Hour	Knots	
6	8	at 5 o'clock made the island of S. Mary's bearing E. S. E.
7	8	
8	8	At 8 Eastern point bore S. S. W. 6 miles distant.

Immediately below these entries the man on watch had chalked the words:

Fanny, My Dear Wife, Frances N.R.

And there the words ended.

Again Deveau interpreted. "It means that by eight o'clock the next morning, exactly twelve hours after the last log entry, the *Celeste* had changed direction, and was now sailing to the *north* — no longer the south — of Saint Mary's, a small island to the east of the Azores. Sometime during the night," Deveau continued, "Briggs altered course and headed north-west, towards the rendezvous-point. The man on watch was Richardson, the first mate — I found some letters from his wife, Frances, in his cabin. He was clearly drafting a letter to her when he was interrupted."

The first mate pointed to the half-completed sentence.

"Michael, this sets the exact time for whatever occurred on the *Celeste*. Eight a.m. on the morning of the twenty-fifth — only a few hours after Briggs changed course. We may never learn what happened, but this was the cause."

321

18

Sunday, 8 December 1872

IT was not until Sunday evening, three days after boarding the *Mary Celeste*, that Callaghan found time to check the galley.

It had taken them this long to get the vessel into some sort of shape. Cold and wet through despite their oilskins, they'd only snatched at catnaps in alternating turns. On the first day, a threatening storm shifted direction and the wind abated, reducing the rollers to no more than an angry swell, allowing them to clear away the torn sails, braces, and loose ropes hanging over the vessel's sides. Although they had taken turns at the wheel, it had been a particularly long and exhausting job for all three. They replaced the binnacle in its position on the roof of the main deck house, facing the wheel. Then the strong smell of alcohol emanating from the hold made Deveau remember the two hatches found open when they first boarded the vessel. Realizing they must have have been removed to allow leaking fumes to escape, he'd insisted on checking the cargo and lashings to make sure that all was safe, and then, rather than sail in fear of explosion, they'd removed both hatch covers again.

All this, and so many other daily chores — pumping the hold dry every morning and evening, repairing the sails, replacing the rigging — had left Callaghan no time to get into the galley. Consequently, they'd been working without any hot food in their stomachs, eating only hard tack brought from the *Dei Gratia*.

But at midday Sunday, Deveau finally declared that the *Celeste* was 'well enough set to rights', and the vital order of the day — while he slept before taking the next watch — was a hot meal of potato-and-onion broth.

Leaving Gus at the helm, Callaghan made his way to the galley, where cooking utensils, potatoes and onions, were strewn across the sodden floor, along with split sacks of rice and flour. Even the stove had been knocked out of place. It took over an hour to get it all back in shape. He lit the stove, then, while waiting for it to heat, began checking the shelves. There was a good stock of provisions: tea and coffee, pork and salt-beef wrapped in muslin, dried apples, cranberries, biscuits. On the top shelf, pushed into the furthermost corner, was a sealed tin.

Callaghan placed it on the table, and, prising the stiff lid off, saw it contained a book, a bottle of ink, and a pen. He read the grandly styled cover: *Voyage across the Atlantic* by Edward Head, Steward on board the brigantine *Mary Celeste*, and smiled sadly to himself. Poor Head had obviously had literary pretensions.

Opening the diary, Callaghan read the inscription to Emma, Head's wife of a few weeks, then, still in his oilskins, he sat down on the steward's bunk and continued.

Reading Head's account of leaving New York, Callaghan noted the steward's puzzlement as to why, on belatedly heading out to sea, Briggs had elected to take the longer, southern route below the Azores, rather than the northern lane.

Numerous pages were devoted to the

terrible weather — the many times it seemed that all was lost; Mrs Briggs and Sophia staying in the main deck house rather than venturing out on deck; the removal of the forehatch and lazarette covers to allow the build-up of alcohol fumes in the hold to escape. Then Callaghan noticed he'd come to Sunday, 24th November, the date of the last recorded log entry, and that Head's diary continued *after* this date . . . way past it . . . into December . . . Saturday 1st, and up to Wednesday 4th — the same day the *Dei Gratia* met the vessel!

Callaghan sat there, his heart quickening as he realized that Head's diary probably held the answer to what had happened on board the *Mary Celeste*.

Taking a deep breath, he turned back to *Sunday, 24th November, 1 a.m.*

Like the previous entries. Head had left it until finishing his duties, writing alone in his galley, with no one else on board aware of the diary's existence.

Sunday, 24 November, 1 a.m.
Captain Briggs had ordered a change of course from tomorrow. We cannot

understand why, because Gilling says it will take us to the north of St Mary Island, and a dangerous shoal known as the Dollobarat, on which the sea breaks with great violence in stormy conditions such as we are experiencing, but whose rocks are hidden under the surface when the sea is calm. Gilling says that with a shifting wind, which is not unusual in these waters, our position might become perilous. We are all very concerned as to why the captain has decided to sail north of the island, instead of sticking to the southward. Gilling says he will ask Richardson to ask Captain Briggs.

Monday, 25 November, 1 a.m. The answer is known. It is exactly like one reads in a book. When Gilling asked Richardson, it seems Captain Briggs had already spoken to the first mate, and so he was able to tell Gilling in confidence, but naturally Gilling told us to allay our fears. It appears that before sailing the captain received a message from a good friend, who is also captain *of a brig sailing from New York to Genoa which left ten days after us, asking Captain Briggs to meet him in the Atlantic, at a point, Latitude 38' North, and Longitude 17' West. It seems there is something he wants to discuss with Captain Briggs before we reach Genoa. We have all been trying to guess what it can be, but our opinions were so varied and far-fetched that we gave up and returned to our duties.*

Tuesday, 26 November, 1 a.m. If anyone finds this book, please —

Coming to the foot of the page, Callaghan realized that Head had written this entry seventeen *hours* after the last log-slate entry, when Richardson had broken off the letter to his wife. He turned the page quickly and read on:

. . . hand it to the authorities. I pray it will bring these evil men to justice. Captain Briggs, Richardson, and Gilling, are all dead, murdered, leaving Mrs Briggs, Sophia, and myself to the mercy — of which they

have none — of the four Germans. At eight o'clock this morning, only minutes after Martens had taken him his breakfast, Captain Briggs, who'd complained of an upset stomach last evening, was taken violently ill. His screams could be heard from every part of the ship and by the time we got to his cabin he was dead. The sight that met our eyes is almost too terrible to describe. He was lying on the floor, his back obviously broken, as the body was bent backward, instead of forwards, just like a snapped stick. Mrs Briggs was near to collapse, but she confirmed that no one was near him at the time. It was like he was having a violent fit, she said, and we were all left puzzled as to what could cause such an awful death.

Callaghan paused, recognizing the unusual circumstances of Briggs's death. Like Kaufmann and Becker it had to be poison, and obviously administered in Briggs's breakfast. But what on earth could it be? A substance so lethal the

328

victim's convulsions were frenzied enough to break the spine in two, yet without the bitter taste associated with known poisons, otherwise Briggs would have spat the food out of his mouth?

We all gathered in the saloon to discuss what to do. Richardson, Gilling and myself were for turning back to the Azores and handing over the body to the authorities. But the Germans wanted to bury the captain at sea, then continue to Genoa and report the matter when we got there. Richardson and Gilling refused, ordering the boat to come about. We went back to our duties, while they retired to the first mate's cabin to discuss the matter further. Minutes later I heard loud yells from the cabin, and rushed back to find Martens standing over Richardson's and Gilling's bodies, with a bloodied sword in his hand. Both their throats had been cut. And Mrs Briggs, who'd run through from her cabin, had fainted on top of them. Then the other Germans arrived.

So, the killer's identity was established at last, Callaghan thought. Arian Martens. And he was no common thug. His methods were those of a professional killer, cold-blooded and ruthless. His German accent almost certainly proved he'd been sent over by Sweeny, rather than hired in New York by Tweed. As all the other evidence also pointed to Sweeny, it was looking as if he'd cut out the rest of the Ring and was acting on his own.

Typically Sweeny. Machiavellian and evil. But no one could go unpunished for ever.

Sweeny and Martens would have their day of retribution.

Callaghan returned to Head's diary:

Martens immediately took control. He ordered the Germans to carry Mrs Briggs back to her cabin, and locked in. I had to scrub Richardson's cabin clean of all blood, then was told to return to my galley and remain there, or forfeit my life. The bodies of Captain Briggs, Richardson, and

330

Gilling, were thrown overboard. As much as I can tell from the direction of the wind, the Celeste is continuing towards the meeting with the brig previously mentioned, although why, I am unable to guess. The captain is supposed to be a friend of Briggs, and will be highly suspicious when he discovers that the captain and first and second mates are all missing. And it is certain Martens cannot meet the other brig with Mrs Briggs and myself still on board to tell of the terrible things we have witnessed. I only pray to God that they will be merciful to little Sophia and allow her to live.

Callaghan felt the old bitterness rising up inside him. Poor Head's supplications had been in vain, proving that there was no one up there listening. But if he was so convinced there was no God, then why did he feel so bitter . . . ?

He closed his eyes, forcing himself to concentrate on the Celeste. Briggs was killed after Martens found out about the rendezvous. The German must have guessed it was with Morehouse, and had wanted not only to prevent it, but also bring the Celeste back on her original course. He'd used poison on Briggs, hoping Richardson would accept the death as a natural, if somewhat violent one, and agree to burying the body at sea, then continue on to Genoa. But Richardson and Gilling had insisted on making for the Azores. A post-mortem would have revealed the poison, so Martens had no choice but to kill them, too.

With the captain and both mates dead, and no way Sarah Briggs and Head could be allowed to live to tell what happened, Martens could no longer sail to Genoa with only his three accomplices on board. His only alternative was to keep the rendezvous with the *Dei Gratia*, and force Morehouse to sail the *Celeste* to Genoa, and claim her as salvage.

But what had happened to the three Germans? And Sarah Briggs? And Sophia? Did the diary say?

Wednesday, 27 November, 1 a.m.
Martens luffing the ship, obviously
making time for the other brig to
catch up.

Thursday, 28 November, 1 a.m.
Sails torn by the wind. Crew too busy
and tired to change setting. Binnacle
smashed by high seas and compass
broken. Martens using Richardson's
compass.

Friday, 29 November, 1 a.m.
Atmosphere very tense.

Saturday, 30 November, 1 a.m.
Goodschaad has confided in me
that he and the Lorenzen brothers
are planning to overpower Martens.
It seems they became involved in
all this when a stranger, another
German like themselves, approached
them in New York and offered them
a large sum of money to enlist on
board the Celeste. He told them
the cargo was required by Germany
— the Fatherland as Goodschaad
calls it — to ensure its new position
of power in Europe, and that another
German, who turned out to be
Martens, would be joining them

in their lodging-house the following day. Martens had been chosen to protect the cargo, and needed fellow countrymen on board for him to converse with and instruct, without any of us understanding what they were saying. But the Germans had not bargained on Captain Briggs and the two mates being killed. Gilling was a friend with whom they'd often worked, and he'd only signed up because they had. Now they realize Martens must kill myself and Mrs Briggs before meeting up with the other brig, and therefore they are planning to take over the ship and sail for the nearest port to give themselves up. They've asked me to promise I will testify in court that they were ignorant of Martens' plans, and had nothing to do with the killings. In the knowledge that my life, and those of Mrs Briggs and Sophia, will be saved if they succeed, I have naturally agreed. But as to whether they are as innocent as they claim, I will leave the court to decide.

The German factor again! But how could two barrels of diamonds, admittedly worth $200,000,000, affect a country as rich and powerful as Germany? The Second Reich, as it was now known, was the dominant military power in Europe today. Only two years ago, her armies had invaded France, forcing the French government to hand over the rich provinces of Alsace-Lorraine, and a massive ransom of 5,000,000,000 frs. to secure their withdrawal.

$200,000,000 was a vast amount, in any country's currency, but it was paltry compared with Germany's total wealth. Yet the German connection to the diamonds could not be denied. As Colleen had observed: it was more than just a coincidence . . .

So, what the hell was Sweeny up to?

Sunday, 1 December, 1 a.m. Goodschaad says that they intend taking the ship over at first light. I pray they will succeed.

Monday, 2 December, 1 a.m. The attempt failed. I saw it all through the window in the galley door.

Martens was at the ship's rail with his telescope scanning the seas. He must have sensed them creeping up behind him, because as Goodschaad aimed an axe at him, Martens moved to one side, slicing Goodschaad's arm open with his sword as the axe embedded itself into the ship's rail. Before Goodschaad could move, Martens put his sword to his throat, and forced the others to surrender. Martens then sent for Mrs Briggs and Sophia, and held the sword to Sophia while the Germans launched the boat. He ordered them all in, and set them adrift. Then, horror of horrors, Martens turned the ship around and aimed for them. I did not see the collision but heard the rending sound as the Celeste cut through the boat, and the terrible sound of their screams. May God have mercy on their souls.

Callaghan closed his eyes, but this only made the dreadful scene more vivid.
He forced his gaze back to the diary.

Tuesday, 3 December. We must be at the rendezvous-point. Martens is sailing the Celeste in wide circles, and constantly sweeping the horizon with his telescope. My final prayer, as I await my end, is that someone will find this diary and use its pages to bring Martens to justice. I commend my soul into God's keeping. Amen.

Realizing now that the mess in the galley had been caused by Head's desperate fight to survive, Callaghan sat for a long time in respectful silence. Then he carefully stowed the diary in his sea-bag, knowing it would be fatal to let Oliver read it. He'd see red, and forget about Desiah Morehouse and the children in his hurry to tear Martens apart.

A few hours later, first light was vainly trying to break through an ominous cloud formation looming up on the black horizon, and Callaghan was out on the *Celeste*'s bows. As the vessel rose to crest a wave, he looked down and saw two long scrape marks confirming Head's account of the collision.

Turning away, he crossed to the stern.

"My watch," he told a tired-looking Anderson. "There's plenty of hot stew on the stove." Anderson grunted his thanks, and headed across the deck to the galley.

Gripping the wheel, Callaghan braced his legs against the ship's pitching, and took stock of the weather. There was the threat of more storms in the air, but the heavy swell had died down. The *Dei Gratia* was still off the port bow, now some 500 yards ahead.

Callaghan looked down at the main deck house, remembering the slice of light he'd noticed coming from the captain's windows. Dare he risk it?

Lashing the wheel, he silently rounded the captain's cabin, then kneeled to peer through a slight tear in the sail canvas covering one window.

The room was dimly lit by an oil-lamp swinging from the ceiling, and the scene that met his eye was totally unexpected.

Wearing a black robe, tied at the waist with a thick red sash, Martens was kneeling, head bowed as though in prayer, in front of the sword, now embedded in the wooden floor.

Callaghan stared, mystified. What the hell did it all mean?

He narrowed his gaze, studying the sword's ornate hilt and trying to memorize the design.

He started with a gasp as a strong hand gripped his shoulder. "Thought you were up to something," whispered Deveau, kneeling beside him. "I could tell from the movement you'd lashed the wheel. What's to see?"

Moving to one side, Callaghan let Deveau take his place. "Looks like some damned Knight Templar in vigil, preparing to meet the Saracens, Oliver commented, straightening up. "Except he's wearing black instead of white. What's it all about?"

What indeed? thought Callaghan. What manner of killer had Sweeny employed? It was like a tableau out of mediaeval times, a throw-back to the Dark Ages . . .

"Hell!" hissed Deveau, pointing out to sea. A rogue wave fringed with white, was bearing down on them! In the early morning gloom, the slate-coloured wall of water looked taller than the *Celeste*'s masts!

Deveau got to the helm first and unlashing the wheel, he spun it swiftly, bringing the bows about to meet the wave head on. Callaghan clutched tightly to the stern rail, holding on for life.

Both men waited.

The huge roller thundered nearer, then its first swell hit the vessel, lifting her up a sheer slope, sheets of water cascading across the deck and slamming into them, nearly sucking them into the wave's icy vortex. For one terrible moment the *Celeste* was perched vertical, her prow pointing up at the dark sky. Callaghan was certain they'd turn completely over, but somehow the *Celeste* crested the wave. She stood still as though suspended, then with a lurch her bows righted, and she plunged down the other side into a grey abyss, hitting the bottom of the trough with a great shudder. Again, the seas crashed over her, but they were through . . . to an angry ocean, with rollers foaming and fighting in all directions, the harbingers of yet another storm coming in off the horizon.

★ ★ ★

First light, and after weeks of being cooped-up inside the *Asia*, Colleen threw a thick tartan scarf over her fur-lined travelling coat, and ventured out on deck, preferring the open promenade to the tobacco-stale air of the saloon.

The winds were still blowing strong, lifting her tresses away from her shoulders and sending them streaming behind her. But this only emboldened Colleen to cross to the ship's-rail and hold on tight, exhilarated by the great waves breaking against the vessel, and dousing her in their salty spray.

Never before had she experienced such storms, especially the last eight days. Roaring gales lashing the seas into a frenzy, creating rollers that completely dwarfed the steamer, lifting her so high, she'd seemed, at times, suspended in space, only to drop her deep into grey valleys, with walls of ocean on either side, until it seemed the ship could take no more. Even hardened passengers who'd been at the gaming tables within hours of leaving New York, had fallen to their knees in terror, invoking Almighty God to come to their aid. Now, with a sudden lull in the weather, God was forgotten, and they were all back at the roulette table, trusting in the wheel of chance instead.

Dark grey clouds rolled low overhead, portents of still more storms in the offing. Looking up at the skies, Colleen prayed for Michael to be safe. If a solid steamship like the *Asia* had come close to foundering, heaven only knew what it was like aboard a hundred-foot wooden brig, at the mercy of the elements, and with a crew of only five to man her. One slip; a sudden high wave . . .

Just the thought of losing Michael for good, was enough to make Colleen confront the truth in her heart. Whatever had happened in the past, she loved him still. And Michael loved her, she had seen it in his eyes. What good was all her caution? Life was too short, too uncertain. Why hold back on the opportunity to make-up, to talk, to whisper, to touch, to kiss, to love? To do so, and it might be gone forever. Yesterday was over, but they still had the rest of their lives before them. Remembering back to their first four years together, the strength of his familiar arms around her, the easy fit of their bodies, perfectly complementing each other, Colleen decided that when — *when*, because no storm could keep him from her — Michael eventually arrived in Gibraltar, her suite was his to share. No more accusations, no recriminations. It was time to start making up for all the wasted years.

19

Thursday, 12 December 1872

DEVEAU pointed to the twin peaks rising out of the sea on the rain-lashed horizon.

"The pillars of Hercules," he shouted, to make himself heard above the winds. "The Rock of Gibraltar to port. Mount Cueta on the starboard."

Callaghan was too exhausted to reply. During the last seventy-two hours of continuous storms, both Sweeny and Colleen had been banished from his mind. Though there'd been no more rogue waves, the fight had often seemed lost as howling winds whipped up seas high enough to swamp the vessel, leaving them chilled and wet through, with no time for sleep, and very hungry, forced to eating hard tack again and no more hot stew. Yet, in spite of the elements, they'd managed to keep up with the *Dei Gratia* — a 'supreme feat of seamanship', Oliver had called it, complimenting both

Callaghan and Anderson — and it was not until yesterday that a sudden, gale-force wind had finally separated the two vessels. Even now, as the Spanish and Moroccan shorelines, and faraway mountain ranges, slipped by on either side of the straits, the weather was still rough.

"Ideal!" yelled Deveau, holding on to the rigging and swaying as the vessel gave a violent pitch. Lashed by the rain, rivulets of water were streaming off his sou'wester and running down his face, soaking his beard and dripping on to his spray-covered oilskins.

"Perfect!" Callaghan shouted back in sarcasm.

The *Celeste* righted herself. "I meant for dropping Martens off," hollered Deveau. "With this wind." The driving spray was forcing him to speak in brief snatches. "And only the three of us . . . there'll be no questions . . . if we sail past Gib . . . into the Med for shelter."

Taking over the wheel from Anderson, Deveau let the *Celeste* run before the wind. Fighting the inflowing Atlantic current, he held her on a straight course, passing between the Pillars, the Rock of Gibraltar towering above them off their port side, and entered the Mediterranean. As they rounded the Point, keeping close to the Spanish coast, the wind slowly abated and the waters of the inland sea became progressively easier. The sky began to clear, and after four weeks of continual storms, the sun appeared through the clouds, sending shafts of golden light down on the grey waters, creating large patches of transparent green crowned with small waves flecked with masses of snow-white foam. Callaghan breathed in the air: my, but it felt good!

They sailed on, searching for calmer waters in which to drop anchor, past small fishing villages with gaily painted boats beached high on the sands, and beyond them, parched brown hills devoid of vegetation. Then they saw the mouth of a large river in the distance, surrounded by a deserted stretch of shore.

"Get ready with the sails," Deveau instructed. "I'll take her in close so we can anchor and rest for a couple of hours. You first, Gus, you look as though you need it."

Having lowered the sails and dropped both anchors within a few hundred yards of Spanish soil, Callaghan leant on the rail and gave an audible sigh of relief. After 3,000 miles of angry grey ocean, it was great to be near to land again, and hear waves gently breaking on the shore, instead of gales howling through the rigging.

Deveau leant alongside him. "Feels good, eh?"

"Incredible."

"So you won't be making a career out of the sea?" Oliver grinned.

"Not at any price," Callaghan replied. "Is Gus inside?"

"Already fast asleep."

"In that case, I'll disappear. I don't want Martens seeing me."

"Why not?" asked Deveau. "He's already seen you once."

"Only briefly, in semi-darkness. And that was before I grew this beard. By the time we reached Genoa, he'll have forgotten my face, especially after another twenty-five days of growth."

From the galley Callaghan watched Martens' dark shape slip out from the main deck house and lower himself over the side. He followed the German's flaxen-white hair to the shore, then the slim, dark, figure loped off across the sands, over a hillock, and disappeared from view.

Callaghan went back out on deck.

"Pity he didn't drown." Deveau spat over the rail into the water.

"And where would that have left Desiah and the children?"

Oliver ignored the question. "When I was in his cabin his eyes never left me, watching me like a snake, ready to stick that damned sword into me if I made any sort of move. And all the time, I kept thinking, just one twist of my wrist, that's all it would take," the first mate held up his strong hands. "But then, I'd remember about Desiah . . ." He half turned. "Now that he's gone, I'll join Gus and close my eyes for a couple of hours. You'd best do the same."

"Later," said Callaghan. "After seeing whether he left any clues."

Entering the captain's cabin, Callaghan found every item reminding him of Sarah Briggs and Sophia, from the melodeon that once resounded to the young mother's playing, to the doll still sitting on the small rocker. How Martens could have lived with these last two articles about, was as puzzling as why he hadn't cleared them away? Perhaps he hadn't even noticed them?

Ignoring the two sea-chests at the foot of the bed, Callaghan pulled the third one away from the wall. Turning it around, he saw 'Arian Martens' painted on the front. Picking the locked clasps open, he began removing the contents, placing everything in order on the bed. When Martens rejoined the vessel, he must find the chest just as he had left it. Four shirts. Four pairs of pants. A woollen shirt. A belt. A cotton cap. A bag containing pieces of cloth and flannel for patching. A razor strop. Overcoat. Light coat. Five waistcoats. Two hats. A pair of half boots in best leather. Six shirt collars.

Nothing extraordinary so far.

Next, Callaghan removed a layer of books, giving each a brief glance. There were thirteen — all in German. Martens was certainly a genuine reader. Yet the idea of an intellectual assassin was even more chilling.

Next was a flute, a lamp, and a sextant inside a wooden case.

Beneath these were two parcels fastened with cord. Checking to make sure the knots were normal, Callaghan then untied them. The first parcel contained a bundle of papers, also in German. Understanding only the odd word, he removed three sheets from the middle and set them aside. Next he opened a canister containing an ancient rolled parchment tied with black ribbon. The scrolled lettering was faint, but again seemed to be in German. The document had a notarized red wax seal, its pattern cracked with age. Callaghan was tempted to take it, then decided it was too dangerous. If it was valuable, Martens might check on it.

He turned to the second parcel which contained two packages tied with cord. In the smaller was a jar labelled Brandreth Pills. New York's latest popular patent pill. He knew them well; advertised to cure every ailment known to man, and very bitter to taste . . .

Bitter!

Callaghan examined the pills. Of course! This was how Martens must have given Briggs the poison. According to Head's diary, the captain had complained of a bad stomach. Martens had probably caused it by putting something in his evening meal. Then, the next morning, when he took in the breakfast, he'd offered Briggs a poisoned pill — well coated by the look of them — knowing that any bitterness would be attributed to the known taste of a Brandreth.

Callaghan removed a pill and put it with the papers.

The last package contained a cloth bag filled with what appeared to be flax-seed. Callaghan emptied one of the desk drawers and poured the contents into it. Hidden in the seed were five shiny-green oval beans, each about an inch and a half in length, with a hard surface and covered in silky hairs. Placing one bean with the Brandreth pill, he added a handful of seed, then emptied the drawer back into the bag.

Carefully replacing everything in the chest, Callaghan relocked it, then slid it across to the door to take to the crew's quarters.

Checking Briggs's desk, he found and removed the letter from David Morehouse, asking Briggs to meet him in mid-Atlantic.

Moving next door to Richardson's cabin, Callaghan gathered up the *Celeste's* papers, navigation book, register, chronometer, sextant — everything the authorities in Gibraltar would expect Briggs to have taken with him if he'd abandoned ship — and threw them overboard.

★ ★ ★

They entered Gibraltar harbour just as dawn was breaking, the Rock casting a giant shadow over the port. As they dropped anchors, they saw the pratique boat approaching.

Deveau focused his telescope. "Captain Morehouse's on board, and he's looking mighty upset. There's also two British soldiers, and a man in a dark suit with a large holdall on his knees." Deveau lowered his glass, and frowned at Callaghan. "Something's happened. I

352

don't like the look of this one bit."

The boat drew alongside. The dark-suited man was the first on deck. Ignoring Deveau, Callaghan and Gus, he crossed to the main mast, and removed a framed notice and a hammer from his bag.

He was followed by two red-jacketed soldiers armed with rifles, who marched across the deck, one to the main deck house, the other to the forrard. Boots crashing on the planks, they about-turned, ordered arms, and took-up sentry positions blocking the entrances, as the man in the suit nailed his notice to the mast.

Morehouse clambered up, face grey and drawn.

"What's going on?" Deveau asked.

"The British are placing the *Celeste* under arrest," said David. He sounded on the verge of collapse. "They don't believe our story. Some jumped-up Admiralty solicitor, Solly Flood, is accusing us of killing everyone on board the vessel, just for the salvage. We're to face an Inquiry into the circumstances, to determine whether or not we're to be put on trial for murder. The guards are here to prevent us removing anything . . . "

"The sword!" Callaghan exclaimed.

"What about it?" asked Morehouse.

"Martens didn't have it on him when he swam ashore."

"Then where is it?"

Callaghan cursed himself for having overlooked it. "It must be in the cabin. Probably under the bed. What if they find it and it's still bloodstained?"

"It's too damned late to do anything about it now, Michael," said Deveau, flatly.

From the top of the Rock came the resounding boom of a cannon.

"What's that all about?" asked Callaghan.

"The morning gun," Deveau explained.

"Welcome to Europe," said Callaghan.

"It's also Friday the thirteenth," Deveau volunteered.

20

STILL weeping silently, Colleen stepped out on to the balcony of The Royal Hotel. Removing her handkerchief from under her cuff, she dabbed her eyes, then looked down on the small cobbled square and postage-stamp size City Hall. Below her, Waterport Street, the port's main thoroughfare, with its mixture of small European shops and Arab bazaars, was crowded with people. She concentrated all her senses on the busy street scene below in an attempt to obliterate the haunting image of a small boat cut in two, and a mother and tiny child hurled into the cold grey Atlantic.

Michael approached from behind, and drew her to him, placing his arms around her and holding her tight. Leaning sideways against him, needing the comfort of his body, Colleen put both arms around his waist, and rested her face against his chest.

Slowly, the everyday scene of the street

below restored her composure. Wiping her eyes again, Colleen turned her thoughts to Michael, and the problems at hand. Taking his arm she led him back inside.

"You must be exhausted. You also look as though you haven't eaten in weeks. Would you like me to order you some breakfast? Then, maybe you'd like to sleep for a couple of hours?"

"Breakfast sounds good. I assume it will be an English one? Bacon, eggs, sausages, fried bread, and whatever else?"

Colleen smiled, despite the gravity of what lay before them. "Of course."

"That would certainly fill the spot. As for sleep, I'll catch up later. Besides, I'm over-tired, and with too much on my mind for rest."

Pulling the bell-cord for room-service, Colleen sat down. "This Arian Martens? How on earth did Sweeny get hold of him?"

"Your guess is as good as mine," Callaghan replied, dropping into the opposite chair. "There's no record of Sweeny ever having been to Germany, but that's not to say he hasn't. The only thing for certain is that he's hired a professional killer in Martens. Three by poison. Two by the sword. Five deliberately, and cold-bloodedly, drowned. As for poor Head, we'll probably never know how he died."

"Evil! Sadistic!" Colleen's tone was filled with repugnance. "Sweeny must have known what kind of man he was employing. That makes him equally contemptible. And guilty under the law."

"Don't worry," Callaghan reassured her. "I'll make sure they both pay."

"Except there's this Inquiry hanging over you, if this Flood man decides to proceed." She leant forward, anxiously. "Shouldn't you confide your identity to him, Michael? Show him Head's diary, let him read what really happened . . . "

"And risk him giving the story to the newspapers, so Sweeny is tipped off? I can see the headlines now: 'Brains Sweeny's diamonds, valued at two hundred million dollars, found on board two New York brigs in Gibraltar. Eleven people murdered.' No, Colleen. I want them both — Sweeny and

357

Martens — and I don't intend losing them."

"But if Flood's an advocate, then surely his concern is to bring the right people to justice? What if you ask him to remain silent until after both Sweeny and Martens have been arrested, wouldn't he agree?"

"Not from what David says about the man. It seems he's more interested in publicity than justice. We're like manna from heaven to him. He probably envisions his name plastered across the front pages of all the leading newspapers, as the man who solved the mystery of the *Mary Celeste* ghost-ship . . ."

They were interrupted by the young bell-hop who took Colleen's breakfast order. "And a large pot of coffee, please," Callaghan called after him, stifling a yawn.

"So, what's your next step?" Colleen asked.

"Find the best attorney in Gibraltar."

"What about Mr Sprague, the United States Consul, he'd advise you. Also," Colleen deliberated, "relations between the States and Britain are pretty good at the moment. I'm sure neither wants a tiny salvage case souring things. Perhaps Mr Sprague would speak to Flood on your behalf, make him realize his case is purely theoretical, and persuade him it would be in the best interests of both countries if the matter were dropped."

"It's worth a try," Callaghan nodded. "I'll discuss it with David and Oliver."

"What about the second Kaufmann telegraph to Sweeny?" Colleen reminded him.

"No need now. Martens no doubt wired him from New York, telling him Kaufmann was dead. If not, then as soon as Martens arrives in Gibraltar, and discovers the *Celeste*'s under arrest and the *Dei Gratia*'s facing an Inquiry, he's bound to wire Sweeny with the latest developments."

"I'd love to see Sweeny's face, when he hears his precious diamonds have been impounded!" Colleen gave a half-laugh. "What do you think Martens will do?"

"He'll hang around for the result of the Inquiry. If we're awarded salvage, then everything is back to normal. But if we're put on trial, who knows? A lot depends on whether they decide to search the cargoes, or release them to their owners."

"I see." Colleen subsided into silence for a moment. "Since you'll be occupied with this Inquiry business over the next few days, what if I start investigating the items you found in Martens' sea-chest? Apart from helping your case, it would give me something useful to do, instead of just sitting here worrying."

"Yes, why not?" Callaghan agreed, rising. "With your experience of researching your novels, you'll be probably be better at it than me."

He withdrew the folded papers from his longbag and handed them to her. "The Brandreth, flax seed, and bean are inside. Where will you find someone to do the translation?"

"I'll try the Garrison Library. But what about the sword hilt? Can you remember the design?"

"I think so." Moving to the writing-desk, Callaghan selected a sheet of hotel stationery, and began sketching. The lines were hesitant at first, but became bolder as he saw the pattern taking shape.

360

"That's as near as I can remember," he said, handing Colleen the drawing.

"It's extremely ornate," she observed.

"That's why I think the design stands for something, and why I'm hoping it won't be too difficult to identify."

"I'll do my best," Colleen promised.

There was a knock on the door. "And now breakfast is served," she added with a smile.

Book Three

Book Three

21

WALKING through Gibraltar, the newspaperman in Callaghan could not help but compare it to New York, contrasting its narrow twisting alleys against the straight, wide avenues back home; its sprawling open market-places to Fifth Avenue's contained emporia; and the low, flat-roofed terracotta villas so different to New York's tall granite buildings pushing ever upward in the current architectural trend. Judging by the babel of languages and exotic apparel — dark-skinned Moors wearing gold ear-rings, turbaned market-traders from India, long-bearded Jews in dark suits and hats — every race seemed to be represented. Their individual cultures maintained, they gave Gibraltar a unique cosmopolitan atmosphere, that was the antithesis of New York's 'melting pot.'

Groups of off-duty British soldiers strolled amongst the crowds, their vivid red coats reminding Callaghan that

Gibraltar was now a British garrison town. The scene of so much bloodshed over the centuries, it had been conquered by many invaders, always in the name of religion. The Roman Catholic 'God' of Spain had lost to the 'Allah' of the Moors, then returned in glory 700 years later, only to be deposed by the Protestant 'God' of the British Empire. Gibraltar's history was certain proof that on earth, power resided with the ruthless, and The Almighty, if He existed, was happy to let them get on with it, despite the suffering to the rest of mankind.

★ ★ ★

"Unfortunately, you could not have chosen a worse opponent than Solly Flood," said Horatio Jones Sprague leaning back in his swivel chair, and looking at them over the top of his half-spectacles.

A dignified-looking man, dressed in a dark, waistcoated suit with a gold watch and chain, the United States Consul drummed his fingers on his red leather-topped desk. On the wall behind him was a large unfurled American flag with hanging gold tassels, its polished stick supported by two brackets.

"The man's seventy-one," Sprague continued. "Hasn't been here long and never wanted the posting. He's Irish by blood, but was born in London, and hoped to spend his remaining years there, enjoying the theatres and the galleries. You can take it from me, gentlemen, Flood won't let this one go. He'll hold on to it like a Jack Russell with a rat. Naturally, I'll do my best to dissuade him, but I'm afraid I can't offer much hope. Conjure up a motive and he'll have thought of it — murder, fraud, piracy — just as long as it gets him the attention of the British Admiralty in London, for a transfer back home."

"Then he's going to find plenty to support his case," said Callaghan. "As we mentioned, there's Briggs's sword under the bed. It's more than likely a souvenir of some past voyage, but from the way you describe Flood, he's bound to make it seem like damning evidence. Plus the scrape marks on the bow and the axe cut in the rail, both of which probably happened back in New York — "

"Lund," the consul interrupted, "for some reason, you've made yourself the general spokesman for the *Dei Gratia*. I must confess I find this rather surprising. I would have thought Captain Morehouse could do his own explaining, or even Mr Deveau?"

David and Oliver fidgeted in their chairs, but remained silent.

"As it happens, sir, my name isn't Lund, it's Callaghan. Michael Callaghan, from New York Police, Detective Squad. I'm investigating two murders which took place back home." Seeing Sprague frown, he dug into his pocket. "Here's my badge and warrant-card. If you want further proof, a telegraph to Captain Irving at Headquarters will confirm my identity. I sailed on the *Dei Gratia* with Captain Morehouse's permission, and this *Celeste* incident could not have come at a worse moment. Especially as I must continue using my alias."

Sprague's face remained stern. "This all sounds most unorthodox. I think an explanation is an order."

Detailing Kaufmann's and Becker's

deaths, Callaghan added that both seemed to point to Peter Barr Sweeny being behind them. Brains was believed to be staying at the Hotel de Genes in Genoa. His reason for this assumption, Callaghan belied, was that a man fitting the killer's description had waylaid David Morehouse in New York, and by threatening the lives of his wife and children, was forcing him to deliver a sealed parcel to the de Genes, addressed to a Peter B. Smith, assumed to be Sweeny. Which was why Callaghan was on the *Dei Gratia*. He thus needed Sprague to telegraph Police Headquarters, to confirm the Morehouses were being protected by the Canadian Police.

"Except, please don't include Sweeny's name," he concluded. "Irving's suspected of being a Ring man himself, and might warn Sweeny I'm on the way. I'm acting under the confidential authority of Police Commissioner General William Smith."

The consul unconsciously resumed his finger drumming on the desk-top as he looked from Callaghan to the badge and warrant-card, then back to Callaghan.

"All right, Callaghan," he said, somewhat reluctantly. "This is crazy logic, but your story's too damned unbelievable for it not to be true, though I certainly intend asking New York for confirmation. But before I do, shouldn't you take Flood into your confidence? If I fail to persuade him to cancel the Inquiry, then once you've taken the stand and sworn the oath under a false name, it will only make matters worse.

"From what I hear of this Solly Flood, sir, telling him I'm investigating two vicious murders would also make matters worse."

"True," Sprague nodded. "Very true." He turned to Morehouse. "Captain? How do you feel about all this?"

"I just want my wife and children safe, sir."

"Mr Deveau?"

"I'm with the captain one hundred per cent, sir," Oliver stated.

"In that case, gentlemen, we'd better start sending some urgent wires." Sprague reached for a telegraph pad and pencil. "The first priority is obviously to establish Mrs Morehouse's safety. So this one is to . . . ?" He looked up at Callaghan.

"Captain James Irving, sir, Detective Squad, Headquarters, New York Police, Mulberry Street."

Sprague repeated the name and address out loud as he wrote them down, then continued: "Callaghan here investigating Kaufmann Becker. Extremely urgent confirm Mrs Morehouse protected Canadian Police." He glanced at Callaghan. "That sufficient."

"Exactly right, sir."

Sprague returned to his pad. "The second priority is to try to undermine Flood by getting the *Celeste* released from custody. So this is to the Board of Underwriters in New York saying . . . now, how can I best word it?" He paused, then again spoke as he wrote: "Brig *Mary Celeste* here derelict. Important send power of attorney to claim her from Admiralty Court." Again he glanced at Callaghan. "How's that?"

"Fine, sir. Let's hope it works."

"We can but try, Callaghan. We can but try. Next, I suggest we send one to my colleague, Mr Spencer, in Genoa. Before the *Celeste* can be released, we

371

will require a copy of her documentation. Might as well use the same wording: American brig *Mary Celeste* here derelict. Important send bill of lading cargo to claim from Admiralty Court."

Callaghan intervened. "Sir, would you also ask for confirmation that Sweeny's staying at the Hotel de Genes?"

"Of course," the consul assented. "Confirm Peter Sweeny Hotel de Genes." His gaze included all three. "No need to add who he is, we've all heard of the man. What about double-checking his whereabouts with our Paris Embassy?"

"That makes good sense, sir," Callaghan agreed.

Sprague scribbled the fourth message. 'Ambassador Washbourne, US Embassy, Paris. Important confirm location Peter Sweeny.'

The consul stood up, and the three of them followed his lead. "They'll be sent today," he promised. "Mr Spencer will no doubt send the bill of lading to Algeciras and I'll arrange for someone to meet the train. As soon as I receive any replies to the wires, especially the one regarding Mrs Morehouse, I'll let you know." Sprague held out his hand to David first. "Meanwhile, Captain, keep your chin up."

"I'll do my best, sir."

"And you, Mr Deveau."

"Thank you, sir."

"Callaghan, if there's anything else I can do, please don't hesitate to ask. In the meantime, I'll arrange an appointment with Flood, but I'm afraid I don't hold out much hope."

"No, sir. Then nor will I," said Callaghan. "Which reminds me there's one thing more. The name of a top attorney?"

"Henry Pisani," Sprague replied, after a brief hesitation. "He's not up to your New York standards, but he's the best Gibraltar has to offer. His address is Galliano Bank Chambers, Cannon Lane."

★ ★ ★

Colleen entered 77 Church Street, a shop with dark window-frames and small panes, and the name W F Roberts, Chemist in faded gold letters over the door. The door-bell jangled as she crossed the stone-flagged floor to the counter. The dispensary's open door revealed a tall thin man pounding at some substance with a pestle.

"Be right with you, madam," he said, wiping his hands on his white overall, soiling it with yellow powder.

"Mr Roberts?" she asked.

"Yes, madam. How may I help you?" he asked, approaching her.

"My name is Callaghan. Mrs. I'm from New York and staying at the Royal Hotel. I've just purchased an old Moorish chest to ship back home." Opening her carry-all, she withdrew a hotel envelope. "I found these items inside, hidden in a secret drawer, and I'm worried they might be dangerous or something? I wonder whether you'd identify them for me?"

"Why not just let me dispose of them?" the chemist asked.

"Curiosity," Colleen smiled. "Actually, I'm a writer, and I thought they might reveal something about what the Moors used to get up to, and maybe provide an interesting storyline? Of course, I shall pay for your time."

The chemist sighed. "Very well, Mrs Callaghan." Accepting the envelope, he peered inside. "The seed looks like ordinary flax seed, but I'll check it. And the bean should be easy to identify from my books of reference. But the pill may be more of a problem. I'll have to subject it to analysis."

"How long will that take?" she asked, affecting polite curiosity. "I'm leaving in a few days' time."

"Late tomorrow. Say six o'clock."

★ ★ ★

Reaching the Garrison Library on Gunners Parade, Colleen approached the uniformed commissionaire.

"Madam?" His upright stance suggested he was an old soldier.

"I wonder whether you can assist me? I need to translate some old papers. They're in German."

"You want Mr Joseph Turner, madam, the ex-librarian. He's retired now, but spends every day, apart from Sundays, in the members' room. Whom shall I say wishes to see him?"

"Mrs Callaghan. I'm an American, from New York."

"If you'll wait here a moment, madam."

Turning smartly the commissionaire marched off down the corridor. Colleen sat down and waited. A few minutes later, the commissionaire returned. "Mr Turner says he will be delighted to see you, madam. If you will follow me."

Leading the way past the reference room, into the wood-panelled stillness of the members' room, the old soldier pointed towards the roaring fire, where a white-haired elderly gentleman, who looked just like Santa Claus, was sitting ensconsed in a low, comfortable-looking, brown hide armchair.

Colleen crossed to his side. "Mr Turner?"

Beaming at her, the ex-librarian struggled out of his chair and held out his hand. "Mrs Callaghan." He spoke *sotto voce* to accord with his surroundings. "Won't you sit down?" He indicated to a chair alongside his, then settling back into his relaxed position, asked, "I understand you have some

German documents you'd like me to translate for you?"

"Actually, if you're able to tell me the subject matter, that may be enough." She took the papers out of her bag. "I'm extremely grateful, and will recompense you for your time."

"Goodness me," the old gentleman chuckled, "I will not require a fee." Removing pince-nez from his top jacket-pocket and clipping them to his nose, he studied each paper carefully, then peered up at her. "May I enquire what is your interest in them, Mrs Callaghan?"

"They were my father's," Colleen replied. "I found them amongst his old papers and brought them with me when I sailed to Europe, in case they were of value."

"I'm afraid not, at least, not of any monetary value. They may however, be of historical interest. Was your father, by any chance, a historian?"

Colleen seized the opening. "Yes, as it happens, he was. That's very perceptive of you, Mr Turner."

The elderly man gave a smile of inward pleasure. "Not really. These papers seem to be extracts from a project he was probably researching. Was he interested in secret societies, do you know?"

"It just so happens he was writing a book on them," she replied quickly, taking Michael's sketch of the sword-hilt from her bag. "I found a drawing similar to this amongst his notes. The original was falling to pieces so I made this copy last night in my hotel room."

Briefly gazing at the sketch, Mr Turner handed it back. "Yes, its shape certainly suggests it was designed for ceremonial, rather than practical use, and probably belongs to some covert sect. All of which implies that your father was researching into the already proven connection between such organizations and the sect mentioned in these documents — the Assassins."

"The Assassins! What a dreadful name!"

"No more dreadful than the reality of their evil deeds, I assure you, Mrs Callaghan."

"Mr Turner, I don't want to impose, but do you have time to tell me something about them?" Colleen asked, certain she was on to a vital lead. "As a hopeful writer, I would like to finish my father's book, if only in memory of his name."

"An admirable ambition," the elderly man approved. Settling even deeper into his chair, the ex-librarian continued, "In that case, let me tell you what I know." Clearing his throat, Mr Turner elaborated. "The Assassins were an Islamic brotherhood of fanatical killers, who existed between the eleventh and thirteenth centuries. Though they've long since passed into history, their methods of recruitment, their indoctrination, and their organization, have provided what can best be described as a blueprint for succeeding secret societies right up to the present day."

"Methods, Mr Turner?" Colleen interrupted. "Can you elaborate?"

"I would only be too pleased," the old man replied. "Initially, they were formed as a Shiite fundamentalist sect . . . "

"You mean, religious?" Colleen almost protested, knowing how Michael would react.

Turner nodded. "Zealously so. They regarded the murder of their enemies as a religious duty. To understand why, one has to go back to the reason for their formation. After the death of the prophet Mohammed in AD six hundred and thirty-two, there was a struggle over who should succeed him. The Sunnis, the orthodox Muslims, believed that the elected Caliphs of Baghdad were the rightful leaders. The Shias, on the other hand, felt that the 'Appointed One', should be chosen from their Imams, the priest-kings, who claimed — and still do — to be directly and spiritually descended from Mohammed, through his daughter, Fatima, and his son-in-law, Ali.

"Anyway, to cut a long story short, some four centuries later, after the death of the incumbent Caliph of Baghdad around the year ten-ninety, a Shiite sect called the Nizari Ismailis decided their claim could be best enforced through a systematic reign of terror and assassination. They established a training-camp in an isolated, impregnable castle called Alamut, meaning Eagle's Nest, high in the mountains, south of the Caspian Sea. Their strength lay in

380

the structure of the organization, headed by the Grand Master — the first being its founder, Hasan-i Sabbah — then came the Da'is, the missionaries, followed by the Rafiqs, the disciples, and finally, the Fida'is, the devotees, who were the actual assassins, trained experts in swordplay, and the use of drugs . . ."

"Drugs?" asked Colleen, scenting another lead.

"Very much so," Mr Turner replied. "The very name Assassins is derived from the word *hashish*. Their knowledge of drugs was remarkable, not only as a means of assassination, but also to control the minds of the Fida'is before sending them out on their murderous missions. First they'd give the Fida'i a drug to make him experience the terrors of Hell, then immediately he'd recovered, they'd give him another narcotic inducing a vision of Heaven — rather like the Jesuits, except that they use the power of their imaginations, rather than drugs." Joseph Turner smiled. "But I'm digressing, an old man's weakness. During this second dream, the Fida'i would be taken to a hidden valley guarded by the castle, specially created to be the most beautiful and fruitful garden ever seen. Marco Polo visited it after the Mongols destroyed the Assassins, and said it rivalled even the Biblical Garden of Eden. Still in a state of semi-consciousness, and believing himself to be in *Assama* — Paradise — the Fida'i would be visited by the Grand Master, the Ayatollah, deliberately clothed in white, and pretending to be Allah. He would tell the Fida'i he'd been specially chosen for a holy mission to kill Sunni leaders, the more the merrier, and that if he was killed in the quest he'd be transported back to Assama, rather than the Hell of his first drug-inspired vision. The Fida'i would then be returned to the castle, where he'd wake up believing he'd seen Allah, then set out on his holy mission, determined to earn martyrdom, and the guarantee of life eternal in some Islamic garden of Paradise."

Colleen frowned, shaking her head. "Hearing all this makes me sympathize with Michael's point of view. When it comes to the Day of Judgement, religion is going to have a lot to answer for."

"Michael?" Joseph Turner queried.

"My husband."

"But one cannot blame religion for the acts of individuals."

"According to Michael, it's the cause of most of our troubles."

"And what about yourself, Mrs Callaghan?"

"I'm a Catholic, but there are times when my faith is sorely shaken."

"But surely it's how each of us responds to religion that matters," the old gentleman persevered. "Otherwise God might have made us all His puppets. But in His infinite wisdom, He gave us free will, to choose our own destinies." Joseph Turner handed back the papers. "Suggest to your husband that he considers the matter prayerfully, Mrs Callaghan, and he may find himself agreeing."

★ ★ ★

Henry Pisani's first-floor office opposite the post office in Waterport Street, was the untidiest Callaghan had ever seen. Worse even than Louis Jennings's at the *Times*. Bookcases overflowing with battered, leather-backed law books; cupboards crammed so full of splitting document-cases the doors would not close; and a plethora of loose files scattered all over the floor. The desk was no better, completely littered with papers and documents, yet the slim, olive-skinned, dark-haired man behind it, had the confident air of one who knew where everything was.

"I shall be happy to represent you, gentlemen," said Pisani, leaning forward across the desk. In his mid-thirties, Henry Peter Pisani was the son of a penniless Italian count who'd married the daughter of a wealthy British army major stationed in Gibraltar. Educated in England from the age of seven, including Harrow, and graduating with a law degree from Oxford University, he'd then returned home to set up his own law practice.

"My fee for salvage claims is ten per cent. But I must warn you our task will not be an easy one. From all accounts, Mr Flood seems to regard you, Captain Morehouse, as a modern-day Blackbeard, and your crew as the most unprincipled villains. No! Please don't misunderstand me." Pisani raised his hand to prevent the indignant David Morehouse from protesting. "This is not my view. I merely emphasize how determined Flood apparently is to see you brought to trial. Nevertheless, because such wild stories are circulating, before we start preparing for the Inquiry, I must ask each of you for confirmation that there is absolutely no truth whatsoever in what Mr Flood is claiming. I trust you will forgive my having to ask such a question, and that you will understand I do so only in your best interests." Henry Pisani sat back, waiting expectantly for their response.

Seeing David and Oliver tensing, Callaghan answered first. "None, Mr Pisani."

The reason Callaghan and Deveau were present at this initial meeting between Morehouse and Pisani was that Michael had been chosen to speak for the crew, while Oliver was representing John Wright.

"Captain Morehouse?"

"None," David growled.

"Mr Deveau?"

"None, Mr Pisani."

385

"Excellent!" exclaimed the lawyer, magically producing pen and paper from the chaos of his desktop. "And now, I would like you to take me through the events, starting from the moment you sighted the *Celeste*. Who saw her first?"

★ ★ ★

"I'd forgotten roast beef could taste that good," said Callaghan, surveying his empty plate. "The Yorkshire pudding went down a treat."

"So I noticed," said Colleen. "Dessert? Coffee?"

"Coffee. Black, with plenty of sugar. I'll ring."

Getting to his feet and tugging the bell-cord, Callaghan pulled back Colleen's chair for her to rise. They both crossed to the two armchairs facing the roaring fire, and sat down.

"So, you're seeing Mr Turner again tomorrow?"

"Yes, ten o'clock. I'd love you to meet him. He's a perfect dear," Colleen added, knowing Michael would take to him.

"I'd like to. Maybe next week. But

now we know there's nothing significant about the papers, there's no need to delve much deeper. Other than identifying the sword — and that's mostly in the hope it might shed some light on the mystery of how Sweeny and Martens ever got together in the first place — the chemist's analysis is by far the more important."

"I don't agree, Michael," Colleen protested, mildly. "I still get the feeling we're missing something. I can't help thinking there's more to those documents than Martens being interested in the history of the Assassins. Don't forget all those other books you saw inside his sea-chest. That's not what you'd expect of a cold-blooded killer."

"And because he's some kind of psychopathic bookworm, you feel the answer lies in books?"

"Well, apart from agreeing that identifying the sword might help explain how Martens met Sweeny, if it *does* turn out to belong to some secret society, as Mr Turner thinks, then it could also tell us much more about our esoteric killer — what he stands for, what his aims are — "

"Colleen," Callaghan interrupted, smiling to soften the harshness of his words. "I don't want to pour cold water on your theorizing, but don't you think you're getting somewhat carried away?"

"In what way?"

"The Assassins, and all the others they spawned, were fanatics dedicated to some religious or political purpose. Martens is Sweeny's hired assassin, and no matter how Catholic Sweeny acts, his only interest in religion is no more than an insurance policy in case it turns out there *is* some sort of life after death. As for politics, well, we both know what motivated him in that pursuit — money and power. But as for him getting involved in European politics, why should he when he's expecting two barrels containing diamonds worth two hundred million. Even Sweeny can retire comfortably and happily on that kind of money."

"Comfortably, yes," Colleen agreed. "Happily? No. The only time Sweeny's happy is when he's doubling and trebling what he's got. As for my getting carried away, don't forget there are a number of questions still needing to be answered. Palermo, for example. One ship bound there, I could accept. But both must surely be more than a coincidence?"

"Maybe," said Callaghan, non-committally. "Anyway it will all be revealed in the end. Meanwhile, what about getting back to the Assassins. You'd only just started on how those religious fanatics evolved into professional killers for hire, when I cut you off."

Colleen opened her eyes wide in mock surprise. "Are you sure you want to hear it? With it being so superfluous and all?"

"But of course," Callaghan replied, in the same vein. "What else is there to do behind the closed doors of a beautiful woman's luxury hotel suite on a cold winter's night?"

Her face became suddenly serious, and she held his gaze for a brief moment before answering, "Other than continuing my story, I can't imagine." Then blushing slightly, she turned to her notes and searched for where she'd left off. "Did I get to the Knights Templar modelling themselves on the Assassins, not only their tiers of organization, but even to the wearing of white tunics, like the Rafiqs, the disciples?"

"You did."

She glanced at the page. "Right. Well, some seventy years after the Assassins first started, the Syrian branch broke away from the Persians, and led by their Grand Master, Rashid Ad-Din Sinan, went from being religious killers, to selling their services for gold. Saladin, or the Crusaders, made no difference, provided the price was right. One of their first victims was the King of Jerusalem and Prince of Tyre, a man named Conrad of Montserrat. As a result, the news of these hired killers quickly spread to the courts of Europe. They were summoned first to Sicily, then various states of Italy, Germany, France, Spain — even a few Kings of England are rumoured to have used them to eliminate their enemies. In fact, it's through this sect that the word assassin became part of our language."

Colleen looked up from her notes. "Both the Syrian and Persian Assassins were eventually wiped out by the Mongols, but long before then, similar secret sects had sprung up in most European countries. In cases like the Knights Templar, their garb was usually white. But when a sect was created for political or religious assassination, they followed the custom of the original Fida'is, wearing black robes with red sashes for their initiation ceremonies, and also the Fida'i methods of killing with the sword, or failing that, poison." She paused, then repeated: "Black robes. Red sashes. The sword. Poison. Just like Martens."

"Just like Martens," Callaghan yawned, with sudden tiredness. "But that brings us back to where we started. Sweeny involved in European politics. Why bother, when he's got a hundred times more than enough as it is?"

"I don't know, Michael. But if Mr Turner and I can identify the sword hilt, maybe it will lead us to the answers." A church clock struck ten. "That reminds me, when Mr Turner was telling me about the religious motive behind the formation of the Assassins, I suddenly thought about the names of the vessels: *Mary Celeste* — Celestial Mary. And *Dei Gratia* — God's Grace, and realized both

391

are religious. Like the Palermo riddle, one vessel I could accept. But for both to have religious names seems more than coincidence."

"Possibly." Callaghan's voice sounded tired, and his eyelids looked heavy. "But do you mind if we discuss it tomorrow? The last eleven days have suddenly caught up with me. I'm dead on my feet."

Colleen knelt beside his chair. "Michael, you'll never make it to the harbour, let alone the *Gratia*. Stay here the night."

There was a knock on the door.

"Wait a moment!" Colleen called out. "The coffee, Michael. That's decided it. Get into bed, and I'll bring your cup to you."

Callaghan needed no second invitation.

After the bell-hop had left, Colleen went into the next room. Michael was stretched out in the large bed, already fast asleep. His bare shoulders showed he was naked. Colleen smiled, her heart soaring, just seeing him there. Kissing him on his brow, she moved to the other side of the bed, and began undressing.

22

SHE was already awake when the morning cannon sent its resounding boom echoing through Gibraltar's narrow alleys. Feeling the chill of winter in the air, Colleen burrowed deeper under the covers, not yet ready to start the day. There was enough light seeping in between the curtains for her to watch Michael sleeping there beside her.

He stirred slightly at the sound of the gun, and moved closer to her. Feeling the heat of his body radiating towards her, Colleen remembered their cold winter mornings in New York, and the way she used to cuddle up to him for warmth, as he held her tightly, but gently, in a snug-as-two-bugs-in-a-rug cocoon. Then they would slowly kiss. And then they would . . .

She started as she felt Michael's arm close over her, then seeing he was still asleep, she smiled and relaxed against him. Through her silk nightdress, she could feel the length of his lean, hard body. Michael turned, drawing her closer to him, his leg parting her thighs. His eyelids fluttered and his hold became slack. His sleep had been deep, and there was a look of dazed puzzlement on his face as he tried to make out where he was.

He was suddenly awake. His eyes flashed open. The room was still too dusky to make out their blueness, but they looked into hers for a long moment, then he smiled. "Good morning, Miss Lowell."

"Good morning," she responded.

Leaning his face forward, his lips brushed hers in a gentle yet searching kiss. She returned it, both of them re-exploring the half-forgotten, yet still remembered fullness of each other's mouths. He drew her closer against him, one hand caressing her back. The pressure of his lips increased and through her nightdress Colleen felt his body responding. Succumbing to his caresses, she became possessed by a yearning, long kept under subjugation, a luxuriating sensual feeling that began

394

deep in the pit of her stomach and slowly spread through her entire body, down to her toes. She pressed her body up against his, and their bodies locked together as one.

The kiss became more searching, as their desire for each other increased, and overwhelmed them . . .

★ ★ ★

Colleen was late getting to the library, but she found Mr Turner in the chilly reference room, wearing an overcoat, and completely absorbed in the thick, heavy book on the table before him. As she reached his side he looked up, smiling with satisfaction.

"I think I've found what you're searching for, Mrs Callaghan. Do you have the sketch with you?"

When she produced it from her bag, he studied it only briefly. "Yes, I thought so," he said, skimming through the book until he got to the page he was looking for, and then showed it to Colleen.

The book title was in block print at the top of the page:

Immediately below it was the Chapter heading:

The Black Knights

Halfway down the ensuing text was a detailed drawing of the filigree hilt of a sword. Though Michael's drawing lacked some of the finer details, there could be no doubt they were the same.

"I came in early, and decided to concentrate on German societies, because of the papers you asked me to translate," explained the ex-librarian. He looked more like Santa Claus than ever, eyes twinkling and face shining with the pleasure of his success.

"Thank you, Mr Turner." Colleen was so thrilled she had to restrain herself from kissing the old man.

"There is quite a bit about them, but I can give you a brief résumé," he offered.

"That would be splendid. Then I can continue researching the pertinent leads — for my father's book," she added quickly.

Pleased to be of help, Joseph Turner's face lit up even more, then placing a hand to his mouth, he gave a customary preliminary cough, and began: "The name Black Knights was their original title, but they now call themselves Totenbund, which means Death League. They are a particularly noxious branch of a German revolutionary movement known as Tugendbund. It's not known when they were first formed, but they certainly existed as far back as mediaeval times. Being political assassins, available for hire, and completely ruthless in the endeavour, they most definitely owe their origins to the Assassins. They have their own particular initiation ceremony, in which the new member kneels before a table with seven lighted candles, and seven swords laid crosswise, then swears the following oath of fidelity, and I quote . . . " Turner peered through his pince-nez at the book: "*'If I become unfaithful to my oath, my brethren shall be justified to use these swords against me.'*" He read on silently for a moment, then looked up. "When the ceremony is over the new member is presented with a sword — a replica of the one I showed you — and a black robe with a red sash . . . "

The sword, the robe, and the sash, Colleen thought. Oh, Michael Callaghan, are you going to have to eat your words!

"The book gives many examples of their ruthlessness," Mr Turner continued, "but let me quote you just one, authenticated by a letter from . . . " — he referred once more to the book — "a Doctor Breidenstein, a leading member of the Tugendbund, to Mazzini in November 1835 . . . "

"Mazzini!" Colleen interjected.

Mr Turner looked up.

"I'm sorry, but the name prompted a question in my mind. Please continue. It will keep until later."

"Are you sure?"

"Positive."

"Very well. As I was saying the letter was to inform Mazzini, that another Tugendbund member, a man named Louis Lessing who lived in the Sihl valley, near Zurich, had been discovered to be selling their secrets to the German government, and had therefore been sentenced to be executed by The Black Knights." Turner closed the book. "Apparently, Lessing's naked body was found staked to the ground. It had a total of forty-nine stab wounds — seven times seven." He explained, "The mystical number of seven is extremely popular with secret societies, and its multiplication as a square root especially so."

"There's a great deal of emphasis on swords," Colleen observed. "Both ceremonial, and as a means of assass-ination. Does the chapter mention whether they use drugs or poison?"

"No," Mr Turner shook his head. "But modern revolutionaries tend to regard themselves more as front-line soldiers, preferring the use of the sword, or dagger, or pistol, rather than mediaeval, Lucretia Borgia-type methods."

"So, drugs remain more associated with the Assassins?"

"Very much so."

"But as far as you know, Mr Turner, would any Black Knight be restricted from copying their methods?"

"I'm no expert on secret societies, Mrs

Callaghan. But provided he achieved the end result, I see no reason why he should not ape them if he so desired."

"I see." Colleen assimilated all this for a moment, then changed her line of questioning. "Mr Turner, when you mentioned Mazzini, were you referring to Giuseppe Mazzini, the Italian revolutionary?"

The librarian nodded. "Yes. The most untiring political agitator in the history of Europe."

"Wasn't he born in Genoa?"

"Born there. Studied there. And died only nine months ago. During his lifetime, the whole Italian peninsula became a veritable hotbed of conspiracy and revolt. The Palermo uprising of '48 was Mazzini inspired. As was Mantua in '52. Milan, a year later, in '53. And then Leghorn and Genoa, both in '57." The elderly librarian recited the dates from memory, without any hesitation. "Since his death, it's rumoured his leadership of the Carbonari has been taken over by someone even more militant. There are more than a few whispers of massive uprising against the rule of Victor Emmanuel, with threat of blood running on the street etcetera, etcetera."

"Carbonari? I assume they're revolutionaries?"

"An Italian underground movement, Mrs Callaghan. In league with the German Tugendbund in the common interest of ridding themselves of the so-called shackles of their existing governments. Between them, they've attracted every fanatic and idealist in Europe; men for whom no project is too fantastic, no vision too unrealistic. And over the last few years, they've also been attracting men of considerable influence and power, mostly Freemasons . . . "

"Freemasonry?" Colleen queried. "I thought it was non-political?"

"Maybe in your country, but not in Europe it isn't," Mr Turner affirmed. "Especially the branch known as the Grand Orients of the Continent, which is so political that both the Carbonari and the Tugendbund hide behind it, meeting in Freemasonry-owned buildings; and there is nothing either Victor Emmanuel or Bismarck can do to prevent them, so powerful is Masonic influence over here, on this side of the Atlantic."

"Goodness! To be that influential!" Colleen exclaimed. "What sort of men are we talking about?"

"Magistrates, lawyers, businessmen, bankers, army officers, and more recently, since the persecution of the Church of Rome, even prelates and priests, despite the Masonic Supreme Being being a weird triune amalgam of the Biblical God, Jehovah, and the heathen gods, Baal and Osiris, hence the name 'Jabulon'."

"Bishops and priests!" Colleen expressed her surprise. "Joining up with revolutionaries?"

"I'm afraid there's nothing unusual in this, Mrs Callaghan. The Jesuits have been doing it for centuries. And now, with Rome under such sustained attack, and the Pope a prisoner in the Vatican, clerics from other orders also see revolution as the only way to restore the Church to its former position of power. There is much talk of popish-inspired plots to assassinate both Victor Emmanuel and Bismarck. Some say this is nothing but evil gossip, but it is hardly to be wondered that others give it credence, especially when the Pope himself seems to be openly inciting violence. Take his most recent speech to his cardinals, at a consistory in the Vatican. It was reported verbatim in yesterday's *Gibraltar Guardian*. There is a copy of it over there on the table, should you care to read it?"

Crossing to the table, Colleen could see the *Guardian*'s headline splashed across the front page:

THE POPE ATTACKS
KING VICTOR EMMANUEL AND
COUNT BISMARCK

"Take time to read the whole article," Mr Turner invited. "In my opinion, it's nothing less than a papal invitation for the faithful to take up arms in defence of the Church of Rome."

★ ★ ★

By the time Callaghan reached Pisani's office, John Wright, Gus Anderson, and Johnny Johnson, were already waiting on the landing.

403

"You're late, Lund. Captain Morehouse and Mr Deveau are already inside," said the second mate, a stickler for punctuality. "Where did you get to last night?"

"Captain's permission, Mr Wright. I met someone I know. Where are the others?"

"They're not required," Wright explained. "Mr Pisani sent a message this morning, saying he only needs the testimonies of the men directly involved."

"In that case, I'd better go straight in."

"Good luck, Charlie," said Anderson, clapping Callaghan on the shoulder. "Keep protecting our interests."

"Thanks, Gus. I will."

David and Oliver, sitting stiffly at attention in the room, both looked relieved to see him.

"Sorry to be late, Mr Pisani, Captain Morehouse," Callaghan apologized. "I'm afraid I was held up."

"That's OK, Lund," David replied, maintaining their pretence.

Pisani indicated the empty chair next to Oliver. "First gentlemen, I have bad but not unexpected news from Mr Sprague. He met Mr Flood last evening and, as anticipated, failed to persuade him to cancel the Inquiry. The date has been set for next Wednesday. The presiding judge will be Sir James Cochrane. He's a fair, but stern man. Apart from being careful how you answer Flood's questions, which I must warn you will be cleverly worded, Sir James is the one you must satisfy." Pisani reached for a pencil. "Therefore, with only three days in which to prepare my case, if I could begin with you, Captain Morehouse . . . "

"No!" David exclaimed.

Pisani looked startled. "I'm sorry, Captain?"

"I can't face him!"

"Can't face him?" Pisani's face cleared. "You mean Mr Flood? Please don't concern yourself about him, Captain. I can assure you that long before Wednesday, I will have briefed you sufficiently . . . "

"I'm not giving evidence, and that's that," Morehouse announced, evading the lawyer's eye.

"Not giving evidence?" Pisani had a

habit of repeating a person's statement as a question. "Confound it, Captain! Do you realize how this will be interpreted? Especially as you're the one claiming salvage! It will be tantamount to confessing your own guilt!"

"I'll take that chance." David's tone was belligerent.

"Do you wish to explain why?" asked Pisani, lowering his voice and regarding his client with bewilderment.

"No, I don't," Morehouse replied, defensively, as he rose and withdrew from the room.

Pisani turned appealingly to Oliver, who was himself looking thunderstruck. "Mr Deveau, can you explain your captain's behaviour, which, to put it mildly, seems to border on the eccentric, if not suicidal?"

"I'm sorry, Mr Pisani," Oliver replied, recovering his composure. "It's the stress he's been under, bringing both vessels to port with half-crews, and now the worry of financial penalties if he fails to get his cargo to Genoa within the maximum time limit."

"Then all the more reason for him to

give evidence, surely?" Pisani argued.

"Leave him to Lund and me, Mr Pisani," said Oliver. "We'll try persuading him."

"I only pray you succeed," Pisani stressed, "otherwise Flood will make great capital of it. Meantime, I'll quickly take both your statements, then allow you to find your captain, while I interview the other three members of your crew."

★ ★ ★

David was waiting for them in the street below. "I'm sorry," he said, his voice flat, but his eyes filled with anguish. "The moment Pisani started asking questions, I realized there's no way I can take the stand."

"But David," Oliver reasoned, "you're only going to make things look worse, as Pisani said. What will happen if the Inquiry goes against us and we're put on trial? Where will that leave Desiah and the children?"

"At least with a fifty-fifty chance," David argued. "But if Flood made me contradict myself, the odds would be nil. I'm OK behind the wheel of a ship, but when it comes to speaking, I get tongue-tied. And my worry over Desiah would only make me worse. If I was sure she was safe, then maybe I'd take the risk." Massaging his furrowed brow, he screwed his eyes closed for a moment, then opened them. "OK, if we hear before Wednesday that Desiah's safe, then I'll testify. But if we don't, you'll have to face the Inquiry without me."

"Then let's hope New York replies," said Callaghan, fervently.

★ ★ ★

"The seed was just flax," said Mr Roberts, "but the pill was pure strychnine. What's more, I'd say it was recently manufactured. It was extremely fortunate it did not fall into the wrong hands."

"Merciful heavens!" Colleen deliberately clapped her hands to her face in horror. "Was it strong?"

"Enough to have killed ten men."

"Gracious! I'm glad I brought it to you," she said. "Mr Roberts, is death by strychnine violent?"

"Not necessarily. Not if it is caused by one of the *strychnos* plants of the order *Loganiaceae*, like the South American varieties *strychnos gubleri* and *strychnos castelnaei*. In such cases, death occurs through respiratory paralysis," he explained, warming to his subject. "But an alkaloid strychnine taken from a convulsant plant, like the seed of the *strychnos nux vomica* — which grows in the East Indies and the Malay Archipelago — or the *strychnos multiflora*, or the bean you brought in, there's a drawing of it my reference book — "

"Was that from a convulsant plant?" Colleen interrupted.

"Most definitely. Found only in the Philippines."

"Mr Roberts, this could be the basis for a great plot," Colleen pretended excitement. "Exactly how would you describe a convulsant plant's effect?"

"Oh, most horrific. Anyone unfortunate enough to take a pill made from a convulsant plant, especially one as strong as you found, would experience such extreme tetanic convulsions that the spine would almost certainly be snapped in two."

"Really!" The method of killing now confirmed, Colleen was anxious to get back to the hotel and concentrate on the wild theory which was occupying her mind, prompted by reading the *Gibraltar Guardian* article.

Mr Roberts watched her go, wondering whether, as a novelist, she would have been interested in the actual name of the bean: *strychnos ignatii*, discovered by Jesuit missionaries in the Philippines, hence its more common name: The Bean of Saint Ignatius.

★ ★ ★

"I found it!" Colleen exclaimed as soon as she'd opened the door to Michael. Her excitement was evident in her tone, yet her green eyes were very serious.

"I take it you mean the sword hilt?" Callaghan said, closing the door.

"It belongs to a secret society of political assassins, who are not only German, but also wear black robes and red sashes. And I think I've worked out the connection between them and Sweeny," she added matter-of-factly. "If I'm correct, it explains how and why he and Martens met. And what we're up against."

"You have been busy," Callaghan smiled, putting his arm around her waist and leading her to a chair. "Let's sit down, and you can bring me up to date."

He listened in silence while Colleen recounted her conversation with Joseph Turner.

"German Totenbund?" Callaghan queried, still not convinced. "Are you certain it was the same design?"

"Absolutely."

"But that doesn't make any sense. What would Sweeny want with a bunch of German political assassins?"

"A common purpose?"

"Such as?"

"To rid Italy and Germany, of their present governments, or more correctly, their dictators."

"Why should he want to do that?"

"Because both Emmanuel and Bismarck have one thing in common. They're persecuting his Church, especially the Jesuits. And Sweeny's not only an ardent Catholic, he's also a fervent Jesuit. I don't know exactly how he became involved, but his reason is to see the Church restored, the Jesuits reinstated, and the Pope released from captivity."

Callaghan shook his head. "I'm sorry Colleen, but I can't accept it. Sweeny — Defender of the Faith! No way! Not unless there was something in it for him."

"Ah, but there is," Colleen replied with conviction. "In fact, he probably has two motives. First, a passport to Heaven, endorsed by the Holy Father, or the Father-General of the Jesuits, against the day when his immortal soul — if he has one — parts company with his mortal coil. This also explains why he chose religious names for his vessels: Celestial Mary and God's Grace."

"And the second?" Callaghan asked, intrigued.

"Financing arms. I'm not suggesting he's investing the whole two hundred million dollars, but enough to ensure the revolution's success."

"He'd have had to be promised a three hundred per cent return," Callaghan remarked. "And guaranteed by the Pope himself." He thought carefully for a few moments. "OK, assuming for the moment that you're right, and that Martens is a member of these so-called Black Knights — or Death League, Totenbund, whatever they call themselves. You think he was chosen by some joint Carbonari Tugendbund revolutionary committee . . . "

"Meeting in some Freemasonry building in Genoa," Colleen interjected. "Mazzini territory, which has a history of revolution as long as your arm. This explains why the diamonds are bound there — to be sold by a diamond merchant who belongs to the movement."

"Let's not get sidetracked," Callaghan suggested. "Let's stick with your original thought. You obviously believe Martens was sent to New York to liaise with Kaufmann . . . "

"No," said Colleen, leaning forward in her chair. "Martens was sent as a bodyguard for Becker."

"Becker? Father Becker?"

413

"Yes. According to Mr Turner, scores of Catholic clerics are joining the movement, seeing it as the only way to remove Victor Emmanuel and Bismarck. I think Father Becker was one of them, and was chosen to go to New York because of his experience as an administrator at the College of Propaganda. Also because he was probably an extreme ultramontane the same as the Pope. Martens was simply his strong-arm protector."

"No, Colleen," Callaghan protested. "I can't buy it. What about his soup kitchen?"

"What about it?"

"Don't you think it's somewhat contradictory for him to have been so concerned for the homeless on the one hand, yet be involved in revolution with the other?"

"Not for someone like Becker. Don't forget I met him and the look in his eyes made my flesh creep. He would have seen the restoration of the Church as sacred a duty as the feeding of the five thousand." Catching Callaghan's smile, she defended herself.

"I'm not condemning my own faith, just the odd fanatic like Becker, who, for some reason, almost always turns out to be a Jesuit. Maybe it's something to do with their training. It's so intensive that every now and again one of them goes beyond the grounds of sanity. Don't forget that Jesuits were involved in the assassination of President Lincoln. And going back only a hundred years, Pope Clement the Fourteenth was killed by poison after he'd suppressed the Society and ordered the papal troops to kick them out of Rome. But it's not the Jesuits alone this time, it's the whole Church, with Pope Pius himself inviting civil disobedience. But see for yourself from this article in yesterday's *Gibraltar Guardian*."

Reaching into her carry-all, Colleen produced a folded newspaper. "Mr Turner brought it to my notice."

Taking it, Callaghan looked down at the headline:

THE POPE ATTACKS
KING VICTOR EMMANUEL AND
COUNT BISMARCK

The article began by reminding its readers of the events leading up to the present situation facing the Roman Catholic Church, quoting from past speeches, first by Francesco Crispi — a leading Italian minister — who advocated 'throwing all cardinals into the Tiber', and that 'Christianity must be purged of the vices of the Roman Church, or else it will perish'; and then by Garibaldi, the Italian freedom-fighter, and friend of the late Mazzini, comparing priests to 'wolves and assassins', and stating that 'the Pope is not a true Christian'.

As to the bulk of the article, it seemed that the Vatican's worse fear — that Rome itself would be lost to the Catholic Church — was about to be realized. The Italian Assembly was expected to vote in favour of a Bill, introduced by the Minister of Justice on 20th November, the main provision of which, according to an exact quote from the Bill, was:

The laws of 1866, 1867, 1868 and 1870, relative to the suppression of religious corporations and the conversion of their property is now to be applied to the province and city of Rome. The property of the religious corporations in the city of Rome are to be converted into inalienable public rentes.

Even before the 1866 ruling, the report continued, some 13,000 church properties — seminaries, churches, monasteries — had been suppressed; after it, another 25,000 were seized. Now, Emmanuel's conquest of Rome, and the 1872 Bill moving for the State to take over all remaining properties, threatened the Church's position in the Eternal City itself.

It had prompted an angry reply from the Pope, in the form of an allocution to a consistory of twenty-two cardinals.

Callaghan could just imagine the scene:

A consistory was the highest of the courts of the Church of Rome, in effect a papal senate, consisting of the whole body of cardinals and presided over by the Pope himself. On this occasion, the consistory had obviously been an emergency meeting, because twenty-two cardinals surely represented only those who resided in the Vatican, plus maybe a persecuted few who'd fled there for refuge.

As he read the extract from the Pope's speech, Callaghan was struck by Pius's emotive phraseology, obviously worded to create maximum effect in newspapers around the world:

The Church continues to be sorely persecuted. This persecution has for its object the destruction of the Catholic Church. It is manifested in the acts of the Italian Government, which summons the clergy to serve in the army, deprives the bishops of the faculty of teaching, and taxes the property of the Church by heavy burdens. This law presented to the Parliament on the subject of religious corporations deeply wounds the rights of possession of the Universal Church, and violates the right of our Apostolic mission.

In the face of the presentation of this law, we raise our voices before you and the entire Church, and condemn any enactment which diminishes or suppresses religious families in Rome or the neighbouring provinces. We consequently declare void every acquisition of their property made under any title whatsoever.

The Holy Father was certainly laying it on thick, Callaghan thought.

But our grief, the Pope had continued, *at the injuries inflicted on the Church of Italy, is much aggravated by the cruel persecutions to which the Church is subjected in the German Empire, where not only by pitfalls, but even by open violence, it is sought to destroy her, because the persons who not only do not profess our religion, but who do not even know that religion, arrogate to themselves the power of defining the teachings and rights of the Catholic Church. These men, besides heaping calumny upon ridicule, do not blush to attribute persecution to Roman Catholics, and bring such accusations against the bishops, the clergy, and a*

faithful people, because they will not
prefer the laws and will of the State,
to the holy commandments of the
Church.

In this, our darkest hour, we
therefore invoke Almighty God to
come to the aid of His Church,
and we thank Him for the activity
of those of our number who continue
to defend the rights of our Apostolic
mission, and do battle against the
iniquity of the oppressors.

Callaghan folded the newspaper, and
looked up.

"Well?" Colleen queried. "What do
you think?"

"Inflammatory, to say the least."

"And that's an under-statement."

Callaghan was near to surrendering.
"OK, assuming Becker *was* involved
— why did Martens kill him?"

"Because he refused to agree to the
death of Kaufmann, a fellow Catholic.
But, by that time, Becker's work was
over, so Martens just killed him as
well."

"Why use a poison?"

"A sword is not the easiest weapon to carry about the streets of New York. And in Briggs's case he used the pill to make it look like the captain died from a violent fit. All of which explains his interest in the Assassins and their use of drugs."

"What about Palermo?"

"A deliberate cover," Colleen suggested. "Sending both vessels there for return cargoes, the normal practice, rather than return with empty holds."

A silence descended as Callaghan dwelt on Colleen's theories.

Colleen broke it. "Martens must have wired Sweeny by now. What do you think he'll do?"

Callaghan looked up. "Guessing, he'll forward the bills of lading to the Admiralty Court, and apply for the cargoes to be released. Until the Inquiry is concluded, both vessels and crews are confined to Gibraltar. But there's no restriction on the consignments. And nothing to stop their legal owners — in other words, the companies Sweeny's hiding behind — from demanding the cargoes be transferred to other vessels, and allowed to sail on to Genoa."

"If he does that," Colleen observed, "then our own plans could end right here."

Genoa

As Don Salvatore Cottone's large yacht entered Genoa harbour, Sweeny stood at the rail, getting his first glimpse of the ancient city known throughout Italy as *La Superba*. Yet he was indifferent to the spectacle of its many-hued, multi-tiered beauty, ascending the encircling hills.

His mind was racing ahead to the messages which should be waiting for him in the Hotel de Genes. As soon as he knew the names of the vessels, and their expected dates of arrival in Genoa, he and Don Cottone could get down to serious discussion of their scheme.

Chewing his unlit cigar, Sweeny inwardly gloated as he thought of its immensity . . . and the huge scale of the rewards.

23

Wednesday, 18 December 1872

"ALL rise!"

The command came from the registrar, Edward Baumgartner. The packed courtroom stood to its feet. Over the years, many salvage claims had been heard by Gibraltar's Vice-Admiralty Court, but — according to Pisani — none had attracted this amount of interest, nor stimulated quite so many rumours: piracy on the high seas, collusion between Captains Briggs and Morehouse to fraudulently claim salvage on the *Celeste*, with Briggs and his crew having been landed at some hideaway on the coast of Spain, or in the Azores, to await their share of the prize money. According to Pisani, these, and other stories even more bizarre had been leaked by Solly Flood himself, in a determined attempt to create maximum publicity and thus ensure the Inquiry received a full and captive audience, with the spotlight very much on himself.

He had certainly achieved his aim, Callaghan thought, as he looked towards the Bench. Every row behind him was filled, and people were even standing some six-deep at the back. Colleen was in the fifth row, and Consul Sprague in the third. The proceedings being an Inquiry, and not a trial, Callaghan and the rest of the *Gratia*'s crew were in the front row, seated in the order Pisani intended calling them to stand: Oliver by the aisle, then Second Mate Wright, followed by himself, Gus Anderson, and Johnny Johnson. Next there was David. Sprague hadn't received a reply from the New York Police, and David was still refusing to take the stand, despite Pisani's exasperated threats of how this would be construed by Sir James Cochrane. Next to David was Orr, then Higgins and finally, young Willard Cleary, his face deathly pale, and his hands visibly trembling.

Pisani was on the other side of the barrier, his papers spread across a wooden table.

Solly Flood stood behind a second

table, to Pisani's right. Callaghan's first glimpse of their 71–year-old antagonist had been only a few minutes ago, when Flood entered the room. Short and round, with a jowly pink face, he was already perspiring copiously beneath his grey wig.

The door behind the Bench opened and Sir James Cochrane entered. He was a tall man, with a long heavily lined face, and looked to be in his mid-sixties.

"Before the worshipful Sir James Cochrane, Knight, Judge and Commissary of the Vice-Admiralty Court of Gibraltar; this day, Wednesday, the eighteenth of December in the year eighteen hundred and seventy-two, this being the day to take evidence of Oliver Deveau, John Wright, Charles Lund, Augustus Anderson and John Johnson, this Court is now in session. Be seated," proclaimed Mr Baumgartner in a loud ringing voice.

The crowd settled down with a muted hum of anticipation.

Clearing his throat, the registrar continued, "The Queen, in Her Office of Admiralty against the ship or vessel called *Mary Celeste* and her cargo,

425

proceeded against as a derelict, is represented by Frederick Solly Flood, Esquire, Advocate and Proctor for the Queen in Her Office of Admiralty. Captain David Reed Morehouse, and the officers and crew of the British brigantine *Dei Gratia*, claiming as salvors, are represented by Henry Peter Pisani, Advocate and Proctor."

Mr Baumgartner sat down. Sir James leant forward. "Mr Pisani."

Pisani rose. "Yes, your worship?"

"I see that Captain Morehouse is not to give evidence."

"No, your worship."

"Hmmm." Sir James regarded him with a puzzled frown. "I assume you have your reasons, Mr Pisani, but it seems strange not to call on the *Dei Gratia*'s captain, and rely instead on the testimonies of her first and second mates, and three of her crew." Sir James sat back. "You may call your first witness."

"Thank you, your worship," Pisani replied, outwardly calm, but Callaghan sensed the tension in his voice at this immediate set-back. "I call Oliver Deveau."

426

Entering the witness-stand, Oliver placed his hand on the Bible, and facing Sir James, swore that "The evidence I shall give will be the truth, the whole truth, and nothing but the truth, so help me God." But his nervousness was obvious, and after completing the oath, he gripped the rail tightly with both hands.

Crossing to the stand, Pisani began with a simple question to put Oliver at ease. "Mr Deveau, would you tell us your occupation?"

"I am the Chief Mate of the British vessel, *Dei Gratia*," Oliver blurted out.

"You may take your time, Mr Deveau," Pisani instructed, in a calm reassuring manner. "Would you now tell us about your voyage?"

Oliver took a deep breath before replying, "We left New York on the fifteenth of November, bound for Gibraltar for orders."

"And your captain's name?"

"Captain Morehouse, Master."

"Thank you, Mr Deveau," Pisani was maintaining a slow pace, attempting to relax the first mate. "Now would you please tell us when you first sighted the *Mary Celeste*."

"On the fifth of December."[1]

"Would you describe the circumstances?"

"I was below at the time. The captain called me and said there was a strange sail on the windward bow, apparently in distress . . . "

"Exactly what time was this?"

"About three p.m., sea time."

Mistake number one, Callaghan thought. They had first sighted the *Celeste* at one o'clock, not three, and it would be recorded as such in the *Gratia*'s log. Three o'clock was when they boarded the *Celeste* the second time. Not that the error was of significance, but it was a sign that Oliver was still nervous, and boded ill for when Flood came to cross-question him.

"What happened next?" Pisani asked.

---

[1] Unlike land time, which started at midnight, sea time started twelve hours earlier, so although the calendar date was 4 December, it was 5 December at sea.

428

"I came on deck and saw a vessel through the glass. She appeared about four or five miles off. The master proposed to speak to the vessel in order to render assistance, if necessary. We hauled up, hailed the vessel, but there was no answer. We lowered the boat and I and two men boarded her. The first thing I did was to sound the pumps which were in good order."

"Did you find anyone on board?" Pisani queried.

Oliver hesitated, swallowed, then declared in a defiant voice, "No, sir. I found no one on board the vessel."

Under Pisani's continual promptings, Oliver continued his evidence, telling the hushed court about finding the hatches off; the three and a half feet of water in the hold; the condition of the *Celeste*'s sails; the binnacle stove in; that everyone's clothes — including a woman's and child's — were still on board, as though everyone had left in a hurry; that there was no sign of the ship's register or any other papers, only the log-book written up to the 24th November; and the log-slate for the 25th which indicated that on that day, the *Mary Celeste* had made the island of Saint Mary.

This took up the entire morning session. During the hour break, apart from exchanging brief smiles, Callaghan deliberately stayed away from Colleen, and remained close to Wright and the rest of the crew. It also seemed prudent to keep detached from David and Oliver, though he answered the latter's "How am I doing?" with a brief word of encouragement. "You're doing fine, Oliver. Just stay calm."

It was the middle of the afternoon before Pisani reached his final question. "Mr Deveau, would you please explain to the court how you erased the log-slate, not realizing it would subsequently be required as evidence of the *Mary Celeste*'s abandonment?"

Oliver turned to face Sir James. "I had to use it to make entries of my own on it, your worship, and so unintentionally rubbed out the entry when I came to use the slate."

Pisani sat down. "Thank you, Mr Deveau. I have no more questions. Your witness, Mr Flood."

As Solly Flood stood eagerly to his feet, Sir James intervened. "Mr Flood, before you examine the witness there are a number of questions which I would like to put to him." Flood sat down again with evident bad grace.

The judge turned to the first mate. "Mr Deveau, exactly what kind of vessel is the *Mary Celeste*?"

"The vessel is a brigantine rigged, your worship, of, I should say, over two hundred tons."

"In your opinion, was she seaworthy?"

Oliver hesitated, before answering, "The vessel, I should say, was seaworthy, and almost a new vessel."

"Did she have a lifeboat?"

"It appeared as if she carried her boat on deck. There was a spar lashed across the stern davits, so that no boat had been there."

"Hmmm!" Sir James stroked his chin. "Rather unusual. What did you do next, after checking the vessel?"

"I went back to my own vessel, reported her state to the captain, and proposed taking her in."

"And as it appears we are not to hear from your captain," Sir James commented, bitingly, "what was his reply, Mr Deveau?"

Oliver's hands again tightened on the rail as he began drawing on the rehearsed replies. "He told me to consider the matter well, your worship, as there would be great risk and danger to our lives, and also to our own vessel."

Sir James turned and looked across the court-well at David. "Nevertheless, after he had been given time to weigh up the salvage claim, he allowed you to persuade him?"

Oliver took his time to reply. "Yes, your worship. He gave me two men, the small boat, a barometer, compass and watch. I took with me my own nautical instruments, and whatever food our steward had prepared. We went on board on the same afternoon, the fifth, and arrived in Gibraltar on the morning of the thirteenth of December."

"The day after the *Dei Gratia*," Sir James remarked. "Being so undermanned, did you not think it advisable to stay together?"

Oliver glanced at Callaghan, then quickly back to Sir James. "When we got into the Straits it came on a storm, so that I dare not make the bay, but laid under Cueta, and afterwards on the Spanish coast to the East."

"And when did you next speak to your captain?"

"When I arrived in Gibraltar, your worship, and found the *Dei Gratia* already here. I had seen her every day during the voyage, and spoke to him three or four times, until the night of the storm when our vessels lost sight of each other."

Sir James scribbled some notes, then sat back. "Thank you, Mr Deveau. Mr Flood, you may continue."

"Thank you, your worship." Slowly getting to his feet, Flood hooked his thumbs into the lapels of his gown in a theatrical gesture and advanced on the witness box. Callaghan saw Oliver swallowing hard.

Flood stared at Oliver for a few seconds before asking his first question. "Mr Deveau, exactly *when* did the *Dei*

Gratia leave New York?" His tone was immediately accusing.

"On the fifteenth of November." Oliver's voice was a pitch higher than normal.

"And by the strangest coincidence," said Solly Flood, introducing a note of incredulity into his tone, "the *Mary Celeste* also sailed from the same port. Do you happen to know the date of her departure?"

"According to the log, she left eight days before us." Oliver hesitated, then added, "Or eleven days."

Flood turned to face the spectators. "Eight?" Playing to the gallery, he gave a deliberate pause, then added, "Or eleven?"

"More or less," Oliver replied.

"Come, Mr Deveau," Flood protested. "As a qualified first mate you surely know how to read a log. Was it eight? Or eleven? Or maybe it was in-between. Nine? Or perhaps, ten?"

"I cannot say," Deveau replied, desperately trying to recall, but failing. "I cannot say what number of days she left before us."

"How very strange. I would have thought a trained seaman like yourself was capable of being more precise," Solly Flood commented sarcastically.

"Tell me, Mr Deveau, still calling on your now proven expertise as first mate, what is your opinion of the *Mary Celeste*'s seaworthiness?"

"I found the vessel a fair sailer," Deveau replied, warily.

"What about the *Dei Gratia*?"

"I would call her a fair sailer also."

"In other words, there was very little or no difference between the two vessels?" Flood concluded.

Oliver hesitated, unsure where he was being led. "I suppose," he finally admitted, "that if both vesels had been equally manned, the *Celeste* would have been faster than the *Dei Gratia*."

Flood seized on the reply. "Yet the slower *Dei Gratia* reached Gibraltar first. What's more, it did so despite a storm, whereas the *Mary Celeste* — to quote your own words . . . " — Flood crossed to his table and selected a sheet of paper — "'dare not make the bay, but laid under Cueta, and afterwards on

435

the Spanish coast to the East'. End of quote."

"There were only three of us," Deveau protested.

"And I would remind you, Mr Deveau, that there were only four, plus the captain and ship's cook, on the slower *Dei Gratia*." Flood glowered at the first mate. "However, be that as it may, we will now move on — or rather back — to how and where you found the *Celeste*. I think you will agree that the shipping lane between New York and the Mediterranean is an extremely busy one. The Celeste left New York some eight, nine, ten, or maybe even eleven days before the Dei Gratia, and, according to her log-slate had been abandoned for ten days before you came across her — yet no other ship on this very busy shipping route appears to have seen her before you arrived on the scene. I must confess I find this extremely difficult to believe, Mr Deveau."

But Oliver remained calm and was not going to be drawn. He gave a dismissive shrug. "We ourselves spoke to only one other brigantine on our voyage, bound for Boston. We did not pass, nor see, any other vessel of a similar class on our outward voyage."

"If that is your story, Mr Deveau, then we must obviously accept it as fact." Flood turned away from the stand, then swivelled back. "Let us move even further back, to the twenty-fifth of November, the day the *Celeste* was apparently abandoned, according to her log-slate. What was the *Dei Gratia*'s position on that particular day, Mr Deveau?"

"I cannot say," Oliver replied, "not without referring to the log. I only know we were to the north of the *Celeste*, somewhere between latitudes forty and forty-two degrees."

"But if you cannot recollect your position," Flood scratched his head in perplexity, "How do you know you were to the north of the *Celeste*?"

"From seeing the *Celeste*'s track traced on her chart," Oliver explained.

"Ah, yes, from the chart, which, if my memory serves me well, showed the *Celeste* to be off the island of Saint Mary? Are you acquainted with

437

the island, Mr Deveau?"

"No," Oliver replied without hesitation. "I have made only one voyage from New York to Gibraltar before, and did not sight Saint Mary's then."

"You are certain?" Flood persisted. "You did not stop off there?"

"I never was at Saint Mary's," Deveau insisted. "Never saw it."

"But as a qualified first mate, could you land on it?" Oliver considered the question, before replying. "I think I could enter Saint Mary's by the help of charts and sailing directions, just as well as any other port to which I have not previously been without any reference to a chart or sailing directions."

"I actually said *land*, Mr Deveau, by which I meant beaching a small boat on a selected stretch of her shore. You specified *enter*. Are you saying you could sail into Saint Mary harbour without having entered it before?"

"I do not know what sort of harbour Saint Mary is," Oliver stated.

Flood walked across to his table. "In that case, Mr Deveau let us leave that point for the moment, although we will

438

return to it later. When you met the *Celeste*, which way was she headed?"

"Her head was westward when we first met her."

"And her tack?"

"She was on a starboard tack."

"Her wheel was presumably lashed?"

"The wheel was not lashed."

"Indeed!" said Flood, in surprise. "What about the wind? From which direction was it?"

"The wind was north."

"And for me to understand the situation properly, you did say that her lifeboat was gone?"

"Yes. One could see where it had been lashed across the main hatch, although that was not the right place for it."

"Nor the easiest place from which to launch, especially with the wheel unlashed," Solly Flood observed. "How do you suppose they accomplished it, Mr Deveau?"

"There was nothing to show how the boat was launched, nor signs of any tackle to launch her." After a full day of cross-questioning, Oliver's voice was suddenly sounding weary.

Flood scratched his head again. "Mr Deveau, on finding the entire ship's complement missing, and this from a vessel which you yourself have already stated on record to be seaworthy, did you consider the possibility that some other vessel might have found her before you, and perhaps killed the crew? For example, when you searched her, did you look for weapons? Swords, knives, or suchlike?"

Oliver passed over the reference to swords. "I do not know whether there were any knives."

"Not even a sharp carving knife, Mr Deveau?"

Flood was obviously trying to make Oliver panic, Callaghan thought, hoping to trip him up in a follow-up question on the sword. But Oliver remained calm, deliberately answering the question as put to him. "All the knives and forks were in the pantry."

"Mr Flood, I rather think we are digressing," Sir James interrupted sternly from the Bench. "If you have a point to make, then please do so."

Flood hesitated, then changed his

mind. "With your worship's permission, I would prefer to return to it at some later stage."

"As you wish, Mr Flood," said Sir James, then turned to Oliver with his own question. "Mr Deveau, do you have any explanation to offer as to why the vessel was abandoned?"

With visible relief, Oliver turned away from Flood and carefully replied. "My idea is that the crew got alarmed, your worship. The sounding rod was lying alongside the pumps. They must have sounded them, found perhaps a quantity of water in them at that moment, and thinking she would go down, abandoned her."

"Hmmm," Sir James reflected. "Abandoned in panic." The darkening windows showed dusk was fast approaching. Flood had returned to his table and was already busy gathering up his papers, as was Pisani.

"One last point, Mr Deveau," said Sir James. "After reaching the straits, exactly how far along the Spanish coast did you sail?"

Flood paused, and watched Deveau

closely as he made his reply.

"We must have run up the Spanish coast some thirty miles after leaving Cape Cueta. Maybe even forty miles."

"A devil of a long way to sail before finding calm waters, Mr Deveau," observed Sir James. "Especially as the *Dei Gratia* was able to make Gibraltar without any trouble." He rose, gathering his gown about him. "However, we will leave it at that for today. I am unable to be in court tomorrow. Therefore, we will adjourn until Friday."

Callaghan glanced across at Flood who was so busy making notes on Deveau's reply, he paused only to stand up as Justice Cochrane vacated the Bench.

★ ★ ★

"Michael?" Colleen murmured, as she nestled against him, and pulled the blankets around her.

"Yes?"

"Why did Flood stop asking about the sword?"

"Where did that suddenly spring from?"

442

"From nowhere."

"And I thought you were dreaming back to a moment ago."

"That was then. This is now."

"Will a man ever understand the workings of a woman?"

"Sometimes. But not always."

"The sometimes is worth it all," said Callaghan, dreamily.

"Mmmm. But why did he?"

"I take it we're back to Flood?"

"Yes."

"Ever see a cat play with a mouse?"

"Deliberately leaving the kill to the end?"

"Until he thinks, that we think, we've escaped his claws. And then he'll pounce, if you can imagine a short fat man pouncing."

"Ugh. I didn't like the look of him."

"I'm not too keen on him myself."

"I wonder what Sweeny's planning?"

"Your mind does wander in the most unseemly circumstances," said Callaghan, stroking her back.

"When are you calling on Sprague?" Colleen persisted, though her voice was a very soft murmur now.

443

"Anytime tomorrow. Why?"

"I thought a lie-in would do us both good."

"I'll need persuading."

"Since when?"

24

Thursday, 19 December 1872

AT the American Consulate, Mr Sprague had received three telegraphs. He showed the first to Callaghan.

New York, 17 December 1872
American Consul, Gibraltar
Canadians still tracing Morehouse.
Callaghan unauthorized Gibraltar.
Irving, Captain, NY Police

"Short and to the point," Sprague commented. "Your captain seems concerned not to overspend police money."

"A recent precaution, I assure you," Callaghan replied wryly.

"Nevertheless it's clear he knows nothing about your instructions from Police Commissioner whatever-his-name-is."

"General William Smith, sir. Nor does he realize there's a connection between Sweeny and the deaths of Kaufmann and

445

Becker. So, there's no danger of him sending Sweeny a warning telegraph." Callaghan sighed. "If only there was no Solly Flood!"

"Yes. I was in court yesterday, and can understand your worry," the consul sympathized. "Unfortunately, I have the distinct feeling he intends to make it last." He handed Callaghan the next telegraph. "I've had it a couple of days, but I knew you were busy with Pisani."

Genoa, 14 December 1872
American Consul, Gibraltar
Documentation sent by rail. Sweeny not here.

O. M. Spencer, Consul

Callaghan looked up in panic. "Not there? Then where on earth is he?"

"Palermo," Sprague replied, giving him the final wire.

Paris, 14 December 1872
American Consul, Gibraltar
Postal redirections suggest Sweeny in Palermo.

Hoffman, First Secretary

446

"Palermo!" Callaghan exclaimed. "What the hell's he doing there?"

★ ★ ★

"That explains why both vessels are bound there," Colleen remarked. "Their cargoes being one barrel over, they can unload the correct number in Genoa, agreeing with the bills of lading, then . . ."

Callaghan poked the fire and the flames leapt up the chimney. "That only explains how, it doesn't explain why." Turning to the butler's-table, he poured the coffee, added milk and one sugar, and handed Colleen her cup.

"Because Palermo's got a history of revolution every bit as long as Genoa's," Colleen replied, settling back into her chair. "From the Mazzini-inspired uprising of '48, to only six years ago, when Victor Emmanuel had to send in gunboats to bombard it into submission. Apparently Palermo is now just as ungovernable as ever, which makes it the perfect place for storing arms, as well as distributing them to both sides of the Italian peninsula."

Callaghan wasn't convinced. "In that case, why bother with Genoa? Why not sail straight to Palermo?"

"I'm not sure," Colleen conceded. "Perhaps Genoa was the original choice and Kaufmann arranged everything accordingly. Then there was a change of plan when Sweeny decided Palermo was a safer haven."

"Maybe," Callaghan agreed reluctantly. "But I still get the feeling there's more to it."

"If Sweeny transfers both cargoes to other vessels, we may never get the chance of finding out," said Colleen, reminding Callaghan of yet another worry.

"It's a mess," he agreed. "The Inquiry. Sweeny hiding somewhere in Palermo. Martens unlikely to reappear unless the proceedings finish quickly in our favour. And Desiah Morehouse still missing."

"Do you think Martens' accomplices are holding her?"

"No," Callaghan shook his head. "Coming from Europe, I doubt he's got any connections in America. Nevertheless, if he is part of some brotherhood of assassins, we can't take the risk. One thing's certain . . . "

Sipping her coffee, Colleen's eyes remained fixed on his face.

"David will refuse to give evidence until she's found. Which isn't going to help the judge decide in our favour. And tomorrow I'll be called to the stand, which means swearing the oath under a false name, and getting deeper into the mire."

25

Friday, 20 December 1872

CALLAGHAN took the stand, swore the oath, and waited for Pisani's first question.

The courtroom was already in dusk, the major part of the day having been spent by Flood continuing to cross-question Deveau, and then Wright, whose replies had mostly repeated the first mate's testimony.

"What is your name?" Pisani began.

"Charles Lund," Callaghan lied, ignoring Colleen's worried frown.

"And your occupation?"

"I am one of the crew of the *Dei Gratia*."

"Mr Lund, would you please recount the events, from the sighting of the Celeste, as concisely as possible. Mr Deveau and Mr Wright have already explained them in considerable detail, and then again in even greater detail in reply to Mr Flood's flood of questions."

There was subdued laughter in court at Pisani's deliberate pun on his adversary's name. Sir James banged his gavel and silence was immediately restored.

"We sighted the *Mary Celeste* on the fifth of December, sea time," Callaghan began. "I was not on watch, but came up from below. I was ordered to board the vessel the second time with the chief mate and Anderson. It was three o'clock when we went on board. We brought the vessel to Gibraltar, arriving on the morning of the thirteenth, and found the *Dei Gratia* already here. We had kept sight of her until reaching the straits, but lost her when the weather began blowing hard."

"Thank you, Mr Lund," said Pisani, returning to his table. "Mr Flood."

Solly Flood stood up, and gave Callaghan a suspicious look. "I must congratulate you, Mr Lund. When Mr Pisani requested you to be concise I doubt even he expected such a succinct, or should I say, well-rehearsed reply. You won't mind if I ask you to elaborate a little."

"Not at all."

451

"Thank you. I am extremely grateful." Flood moved out from behind the table. "Now, Mr Lund, according to the testimonies of Mr Deveau and Mr Wright, we are being asked to believe that only three persons — Deveau, Anderson and your goodself — sailed the *Celeste* to Gibraltar. A most remarkable achievement," he added with considerable irony. "One could even place it in the category of extraordinary. However, in your concise statement, you said that you kept the *Dei Gratia* in sight until reaching the straits. How many days out of Gibraltar would that have been, Mr Lund?"

"About two days."

"Two days? Are you sure?"

"I think so," Callaghan deliberately hedged, realizing that Flood was leading up to something.

"Mr Wright stated three?"

Callaghan shrugged. "It may have been three."

"Two days ... or three. Perhaps, like Mr Deveau's memory on leaving New York, it could have been five, or even ten?"

452

"It was neither ten nor five days," Callaghan replied calmly. "To the best of my recollection it was two or three."

"I see. Two." Flood gave his now familiar pause. "Or three?"

"I'm sure it was two."

"Sure, but not one hundred per cent certain. Nevertheless, now within sight of land, you suddenly lost sight of each other? Yet for six hundred miles of open sea you managed to sail together side by side?"

"It was bad weather," Callaghan reminded him.

"It must have been," Flood agreed, sarcastically. "Obviously much worse than the Atlantic. So bad, according to Mr Deveau, it forced you to sail some forty miles into the Mediterranean. Yet, peculiarly, not too bad to prevent the *Dei Gratia* from entering Gibraltar and registering the claim for salvage, eh Mr Lund?"

Flood glared at him, trying to goad him into replying, but Callaghan refused to be drawn, letting silence provide his answer.

The Queen's Proctor immediately

453

reverted to his familiar line of questioning, starting with Callaghan's first sighting of the *Celeste*, and continuing through to the voyage to Gibraltar, with questions about the sail-setting, the amount of damage suffered by the vessel, the depth of water in the hold, and how long it took to pump her dry, in an obvious attempt to get Callaghan to contradict the previous evidence of Oliver and Wright. But Callaghan persisted in giving Flood the briefest of answers, until eventually, with the light continuing to fade inside the courtroom, the Queen's Proctor gave up and returned to his table.

"Mr Pisani," said Sir James Cochrane from the Bench, "I suggest we examine your two remaining witnesses tomorrow."

Their advocate rose to his feet. "As your worship wishes."

"Mr Flood," Sir James queried. "I take it you have no objections?"

"None, your worship."

"Very well." Sir James banged his gavel. "This court is adjourned until tomorrow, Saturday, the twenty-first of December."

26

Saturday, 21 December 1872

THE last day, and Callaghan noted the courtroom was even more crowded. Anderson was immediately called to the stand and Pisani began in the usual pattern, asking him to state his version of the events. Then Flood cross-questioned Gus, probing for contradictions between his version and the previous testimonies. Eventually the Queen's Proctor asked how long it had taken to straighten the *Mary Celeste*, before making for Gibraltar.

"We got under sail the same night," Gus replied. "But it took us two or three days before we got her all right. We had to pump her out first."

"What is your opinion of the Celeste?" Flood asked.

"The vessel was in a fit state to go round the world," Gus volunteered to Callaghan's dismay.

"Was she indeed?" Flood commented, raising his eyebrows. "Which makes even more difficult to believe that Captain Briggs and his crew could have voluntarily deserted her in mid-Atlantic and taken to the lifeboat, especially with his wife and small child on board. Thank you, Mr Anderson, you may stand down."

Still not having made any move to sensationalize the proceedings, Flood resumed his seat.

The final witness was the Russian-born John Johnson. Aware that his witness had only limited English, Pisani kept his promptings to a minimum, and sat down.

With slow deliberation Flood got to his feet, placed his hands behind his back under his gown and stated: "I have no questions to ask this witness, your worship. However, I would ask your permission to recall Oliver Deveau to the stand."

Callaghan saw Oliver stiffen and blanch with sudden shock.

"For what purpose, Mr Flood?" Sir James questioned.

"To settle the question regarding the

Dei Gratia's position on the twenty-fifth of November, your worship, the day the *Mary Celeste* was supposedly abandoned. Furthermore, in order to facilitate my examination of the witness, I would be very grateful if Mr Pisani would let me have sight of the *Dei Gratia*'s log."

"Certainly you may see the log if you so wish, Mr Flood," said Sir James.

"Thank you, your worship. I have asked for it twenty times a day, but unfortunately have not been able to procure it."

Pisani sprang to his feet. "Your worship, the log is here in court and has always been accessible to the Queen's Proctor."

"Then I cannot see what objection there could have been to its production, Mr Flood," Sir James admonished, obviously suspecting the advocate of some courtroom trickery. "Please avail yourself of it. In the meantime, Mr Deveau will resume the stand, remembering that he is still on oath."

While Flood walked over to Pisani's table and picked up the *Dei Gratia*'s log-book, Oliver crossed the floor and entered the witness box.

Flood approached the stand, and handed Oliver the open book.

"Would you confirm whether this is the log of the *Dei Gratia* and in whose hand it is written?" the Queen's Proctor requested.

Oliver glanced down, then faced the Bench. "The book now produced is my ship's log, and is in my handwriting up to the fifth of December, the day I left the ship."

"Would you now read out the position of the *Dei Gratia* for both the twenty-fourth and twenty-fifth of November?"

Oliver looked down at the open page. "On the twenty-fourth our latitude was forty-one degrees, forty-nine; longtitude, fifty degrees, fifty-six. For the twenty-fifth of November, latitude was forty-one degrees, fifty two; longtitude, forty-six degrees, fifty-three."

"Thank you, Mr Deveau," said Flood, recovering the book. "You may stand down." Looking puzzled, Oliver stepped down from the box and headed back to his seat.

Solly Flood meanwhile approached the

Bench and addressed Sir James in a voice intended to carry to the back of the room. "With your indulgence, your worship, I would now seek your permission to meet in the privacy of your chambers, in order to discuss certain new and alarming matters relating to this case."

"Is this necessary, Mr Flood?" Sir James demanded.

"Respectfully, yes, in my opinion, your worship."

Sir James's expression remained stern. "I trust that my opinion will concur with yours, Mr Flood. Mr Pisani?"

Their advocate stood. "Yes, your worship?"

"I would be obliged if you would accompany us."

The instant the door closed behind the three men, the courtroom burst into a hubbub of simultaneous conversations, with spectators huddling into various groups to discuss this latest twist of events. Morehouse leant across his seat, his face suddenly drawn and anxious. "What the hell's he up to?" he demanded, at once realizing it was the sword. Aware of Wright and the others watching them, Callaghan shrugged as though ignorant of what was happening, and facing around towards Colleen, whose worried expression betrayed her fears. The minutes slowly ticked by, then the door suddenly opened, and Mr Baumgartner called out, "All rise."

The three men re-emerged. Sir James Cochrane with a grave face; Flood looking exultant; and Pisani obviously very angry. Callaghan saw that the lawyer was avoiding looking towards them, and reaching his table, he turned and faced the Bench.

Sir James remained standing, and announced, "Certain evidence has been brought to my notice respecting this vessel which make further investigations imperative. These will commence Monday. This court is therefore suspended to await the results of these findings. All parties to the claim for salvage are hereby ordered to remain in Gibraltar and are not, under any circumstances, to leave this port." Sir James banged his gavel down hard. "This court is adjourned until further notice."

The courtroom erupted into a babel of voices as soon as Sir James had exited. Solly Flood turned to regard the *Dei Gratia*'s crew in triumph, hands on hips, and a gloating smile on his face.

David stepped straight over the barrier, and made for Pisani, followed by Callaghan, Oliver and the rest of the crew.

"What happened in there?" David demanded.

"You mean apart from the inconsequential matter of the sword found under Captain Briggs's bed?" Pisani answered with glaring sarcasm. "Plus the coincidence of it being bloodstained, and the apparent discovery of fresh bloodstains on the floor and walls of the first mate's cabin, all of which are to be analysed by Doctor Patron, Gibraltar's leading physician."

He paused in an attempt to control his temper. "There are also unweathered scrape marks on the *Celeste*'s bows, but these need not give you any concern, despite the fact that Mr Austin, the Admiralty's surveyor, regards them as the

461

type of damage consistent with slicing a small boat in two. And there is also concern over a deep axe-cut in the rail, which also appears to be recent."

Hitching up his gown, Pisani busied himself with his briefcase "With Christmas approaching, I won't spoil it by going any further, Captain Morehouse, but should you wish me to continue representing you, I suggest you call to see me as soon as the celebrations are over. If I'm to prevent you — and your crew — from being indicted for murder, then the sooner the better we start preparing for the Inquiry's resumption."

Picking up his case, Pisani began to leave. "I would wish you all a Merry Christmas, but perhaps this is not exactly the opportune moment."

* * *

The dark clouds over the Rock seeming to typify their gloom, Callaghan paused outside the court-house with David and Oliver, watching the crew thread their way down the narrow Governor's Lane as they headed back to the harbour. He searched for Colleen, but could see no sign of her.

"The way things are going, we'll soon be facing the rope," David exclaimed despairingly. "If only I knew Desiah was safe, I could explain what really took place. What do you think's happened to her?" He turned to Callaghan, his voice low and desperate. "What are the police doing to find her — "

Jostled from behind, David stumbled, then recovering his balance, he held out a crumpled piece of paper. "Someone pushed this in my hand!"

Callaghan took the note, and aware of Oliver looking over his shoulder, read the pencilled message:

Leave on *Dei Gratia* without me soon as ship's orders received. Arrive Genoa 15th January.

"Martens!" Oliver snarled, turning and scanning the sea of heads around them. Quickly handing the note back to David, Callaghan leapt on to the court-house steps, and immediately saw a man shrouded in a black robe forcing a path through the crowd.

"Over there!" Oliver yelled, running after the figure.

"No!" Callaghan shouted. The last thing he wanted was for the German to be caught. But Oliver was already closing on his quarry. Callaghan went after him. Reaching him just as Oliver was stretching to grab the man, Callaghan slammed into the first mate, and all three fell to the ground. Before Callaghan could stop him, Oliver pulled back the man's hood, revealing the frightened face of a dark-skinned Moor.

"Where is he?" Deveau grabbed the man by the throat. "Tell me, or by hell I'll make you talk."

As the Moor clawed at his neck, trying to tear the hand away, his eyes rolling in fear, Callaghan prised Oliver's fingers loose.

"Where is he?" Oliver demanded again. "The man who gave you the message?"

"Not know," the Moor stammered. "He paid money, said give paper, then run fast."

Callaghan pulled Oliver to his feet as

the Moor scuttled into the watching crowd.

"You tried to stop me," Oliver accused.

"Don't be crazy," Callaghan half-laughed. "I was after him too, but I tripped. Come on, let's get back to David."

David was leaning against the court-house wall, the note still in his hand. "The fifteenth is three weeks away," he commented. "Yet Genoa's no more than a ten-day journey, fourteen at the most. What's Martens up to?"

"More to the point, how will Flood react after we've left?" said Callaghan. "Will he wire Genoa and have the police waiting?"

David regarded him intently. "You're not suggesting we agree?"

"We've no choice," Callaghan stated. "Not with the threat still hanging over Desiah and the children."

"But the judge just warned us not to leave!"

"We've no choice," Callaghan repeated. "I've been expecting Sweeny to do something for days, but I didn't anticipate this."

"I've got a suggestion," Oliver intervened. "Michael, John, Gus, Johnny and myself have already given evidence. What if we go, taking Orr, Higgins and Willie with us, leaving you here to explain to the court?"

"Explain!" David protested. "Explain what, for hell's sake?"

"Anything. Just as long as it keeps Flood off our backs."

"For example."

"I don't know," said Oliver. "What about saying you were forced to instruct us to sail to Genoa, because you would have been bankrupted if the cargo remained tied up here any longer?"

"That might work, David," Callaghan agreed. "Especially if you tell them we'll return as soon as the cargo's been unloaded."

"We?" queried Morehouse, expectantly.

"OK. Oliver and the others."

"And how will I explain your absence when they get back?"

"Tell them I fell overboard or something," replied Callaghan, at the same time realizing that if he was successful in capturing Sweeny, it would

466

invalidate any further proceedings.

David was silent, wrestling the conflict in his mind. "All right," he finally conceded. "But Flood's not going to like it. Nor the judge. This is a British court of law we're flouting."

"Damn Solly Flood!" said Callaghan, feeling his Yankee spirit rebelling. "And damn the British!"

★ ★ ★

Born and bred in Gibraltar, Walter Simms had worked in the offices of Turner & Co (Gibraltar) Limited, Shipping Agents, at 67 Irish Town, from the age of fifteen, nigh on forty years now. Since the advent of the telegraph he'd seen Gibraltar become a busy calling-in port for commercial vessels plying the Atlantic and Mediterranean sea-routes, a pick-up for new shipping-orders negotiated after their last port of call. Much of Turner & Co's work came from acting as intermediaries for the shipping-agents of other countries, and Walter Simm's job was to ensure the necessary paperwork was always ready for the masters of vessels

467

waiting in the harbour.

Walter Simms loved his work. It put him in touch with almost every port in the western hemisphere, and many in the east as well, and gave him the feeling of travelling the world, despite hardly ever leaving the Rock.

Today, however, was not enjoyable. The European partner of the firm of Meissner Ackermann & Co of Hamburg and New York, was making Simms uneasy, and he was impatient for the meeting to be over. It wasn't so much the man's disquieting appearance — mesmeric slate-blue eyes, abnormally fair skin and hair — it was the way he was looking straight through Simms, sending a coldness right down to the base of his spine, and making him shiver.

"Right, Herr Meissner," said Mr Simms, in a forced, businesslike manner, averting his gaze from that of the albinotic German. "Your papers are in order. First, which is the port of destination?"

"Genoa," came the whispered reply.

Even the voice sounded sinister, thought Simms, hurrying on. "The consignees

468

are presumably yourselves, Meissner Ackermann?"

"Correct."

"Negotiated price? In British money, if you know it?"

"Seven shillings and threepence a barrel."

"Is the cargo to be dispatched to Hamburg, or remain bonded in Genoa?"

"Bonded."

"The name of the vessel?"

"It was the *Dei Gratia*." Mr Simms looked up sharply. The news of Sir James Cochrane's restriction on this vessel was already common knowledge throughout Gibraltar.

Herr Meissner continued, "We cannot wait for the cargo to be held up here, and are arranging to have it transferred to another vessel."

"And the name of the new vessel?" Walter Simms asked.

"It is not yet decided. We are awaiting tenders."

"In that case," Mr Simms volunteered, "I'll leave it blank."

"When will the new papers be ready?" Herr Meissner asked.

Walter Simms calculated. Tomorrow was Sunday. And Herr Meissner had still not found an alternative vessel. "Monday morning?"

"No later?" Although the German intoned the words, Walter Simms got the distinct feeling he'd been given an ultimatum.

"Certainly not," he promised. "Monday, first thing."

"I will collect them myself."

"Certainly, Herr Meissner. I will ensure they are ready." Even if I have to get here early, Walter Simms thought to himself.

★ ★ ★

Horatio Jones Sprague stood in the window of the American Consulate, looking up at the blanket of mist hanging over the top of the Rock. On days like this, Gibraltar felt like a prison, and he was always glad when the fog lifted and he could see the sky above.

He turned back to Callaghan in the room. "Things are looking black for you, my friend. If only you'd tell them your true identity, then Sir James might believe

470

in your innocence and rule in your favour, especially if Police Commissioner Smith telegraphed him, confirming everything?"

Knowing he would soon be gone, Callaghan felt dishonest keeping up the pretence with Sprague, but he had no alternative. The United States Consul could not be told of their plan. Should he want to help, his diplomatic position made it impossible. "I dare not, sir. Having now seen what kind of man Solly Flood is, I doubt he would keep it confidential."

"He would have no choice, not if Sir James ordered him."

"That's assuming Sir James believed us, sir, and there's no guarantee he would. Besides, Flood seems to have a natural flair for leaking information."

Sprague sat down. "So what do you intend?"

"Pisani has agreed to continue representing us. We still hope to win."

"I don't know if that's wise," the consul remarked. "He looked very angry leaving court. It's no good having an advocate who's no longer on your side."

"I'll discuss it with David and Oliver."

Callaghan paused. "Your message referred to a telegraph?"

Sprague handed him a printed cable. "From Mr Spencer in Genoa. It arrived while we were in court."

Callaghan looked down at the paper in his hand.

Genoa, 21 December 1872
American Consul, Gibraltar
Rechecked. Sweeny Cottone now here.
O M Spencer, Consul

"Genoa," he commented. "I wish he'd make up his mind. I'd also like to know who this Cottone is. This isn't the first time his name's cropped up."

"I'm afraid I have no inkling," Sprague replied. "Would you like me to wire Mr Monti, our Consul in Palermo, and ask him for details?"

Callaghan thought swiftly. "Yes, sir. That would be appreciated. Especially if he could prepare a dossier on the man, preferably two, sending one to Gibraltar, and the other to Mr Spencer in Genoa."

"Genoa?" Sprague queried. "Is that necessary?"

"Just in case, sir. Call me a supreme optimist, but I think we'll be in Genoa sooner than everyone thinks."

★ ★ ★

Father Shaw was facing a terrible dilemma and it was tearing his very soul apart. Through the fine-meshed grille, in a whispered tone that was making him shiver, a penitent was confessing his appalling sins, and would soon be asking for absolution.

This would be his moment of decision, when the transgressor asked to be made clean in the sight of God, and the dilemma would have to be resolved.

Father Shaw had served as a priest for nearly forty years, and in that time had heard many thousands of confessions, but never anything like this. Never before had his heart pounded so badly, nor had he ever been so sickened.

Nothing in his sheltered life had prepared him to deal with such evil.

The only child of devout Catholic parents, his vocation had been decided for him at birth. Having accepted, early

473

in his childhood, that his life would be spent in the service of God, Father Shaw had been content — especially during these last seven years in Gibraltar at The Sacred Heart of Jesus, where the cloistered atmosphere of both the cathedral and town had so suited his nature — to remain a humble priest, caring for the poor, the sick and the dying, also hearing the confessions of the penitent, and granting absolution according to the power vested in him by the Church.

The power vested, this was the root of the terrible burden now thrust upon him. In his agony of mind and spirit Father Shaw could feel his chest — aggravated by his recent poor health and diagnosed by his physician as a weak heart — rapidly tightening with the stress of his responsibility, and breathing was becoming more difficult by the second.

Scriptural authority for his power to absolve sins, granted by the risen Christ to His Apostles, and thus to their successors, was in the Gospel of Saint John, Chapter 20, verse 23: 'Whose soever sins ye remit, they are remitted unto them'.

Not that the penitent was absolved from temporal punishment for his actions. For was not King David told that although 'the Lord has caused thy sin to pass away' — in David's case, adultery and murder — he would nevertheless have to pay for his crime here on earth, because 'the son that is born to thee shall surely die'.

Nevertheless, priestly authority to absolve sins was efficacious for the life to come, so that in Heaven, deeds which on earth were scarlet, would be 'as white as snow'.

But this power, bestowed by the risen Saviour to His Apostles, did not stop there, for He had gone on to tell them: 'Whose soever sins ye retain, they are retained'. Consequently, through his priestly line of succession, Father Shaw not only had the power to grant God's absolution, *he also had the power to refuse it!*

It was an awesome responsibility.

It all rested on whether he believed that the whispered voice on the other side of the grille belonged to a true penitent, confessing under the burden of supernatural sorrow for his wrongdoings.

And Father Shaw did not believe it. Hence his anguish.

The sacrament had begun in the normal way with the unknown voice requesting: 'Pray, Father, bless me, for I have sinned'; and Father Shaw repeating the prescribed blessing: 'The Lord be in thy heart and on thy lips, that thou mayest truly and humbly confess thy sins, in the name of the Father, and of the Son, and of the Holy Ghost'.

This had been followed, to Father Shaw's increasing horror, by an account of two murders in New York, and the terrible way they had been perpetrated. He had clutched his stole, and begun praying with all fervour: 'Almighty God, if it be possible, let this cup pass from me', echoing the words of Christ at the Garden of Gethsemane, and feeling such agony of soul that the sweat ran down his forehead. He had raised his hand to wipe the beads off, almost expecting them to show blood, as had happened to the Blessed Son when He begged the same prayer of His Father, and God had sent down an angel from Heaven

476

to strengthen Him. But no similar angel of mercy had entered the confessional, and Father Shaw was left to decide in his own strength.

And now — Father Shaw almost collapsed with revulsion — the whispered voice was confessing to the terrible murder of Captain Briggs of the *Mary Celeste*, the brigantine recently brought into Gibraltar by the crew of the *Dei Gratia*, all of whom were now under suspicion of a crime which they obviously had not committed.

O God, Father Shaw begged, as his heart pounded even faster, *please grant me Thy strength and Thy insight*. Fighting to control his breathing, he tried to examine the dilemma doctrinally. Contrition fell into two categories: perfect contrition which came from the penitent's genuine love of God; and imperfect contrition, which sprang from lower motives, mainly the fear of eternal damnation. The latter, though not sufficient in itself to effect reconciliation with God, nevertheless became sacramentally efficacious by the priestly pronouncement of absolution.

But the man on the other side of the grille was seeking to create a third category: justified contrition — claiming his actions had been necessary to rid Italy of King Victor Emmanuel, and Germany of Count Bismarck, thus restoring the Holy Church back into the purposes of God. Father Shaw was horrified by the man's reasoning. Even Judas Iscariot, the evil 'son of perdition', had shown remorse for betraying the Son of God, hurling his tainted thirty pieces of silver down on to the floor of the temple, and then hanging himself.

But this man was evidencing no sign of contrition — either perfect or imperfect — only cataloguing his actions.

The first and second mates . . .

Father Shaw shielded his face in horror.

Three German seamen . . . a woman . . . and her child.

The band around Father Shaw's chest tightened, and he was finding it difficult to breathe. He wanted to tell the penitent that he was no longer able to hear confession, that the question of absolution would have to be referred to

478

the bishop, but the pain was so acute he was unable to utter a sound.

The steward forced to the ship's rail at the point of a sword, then made to jump in the ocean, and left to drown.

With this, the recited list of sins was ended, and the voice whispered through the grille: "For these and all my other sins which I cannot now remember, I ask pardon of God, and penance and absolution of you, my ghostly Father."

Pardon! Father Shaw rebelled at the thought. The man was nothing more than a cold-blooded, calculating killer, and did not merit pardon. Not from the bishop, nor even Holy Father himself.

What was more, even in his pain, Father Shaw had discerned the omissions in the man's plea. No admission of being 'heartily sorry', no promise to 'purpose amendment in the future', nor was the request for pardon made 'humbly'. Father Shaw thought of the nine innocent men who might yet be indicted for murder. As a priest he was under the 'seal of confession' never to break his vow of silence, not even on pain of death. But was it possible that his decision not to grant absolution, might in some way negate his holy vow?

The fate of nine innocent men lay in his hands.

Father Shaw knelt to pray for God's guidance, and tried to spread his arms out, to adopt the position of Christ on the Cross. A sudden, violent flash of pain shot across his heart. He sank back on his heels in the corner of the confessional, clawing at the constricting band encircling his chest, squeezing the breath from his lungs.

The curtain opened, revealed a man dressed completely in black. His hair was so fair it was almost white. He knelt down, his pale-blue eyes staring into Father Shaw's with a frightening, hypnotic intensity, and the priest instantly realized he had been listening, not to a cold-blooded killer, but to a psychopath . . . a madman, who even now was committing further profanity.

Father Shaw tried desperately to resist, but his limpless hand was lifted to the man's own breast, and then guided to make the sign of the Cross, while the man intoned the words which Father

Shaw had determined to refuse: "*Deindi ego te absolvo a peccatis tuis, in nomine patris, et filii, et spiritus sancti. Amen.*"

Father Shaw opened his mouth to condemn the act. The man's hand loomed down over his face, choking the words, closing his nostrils tight between thumb and first finger.

And a black veil descended before Father Shaw's eyes.

★ ★ ★

They were standing on the hotel balcony watching the street below rapidly empty of people as the shops closed, and the wares on display in the market-place were packed up on assorted mules and carts. The Spanish vendors had long since left, to return across the border before the evening gun fired at half past five, and Gibraltar's fortified gates closed for the night. A sudden quietness descended over the previously bustling town, and a chill breeze blew in from the harbour. Colleen shivered and went back inside, followed by Callaghan who closed the casement windows. Returning to her chair by the fire, Colleen held her hands to the warming flames. "Are you sure Flood won't place a guard on the *Dei Gratia?*" she asked.

"He hasn't so far," said Callaghan, sitting in the chair facing her. "His mind is so taken up with bringing us to trial that the thought of our leaving doesn't seem to have occurred to him. Though it didn't occur to me either. Only Sweeny could have come up with it. I was expecting him to do it legally, but I should have realized that acting within the law is not his way."

"There's going to be a great furore when they realize you've sailed. What if the Italian police are waiting for you in Genoa?"

"I'll face that if and when it happens," replied Callaghan. "At the moment I'm more concerned Sprague may cancel his request to the Palermo Consul for the dossier on Sweeny's travelling companion, or that Spencer in Genoa will refuse to give it to me."

Colleen had been pondering this same possibility. "Why not write Sprague a letter, telling him that when David

482

ordered the *Dei Gratia* to sail, you decided to take advantage of the opportunity to get to Genoa, but that for obvious reasons you were unable to let him know beforehand? I'll have it delivered to him the morning after you sail, once I'm certain you've got safely away." She continued, "As for Cottone, he's obviously some leading Sicilian revolutionary, it's the only explanation that fits. But just in case Sprague does change his mind, I'll make enquiries when I get to Genoa."

Callaghan nodded. "The letter's a good idea. But I'd rather you stay close to the Hotel de la Ville. It's far enough from the de Genes for you not to bump into Sweeny by accident."

"If that's what you'd prefer," Colleen agreed, without argument, surprising Callaghan. Before he could question it, she commented, "So I was wrong about Palermo, after all?"

"Not really," Callaghan replied. "It's odds on Sweeny and Cottone will return there after selling the diamonds. It still makes good sense as an arsenal, and a centre from which to distribute the arms."

"But why has he added ten days to your sailing time?"

"Maybe he needs extra time to organize the selling arrangements, and prefers leaving the diamonds safe in the *Dei Gratia*'s hold until everything's been arranged," Callaghan speculated.

Colleen looked into the fire. "It's Christmas Day in four days' time," she said quietly. "You'll probably be at sea, and I'll either be in a strange hotel in Genoa, or on my way there by train."

"There'll be other Christmases," Callaghan promised. "We've a lifetime of them ahead of us."

"Provided nothing goes wrong," she said, seriously.

"Trust me, nothing will."

27

Monday, 23 December 1872

SHORTLY before midnight on Monday, 23 December 1872, with First Mate Oliver Deveau at the helm, the *Dei Gratia* slipped her moorings and sailed silently out of Gibraltar harbour. The moon was hidden behind dark clouds, and her departure was unnoticed. Once safely out into the bay, Deveau ordered full sails to be raised. A short while later they had rounded Europa Point, and were heading east towards Genoa, 854 nautical miles away.

Genoa

In Genoa, the moon was hovering above the Hotel de Genes out of a cloudless, starry, midnight-blue sky. Wearing a maroon smoking-jacket, and secure in the knowledge that Bruno was sitting guard outside his door, Salvatore Cottone was standing by the window, looking down at the deserted Piazza Carlo Felice, smoking a long corona, and thinking about Sweeny and his diamonds.

The attorney from New York did not appeal to Don Cottone. From the first moment of their meeting, he had taken a personal dislike to the man. Uncouth both in mannerisms and speech, Sweeny grated on his sensibilities. Salvatore Cottone's preference was for people of refinement, a trait inherited from his distant Norman ancestors. Thirty-eight years ago, when he was only twelve, this quality had been recognized by his father's employer, the Baron Inglese. As a consequence, the Baron had made himself responsible for the young Salvatore's education, teaching him to read and write, then paying for him to attend college, and finally encouraging him to enter a Dominican seminary to train for the priesthood.

Life was strange, Don Cottone reflected. Had it not been for the death of his father curtailing his studies, followed seven years later by his uncle's demise — a traumatic event which had dictated the course of his life — he would today have been a priest. And probably content to be one.

His thoughts returned to Sweeny. Don Cottone had to admit that his plan was brilliant, offering untold rewards. There was no denying his razor-sharp intelligence, nor his talent for devising an almost limitless variety of subsidiary schemes.

Also to be considered was his meeting with Father-General Beckx, which Sweeny was somewhat prone to boast about — another unpleasant trait — but which should, nevertheless, guarantee the beginning of Victor Emmanuel's end. This would lead to his eventual downfall, and Sicily would be returned to the Sicilians, as it should be: a different people, a different language, a different culture, and a different way of life.

Salvatore Cottone moved away from the window and sat in a chair by the still flickering fire.

Consequently, he'd kept his distaste for Sweeny well hidden behind an impenetrable mask. Not once during their negotiations had he allowed the American to suspect how near he was to being separated from his diamonds, and the proceeds utilized to effectuate the plan without him.

But the die was now cast. Back in Palermo, handshakes had been exchanged. And the hand of Don Salvatore Cottone was more binding than an impressed seal. Above all else, it was a matter of family honour. As head of the family he would never disgrace that honour. Nor was he a man who would ever break his sacred word.

* * *

With Sweeny having taken the entire floor, Cottone's son-in-law, Carlo Maranzano, was lying in bed in his room further down the corridor. The sheets were still warm from the supple body of the young Genoese woman, girl — she could not have been more than sixteen — smuggled up the backstairs by Guido, one of his two bodyguards.

His burning physical needs having been sated, Maranzano was staring up at the ceiling, thinking of how the situation would be dealt with if he, not Cottone, was in control. Frustrated by his father-in-law's constant state of self-discipline — instilled in him by his five years in the Dominican seminary — and his long, silent, brooding analysis before deciding on any course of action, Maranzano wanted to take advantage of the people's simmering mood of rebellion, and get them out on the streets again, like six years ago. Admittedly, many had died when Emmanuel sent in the gunboats and shelled the capital. But if Cottone had persevered, instead of calculating the cost, calling a strategic halt in order to revert back to guerilla warfare, they would have won eventually, and Sicily would not now be ruled by a Piedmontese outsider.

As for the man from New York, he was also a foreigner, and as such the code of family honour did not apply. He should be disposed of, and the proceeds of his diamonds used solely to liberate Sicily. None of it should be diverted to any other cause. If only he was in control, Maranzano brooded, then not a single franc would go to mainland Italy, the Church, the Pope, or Father-General Beckx and his Jesuits.

Let them go their own separate ways.
And leave Sicily to Sicilians.

Book Four

28

Wednesday, 15 January 1873

AS Genoa drew nearer across the water, a shaft of sunlight broke through the early morning clouds, framing the port like a painting. Built into an amphitheatre of hills encircling the wide bay, the city was a jumble of red, green and earth-brown rooflines, and towering white church domes, and rounded cupolas. Villas with hanging gardens and wooded terraces, dotted the slopes above, and higher still, silhouetted against the skyline, stood Genoa's ancient fortress walls, interspaced by tall grey watchtowers.

Outside the harbour were three steamships riding at anchor. Beyond them, on the other side of the protecting mole, the inner port was full of sailing vessels, tied up alongside quays, loading or unloading cargoes.

A small vessel appeared from behind the port-light at the end of the mole, and headed towards them. "The pratique boat!" Oliver shouted. "Lower sails!"

Having satisfied the officials of their clean bill of health, the *Dei Gratia* was guided to an empty berth, and finally tied up at journey's end, 4,060 nautical miles from New York.

There was no one waiting for them. Nevertheless, not knowing what action Gibraltar had instigated in response to their flight, Oliver was anxious to register with the port authorities prior to officialdom descending upon them. And with unloading certain not to start until tomorrow at the earliest, Callaghan was impatient to see Colleen, before becoming a tail to the last barrel of diamonds.

Threading their way through the crowded dockside, the two parted company, and twenty minutes later, Callaghan was paying-off his cab at the Hotel de la Ville.

Apart from a few loitering guests, the black-marble-floored foyer was quiet as Callaghan approached the desk. The clerk, an immaculately dressed young man, looked up, and gave a slight frown at his rough appearance.

"May I help you, *signor*?" he queried in an indifferent tone.

"You have a Mrs Callaghan registered?"

"Yes, *signor*." Then glancing at the key-board, he added, "But I am very sorry, *signor*, Mrs Callaghan does not appear to be in."

Callaghan was momentarily puzzled. Colleen wouldn't have gone to the port after they'd agreed to meet at the hotel. Obviously she hadn't expected him this early.

"Did she leave a message?"

The clerk turned to the pigeon-rack. "No, *signor*."

"In that case, I'll wait in the lounge."

Looking dubiously at Callaghan's sea-stained clothes, the man replied with obvious reluctance. "Very good, *signor*. When Mrs Callaghan returns, whom shall I say is waiting?"

"Her husband."

Entering the albescent-marble-floored lounge, with its gold velvet chairs and heavy chandeliers, Callaghan sat in the corner facing the foyer.

Twelve o'clock, twelve-thirty, one o'clock — an ornate mantelpiece clock struck every half-hour. By now the lounge was busy with guests coming to and from luncheon, looking askance at the weathered sailor in the corner. By one-thirty, Callaghan had had enough. He returned to the desk. "Does my wife usually stay out the whole day?"

"I am afraid I cannot say, *signor*."

Callaghan hesitated, beginning to feel uneasy. Colleen had known that the *Gratia* was intending to dock early, and this wasn't like her. "Do you exchange American dollars?" he asked, deciding to give her just a bit more time.

"Of course, *signor*."

"Here's ten. Would you order me some coffee and sandwiches: veal, chicken, whatever you've got."

By six o'clock, darkness had descended outside and Callaghan was becoming more restive by the minute. The lounge was again filling with guests, now elegantly dressed for dinner, and sipping their aperitifs as they discussed the menu.

At seven-thirty, Callaghan returned to the reception desk where there was a new clerk on duty. Requesting a pen and paper, he quickly wrote Colleen a note, asking her to remain in the hotel until he returned. Then he went outside and instructed a waiting cab to take him to the Piazza Carlo Felice, where Sweeny was staying at the Hotel de Genes. There was no reason to suspect that Colleen's absence was anything to do with Sweeny, Callaghan told himself. Even so, there was nothing more he could do tonight except keep watch on the hotel and make sure the elusive scoundrel didn't slip away just as the net was closing in on him.

A hundred yards alongside the harbour, with the reflections of cabin-lights and mooring-lamps glistening on the still waters, the carriage turned left into a city of contrasts. Though alive with modern-day traffic of cabs and coaches, the ancient cobblestoned streets were dominated by tall, ancient buildings, and vast mediaeval palazzos with great stone balconies tiered one above the other. Many of the side alleys were so dark and narrow that only sedan-chairs, preceded by lantern-bearers, were able to enter.

The cab stopped in a large busy square and Callaghan descended, paying the one-franc fare. Immediately recognizing the large edifice in the far right corner, with its colonnaded entrance crowded with men and women in evening clothes, as the Teatro Carlo Felice opera house, this placed the Hotel de Genes as the well-lit building tucked into the opposite corner.

Callaghan hesitated, wondering whether to go inside. His two-month beard and seaman's clothing should make him unrecognizable. Then, deciding it was too risky, he crossed the piazza, and hid in a dark recess between two buildings from where he could watch the hotel entrance.

Four hours later, a clock struck midnight and Callaghan had seen no sign of Sweeny or Martens. There had been a brief shower and the damp cobblestones were reflecting the light of the half moon.

By two o'clock, the hotel was mostly in darkness, and Callaghan was feeling the strain of his long day. When the one remaining cabbie suddenly jigged his reins and began moving off, he ran after the coach. "Hotel de la Ville."

The same clerk was on duty, and Callaghan's heart skipped a beat when he saw his note was still in the pigeon-rack. Nevertheless he asked, "Has Mrs Callaghan returned?"

The man glanced at the key-board. "No, *signor.*"

The lounge was empty and in darkness. Settling into the same chair as earlier, Callaghan waited for day with a growing conviction that something had gone terribly wrong.

By nine, the room was filling with guests, but there was still no sign of Colleen. Callaghan hurried to the cab rank, knowing there were only two places she could have left a message — the port, or the US Consulate on the other side of the city.

"*Dove, signor?*"

"Porto Franco."

As Callaghan approached the *Dei Gratia*, he saw that unloading had already started. Pulled by a horse-operated hoist, a heavy net of barrels was being lifted out of the hold, and lowered on to an almost full cart, where two men were waiting to receive it. An empty cart, with two more wagoners, was standing-by for the next load.

Oliver was on the dockside and seemed to be arguing with a tall, slim man in his late thirties, wearing a long dark overcoat and black top hat. As Callaghan drew nearer, he heard the stranger's clipped English accent above the surrounding noise. "I repeat, Mr Deveau, that by leaving Gibraltar in direct contravention of Sir James's restrictions, both you and Captain Morehouse have violated the court's authority."

"We had no choice," Oliver growled in reply. "We had to get the cargo to Genoa on time."

"On time! But, Mr Deveau, you are ten days' overdue!"

"The vessel sprang a leak," Oliver lied. "We had to call in at Palma for repairs."

"You *are* having an adventurous voyage!" The Englishman's civil tone was steeped in sarcasm. "Be that as it may, the Inquiry has been suspended until your return. Unless, that is, the Court tires of waiting, and Sir James announces his verdict without you. In which case, your flaunting of his authority will most certainly be taken into consideration, and you and Captain Morehouse could find yourselves facing grave charges. Extremely grave charges, Mr Deveau, I trust I am making myself clear."

"Very," said Oliver. "As it happens, I intend getting back as soon as we finish unloading. In fact, I've engaged extra wagons to hurry things up."

"The sooner you go the better, Mr Deveau. I'm only sorry the Italian law does not empower me to send you back under escort. And if you have any regard for your captain, you'll return in shorter time than it took you to get here. In the meantime, I will telegraph Gibraltar to say you'll be there before the end of the month, and trust that this will prevent them proceeding without you. I bid you good day, Mr Deveau."

Turning, the man marched away stiff-backed, with the walk of an ex-military officer.

Callaghan crossed to Oliver's side. "I take it that was the British Consul?"

"Yes. Montague Yeats bloody hyphenated Brown. But forget about him. What about you? You're looking drawn."

Callaghan asked about a message from Colleen, to which Oliver replied in the negative, suggesting, "Have you tried the consulate?"

"That was my next call. But it looks as though unloading's well under way?"

"Managed to get started yesterday," Oliver confirmed, "I was expecting you back." He indicated the waiting cart. "You're only just in time. That'll be the last."

Colleen, Callaghan's mind raced. What the hell do I do now . . .

Oliver cut across his thoughts. "Here's someone else heading towards us."

Callaghan turned. Forcing his way along the quayside, and very obviously in a hurry, the man was middle-aged, medium height, tubby, with a round, tanned face and completely bald, without even hair on the sides of his head. He was wearing a waistcoated light-grey suit, and carried a rounded leather dispatch case.

"Are either of you with the brigantine *Dei Gratia*?" His accent was American,

502

probably New England.

"I'm her first mate, and acting master," Oliver replied. "The name's Deveau."

The man held out his hand. "Pleased to meet you, Deveau. I've read all about you in a detailed report from Mr Sprague. My name's Spencer. I'm the American Consul in Genoa. Sorry to hear about your troubles. You should be commended for bringing the *Celeste* into port, not made to face an Inquiry. But that's typical of the British. I'm looking for a Michael Callaghan of the New York Police . . . "

"I'm Callaghan, sir."

Quickly grabbing hold of Callaghan's arm, Consul Spencer pulled him aside. "Is there somewhere we can talk? It's mighty urgent!"

Oliver had overheard. "Use David's cabin, Michael."

"Thanks, Oliver. Let me know when the last wagon's full."

"Will do," Oliver promised.

Entering the cabin, Spencer dropped into one of the armchairs. "Close the door," he instructed, placing his case on the floor.

Callaghan slammed it and asked, "Is it my wife, sir?" "You've just answered my question, Callaghan." The American spoke hurriedly. "I thought the same surname was too much of a coincidence. I'm afraid I've got bad news."

Callaghan's heart plummeted. "She's not . . . ?" He left the rest unspoken.

"No, she's not," Spencer blurted. "Sweeny's got her. He's holding her in return for information. He's given me thirty-six hours to reply, and a warning not to contact the police. It arrived at the Consulate two hours ago, only moments after I'd read in the newspaper that the *Dei Gratia* arrived yesterday. Knowing about you and your mission from Mr Sprague's letter, and seeing that Sweeny's hostage had the same surname, I came straight here instead of waiting for you to come to me." Extracting a handkerchief from his pocket, the consul dabbed his forehead, then pulled out his watch. "There's already less than thirty-four hours left, Callaghan."

His bewildered mind was racing with all manner of questions, but Callaghan pushed them all to one side.

"What information is Sweeny demanding, sir?"

"Some details from Mr Sprague. Unspecified until I agree to comply."

Sprague! It was obviously to do with the *Celeste*. But what the hell could Sprague tell Sweeny that he hadn't already been told some fourteen days ago by Martens, when the killer arrived in Genoa?"

"Then what?" Callaghan queried.

"I telegraph Sprague with the details. Hand over the reply. And your wife will then be released. If I refuse, she won't be seen again."

"Not seen again!" Callaghan erupted. "Sweeny wouldn't dare . . . "

"No, but Cottone would!"

Callaghan stared at the consul. "Cottone? He's not that ruthless? Surely?"

"And more!"

"A revolutionary?"

Spencer looked puzzled. "Cottone a revolutionary? What gave you that idea?"

"You mean he's not?"

"Anything but."

"Then what is he?" "Mafia."

It was Callaghan now who looked mystified. "Mafia?" he repeated. "Who or what the hell are they?"

"Like no other organization you've ever heard of before," Spencer replied, pushing a finger under his stiff collar as though attempting to loosen it. "It's only since Victor Emmanuel took over Sicily that the world outside has got to hear of them. A number of investigative articles have recently appeared in leading Italian newspapers, but for the most part their activities are still shrouded in secrecy. However, I once served a year in our Palermo Consulate, so I know just how ruthless they can be. Hardly a day went by without someone being killed, and the body left on the street as a warning, with no one — not even the police — daring to remove it until they said so."

Callaghan dropped down hard into the opposite chair. "And that's who this Cottone is? Some sort of leading Mafia figure?"

"Somewhat more than that," said Spencer, loosening his collar for the second time. "It's rumoured he's the *capomafia* — the supreme boss — of the whole caboodle, seemingly the first in Mafia history."

"History?" Callaghan repeated, his instinct picking up on the word, but his thoughts on Colleen, and how to deal with this unexpected development.

The consul nodded. "Yes. They've been around for centuries. In fact, to realize what we're up against, it would help you to know something about them?"

"I'd prefer discussing how to free my wife, sir."

"Did you fight in the war, Callaghan?"

"Almost two years."

"Then you must be aware of the golden rule: know your enemy. It not only applies to the science of warfare, but to every walk of life, especially when you're facing someone as powerful as Cottone, and an organization as ruthless as the Mafia."

Assuming his right to continue, Spencer leant forward as far as his stomach would allow. "They go back to the eleventh century, when the Normans took over the island and seized all the lands, forcing the people into serfdom. Some of the more partisan-minded Sicilians decided to resist — rather like Robin Hood — and

507

escaped with their families into the hills, from where they set up camps in what they termed *mafias* — it's derived from the Arabic *mafie*, who occupied the island before the Normans and means 'place of refuge'. After the Normans came the Spanish, but by now the various resistance groups — or *cosche*, their word for 'families' — had divided the island up between them, each controlling a particular area, with the father at the head, followed by his sons, then sons-in-law, cousins, nephews, and finally loyal friends. In order to exist, each group had to have the backing of the peasantry living in their part of the island, which they bought by sharing their booty with them. But in return, they demanded the people's silence — they call it *omerta*, it literally means 'being a man' — which under no circumstances permitted recourse to the legal authorities, or even the slightest co-operation with them. To give you some idea of the loyalty demanded — both then and now they have a proverb, which, if you'll forgive my pronunciation, goes something like this: *L'omu ch'e omu non rivela mai mancu si avi corpa di cortella,* which means: 'The man who is really a man reveals nothing, not even with a dagger through him'."

"Nice people," said Callaghan, dismissively. "But with respect, sir, although this is all very interesting, it doesn't help Colleen."

"Hear me out first, Callaghan," Spencer insisted. "As I said only a moment ago, to discover the enemy's weaknesses, one should first be apprised of all there is to know about them. Shall I continue?"

Callaghan hesitated, then abruptly nodded.

"Right. Where was I? Oh, yes. Over the years their control of Sicily — and the people's fear of them — has grown to such an extent that they now virtually rule the island. The owners of most of the estates have been forced to hand over the management to the various Dons — the name of respect by which the head of a 'family', or *cosca*, is known. Incidentally, the name Mafia is a collective title given to them by outsiders, which they themselves do not acknowledge. To them, every *cosca* is a separate 'family', each opposed to the other. The Don is the *capocosca,* which means 'head of the family'. What's more, in order to exercise greater control over his territory, it's quite common for a Mafia Don to have one son go in for the law, and another into the priesthood. In fact," the consul stressed, "as most Sicilians are devout Catholics, to have a priest as a son can be of great prestige, and in some families, when the Don dies, it's not unknown for the priest-son to leave the Church and succeed him."

"The damned Church again," Callaghan said. "Everywhere I go, it keeps cropping up."

Spencer looked slightly shocked. "This *is* Italy," he reminded. "Here the Church is — or at least, was — an integral part of the fabric. And old habits die hard."

"I didn't just mean Italy," Callaghan stated. "It started in New York, and has continued ever since."

"You sound very antagonistic towards it," the consul observed.

Callaghan shrugged. "Just making a comment. But as I said before, none of this helps Colleen. Especially as she's being held by some criminal organization, who probably don't care whether . . . "

"Strangely enough," Spencer cut across him, "they don't consider themselves criminals, rather as protectors of the peace. They have an extremely well-organized tiered system of control. Below each Don is a *consigliere*, an advisor; followed by the *caporegime*, the lieutenants; then the lower echelon, the *mandatari*, who carry out the instructions."

"More to the point, sir," Callaghan intruded, impatiently. "Are they capable of cold-blooded murder?"

Withdrawing a photograph from his case, Spencer handed it to Callaghan. It showed a moustachioed man standing on a barren hillside, with his foot planted on the chest of a male corpse in the pose of a hunter standing over a dead animal. He was wearing a woollen-lined jacket, and baggy trousers tucked into leather boots. Over his chest and shoulders were crossed bandoleers full of ammunition, and in the crook of his arms he was holding what looked like a sawn-off shot-gun.

"It's called a *lupara*," said Spencer. "It's a most fearful weapon, specially made to be hidden inside clothing. Sprays lead pellets and makes one hell of a mess. Take a look," he invited.

Callaghan looked at the corpse, riddled with bullet-holes, and surrounded by a pool of blood.

"Not a pretty sight," Spencer commented.

"I've seen worse," said Callaghan, handing the photograph back.

"That's the value they place on human life," the consul stated. "Murder's an everyday event to them. It means no more than swatting a fly. What's more, they have a practice of making the punishment fit the crime. A man has only to betray their secrets, and his body will be found with the tongue severed and eyeballs torn out. As for raping or seducing a female of the family, then . . . "

"OK, sir," Callaghan snapped. "You've made your point. So they're killers. At least with men. But what about women?"

"No . . . " Spencer hesitated. "I'm afraid they deal differently with women?"

"How different?"

Spencer loosened his collar. "Houses of ill-repute."

"Brothels!" Callaghan felt as though he'd been struck.

Spencer's expression was sombre. "It's one of their main sources of income. They have them right across the island. Palermo. Messina. Catania. All the major towns."

Callaghan sprang to his feet, knocking his chair over. "Then we've no choice but to agree. Provided Sweeny keeps to his side of the bargain?"

"Why shouldn't he?" Spencer asked.

"Sweeny! He's never kept his word yet. Why start now?"

"Surely, if he gets his information?"

"But what if Mr Sprague doesn't have it?"

Spencer rubbed his bald head, perplexed by the possibility.

"Sir, I have a suggestion." Callaghan leaned forward, capturing Sweeny no longer important. "It will involve your co-operation?"

Spencer waited for him to proceed, his eyes narrowing warily.

"If I can discover where they're keeping Colleen, then maybe I can break her out. The only way to do this is for you to continue negotiations with Sweeny, and insist on seeing Colleen to ensure she's alive. Then, they'll either have to bring her to you; or, more probably, you to her. Whatever action they take, I'll be hiding outside the consulate — "

"Callaghan! I evidently didn't make myself understood," Spencer protested. "You don't have the slightest conception of the sort of people we are dealing with here. Forget your East-Side criminal. They're children by comparison. Cottone is constantly protected by two personal bodyguards, as well as his son-in-law, Carlo Maranzano, who's also accompanied by two bodyguards. They've taken over the entire wing of the Hotel de Genes, and are guarded by at least four more *mafiosi*. Every one of them will have sworn absolute obedience to Cottone, by cutting their wrists and allowing their blood to drip on to a paper replica of a saint, and reciting a sacred oath to sacrifice their lives to Cottone, if he orders them to."

Spencer paused for Callaghan to understand the reality of the situation. "This is what we'd be going up against.

They may not be fanatics in the visionary sense of the word, but they come pretty close. Not the sort of people to tangle with."

"Maybe not. But we've a woman's life at stake here," Callaghan argued. "Besides, and with respect, sir, the worst you're facing is a bumpy coach ride, probably blindfolded. They'll need you alive to wire Sprague. The risk is all mine. And once I find where they're keeping her, I can always come back for the police."

Spencer massaged his furrowed brow as he wrestled between his instinct for self-preservation and his desire to be brave. "Very well," he agreed, with an air of resignation. "I'll send Sweeny a message as soon as I get back to the consulate." Removing a second folder from his briefcase, Spencer handed it across. "It may help you to read this dossier on Cottone. Mr Sprague wasn't too pleased about you leaving Gibraltar without confiding in him, but he understood your reasons, and, as you see, did not withdraw his request for the information on Cottone."

Taking the file, Callaghan began reading the notes:

SALVATORE COTTONE

Born Monreale 1821, son of the gabelloto (estate manager) for Baron Inglese. Educated by Baron Inglese in return for father's success managing the estates. From college went to Dominican seminary to study for priesthood. Speaks English.

Left seminary aged 23 on death of father, and returned to Monreale as gabelloto. Married. One daughter. No sons.

Monreale: Situated above Palermo. Seat of Catholic bishop with history of clergy protecting local cosca in return for financial support. The most important of the Sicilian cosche, controlling irrigation to local orchards and vineyards; also roads from interior into Palermo, receiving pizzo — protection money — on all goods passing through.

Cottone became Don of Monreale cosca at the age of 30 on assassination of uncle by rival *cosca*. After avenging uncle's death, Cottone next began a *burrusca* — *Mafia power war* — to control Palermo and the waterfront, then gradually took over the villages surrounding Palermo; including Northern Palermo and the coastal road from the west; Monreale, Montelepre and Misilmeri, controlling roads from the interior; and Villabate and Bagheria, controlling coastal routes from the east.

Cottone believed to be *capomafia* — supreme boss — first in Mafia history. In 1867, brought Castellamare *cosca* under his influence by marrying his daughter to Carlo Maranzano, son of Castellamare Don.

They have one son, named Salvatore after Cottone, born 1868. Maranzano presumed to be Cottone's heir-apparent.

So this was Sweeny's new partner in crime! Callaghan thought. Don Salvatore Cottone, ex religious student, now *capomafia* of Palermo and most of north-western Sicily. Which reminded

517

him of Colleen's theory.

"Would Cottone and his Mafia have anything to gain by getting rid of Victor Emmanuel?" he asked.

"Everything to gain and nothing to lose," Consul Spencer replied. "Emmanuel's doing his level best to stamp out the Mafia, sending in troops to 'purge the island', to quote his words. There's a bloody fight for control taking place there at the moment, with the army holding on-the-spot tribunals and executions, and the Mafia retaliating with political assassinations."

That confirmed Colleen's theory, Callaghan decided. An unholy trinity of men: Martens, Cottone and Sweeny; with a multiplicity of purpose. *Sabulon* instead of *Jabulon*, with Satan replacing Jehovah. *Sa*: the adversary, Martens, for the revolution; *Bul*: lord of a place, Cottone, whose aim was to restore Sicily to his sole control. And *On*: of the underworld, duplicitous Sweeny, helping to restore the church to power and receive his passport to Heaven, while accruing a healthy profit on the sale of arms to the revolution.

Spencer handed him two more photographs. "The top one's Cottone."

Callaghan looked down at the portrait of a handsome nobleman, with silver-grey hair and a small pointed beard.

He studied the aristocratic face in detail. It was not at all what he had expected . . . and yet, there was something disturbing about the dark eyes staring coldly into the camera, or was it merely the superior pose of a man used to command? Don Cottone's features reflected the mixed blood of his ancestry: The hauteur of a Norman baron with his imperious nose and the dark dispassionate gaze of an Arab. A deadly combination.

The other picture showed three men posing together on the steps of a huge white villa. The man in the middle was heavily built, at least six inches taller than the others. The man on his right was thin with a long, mean face, while the other was squat, his black hair plastered flat with grease. All three were holding *lupari*, except the taller man's weapon was silver-patterned, presumably to show his elevated position in the Mafia echelon.

"The tall one's Carlo Maranzano," Spencer stated. "The others are his bodyguards, from his father's Castellamare *cosca*. They're all dangerous, but be particularly wary of Maranzano. He's reputed to be a sadist, as well as a killer."

Callaghan studied the face carefully, noting the thick sensual lips which hinted at a cruel nature.

"Michael!" Oliver's voice bellowed down the companionway. "The last cart's moving off."

Callaghan jumped to his feet. "I have to go, sir. I'll see you later at the consulate."

Oliver was waiting with Callaghan's sea-bag and a folded parchment. "It's a map of Genoa," he explained. "It might come in useful." He clasped Callaghan's hand in a tight grip. "Take good care."

Callaghan returned the pressure. "Thanks Oliver. And don't worry about Flood. Whatever happens, I'll stop in Gibraltar on my way back, and explain everything to the court. After that, the *Mary Celeste* mystery will be a thing of the past."

29

THE wagon slowly trundled across the cobbles, both wagoners looking straight ahead towards the dark warehouse area to the east of the harbour. Following from a distance, Callaghan kept to the quayside, passing under the jutting prows of vessels berthed along the docks.

Reaching the towering mass of warehouses, the cart disappeared into a narrow opening between the two front buildings. Still keeping a safe gap between them, Callaghan entered the alley. The buildings loomed high above him, their stonework, black with centuries-old grime, shutting out the daylight. Twisting passages led in all directions, making a most confusing maze.

Up ahead, the wagon turned into a warehouse that looked even older than the rest, its arched entrance dark and low like a crypt. Along the side of the building were a number of small windows. Callaghan crossed the alley, rubbed dirt off a grimy pane, and peered through. The light inside the building was dim, but he could see the previous loads of barrels stacked against the far wall. The final wagon stood in the middle of the floor, next to a small mule-cart, its driver seated. The two wagoners quickly lifted a barrel on to the cart, securing it with rope. The driver flicked his reins and drove out of the warehouse.

Edging to the corner of the building, Callaghan watched as the cart turned towards the city. The driver was young, with skin so pallid it glowed white. He was staring straight ahead with a strange fixed expression as though he were in a trance. Callaghan let him get fifty yards ahead, then followed.

The alley eventually opened into a cobbled square with an archway in the wall, guarded by two officials wearing red uniforms and cockaded hats. Without turning his head, the driver produced a piece of paper. One of the customs-guards glanced at it, then waved him on.

As Callaghan hurried across the cobbles, both men looked towards him, but seeing only a seaman with no baggage to search, they ignored him.

Callaghan found himself in a narrow busy street, its pavements cluttered with canvassed stalls, the vendors vociferously exhorting the quality of their particular produce to the crowded passers-by. For a moment Callaghan was overwhelmed with the noise, then continued after the cart, already some distance up the street. Hurrying after it, he came parallel with the driver, and again noted the peculiar way the young man was staring fixedly ahead, as though oblivious of everything around him.

The cart entered a wider even busier street, with a plaque high on the wall of the corner building reading Via San Lorenzo; then made a left turn, into another narrow, twisting alley. Callaghan again allowed it to open a safe gap, then ran across the street, and entered the dark byway, but the cart had disappeared. Hearing the distant rumble of its wheels, he chased after the sound, only to find himself in a dark mediaeval city, where time had seemingly stood still, despite the passing of centuries: a labyrinth of tight, cobbled byways, connected, and intersected, between tall, gloomy buildings, all appearing to lean towards each other, blotting out the light, and as silent as the grave.

The sound of the cart now seemed to be coming from every direction. Callaghan hesitated, not knowing which way to go, when suddenly the rumbling ceased.

Desperately, he ran through a low archway into a small, deserted square with dark cramped exits leading out from its other three corners. Callaghan sped down the passage to his left, but it humped over a stone bridge, narrower than the cart. Doubling back, he tried the next exit, but it led to a dead end. Despairing, he fled along the final route, around a corner, and saw that it petered out into an arcaded alley between two buildings — but wide enough for the cart.

Over the entrance was a black marble tablet. Though the carving was partly worn away with the passing of time,

Callaghan could trace the sideways figure of a bearded man in a loin-cloth with seven swords impaled into his body: three in his back, one in his chest, two in his stomach, and one into his crotch.

Callaghan stared up at it. Seven swords? The emblem of the Black Knights?

Removing his seaman's knife from its sheath, he crept down the long dark tunnel, then peered out at a closed courtyard full of weeds and cracked, broken slabs. Across the quadrangle was a large, crumbling, L-shaped palazzo. Centuries old, with inlaid black and white marble, it must once have been magnificent, but was now a ruin of chipped plaster, broken windows, and doors hanging off their hinges. Completing the horseshoe of buildings, was a long, dilapidated stable-block, its roof falling in. The mule cart was tied to a post outside, but the barrel was gone.

Callaghan looked back at the palazzo, wondering how many men were inside. The driver for one. Maybe also Martens and other Black Knights? Plus Sweeny?

And possibly Cottone, Maranzano and their bodyguards? The courtyard was too open to chance going any nearer, and with Colleen's life at stake, the odds were too high.

Sheathing his knife, Callaghan turned back up the tunnel. It made more sense to get to the Consulate and wait for Sweeny to contact Spencer.

★ ★ ★

Inside a dark room on the palazzo's first floor, slate-blue eyes looked down on Callaghan in the courtyard. One hand clasped the ornate hilt of a dagger, while the other gripped the blade so tightly, a pool of blood was forming in the watcher's cupped palm as he recognized the interloper.

Only six weeks ago he'd held the point of his sword to the man's throat. One thrust then would have finished him. Whoever he was, he was obviously no mere seaman.

On the floor was an open chest of diamonds. The palazzo was to have served as a base until they'd been sold on the Exchange. Now they would have to be moved, and the sale postponed.

All because of one man.

The grip on the blade tightened.

He would not escape the next time.

Blood overflowed from the watcher's hand, dripping on to the floor. He stared at it, then deliberately increased the pressure on the blade, at the same time moving his hand so that the drops fell on to the diamonds.

Purchased by blood.

Fiesole

The sun had long since fallen behind the hills of the Arno valley and the room was in darkness, apart from the dim light of the single candle on the desk. Whenever he was reading 'Week One' of Saint Ignatius's *Spiritual Exercises*, Beckx preferred it this way. It helped him to imagine all manner of demons and evil spirits lurking in the blackness of the corners, and gave him the terror-feeling of Hell which Loyola's manual demanded.

Since receiving Father Becker's tele-graph, Beckx had followed the Blessed

527

Saint Ignatius's example, and locked himself away from the affairs of the world to prepare himself for the re-emergence of the Society, once Victor Emmanuel had been overthrown.

He opened his faded copy of the *Exercises* — a 250–year-old, dark leather-bound Latin translation of Loyola's original, Castillian edition — which he treasured above all the other books in his library, including the Bible.

Beckx particularly liked its disciplined teaching. Loyola had been a soldier before his miraculous conversion while recovering from battle wounds. His whole upbringing until then had revolved around the bearing of arms, and naturally the feeling of military discipline was in every page of the book. Beckx approved of discipline; it created efficiency. He also agreed that in the same way a body was strengthened by physical exercises, so could the spirit be infused by spiritual exercises.

Beckx also approved of the way Loyola had divided the *Exercises* into weeks. During their training, Jesuit novitiates were locked away in complete isolation and total silence, allowed to converse only with their confessor, and the director of the retreat. The manual's procedure was imprinted on Beckx' memory:

Week One: The purgative week, when the novitiate is to exercise his imagination to actually seeing, and experiencing for himself the terrors of Hell, to impress upon him the supreme folly of mortal sin.

Week Two: The ultimate contrast, when the novitiate concentrates his imagination to be living with Christ in Galilee, feeling himself to be walking the same dusty roads, to the point where he can feel the dirt on his feet, and then entering the same villages and towns to preach to the people.

Week Three: When the novitiate is to exercise his imagination to experience the many anguishes of Christ, transporting himself to be sitting around the table at The Last Supper, sweating drops of blood in the Garden of Gethsemane, suffering the pain of being scourged, and then the dreadful agony of the Crucifixion.

Week Four: When the imagination is exercised to actually smell the immeasurable fragrance and sweetness of the Godhead, the purpose of which is to make the novitiate realize that his ultimate reward for accepting his vocational call will be eternal union with God.

This was the point at which the novitiate entered into the state of true sanctity. Unfortunately, yet inevitably, there were those who condemned the *Exercises*, Beckx thought sadly, claiming that their effect on susceptive minds could lead to madness. One living American historian had recently gone so far as to call them 'a psychological masterpiece'. But that was absurd. Such lay-people did not appreciate the care which went into the selection of candidates. Only healthy young men of sound mind were chosen, men like Father Karl Becker, well able to submit to the intensity of their ten-year training.

The American historian's blasphemous

judgement only displayed his ignorance of why and how Saint Ignatius had been guided to write *The Exercises*. The *why* was because it was the time when Luther and Calvin had been preaching their heresies, telling people that the way to God was by faith alone, and not through belonging to God's one and only Holy Church on earth: the Church of Rome.

As for the *how*, this was even further proof of God's divine blessing on the formation of the Society.

Seeking isolation away from the world, and all its pleasures, Loyola had found a cave outside Manresa in Southern Spain. With him he had a copy of Garcia de Cisneros' *Exercises of the Spiritual Life*. Cisneros was a former abbot of the monastery at Montserrat. Reaching for his copy of the book, which was always on his desk, Beckx opened it to the descriptive passage that most appealed to him:

Picture to yourself the torments of Hell, as well as Hell itself: A desolate place deep under the Earth, like a fiery crater or gigantic town, shrouded in terrible darkness, blazing with dreadful flames. Cries and lamentations which pierce to the very marrow fill the air. The unhappy inhabitants whose pain and torments no human can describe, are eternally burning in raging despair.

No wonder it had inspired Ignatius to subjugate his body to the same plane as his spiritual mind — praying on his knees seven hours every day, wearing a vest, interwoven with sharp irons, next to his skin, and a crucifix of nails on his breast, so that when he was tempted to lie down on the damp cave-floor to sleep, they pierced his body, drawing blood, and making him conscious of the weakness of the flesh.

But Ignatius's self-discipline had been rewarded. When the time came for him to write the *Exercises*, a vision of the Blessed Virgin had appeared before him and remained with him, dictating every word for Ignatius to write down. Together, they had divided the manual into weeks, then specified the exact nature of each exercise. Beckx especially favoured those for the first week, the purgative week, when the mind of the novitiate was most receptive. Turning to his copy of the *Exercises*, he opened it at the exact page:

The first point consists in this: that I hear with the eye of the imagination, those enormous fires, and the souls, as it were, in bodies of fire.

The second point consists in this: that I hear with the ears of the imagination, the lamentations, howlings, cries, and the blasphemies against Christ Our Lord and against all His Saints.

The third point consists in this: that I smell with the sense of smell of the imagination, the smoke, brimstone, refuse and rotting things of Hell.

The fourth point consists in this: that I taste with the sense of taste of the imagination, the bitter things, the tears, sorrows, and the worms of the conscience in Hell.

The fifth point consists in this: that I feel with the sense of touch of the imagination, how those fires fasten upon and burn souls.

Beckx smiled. It was masterly.

Having completed his work, Ignatius had journeyed to Rome and shown it to Pope Paul III. The Holy Father had given it his papal blessing, and thus it was that the Society of Jesus, the greatest teaching Order ever known to man, had come into being.

And with what success, Father Beckx thought, smothering a pang of pride. The Society had turned back the tide of the Protestant Reformation; repressing heresies, and spreading the gospel of Rome to the four corners of the globe.

What the Church needed today, in her present moment of crisis, the Jesuit General brooded, was someone with the extraordinary zeal and selfless dedication of Saint Ignatius.

Staring into the darkness, Beckx' thoughts again turned to Father Becker.

30

The United States Consulate,
1 Salita Cappuccini,
Acqua Sole.

MR SPENCER was sitting at his red-leather-topped desk, writing by the light of a green-globed, shiny brass oil lamp, as Callaghan entered the study. Seeing a warm inviting fire in the white marble fireplace, Callaghan crossed to the hearth and stood with his back to the flames as he waited for the consul to raise his head.

"Did you sleep?" Spencer queried.

"Only rested. I won't be able to go off until Colleen is safe. What time will Sweeny's carriage be here?"

"Ten," replied the consul, his strained voice betraying his nervousness.

Callaghan tried calming him down. "Don't worry, sir. Just keep remembering that Sweeny needs you to send the wire to Mr Sprague."

Mr Spencer gave a wry smile, but his eyes remained serious. "So I continue telling myself, Callaghan, but it doesn't help any." He indicated to the paper on his desk. "I thought I'd make my will, just in case. Would you witness it for me?"

"Of course, sir. But I don't think you need worry about it for a good many years, yet."

"Always wise to be prepared for the worst, Callaghan. Meanwhile, I received another wire from Mr Sprague. Something about Captain Morehouse's wife being found safe with relatives in British Columbia. Does that mean anything to you?"

"Yes, sir. It's too long to go into, but it means that I'm now free to confront Sweeny with everything I've got — no holds barred. Which reminds me, do you have a pistol?"

Spencer nodded. "Only as a keepsake. A Colt .45 from the war. I keep it locked in my desk."

"Is it oiled, sir?"

"Oiled and wrapped. With bullets."

"May I borrow it?"

"Certainly." Spencer unlocked the middle drawer, and withdrew an oilskin-wrapped bundle which he handed to Callaghan. "I should have thought of it myself. It will help to know you're not only behind me, but that you're also armed."

Unwrapping the parcel, Callaghan inserted his finger through the trigger guard, and tested the revolver's balance. Checking the cylinder to make sure it was unloaded, he held the barrel against the light from the desk-lamp, and peered down it, happy to see no sign of rust. Placing two bullets in his pocket, he loaded the other four into the chambers, ensuring that the hammer was resting over an empty one, and that the next was also empty. Then he thrust the pistol under his trouser-belt.

"Time to be off, sir. But first, may I ask a favour?"

"Of course."

"In my sea-bag, upstairs, there's a diary. If I'm not back within twenty-four hours, would you forward it to Henry Pisani in Gibraltar, David Morehouse's advocate? Now that Mrs Morehouse is safe, Mr Pisani will be able to use it as evidence to end the Inquiry."

Spencer frowned. "All very mysterious, Callaghan. Why was it not produced before?"

"Sweeny's people threatened to harm Captain Morehouse's wife and children. But now that we know they're being protected, will you do it, sir?"

"By all means. Nevertheless, I should . . ."

"Sir, it's nine forty-five," said Callaghan heading for the door. "I'd like to be well hidden before the carriage gets here, just in case they have someone following."

Spencer opened his mouth to pursue the matter, then remembered his will. "Wait a moment, Callaghan," he protested, holding up the document. "I need your signature."

"You need two, sir."

"You're nearest the door. Call my housekeeper."

★ ★ ★

From behind the bushes of the Villa Negri municipal gardens, opposite the consulate, Callaghan watched the black

538

carriage arrive. Black curtains were drawn over the windows, hiding whoever was inside. No one descended. And the dark-suited driver remained seated.

The consulate door opened and Spencer appeared, framed against the light inside the building. He pulled the door closed, and became a dark outline as he walked down the pathway and disappeared into the coach.

Callaghan heard the door shut, then the carriage pulled away. Despite the late hour, the streets were still busy, and the coach proceeded at a crawl. Remaining hidden in the bushes, to make sure it was not being followed, Callaghan waited until the coach turned right, heading towards the city centre. Sprinting across the gardens, he crossed the piazza, then down a side-street, finally emerging behind the coach in the wide avenue leading to the Piazza Carlo Felice.

Still restricted by the traffic, the carriage continued across the Piazza, passing Sweeny's hotel in the near corner, then exited into the Via Sellai. Turning right at the statued Palazzo

Ducale, the Palace of the Doges, it then proceeded down the Via San Lorenzo, now unmistakably heading towards the harbour.

Suddenly veering left, the coach entered a dark alley. Keeping close to the walls of the buildings, Callaghan followed. At the far end of the narrow street was a high brick wall. Beyond it, Callaghan could see the tall shapes of the bonded warehouses outlined against a cloudy sky. The arched gateway was closed, but it was not the one through which he'd followed the mule-cart.

A customs-guard emerged through a small door in the gateway. He exchanged a few brief words with the driver, then went back inside. Seconds later, one half of the double gates slowly swung open. Callaghan waited for the guard to cross to open the other, then swiftly and silently slid along the right rear side of the coach. With the darkness of the surrounding building giving him extra concealment, he followed the coach through the gateway, across the small square, and into a dark narrow alley. Falling behind again, Callaghan allowed a small gap to open between them. Its wheels resounding on the cobbles, and bouncing off the walls of the empty alleys, the coach continued down one black byway after another, finally entering a blind alley and passing through a low archway into the walled yard of a tall warehouse. Wheeling around in a tight circle, the carriage stopped alongside a side door, where a faint flickering light shone through the dirt-covered windows.

Stealing into the compound, Callaghan found a dark corner from where he could watch.

The coach door opened and a dark-suited man descended, followed by Spencer, now blindfolded, hesitatingly feeling for the steps with his feet until he reached the ground. The man grabbed his arm, and as he led him into the building, Callaghan caught a brief glimpse of casks and barrels scattered across the warehouse floor.

The driver remained seated, not moving. Minutes passed, then the door opened, and Spencer and the man reappeared. Still blindfolded, the consul paused deliberately before climbing into the carriage and gave a single cough.

Callaghan heard the prearranged signal. Only one guard.

Watching the coach disappear into the labyrinth of winding alleys, he settled back to wait.

After an hour, he decided it was safe to emerge. Creeping up to the door, he pressed slowly down on the latch, taking care to make no sound.

He sensed, rather than heard, someone behind him. Before he could turn, a violent explosion of pain flashed through his head, and everything went black.

★ ★ ★

He came to slowly, rising out of a bottomless pit, only to slide back into darkness, then, as he neared the surface again, he became aware of his head resting on something soft, and a hand gently caressing his forehead, fingers brushing lightly through his hair.

Recognizing Colleen's perfume, and that his pillow was her lap, Callaghan slowly opened his eyes. The light was dim, a flickering glimmer silhouetting her head and shoulders, yet reflecting the golden highlights of her hair.

He tried sitting up, but the movement was too sudden, and a sharp pain stabbed across his eyes, forcing him to lie back down.

"Stay still," he heard Colleen whisper.

After a short while, he tried again, this time more slowly. Pushing his palms against the straw-covered floor, he straightened to a sitting position and saw they were enclosed in a hastily erected barricade of crates with a top row of casks. The light dancing on the high ceiling came from beyond the barrier.

The whole of his head a dull ache, Callaghan gingerly touched his neck, unable to restrain a sudden indrawn breath at the tenderness there.

"Shouldn't you lie still a while longer?" Colleen asked.

He tried a reassuring smile, but his facial muscles were too numb to sustain it. "I'll be OK. It's easing by the second." He reached for his belt, but both the revolver and knife were gone. "I must be getting past it. I should have realized they'd have someone outside, but whoever he was, he was good. I waited at least an hour, but he never made a sound."

"It was the thin one. With a mean, ferret-like face."

"I'll remember that." After three and a half weeks apart, there was so much Callaghan wanted to say, but this was neither the place nor the time. "Are you OK? You're not hurt?" he asked, seeing only concern for him in her dark green eyes.

Colleen smiled. "Yes, I'm OK. Only my pride's hurt at getting caught."

"What happened?" Keep talking, Callaghan told himself, the best antidote to pain and panic.

"My own stupidity," Colleen confessed. "After a week of hiding in the hotel, I began to feel claustrophobic. I decided to find out about Cottone, just in case Sprague withdrew his offer to help. So, I decided to go to their hotel and take a quiet chair behind a palm in the corner of the lounge, hoping to see the man . . ."

"And size up the enemy," said Callaghan. "To quote an old army

544

instruction much used by Consul Spencer."

"I confess it was foolish," Colleen sighed, "but I wanted to be doing something. Anyway, I hadn't been there an hour when Sweeny suddenly sat down in the next chair, and asked me what I was doing there? My mind went a complete blank. Instead of saying I was on a European tour, and what a coincidence it was meeting him, I told him I'd come for an affidavit clearing Father's name. He made some hypocritical expression of condolences, then without warning . . . "

"He asked how the hell you knew he was in Genoa?"

"Exactly," Colleen replied, wryly. "I fell back on the tour explanation, saying I'd seen him in the street, and come to the Hotel de Genes in search of him, knowing it was the best hotel in Genoa. Even as I spoke I realized every word was a contradiction. But Sweeny pretended to believe me, and said he'd think about the affidavit, then asked for the name of my hotel. I gave him the name of another one, and quickly left. I remained in my hotel room for a couple of days, but when nothing happened, I chanced going out for a walk after dinner. Some two hundred yards from the hotel, a coach stopped alongside me. I was bundled inside, and since then I've been stuck here, with no explanations, until Mr Spencer came here a short while ago, asked if I was unharmed, then went away, after reassuring me I would soon be free." Colleen grabbed hold of Callaghan's arm. "Michael, what's going on? Why am I being held here . . . " Her voice tailed off.

Placing his arm around her, Callaghan drew her head on to his shoulder, and held her tight. "Don't worry," he whispered. "Everything will be all right." The promise was made with a confidence he was far from feeling.

"No, Michael," Colleen insisted, fighting to prevent her voice from breaking. "You must tell me what's happening."

"OK," Callaghan agreed, realizing she had a right to know, and proceeded to bring her up to date, telling her also that Sweeny was holding her as ransom in return for information from Mr Sprague.

"What information?" Colleen asked.

"Presumably about the *Celeste*."

"But surely Martens can tell him everything he needs to know?"

"That's what I thought. Has Sweeny been to see you since you were brought here?"

"No." Colleen stated, but adding. "When we met in his hotel, he seemed very edgy."

"Probably wondering whether Cottone can be trusted," Callaghan speculated. "It can't be everyday a Mafia Don is asked to safeguard a hundred million dollars worth of diamonds."

"That doesn't explain what he wants from Gibraltar," Colleen remarked. "Nor what will happen to us if Sprague doesn't have the information."

"Hopefully, we won't be around to find out," Callaghan replied, slowly rising to his feet and making for the barricade. Through a gap in the crates, he could see Maranzano's other bodyguard, the squat, greasy *mafioso*, sitting on an upturned wooden box by a large crate on which stood a single oil lamp. He was whittling at a piece of wood with his knife, his *lupara* propped alongside him against the crate. There was no sign of ferret-mean, nevertheless it would be impossible to get over the barrier and reach squat-and-greasy before he picked up his gun.

As Callaghan turned away, another pain shot through his head, and that decided it. He returned to Colleen and stretched out.

She lay alongside him, her arm round his chest. "Still hurts?"

"A little. There's only one guard on duty. Where's the other?"

"He'll be somewhere nearby, resting. What are you planning?"

"Our escape," Callaghan replied, drawing her to him. "But we'll leave it until morning. Now let's try getting some sleep."

31

Friday, 17 January 1873

FROM the dim light seeping through the window, Callaghan saw it was approaching dawn. He looked around their makeshift prison, from the centuries-old paved floor to the planks of wood stacked against the corner walls, then he spotted the tool he wanted, a rusted piece of metal hoop.

Alongside him, Colleen stirred, then slowly sat up. "How's your head?"

There was a slight ache and a certain stiffness, but no pain, as Callaghan turned towards her. "Much better."

He stretched out for the hoop. The rust was only on the surface, the metal underneath was still strong.

"What are you intending to do?"

"Test Archimedes' words: 'Give me somewhere to stand and I will move the earth'. I only hope he was right."

Callaghan crossed to the barricade and saw ferret-mean was on guard, sharpening his knife on a piece of stone.

Crouching down he examined the mortar around the paving-stones. It all looked brittle. Selecting a slab next to one upon which two crates and a cask stood, Callaghan inserted the metal into a crack and slowly began loosening the cement, taking care to make no sound.

Removing the surrounding mortar, he dug away enough earth to slip both hands under the slab, then pulled upwards, but the stone refused to budge. Putting all his muscle into a second attempt, he felt it lift, grating noisily as it came free. He quickly scattered some straw over the area, and peered through the barricade. Ferret-mean was armed and on his feet, looking towards the barrier.

Returning to Colleen, Callaghan lay down, and closed his eyes as he heard ferret-mean approach the barricade. Colleen turned over in sham restlessness, rustling the straw. Satisfied they were still asleep, the *mafioso* returned to his post, the box scraping the floor as he sat down.

After a few moments, Callaghan returned to work on the slab, while

Colleen kept watch at the gap in the barrier.

"Wait! They're changing over. The mean-looking one's going to lie down . . . no, he's not! He's coming back. Someone's come in . . . " She turned to Callaghan, fear in her eyes. "It's one of the men you described. The son-in-law."

Joining Colleen, Callaghan watched Maranzano approach his two men. Bulging with muscles, he was even taller than his photograph had suggested, well over six feet, with dark olive skin and black wavy hair. Opening his coat, he removed his silver-filigree *lupara*, propped it against a nearby crate, and said something to ferret-mean, nodding towards the barrier. Expecting Maranzano to enter the prison, Callaghan prepared to retreat, but then, surprisingly, Cottone's son-in-law turned a crate over and sat down . . . His two bodyguards sat opposite, and the three began talking quietly together, leaning forward in a huddle.

"Why doesn't he want to question you?" Colleen whispered.

"Maybe he has to wait for Cottone,"

Callaghan speculated. "In the meantime, do we get food? I could eat the proverbial horse."

"Mid-morning and mid-afternoon. No meat. Just bread, cheese, and cheap wine."

"In that case, we may as well retire to our bed-chamber. Unless there's somewhere else you'd prefer to go?" he continued, trying to lighten their desperate situation. "Delmonico's?"

"A bath," Colleen replied, longingly. "I'd give anything for a long, hot, soapy bath."

"Tonight, in the consulate," Callaghan promised. "They have a marble one that's the last word in luxury."

"Big enough for two to share?" asked Colleen, joining in the pretence.

"Easily."

"Mmmm. Just the thought of having my back sponged. Bliss."

Judging from the sun's ascent, several hours passed. Then they heard the door opening and closing, followed by more footsteps crossing the stone floor. Callaghan met Colleen's expectant gaze, and slowly they crept to the barricade to

552

look through to the other side.

Though it was a year, two months and two weeks since Callaghan had last seen him, Sweeny had not changed. Still the same short, rounded shape wearing a black coat, his thick black hair escaping from under the habitual black hat, and the black walrus moustache hiding his ugly face.

The silver-haired man alongside him was obviously Cottone. Slim, about five feet nine in height, he wore a long dark overcoat, but no hat. His face was leaner than in his picture, the nose more hawk-like, increasing the impression of a cruel nature. Flanked by two bodyguards, his whole attitude denoted detachment and superiority. The *mafiosi* were both short and burly, their stolid faces cold to the point of being expressionless. One had dark Moorish features; the other a round, flattish face, with Asiatic-looking eyes. Each man carried a *lupara*.

Maranzano and his men were already on their feet as Cottone approached, asking his son-in-law a question. Maranzano replied by picking up Spencer's Colt .45, and indicating towards the barricade.

Callaghan noticed the scene was enacted with the minimum of words, and the briefest of gestures, which, he decided, must be a peculiarity of the Mafia.

Removing a cigar case from his inner overcoat pocket, Cottone selected a corona. The Asiatic *mafioso* swiftly produced a box of matches, and lit the cigar. Cottone drew on it for a moment, then slowly exhaled a wreath of smoke, and gave a single nod. The man immediately headed towards the barricade, followed by Maranzano's two bodyguards.

Placing a protective arm around Colleen's shoulders, Callaghan drew her away from the barrier.

A section of the wall was swiftly removed and from the other side, the Asiatic *mafioso* gestured with the barrel of his *lupara* for Callaghan to come through into the warehouse. Colleen tried to follow, but she was blocked by ferret-mean. As the *mafioso* prodded Callaghan towards his Don, he was aware of Cottone's dispassionate appraisal, and Maranzano's more hostile scrutiny. But his main focus was on Sweeny, who was studying him with a puzzled expression, the bushy eyebrows narrowed in a familiar scowl, then as he penetrated the beard, recognition suddenly dawned.

"Michael!" he exclaimed, in a deep, snarling tone.

Seemingly undisturbed by Sweeny's knowledge of the prisoner, Cottone's expression remained unchanged. Maranzano, however, turned to look at the New Yorker.

"*Buon giorno*, Sweeny. Sorry I can't add *benvenuto*," Callaghan said.

Sweeny's scowl deepened. "First, Colleen. Now you. And carrying a gun, too. What the hell's going on, Michael?"

"Just missing you, Sweeny. It's been over twelve months. And you were in such a hurry, we never got to say goodbye."

"Cut the humour, Michael. You're in no position to joke. And how come you both knew I was in Genoa? There's something funny going on here, and I don't like the feel of it."

In a flat voice, with no trace of inflexion, and his eyes never leaving

Callaghan, Cottone asked, "You know this man?"

"Sure," Sweeny replied. "We're sorta related. He's married to my niece over there. Got some personal vendetta against me. He's also a cop."

Cottone's only visible reaction was a narrowing of his dark gaze, but a brooding coldness emanated from within him. Sensing the tension, Carlo Maranzano questioned his father-in-law. Despite speaking Italian, Callaghan understood none of the Sicilian's brief reply, apart from the word *polizia*, to which Maranzano reacted angrily, drawing his hand viciously across his throat. Cottone ignored him and Maranzano flushed with anger at this rebuff in front of the four lower echelon *mafiosi*. For a moment, he seemed poised to protest further, then he stepped back, his olive complexion darkening with resentment.

"You ain't answered my question, Michael?" Sweeny growled. "I'll ask you one more time, or maybe you'd like Nino to persuade you." Sweeny gestured towards Cottone's bodyguards, though which man was Nino was impossible to guess, since neither reacted to hearing the name. "I'm told he's expert with a stiletto, peels the skin off in strips. Even the Apaches back home have got nothing on him. As for anyone hearing your screams, he's got his own way of preventing this — stuffs a cloth in your mouth, making you choke on them."

Behind him, Callaghan heard Colleen cry out. Then he noticed Cottone give the briefest of nods. Spinning round, Callaghan saw ferret-mean putting the barrel of his *lupara* to Colleen's throat, choking her protests.

Angrily, he turned back to Sweeny, his only thought now to accomplish Colleen's release. "OK, whatever you want to know." He spoke through gritted teeth. "But first, I want Colleen taken to the American Consulate, and a letter from Spencer confirming she's safe — "

"You're surely not trying to *negotiate*!" cried Sweeny, lapsing into his East-Side accent with incredulity. "You obviously can't have been listening, Michael. I've only got to let Nino get to work on you, and you'll be begging to talk."

His anger back under control, Callaghan

was two moves ahead. "In return I'll wire Gibraltar asking Sprague to give you whatever you want to know."

"Gibraltar! Sprague!" Sweeny's eyes became slits. "How do you know about them?"

Callaghan gave a deliberate shrug. "Sprague. The *Mary Celeste*. The *Dei Gratia*. There's not much I don't know, Sweeny. I also know about Father Becker and Martens and Kaufmann . . . "

Sweeny stepped forward, furious. Cottone snapped his fingers, and a long-bladed stiletto suddenly flashed in the Moorish-featured *mafioso*'s right hand. As Sweeny grabbed the lapels of his jacket, Callaghan restrained his impulse to push him away, knowing the *mafioso* would make him suffer for it.

"Kaufmann! What about Kaufmann?" Sweeny demanded.

"Ask Martens. He killed him."

Sweeny's face registered shocked horror. "Kaufmann's dead?"

"Come off it, Sweeny, you know damn well he is!"

Sweeny's grip on his lapels tightened.

"And how should I know that, Michael?" he grated.

"Like I said, from Martens."

"And who the hell's Martens?"

Sweeny had always been good at play-acting, but not this good. Callaghan was puzzled. Why bother, when he held most of the aces? Unless he didn't . . . ?

"OK," Callaghan replied, still perplexed. "So that's not his real name. I'm talking about the albino killer you sent to New York to protect the diamonds."

"Diamonds!" Sweeny shook him. "What the hell d'you know about the diamonds?"

"Drop the act, Sweeny. Martens must have . . . "

Sweeny slapped his face. "Michael. I ain't telling you this again. I don't know any Martens."

Though reeling from the blow, Callaghan's thoughts were racing. Sweeny very obviously knew nothing about the German! It looked as though the supreme double-crosser had himself been double-crossed. Hell! Not only might there be a way to negotiate Colleen's release, but also of buying time to make his own escape.

"You expect me to believe you?" he challenged.

"What'll it take?"

For Sweeny the politician, lying was first nature. But Sweeny the ardent Catholic would never perjure himself.

"Your sacred oath."

Releasing his hold on Callaghan's lapels, Sweeny made the sign of the Cross against his breast, raised his right hand, and began reciting . . .

★ ★ ★

"When we get him, I'll make sure Nino takes a long time to make him pay," Sweeny rasped, when he had finished. "Still, I gotta hand it to you, Michael, you've certainly been busy. But what the hell. If you hadn't sent me that wire, we'd still be waiting in Palermo for two unknown vessels to appear." He paused, deep in thought. "So, apart from us here, there's only Morehouse and Deveau in the know."

"They only know the cargoes are connected with you, but nothing about the diamonds," Callaghan lied.

560

Throughout the account, Cottone's expression remained detached and unreadable. Maranzano looked curious, but having suffered one rebuff, refrained from asking questions. As for the four *mafiosi* they obeyed the *omerta*: hearing nothing and seeing nothing that could implicate their Don.

As Sweeny began pacing the floor, Callaghan silently assessed the position. Impatiently awaiting a second wire from Kaufmann, it was now clear what Sweeny had wanted from Sprague — a list of all vessels sailing from New York which had stopped-off in Gibraltar since the beginning of December. But now, apart from knowing the names of both vessels — immediately recognizing them as the ones involved in the great sea mystery, reported on in all the local papers — and that Martens had already succeeded in stealing the *Dei Gratia*'s diamonds; more importantly for Callaghan, Sweeny fully realized the possible threat of the *Celeste*'s cargo being searched, and of the second one hundred million dollars worth being discovered by Solly Flood's surveyor.

Sweeny was still pacing the floor, desperately trying to think of a way to salvage the situation.

It was time to make his move, Callaghan thought. A deliberate gambit which would give him the time he needed . . . provided Sweeny believed him.

"Finding Martens will be like looking for a needle in a haystack," he said. "And without the *Celeste*'s bill-of-lading you won't — "

"Don't worry about that stinking priest-killer," Sweeny growled. "We'll find him sure enough. Thanks to you, he's no idea we're in Genoa. If he's not in that palazzo, we'll get him when he tries to sell the stones on the Exchange. And when we do, he's sure as hell gonna wish he'd never messed in Peter Sweeny's affairs." He stopped his pacing, and continued to think out loud. "What worries me is them authorizing a search of the *Celeste*'s cargo before we find him and get her papers to Gibraltar."

"I can prevent that with a single telegraph," said Callaghan. "Provided you release Colleen."

Cottone's eyes narrowed, while Sweeny

spun to face Callaghan. "You bluffing?" Brains threatened.

"No."

"It's on the level?"

"Yes."

"How?"

"Sprague has power-of-attorney over the cargo. He was appointed by the Board of Underwriters in New York. He's also had a copy bill-of-lading sent to him from Genoa, and can have the cargo transferred to another vessel whenever he chooses."

This was the fabrication which Sweeny had to believe. The truth was that Winchester, the *Celeste*'s major shareholder, had instructed the Board to refuse Sprague's request, and was already on his way to Gibraltar to represent himself before the Inquiry.

Sweeny's brows met in a suspicious scowl. "So why doesn't he?"

"He's waiting for my telegraph."

"Then what's to stop me sending one and signing your name, like you did to me with Kaufmann?"

"The wire has to include a coded word, known only to Sprague and myself,"

Callaghan said simply, wearing his best poker face.

Sweeny leaned into him pugnaciously. "That doesn't require any deal. Thirty seconds with Nino, and you'll be shouting out the word."

"And how will you know I've given you the right one?"

"I didn't say anything about Nino killing you. Just peeling you. All we have to do is keep you alive to see if the wire works. If it doesn't, then I promise you, you'll give us the correct word next time, especially after — "

"Signor Callaghan," Cottone intervened, his low, dispassionate voice immediately silencing Sweeny. "What if Consul Sprague telegraphs Consul Spencer for confirmation of your message?"

"He won't," Callaghan stated. "Not if my wire's got the codeword. But even if he did, Spencer would co-operate to effect my release."

"Release!" Sweeny spat out the word. Snatching up Spencer's Colt revolver, he thrust the barrel under Callaghan's chin. "Michael, if you think you've got any chance of being . . . "

"I know that, but Spencer won't."
Turning from Sweeny, he faced the
capocosca: "So, Signore Cottone. Are
we agreed?"

Cottone studied him in silence for
a moment. "I see you also know my
name, Signor Callaghan. It is a great
pity you were not born a Sicilian." He
gave a shrug of his shoulders. "Sadly, I
cannot agree to release your charming
wife until our vessel has been loaded with
the *Celeste*'s cargo, and also returned to
Palermo. The sooner the wire is sent, the
sooner this will be. Unfortunately, as we
have no writing material here, there will
be a short delay while Signor Sweeny
returns to the hotel. In the meantime,
if you require anything?"

"Breakfast," Callaghan replied calmly,
trying to keep his elation from being
expressed in his face. "We haven't eaten
since yesterday."

Don Cottone snapped his fingers.

★ ★ ★

Lowering her bottle of wine, Colleen
asked, "Do you think Kaufmann was

565

in on it? He was a German and a Catholic, and probably as much opposed to Bismarck's *Kulturkampf* policy as Becker."

"If he was, there would have been no diary memos to wire Sweeny," Callaghan replied, tearing off a hunk of bread to go with the cheese. "Sweeny's original instructions were for the two vessels to sail to Marseilles. But, after agreeing to meet Cottone — for some other reason than we thought — he altered them to Palermo, with both ships calling in to Gibraltar to await further orders, presumably in case he changed his mind again if he and Cottone didn't get on. But then Martens stole the diamonds and made Kaufmann divert the vessels to Genoa, with the *Gratia* calling into Gibraltar to wait until the *Celeste* had been unloaded without incident, and her stones were safe. However, the memos suggest that Kaufmann planned to wire Sweeny with all the facts, after the *Celeste* had sailed, so he and Cottone could meet the Celeste, fix Martens, and discharge the exact number of barrels as per the bill-of-lading, leaving the *Celeste* free to sail to Palermo with the diamonds still in the hold. It would have been the same with the *Dei Gratia*, when she finally arrived from Gibraltar. Unfortunately for Kaufmann, Martens had already decided he was expendable."

"That makes sense," Colleen agreed, helping herself to some more bread and cheese. "But if Sweeny and Cottone are not involved in revolution, what's their connection? How did they ever meet in the first place? What has Palermo got to interest a man with two hundred million dollars? And what's Sweeny got to offer the *capomafia* of all Sicily?" she paused, thinking out loud. "Unless . . . unless Cottone's planning to steal — " Her eyes widened with sudden conviction. "Maybe that's it! He's not interested in Sweeny, only in his diamonds!"

"Who knows," Callaghan replied. "There's been more twists in all this than a tangled piece of rope, and it's not over yet." Finishing his wine, he stretched out on the hay. "As soon as Maranzano leaves, we can get back to testing Archimedes. All this talking between him and his bodyguards is making me uneasy." The three men had returned to their huddle the moment Cottone and Sweeny left; "Whatever he's up to, I'd prefer to be out of here before it happens."

It was late afternoon before they heard Maranzano leave the warehouse. Dusk was descending, and the oil lamp was casting fluttering shadows across the ceiling. Callaghan gently roused Colleen, who was sleeping by his side. "It's time."

Squat-and-greasy was on his own, still whittling his piece of wood. Ferret-mean had either left with Maranzano, or was resting.

While Colleen kept watch, Callaghan returned to his stone slab, slowly prising it loose until it was vertical, then edging it towards him an inch at a time, he lowered it down on to the slab behind.

Kneeling alongside the shallow hollow left by the stone's removal, he began digging under the slab on which the two crates and cask were resting. Eventually satisfied that the resulting cavity was deep enough, he crossed to the wooden planks stacked in the corner, and selected the stoutest. Inserting one end under the slab, he lowered the beam down on to the two slabs on the other side of the hollow, and stepped back to examine the angle. He would have preferred it steeper, nevertheless the plank was long enough to extend well past the two-slabbed fulcrum, which should create sufficient upthrust to topple the crates forward and leave enough of a gap for a break to freedom. The only uncertainty was the element of surprise. Would squat-and-greasy be startled enough to be momentarily incapable of reaction, or would his response be immediate? His *lupara* was less than an arm's length away.

Finding a stout piece of timber to use as a weapon, Callaghan returned to his makeshift lever. Colleen glanced through the gap, then nodded as she moved clear. Bending his knees poised to land the whole weight of his body on the plank, Callaghan froze as he heard the warehouse door. Colleen moved swiftly to the spyhole, then spun back. "Sweeny!"

Quickly removing the plank, Callaghan placed it on the floor, while Colleen scooped up an armful of straw and scattered it over the two slabs and the hollow.

A cask was removed in the barricade, then Sweeny's face appeared above the second crate. Between his lips was an unlit cigar which he was rolling from side to side. Placing a sheet of paper and a pencil on the crate, he stepped back and raised Spencer's revolver for Callaghan to see he was armed. Removing his cigar, he spat away some dry pieces of tobacco stuck to his lips, then gave an unpleasant leer. "I sure hope for your sake this telegraph works, Michael. I wouldn't like to be in your skin, or stripped of it, if it doesn't."

Callaghan ignored him, and penned a message to Sprague, giving him the go-ahead to use his power-of-attorney to transfer the Celeste's cargo.

"What's the name of your vessel?"

"*Santa Rosalia.*"

"When she can leave?"

"Tomorrow."

Callaghan completed the wire and handed it to Sweeny to read.

"Which is the codeword?"

570

Callaghan forced a laugh. "Come on, Sweeny, you didn't expect me to fall for that?"

"Worth a try," Sweeny growled. "You might have slipped up and told me." Placing the message in his pocket, he took out a box of vestas and lit his cigar. After a couple of puffs, he removed it and studied the lighted end. "We searched the palazzo; place was empty. But you should have told me about that emblem, Michael."

"The Black Knight crest?"

"Is that what you thought it was?" Sweeny sneered. "You went to the wrong school, Michael." He took another pull at his cigar. "A couple of days, and the *Gratia*'s diamonds will also be back in my possession. Then we can all be on our way back to Palermo, to get ready for your funeral."

Realizing Sweeny was in an expansive mood, Callaghan decided to needle him, hoping his weakness for boasting would loosen his tongue. "I hope you and Tweed enjoy Sicily. Assuming Cottone allows you to, once he's got his hands on the diamonds."

"Tweed!" Sweeny snarled. "That has-been! Don't tell me you thought he was involved? It's all mine, Michael. I was the brains behind the Ring so I earned it fair and square. What's more, you sure as hell don't think that this is all about Peter Barr Sweeny retiring out to grass in Palermo? Listen good. Twelve months from now I'll be back in New York. And not just me, but Cottone and his boys as well. This Victor Emmanuel's making things a little hot for them in Sicily at the moment, so I've persuaded them to transfer their business to the other side of the water . . . "

"New York!" Callaghan exclaimed, genuinely aghast. "Forget it, Sweeny! New York wouldn't have you back, not in a million years!"

"Not have me back!" Sweeny hurled his cigar to the floor. "Let me tell you something, Michael, they're *begging* me back. My Paris attorneys are already finalizing the deal, part of which includes immunity from prosecution. And when I *do* return, you sure as hell don't think I'm gonna be satisfied with just New York. No way! Listen, what with my expertise and Cottone's organization, we're planning on taking over every major city throughout the entire United States. What's more, with what I now know about Martens, the percentage I'd agreed to give Beckx, well, he can damn well whistle for it. I'll give it to the American Church instead."

And with this enigmatic remark, Sweeny ground his cigar into the floor with the heel of his shoe, and turned and made for the exit. Callaghan watched the door close, then made his way back to Colleen as the *mafioso* replaced the cask.

"Michael, you don't believe him?" Colleen's eyes were wide with shock. "New York wouldn't be so stupid as to let him back? No, it couldn't! Not after all he did!"

"It's crazy!" Callaghan replied, still absorbing the blow, and at the same time pondering Sweeny's final remark. "When I said it wasn't over, I never expected this twist. But at least we now know what they're up to. Hell's bells — introducing the Mafia into the States!"

"We must get to Spencer for him

to telegraph Washington," said Colleen, urgently. "Surely Congress can overrule New York and prevent this from happening."

Though Callaghan agreed, his thoughts had swiftly moved on to a more immediate but equally sinister factor. By revealing the plans in front of Colleen, it was obvious that Sweeny and Cottone had no intention of releasing her. Now was their only chance to escape and there was no time to lose. Maranzano might return at any moment.

Dropping to his knees, Callaghan removed the straw around the cavity, then quickly set the plank in place. Colleen peered through the gap. And again the warehouse door opened.

"It's Maranzano," Colleen whispered over her shoulder. "There's someone with him." She spun around. "He's blindfolded!"

Callaghan joined her at the spy-hole. Maranzano was prodding a dark-suited man between the shoulders with his *lupara*, propelling him towards the oil lamp. In the dim light, the man appeared to be young, dark-haired, with olive-skin.

The greasy-haired *mafioso* stood up, grabbing his *lupara*, as Maranzano forced the prisoner to sit. Ferret-mean entered the circle. Maranzano uttered one word to him. Placing his *lupara* against a crate, ferret-mean removed the prisoner's blindfold. Maranzano put the muzzle of his *lupara* against the young man's temple and asked him a question. The man shook his head. Resting his weapon next to ferret-mean's, Maranzano gave the *mafioso* a brief nod. Removing a thin piece of rope from his pocket, ferret-mean looped it and threw it over the prisoner's head, pulling it tight around his neck. The young man clawed at the *garotte*, his head rocking violently from side to side. The *mafioso* relaxed the cord, and Maranzano repeated his question. But again the prisoner refused to reply. Ferret-mean reapplied his *garotte*. This time, the young man's struggles were less violent, the strength sapping out of him.

"Michael, we must do something!"

Callaghan crossed swiftly to the plank. Flinging himself up, he landed heavily with both feet, tilting the slab. The top cask crashed to the floor, splintering open, it's contents splashing over the three *mafiosi* and their prisoner. The middle crate fell off, the bottom one slid forward, and Callaghan hurled himself through the gap. The greasy *mafiosi* was nearest; he'd dropped his *lupara*, and was clawing at his eyes. Picking up the gun by the barrel, Callaghan swung it around, breaking the man's skull. Ferret-mean was scrambling on the floor for his weapon. Callaghan brought the butt down on the man's neck, and heard the bone snap. Throwing himself sideways, Callaghan was already cocking the *lupara*'s hammer as Maranzano snatched up his shot-gun and swivelled around, arcing the twin-barrels towards him. Callaghan pulled the trigger first. The shot tore a huge hole in Maranzano's chest, hurling him backwards amongst the empty boxes and barrels, where he lay, staring sightlessly up at the warehouse ceiling.

The young man crossed over to Maranzano's body, and looked down at it for a moment, then, kneeling, he made the sign of the cross, and recited in Latin: *Requiem aeternam dona ei, Domine. Et lux perpetua luceat ei.* The prayer over, he spat twice, first in Maranzano's right eye, then his left.

Hearing Colleen's cry of horror, Callaghan turned and saw her leaning against the barricade for support, staring at the man with open disgust. Then she gave a warning cry: "Michael!"

Callaghan spun around to see the young man pointing Maranzano's *lupara* expertly straight at him. His eyes never leaving Callaghan, he backed across the floor, then out through the door.

Colleen ran to Callaghan's side. "Michael! He was a priest! What he did was revolting! And why did he hold the gun on you? What does it all mean?"

Callaghan remained silent for a moment, then finally gave a wry smile. "I should have seen it all sooner, Colleen. That's the second twist in less than an hour. I wonder if there's any more?"

"Twist? What twist."

"The emblem. Sweeny took one look at it, and worked it all out, while it's been staring me in the face for two months and I never saw it."

"Saw what?"

"Who Martens is."

"Who he is! He's a Black Knight. A political assassin. We already know that."

"Yes, but he's more than that. Infinitely more." Callaghan got to his feet. "I'll explain it all when we get to the Consulate. In the meantime, Cottone's going to be wanting to avenge the death of his son-in-law, so the sooner we're away from here, the better."

Stopping only to pick up a *lupara* and bandoleer, and stick a knife in his sheath, Callaghan hurried Colleen out of the warehouse.

32

"YOU may leave it with me, Callaghan," said Spencer. "I will write Washington a full report and have it dispatched by the first available steamship. Rest assured that neither Cottone nor his *mafiosi* will be allowed to enter our country."

"Thank you, sir."

The consul thoughtfully swirled the amber liquid round his brandy glass. "And now, what about Martens?"

Increasingly concerned by Callaghan's and Colleen's nonappearance, Spencer had not waited the twenty-four hours to read Head's diary. Horrified by the account, and convinced that Callaghan had become another of Martens' victims, he'd been on the verge of calling the Genoa police when they'd arrived at the consulate. He was now fully informed of the entire affair.

Callaghan placed his empty glass on a side-table.

"Sweeny started it," he began, "by boasting he knew how to find Martens." Colleen turned away from the fire, anxious not to miss a word. "As soon as he'd left, Maranzano brought in a prisoner and began torturing him to make him talk. Later, when I realized he was a priest, everything suddenly fell into place. Including the emblem, which Sweeny recognized — it's nothing to do with any Death League. It's a Jesuit emblem; I vaguely remember seeing it as a boy in school. It's intended to illustrate the seven deadly sins, with the swords placed in various parts of the body supposedly identified with each temptation: pride, wrath, envy, gluttony, avarice, sloth, with the seventh, in the crotch, for lust."

"You mean that the palazzo was once owned by the Jesuits?"

"Yes, sir. Probably a seminary."

"Well at least it confirms Martens connection with Father Becker," said Colleen.

"It does. But not the way you imagine, Colleen."

"What do you mean?"

"Martens and Becker are one and the same man."

Colleen stared. "But that can't be! Father Murray identified the body; and he conducted the internment service."

"Yes. That blinded me too. I can only guess that despite what he said, Murray must be an ultramontane, and either knew, or guessed, what was happening. In fact I think he deliberately misled me, to put me off the scent. The body at the foot of the bridge was that of the real Arian Martens. If I'm right, he was an ordinary German seaman, who just happened to resemble Becker. Becker murdered him for his papers — "

"If I'm following you both correctly," Spencer interrupted them, are you saying the killer's a Jesuit priest?"

"I'm afraid so, sir," Callaghan replied. "On the *Mary Celeste*, I saw him kneeling in front of a sword. Colleen later identified the hilt as that of the Black Knights, and I assumed he was carrying out some form of ritual ceremony, but looking back on it now, it's more likely he was using the hilt as a substitute Cross."

581

"Then he's not a Black Knight after all?"

"On the contrary, he's very much a Black Knight, Totenbund, Death League, call them what you will. it's my guess he joined them in Berlin to help restore the Church, and free the Pope. By coincidence, Beckx chose him to sail to New York, in order to liaise with Kaufmann, and get Sweeny's diamonds safely shipped to Europe. If I'm right, Sweeny intended donating a percentage of the two hundred million — say ten per cent, that's twenty million, one hell of a lot of money — to Father-General Beckx to help the cause of restoring the Church, and freeing the Pope from the Vatican. However, unknown to Beckx, Becker was already up to his eyeballs in the revolutionary movement. Having reached New York, he became greedy, and decided to divert the entire two hundred million to the cause — Cause with a capital 'C'. He forced Kaufmann to co-operate, probably by threatening the life of his wife; and the rest you know."

"You must be mistaken, Callaghan,"

Spencer frowned. "It seems inconsistent for a man to be both priest and killer."

"Not really, sir. We are all of us part good and evil, as I know to my own cost. I recently let the bad side of my nature take away four years of my life that could have been wonderful." He gave Colleen a rueful smile. "With Becker, the separation is obviously more extreme. Having worked in the College of Propaganda in Rome, he's probably a hyper-ultramontane who regards Victor Emmanuel's imprisonment of the Pope, and Bismarck's *Kulturkampf* policy in Germany, as akin to blasphemy. In fact, it's more than likely he considers both men to be instruments of the Devil, being used to spread darkness across Europe. He would regard their removal as a holy victory in the fight against Satan."

"Bit beyond me, all this," Spencer muttered. "I'm Episcopalian. Rarely go to church, especially since arriving in Italy."

"Just think of him as a fanatic, sir, a latter-day Ignatius Loyola, whom, I rather suspect, he's trying to emulate."

"Come, come, Callaghan," Spencer

protested. "That's a bit much, comparing a killer to a revered saint."

"Perhaps so," Callaghan conceded. "Nevertheless, there are certain parallels between the two. Especially in the situation facing the Catholic Church, both now, and some, three hundred and fifty years ago, when Ignatius came to its rescue."

"Such as?" Spencer demanded.

"As I'm sure you know, sir, the Catholic Church was losing ground to the Protestant Reformation. The Church's prestige had sunk to an all-time low, partly through a succession of corrupt, worldly popes. People began parting company with Rome, slowly at first, then in ever increasing numbers. Then Ignatius suddenly arrived on the scene to stop the rot. Prior to his religious conversion, he was a Spanish soldier, so I suppose it was inevitable that his way of tackling the problem was more military than spiritual. Having devised what can best be described as the Jesuit manual, known as the *Spiritual Exercises*, with its concentration on the terrors of Hell and . . . "

"Ah, yes," Spencer protested, "but dammit, Callaghan, that was hundreds of years ago, when people still believed in hell-fire and demons. Modern thinking is quite different."

"Not Jesuit thinking," said Callaghan. "I once had to research the Order for my father's newspaper. Their indoctrination methods are still unchanged to this day. Becker will have undergone the same intensive ten-year training. They also have a maxim: 'The end justifies the means'. Over the years, some Jesuits have used that phrase to justify even regicide — "

"Oh, come!" Spencer objected. "I cannot accept that!"

"This is not an opinion, sir, but historical fact. Henry the Fourth of France was the victim of a Jesuit plot. There was even a pope, according to Colleen's Gibraltarian librarian. And more recently, our own Abraham Lincoln. I could go on . . ."

"No, that's quite enough," said Spencer hastily. "I'm beginning to be persuaded. In which case, we are also dealing with a man of considerable intellect, which

585

makes him infinitely more dangerous than a common assassin."

"And a man with a very strong motive, when you consider the way the Jesuits have been persecuted of late, thinking he has right on his side. And as we know from history, there's nothing worse than a fanatic fighting for a cause he believes in. Calvin had a man named Servetus burnt at the stake just because the poor guy disagreed with him on the doctrine of the Trinity. As for Becker, with the militant speeches the Pope's been making recently, he probably can't wait for the revolution to get started. I've a hunch he's set up his own body of Jesuit soldiers, like Loyola, except that in Becker's case, he's training assassins, not missionaries."

"Trained assassins!" Spencer jerked upright. "What makes you think that?"

"Some papers I found in his sea-chest. They were in German, but Colleen had them translated. They referred to an ancient Islamic sect of fanatics called the Assassins. Becker had obviously been studying their methods — "

"I've read about them," Spencer

586

interrupted. "A body of Shiite funda-mentalist killers. Their leader used to test their obedience by ordering men to leap off the nearest cliff to their deaths. He also indoctrinated them with drugs."

"Yes, sir. Their methods of killing were sword and poison. As you know from Head's diary, two of Becker's victims had their throats slashed, while Briggs and the two in New York were killed with strychnine pills, each strong enough to kill ten men."

"Yes," Spencer pursed his lips. "Then we're really dealing with a psychopath." The consul paused for a moment, reflectively. "I wonder which side of his nature is predominant? Jesuit? Black Knight? Or Assassin?"

"Maybe all three personalities existing together within one body, if that's possible."

"Dubious," Spencer frowned, not so certain. "However, be that as it may, what made him copy an Islamic sect? It seems a strange thing for a Jesuit priest to do?"

"I'd say he was trying to emulate Loyola."

"In what way?"

"According to the sceptics, the *Spiritual Exercises* — and their emphasis on experiencing Heaven and Hell — were stolen from Islam, rather than dictated by the Virgin Mary, as Ignatius claimed. It's sometimes described as the Jesuits's Koran. At the time of Loyola's conversion, Southern Spain was just emerging from eight hundred years of Muslim rule, so he would have been fully conversant with their training methods, many of which are similar to ones found in the *Exercises*."

"So Becker decided to follow him? On the principle of what was good enough for Saint Ignatius was good enough for him?"

"Something like that, sir. In his quest, he unfortunately found the Assassins, who were exactly what he was looking for, with their short-cut methods of indoctrination by drugs. Unlike Loyola, Becker doesn't have ten years to train his recruits. He wants them ready yesterday. Which is why I'd lay ten to one that somewhere out there, he's got a training-camp rather like the Assassins *Alamut*."

"With what precise aim?" asked Spencer, perplexed.

"I know it will sound far-fetched, sir," Callaghan replied, "but I suspect his primary objective is to exterminate leading Italian and German politicians, with the main targets being King Victor Emmanuel and Count Bismarck."

"Good heavens!" Spencer jumped to his feet and paced the room. "If you're right, Callaghan, this is serious, damned serious. It may be the lesser of evils to let Sweeny and Cottone find him."

"That may not solve it," Colleen suddenly spoke out. "Sweeny considers himself to be religious. And Becker's a priest. Sweeny's only concern is to retrieve his diamonds, and get on with his plans to bring the Mafia to the States. If he does find Becker, I suspect he'd let him go, rather than have him killed. And that should also suit Cottone, who'd like nothing better than have Becker assassinate Victor Emmanuel, with the blame laid on the Church, not his Mafia."

Spencer massaged the top of his bald head. "That's a point," he conceded.

"So, where do we go from here?"

Callaghan shrugged. "I'm not too sure, sir. Sweeny said he knew how to find him, but I've no idea where he's likely to start."

"Probably the Catholic churches," Spencer suggested, "in the hope of finding some other priest in the know."

"But I thought all the churches were closed?"

"For worship," the consul explained. "But many of them are rich in treasures and paintings. In such cases, priests have been retained as paid guardians of the State. There are a large number of wealthy churches in Genoa. In the meantime," he continued, "I'd better write to my colleague in Florence, requesting him to go to Fiesole, and inform General Beckx that his emissary has turned into a renegade. I'll also acquaint the Genoa authorities of our suspicions, asking them to confine Sweeny and Cottone to their hotel, and appealing for their assistance in the search for Becker."

"How long will all that take them, sir?"

"At least twenty-four hours."

Callaghan stood up. "That's too long, sir. Sweeny's already got a head start on us. Things could start happening before then."

Colleen rose from her chair and came to his side. "Michael, what do you intend doing?"

He smiled to reassure her. "Only keep a watch on the hotel."

"But what if something transpires before help arrives?"

His smile faded. "I don't know. Let's just hope nothing does."

Colleen took his hand in hers. "Be careful. Don't forget that Cottone's probably already looking for you to avenge Maranzano. Her grip became tighter. "I won't feel safe until we are back home again."

"I'm afraid Cottone won't be stopped by an ocean, Mrs Callaghan." Spencer looked up from his desk. "Unless we find some evidence to put him away under lock and key, he won't rest until his family honour has been satisfied, even if it means sending his *mandatari* all the way to New York."

Seeing the stark fear in her eyes, Callaghan drew Colleen to him. "Don't worry," he murmured, despite the knot in his stomach. "Fate has been kind so far. It's not going to deal us a losing hand now."

Colleen returned his embrace. "God, Michael," she whispered. "Not fate."

★ ★ ★

The dark, unlit façade of Sant Ambrogia looked down on the black coach and horses waiting outside. Bruno sat on the driver's seat, his Asiatic eyes staring impassively at the building. The windows of the church suddenly reflected the flickering light of a candle. Bruno looked away, glancing around the empty piazza, knowing he would not have much longer to wait.

Inside the building, the Moorish-faced Nino watched the transept door open as a cassocked priest emerged, carrying a gold candlestick in front of his chest, his hand cupped around the flame to prevent it blowing out. The glow revealed the church's ornateness: marble and mosaic walls, ceilings covered in richly coloured frescoes, a high altar with four monolithic columns of black marble, and a number of large paintings.

The priest stopped before one of Saint Ignatius healing a demoniac. Kneeling in front of the painting, the priest placed the candlestick on the floor, then crossed himself and bent his head to pray.

Nino stepped out of the darkness. Placing his stiletto against the priest's throat, he forced the young man to his feet, then thrust him towards the main doors.

Before emerging into the night, Nino glanced out. The piazza was deserted. He hurried the priest into the waiting carriage. Flicking the reins, Bruno sped across the square, and into the Via Sellai.

As they entered the Piazza Carlo Felice, the moon emerged from behind a cloud and lit up the square. Without turning his head, Bruno saw the man in seaman's clothing hiding behind a pillar of the Teatro Carlo Felice, and immediately recognized him. Still looking straight ahead, he drove past the front of the hotel, then turned into the tunnel leading to the rear courtyard and the back stairs.

★ ★ ★

It did not take long for Nino to make the priest talk. No longer than it took to force the needle-sharp point of his stiletto under the nail of the young man's index finger, and prise it off. Had it not been for the face-towel stuffed into his mouth, the priest's screams would have woken the entire hotel.

When the young man recovered consciousness, he immediately revealed where Becker was hiding.

From his chair by the fire, Don Cottone looked across at Bruno. The mafioso slightly parted the window curtains. "*Si, padrino*, he is still there."

In the opposite chair, Sweeny stopped chewing his unlit cigar. "Why don't we just send Nino across to finish him off?" he asked. "Then tomorrow, once we've got the stones, we can let Becker go. He ain't gona do us any more harm."

The glow of the fire shone on the

594

silver-work of Maranzano's *lupara*, lying across Cottone's lap. "It is a matter of family honour," he stated, in a voice devoid of emotion, "which only I can satisfy."

33

IN the semi-darkness of the Teatro Carlo Felice's pillared entrance, Callaghan stamped on the paving-stones to restore his circulation. It had been a long cold night, but across the square the hotel was coming to life. Lights were showing in the staff's attic windows, most of the ground floor, and a number of the guests' rooms.

Stifling a yawn, he dug into his pocket for the last of the bread provided by Spencer's housekeeper. He ate it, thinking longingly of a hot bath and a five-course meal.

Then Callaghan saw the Asiatic Bruno and a black-cassocked priest emerge from the hotel tunnel, and head across the square. The priest was looking around with nervous, spasmodic movements, and his right hand was bandaged. They entered an avenue leading out of the south-east corner of the piazza. Despite the early hour, the streets were already filling with people and horse-traffic, and the rising sun was swiftly dispersing the flecked grey winter clouds.

Quickly checking the weapons hidden under his jacket — *lupara*, bandoleer — and the knife in its sheath, Callaghan moved out from behind the pillar. Staying close to the walls of the buildings, he followed the two men into the Via Giulia Stefano, keeping about a hundred yards behind.

From his first-floor window, Cottone watched Nino cross the *piazza* and follow the American. He waited until Nino had rounded the corner, then inserted two bullets into the empty chambers of the pistol held in his right hand.

Unaware he was being tailed, Callaghan hid inside a shop doorway as he saw Bruno and the priest turn into a stable-yard. A few minutes later they reappeared, on a mule-cart — the same one used to carry the barrel from the warehouse to the palazzo, he recognized the markings. The priest was driving. Jerking the reins, he pulled the mule left, heading towards a narrow gateway in a fortified wall at the far end of the Via.

597

Callaghan followed the cart through the arch, along a curving street, then through another gateway in a second fortified wall. The morning sun had driven away the clouds, and the sky was a brilliant azure.

Crossing an old stone bridge over a wide, swift-flowing river, the road now turned to dust, climbing above the city out into the country, leaving its white palaces and villas all huddled together far below. Beyond them, the wide blue bay stretched to a hazy, distant horizon.

There were many on the road, some going in the same direction as themselves, but most were journeying towards the city. Farmers with wagons, some empty, some full of produce; drovers herding animals, or packed mules; peasant-women with baskets full of fruit on their heads and tired children around their feet; and every once in a while, the more fortunate in a carriage and pair.

The cart lumbered on — with Bruno looking straight ahead, and the priest sometimes jigging the braces but hardly encouraging the mule to move any faster. The coast road was filled with the most breathtaking scenery Callaghan had ever seen; cliffs climbing so precipitously that the route was often forced through dark, jagged tunnels hewn out of the rock, before emerging into the sunlight and the luxuriant vegetation of chestnut trees, cypress, firs and palm trees, the Mediterranean appearing between their branches, its coastline indented with coves, and its waters reflecting the deep blue of the cloudless winter sky.

Sometimes passing an old watch-tower, and on one occasion, the ruins of an old castle, the road continued towards a distant, green, tree-covered promontory jutting out into the sea.

The sun had passed its zenith before they finally reached it. Turning into a dirt track, the cart proceeded across open ground, heading towards a forest of pines, that seemed to cover the whole of the peninsula. Far below, the Mediterranean stretched away into the distance, its white crested waves breaking against the rocky shoreline.

From the shelter of a large chestnut tree, Callaghan watched the cart disappear into the trees. Alongside the track was a dry, deep ditch. Sprinting to its cover, he crept along it until he reached the forest's edge.

Hiding behind a large boulder, Nino watched the American climb out of the ditch and dart into the trees. Selecting some stones, he swiftly built a cairn as a signal for his *padrino* to wait there in his coach.

Callaghan slipped from tree to tree, taking care not to tread on any loose twigs, following the cart track deeper into the forest, until the path dipped into a glade and stopped. Callaghan could see the mule between the shafts of the cart, tethered to a low-hanging branch, but there was no sign of the two men. Suddenly, from the slope above, he heard stones clattering down towards him. Climbing towards the sound, he crested the brow, and, through the trees, glimpsed Bruno and the priest disappearing deeper into the forest.

Using the tree-trunks as cover, Callaghan followed them, zig-zagging up slopes, then down into hollows, the thick shadows of the trees, broken by shafts of sunlight, across the floor of the forest.

From faraway he could hear the sound of the sea. Then the crashing of waves against rocks began to grow louder. More light filtering in through the trees told him they were nearing the end of the headland, and Callaghan knew it was time to make his move.

Ahead of him, the two men were nearing a rocky hillock, with a faint path skirting it to the left. As the priest led Bruno down the track, Callaghan sped ahead to the right, weaving between the trees. Reaching the other side before them, he hid behind a thick shrub, under an overhanging outcrop of rock. Placing his *lupara* on the ground, he unsheathed his knife. Seconds later, the two appeared around a corner of the track, the priest still leading.

As they drew level with Callaghan, the priest suddenly picked up the skirts of his cassock and started running down the track. In one swift movement, a stiletto appeared in Bruno's hand, his arm drew back, and the knife flashed through the air. The priest fell, the blade embedded between his shoulder-blades. His body rolled down a steep bank and thudded against a tree. As Bruno crossed to the edge of the path to look down, Callaghan crept up behind him, threw his left arm around the man's throat and brought his knife upwards under the ribcage, into the heart. Bruno's body sagged, then toppled down the slope, on top of the priest's corpse.

Wiping the blade on the grass, Callaghan went back for the *lupara*, to find a small boulder had fallen off the outcrop on to the weapon, breaking the trigger and bending the barrel. Cursing Fate, Callaghan unfastened the bandoleer, and threw it on the ground.

Nino watched the American turn away and head for the edge of the forest. By dropping the rock on the *lupara*, he'd not only disarmed him, but also obeyed his *padrino*'s order to give the man no reason to suspect he was being followed.

Reaching the treeline, Callaghan looked out over the panoramic sweep of the Mediterranean. To his left the shimmering bay extended far back to the distant mainland; and through the huge chestnut trees draping the hillside to his right, was a vast blue expanse of water, spreading out as far as the eye could see.

At the extreme edge of the headland, almost hidden by the lush vegetation, rose the walls, battlements and rounded watchtower of an ancient castle.

Becker had chosen well, Callaghan thought. If the Assassins' *Alamut* had been the most beautiful spot since the Garden of Eden, then this was surely its successor.

He gazed at the castle, noting the magnificent chestnut tree that stood against the western wall, its branches overhanging the battlements. Calculating it would be dusk in about two hours, he settled down to wait.

From behind a tree about a hundred yards away, Nino stared impassively at the castle, then back to the American. Knowing the man could do nothing until dark, Nino turned away and headed back through the forest to meet his *padrino*.

★ ★ ★

Callaghan let go of the branch and dropped the few feet to the battlement.

603

Finding the heavy wooden door to the tower unlocked, he quickly passed through and emerged on a landing halfway up a curving flight of stone stairs. At the top was a solid wooden door with large iron hinges, studded with huge nail-heads. He climbed up and cupped his ear to it, but there was only silence. Returning to the landing, he began inching his way down the spiral steps, hardly daring to breathe. He rounded a corner, on to a long arched gallery of dark wooden doors, each with a solid, eye-level hatch.

From behind the first door, he could hear wailing and moaning. Opening the hatch, Callaghan peered through to nine young men in brown homespun robes, all in various stages of paroxysmic agonies. Three were writhing on the floor. Four were huddled against the walls with their knees drawn tight into their stomachs. And two were just staring terror-stricken into space.

Hurriedly closing the hatch Callaghan approached the next door. Again there was moaning, but this sounded very different from the first. Softer, gentler, like the sighing of people in supreme ecstasy. Through the hatch he saw seven men — all young like the others, but wearing white robes — lying down on mattresses spread across the floor. The look on each face was of extreme bliss, and three had their arms stretched out in adoration towards someone only they could see.

Hearing a door open behind him, Callaghan turned and saw five young men, wearing black robes with red sashes, in the gallery. One was the man who had driven the cart to the palazzo. Each had a sword in his sash. They stood still, staring zombie-like at him, then, drawing their swords, they advanced on him, blocking the way back to the battlement.

The only escape was down. Callaghan turned and ran along the gallery. As he reached the stairs he could hear them in pursuit, but only the sounds of their feet, no voices, and therefore all the more eerie. Tearing down two flights, he found himself in another large hallway of closed doors and, at the far end, a long corridor.

He dashed down it, but there was no

sign of an exit. Behind him, he heard the men closing in on him. Feeling like a trapped animal, he turned to face them, then saw some stone steps to his left, leading down to an open door. Desperate, he took them two at a time, and came into a huge, high-ceilinged scullery with a stone-flagged floor. The door was thick and stout and had a heavy iron lock with a key. Callaghan slammed it shut and turned the key — it would buy him precious minutes. In the far corner were two more doors. The first revealed a large food store; the second opened to another flight of stone steps. Almost falling in his haste, he raced down them to a stone-walled passageway, leading to a heavy wooden door. Callaghan wrenched it open. The fading light, filtering in through two slits in the greystone walls, showed a low arched cellar thick with cobwebs and dust, with a tarpaulin-covered stack in the middle of the floor.

But there was no way out.

Above him Callaghan heard the distant pounding on the scullery door. Constant, rhythmical beats, with the slow regularity of a church bell. Callaghan was under no illusions as to what Becker would do to him. Remembering Kaufmann's and Martens' broken and twisted bodies, Callaghan felt a cold shiver crawling up his spine. Determined not to succumb without offering resistance he lifted the tarpaulin, hoping to find something more substantial than a knife to use as a weapon.

Looking down upon the crates of explosives, detonators, coiled fuse wires, boxes of vestas, Callaghan saw all the proof of Becker's revolutionary intentions and, maybe, the way to prevent him.

OK, so it meant he would be blown up with them, but surely that was preferable to any of Becker's Assassin methods. Reaching for his knife, he paused. If he used a whole coil of wire the explosion would be delayed, giving him a chance to escape.

Connecting the detonators, Callaghan lit the fuse, then quickly returned to the scullery, closing the cellar door. The hall door was still resisting the battering, but the lock was beginning to come away.

Withdrawing his knife, Callaghan stood

in the middle of the floor and waited.

The lock gave, and the door burst open. Swords drawn, the five priests advanced on him slowly in a half-circle. Callaghan dropped his knife in a faked gesture of surrender, anxious to get out of the scullery before the explosives went off.

Indicating with their swords, the priests forced him back up the two flights of stairs to the gallery, then up the spiral steps to the room at the top of the tower. Knocking on the iron-studded door, they were bidden: *"Herein!"*

From his earlier study of the castle, Callaghan knew it to be the uppermost room, high above the battlements. The walls — broken by one full window leading on to a large stone balcony — were rounded, with no corners. The furniture was austere, two wooden chairs on bare floorboards, a simple bed, and a dark oak table behind which sat Karl Becker, wearing his black robe and red sash.

He looked up from a large, black, leather-bound Bible. On the table, in a plain pewter holder, was a single candle, its flickering flame lighting only the prominent features of his face, leaving the hollows in shadow. The visual effect was one of evil. On the wall behind him was a carved wooden Cross, bearing the figure of the crucified Christ.

On the floor was an open chest inside which a hundred million dollars worth of diamonds glinted in the moonlight. A number appeared to be tinted red, as though reflecting all the blood which had been shed.

His slate-blue eyes mirroring the candle-light, intensifying his unblinking gaze, Karl Becker looked up at Callaghan.

"How did you find me?" he whispered.

Callaghan stared back, trying to defeat the hypnotic gaze. With an effort, he tore his eyes away, and glancing to his left, noticed four ancient engravings, similar to the ones in the library of Saint Francis Xavier in New York.

The first was of men and women with terror-stricken faces clawing and screaming to escape the flaming pit of Hell, their way barred by thick iron grating, and threatened by a bolt of lightning from the black skies above.

The second showed a young man, his left arm held by an angel and his right by a demon, being persuaded to choose between two visions: one a pathway leading to Heaven, the other of souls burning in Hell.

The third depicted Christ, surrounded by His followers, holding His Cross in front of Him like a standard-bearer entering battle, as He confronted Satan and an army of demons.

The last engraving showed a stairway filled with men who had chosen to fight for Christ, each bearing a Cross, as they ascended to Heaven to claim their eternal reward.

"Have you come alone?" Karl Becker leant across the table, his pupils distending as they bore into Callaghan's, then, in a threatening, muted voice, asked, "How much do you know?"

"Everything," Callaghan replied, conscious of the seconds ticking away to the explosion. If he could just keep the psychopath talking until it happened, the battlement and the trees were only a short flight away. "I know your name: Karl Becker. That you are a Jesuit priest. That you murdered a diamond merchant named Kaufmann, and a German seaman named Martens. And the entire complement of the *Mary Celeste*. All for two barrels of diamonds. I also know your motive. To finance a revolution to remove Victor Emmanuel and Bismarck, and restore the Church.

"Tell me," Callaghan deliberately challenged, "aren't you going against all Christian teaching? I thought it said in the Bible — somewhere in Romans — that all governments are ordained of God, and that those who refuse to obey the law of the land are therefore rebelling against God's holy will?"

Becker continued to stare at him, then suddenly pushed his chair back, and stood up. Crossing the room, he opened the window. Hanging low in the sky, the pale moon shone through the trees, casting dark shadows across the balcony. From far below, came the sound of waves crashing on the rocks.

"Come here," Becker whispered, stepping outside.

Callaghan followed him. The balcony protruded high above the castle, with a

611

sheer drop down past the cliffs to the sea far below. Casting a silver glow across the dark waters, the moon lit up the bay as clearly as daylight. The night-blue sky above was full of stars, and the faraway mainland mountains speckled with a myriad of flickering lights. Callaghan had a strange unearthly feeling of being suspended over the whole scene. He stepped back.

"I see you feel it," Becker murmured. "What does it say to you?"

Still feeling as though he was falling, Callaghan shook his head.

Becker gave a thin smile and answered his own question, quoting from the Bible: "*And the Devil took Christ up into an exceeding high mountain and sheweth him all the kingdoms of the world, and the glory of them.*"

Turning from Callaghan, he stared out over the view, the look in his eyes suggesting he was far away. Surely, Callaghan thought, recognizing the passage from the Temptation of Christ by Satan, the madman wasn't identifying himself with Christ in the wilderness?

Suddenly Becker continued: "*And the*

612

Devil saith unto Him, 'All these things will I give thee if Thou wilt fall down and worship me'. Then said Christ unto him, 'Get thee behind me, Satan, for it is written: Thou shalt worship the Lord thy God and Him only shalt thou serve'."

Becker's eyes now burned feverishly into Callaghan's. "Thus you have your answer. Having refused to bow the knee to His enemy, Christ took up His Cross and became the victor over Satan. And following the example of our militant Lord, I also refuse to bow the knee to those who seek to destroy His Church."

Callaghan deliberately interrupted, wondering when those damned explosives were going to blow. "But surely, did He not also say: '*Blessed are the merciful for they shall obtain mercy, and blessed are the peacemakers for they shall be called the children of God*'?"

"But first must come the victory over evil!" Becker returned, exultantly. "This our Lord clearly foretold when He warned: '*Think not that I come to send peace on earth. I come not to send peace, but the sword*'."

"But that's a false interpretation,"

Callaghan dragged out the argument. "You know the rule for obeying Scripture: add nothing to it, take nothing from it, change nothing in it. When Christ said that, He was not claiming to be the instigator. He was warning His disciples that by preaching His Gospel, they would incur Satan's wrath, and that the Devil would resort to every means possible to oppose them, even the sword. Surely," Callaghan paused, realizing he was defending what for years he'd been denying, "the religion of Christ is based on love, not, as you would have it, the destruction of those whose views do not agree with your own? As a result, you have yourself fallen into Satan's trap and murdered an innocent child."

Becker smiled. "'*Blessed are those whom men shall revile and persecute*'," he quoted softly, "'*and say all manner of evil against falsely, for the sake of Christ*'. The child was sacrificial in the greater cause, as were the children of Bethlehem when they were slain in order that Christ might live, thus fulfilling the words of the prophet: '*that in Rama, there was heard lamentation and great mourning, Rachel weeping for her children'*."

The man's definitely deranged, Callaghan decided, looking into his feverish eyes, then returning into the room.

Becker remained staring at the view, then suddenly stepped back through the open window, and came right up to Callaghan. His eyes were now icy cold. "But we are not here to argue doctrine. Apart from yourself . . . " he whispered, his tone threatening, "who . . . else . . . knows?"

"God?" Callaghan replied.

Becker studied him, his face showing no emotion. Then he walked over to the table and opened a small oak chest from which he took three cloth bags, two in differing shades of brown, and one black. Untying the darker brown sack, he withdrew a pinch of grey powder, then nodded to the priests. As two grabbed Callaghan's arms, Becker approached him with the powder. "*Ololiuqui*," he stated. "From the seeds of the Mexican *Ipomoea violacea*. Mixed with black henbane it produces a foretaste of Hell which can persuade the most stubborn to confess the truth."

He turned to the priests. "*Halt ihn fest!*"

Dragging Callaghan down to the floor, four priests pinioned his arms and legs, while a fifth held his head firm and squeezed his nostrils tight. Kneeling alongside him, Becker prised Callaghan's mouth open and poured in the powder, forcing him to swallow. It was extremely bitter.

Straightaway Callaghan felt himself begin to shiver. Then came giddiness, followed by a feeling of numbness, and a painful sensitivity to even the dim light of the candle. He closed his eyes and found he was falling, falling, falling, into a deep dark pit which was blacker than the darkest night. From its bottom emanated the most terrible sounds, the cries of all the eternally damned wailing with the heart-breaking pain of souls in torment. Even as he fell, twisting and turning ever deeper into the void, Callaghan tried putting his hands to his ears to shut out the awesome howls, but was unable to move them. Suddenly the pit widened into infinity, and coming towards him out of the blackness was a consuming fire. In its centre were the inhabitants of Hell: pleading faces looking upwards, arms and claw-like fingers outstretched; and dancing around them, oblivious of the flames, were cackling fiends and demons, creatures more monstrous and frightening than any imagination could conjure. And there, in the midst of them, Callaghan suddenly saw his own face, the skin slowly peeling off in the heat, layer by layer, until only a staring black eyeless skull remained. Then the flames started on his body.

Through it all he could hear and feel his heart pounding, and his mind being deprived of all reason. Then came Becker's voice, insistent, whispering: "Who else knows? Tell me, and you will be released from the fire."

As the flesh parted from his body, leaving only a skeleton, a part of him screamed to tell Becker everything, but his stronger half fought back, not allowing him to speak.

Slowly the visions grew fainter, floating away as though on a cloud. And then they were gone.

Callaghan surfaced in the room, his

clothes soaked with perspiration. Becker was leaning over him, with a pinch of brown powder between his fingers.

"Extremely resistant," the Jesuit murmured softly. "But having survived Hell, we'll see what a taste of Heaven can achieve." Again forcing Callaghan's mouth open, he let the powder pour slowly out of his hand. "Peyote, from the Mexican cactus *peyotl* of the genus *Lophophora*."

This time, Callaghan, felt a wonderful sense of anticipation, then an overwhelming exhilaration combined with rapture. Before his eyes the walls of the room slowly dissolved into a mighty yet inaudible stream full of indescribably beautiful colours which were not of this earth. He could feel himself smiling in pure joy at the sensation of sheer bliss. He tried to fight it, but the feeling was too strong. Bathed in a glittering silver glow he floated through air that was both scintillating and purifying, towards a distant, radiant glow that he knew, from the heavenly music emanating from it, must be eternal, holy, the ultimate. He wanted to experience it more than anything he'd ever known.

"Tell me who else knows," he heard God ask, in a voice so gentle, and so full of love he wanted to cry. "Tell me, and you will enter into my Kingdom."

With tears streaming down his face, Callaghan held nothing back, telling God about Colleen waiting in the consulate, and Sweeny and Cottone in the Hotel de Genes.

Slowly the light faded. Callaghan stretched his arms towards it but it was now no more than a distant speck. And then it went out.

Callaghan found himself back in the room, feeling strangely fresh and alive, with none of the after-effects normally associated with drugs. Everything he'd experienced was clear in his mind. Was there a Heaven out there somewhere, he wondered, or had it simply been a hallucinatory experience?

"*Bring ihn hier!*" Callaghan heard Becker command, then felt himself being raised to his feet. He looked across the room and saw Becker out on the balcony with the black bag in one hand, and a brown pill in the other.

The strychnine pill!

Callaghan fought desperately to free himself, but the priests' combined strength was too much for him. They dragged him through the open window, and he heard the sea pounding against the jagged rocks underneath.

"Heaven?" Becker asked. "Or Hell? You've seen them both. Which will you find yourself in?" He paused. "I think . . . "

O, God! Callaghan cried out inwardly, the plea coming from the very depth of his soul. *Please save me!*

" . . . Hell!" said Becker, raising the strychnine pill.

Please! O, please God, please, please help me!

As the pill touched Callaghan's lips, he heard a shot, then saw Becker stagger back over the balustrade and plunge into the black depths below.

Jerking himself free from the clutches of the silent priests, Callaghan spun around. Don Cottone was standing in the room, a smoking pistol in his hand. Behind him stood the Moorish Nino and four other *mafiosi*. The *capomafia* looked at Callaghan with cold eyes, then raised the pistol, and pointed it at his chest.

"A life for a life," he stated, with no inflexion in his voice.

The barrel moved slowly upwards until it was aimed straight at Callaghan's head. Cottone pulled the trigger. The bullet whistled past Callaghan's ear, into the darkness.

Throwing the pistol at Callaghan's feet, Don Cottone walked out of the room.

34

"WHY did he do it?" Callaghan asked.

He was standing with Sweeny by the open window, the lights still glimmering across the bay. Nino and the chest of diamonds were long gone. The other *mafiosi* were in the cellar, removing the dynamite. The one sent down to discover why the charge hadn't detonated, had returned with a half-burnt coil, a fault in the wire having extinguished the spark. Providence? Callaghan had wondered. Who knew? Who ever knew? Only someone infallible. And no one human born could ever be that.

"Why did he do it?" he repeated, thoroughly perplexed.

Sweeny gave him a twisted grin. "To satisfy some stupid debt of honour, that's why. The priest you saved in the warehouse was his favourite nephew, his dead brother's son — "

"His nephew! He wasn't one of Becker's men?"

"Hell, no! Did you think he was?"

"Something like that."

Sweeny looked surprised. "You've certainly been getting it all wrong, Michael. He's the one who introduced me to Cottone. I met him by accident in Notre Dame Cathedral in Paris. He's also Cottone's heir, the one chosen to succeed him. It was never Maranzano, which is why he was plotting to take over. The nephew found out about the plan, and rather than risk Maranzano intercepting a telegraph, took the first available ferry from Palermo. But one of Maranzano's pals took the chance of wiring him. Maranzano was waiting for Cottone's nephew at the dockside, and was grilling him to reveal all he knew, when you broke out. According to Cottone's crazy code, he owed you two lives. His own — which he paid off by killing Becker — and his nephew's — "

"Which he settled by deliberately missing me?"

"Yes. Stupid, ain't it?" Sweeny growled. "Anyway, it means we're all even, and we can all go home. Except for one last thing."

Sweeny picked up the Bible and the candle from the table and stepped out on to the balcony.

"*I cast this man out from the fellowship of the Church*," he intoned. Opening the Bible, he ceremoniously closed it. Then he threw the lighted candle over the balustrade towards Becker's body sprawled down on the rocks below.

Callaghan recalled a vivid scene from his childhood, of a ceremonial service at his church to excommunicate a member who'd fallen from grace. After pronouncing the dreadful sentence, the priest had closed the Bible, symbolizing the book of life, then extinguished a candle by throwing it to the floor, to show that the light of the soul had been removed from the sight of God, and finally he tolled a bell as a death-knell for one who had died. For months afterwards, Callaghan had had nightmares about it.

By the Bell, Book and Candle, thought Callaghan. Was it that easy for Sweeny to erase a renegade priest from the Church's roll-call? If there was a final Day of Judgement, would it be that easy then?

"I'll ring the bell when I get back to Palermo," said Sweeny as he re-entered the room. "I was gonna give one per cent to help get the Church restored — two million, that's a hell of a lot of money, but Becker got too greedy. I might still give it to the Church back home, but I'll give it some further thought first."

"If you do, make it one per cent of a hundred million, not two," said Callaghan. "On the way home I'm calling into Gibraltar to help close the Inquiry. So you can forget about the barrel on board the *Celeste*."

"Win some, lose some," Sweeny shrugged, slipping back into his East-Side accent. "Besides, that's peanuts compared to what we're gonna make over the next few years. Especially with Becker's drugs. After seeing those priests high on that heaven powder, it's gotta be the biggest potential money-spinner of them all."

Callaghan stared at him. "You don't still believe you're going to be allowed back into the States?"

"Sure. Why not?"

"Listen, Sweeny, by the time this story gets out . . . "

"What story?"

"This one. About the *Mary Celeste* and the *Dei Gratia*."

"Who's gonna publish it?"

"The *New York Times*."

"Michael, now who the hell's gonna believe you. Renegade priests. Barrels of diamonds. A deserted castle. Drugs. A plot to assassinate Bismarck and the King of Italy. And an organization called the Mafia that no one back home's even heard of . . . yet. Can you really see the *Times* publishing such a crazy story?"

"I've got the evidence to prove it, including the occupation of this castle."

"We've already almost emptied it," Sweeny sneered. "The priests will be taken to Palermo on Cottone's yacht until the effects of the drugs have worn off. The corpses will be disposed of, and, in a couple of hours, there'll be no sign of any occupation at all. Everything, except the explosives, which Cottone can use, will be at the bottom of the sea."

"I've got a diary to back it up."

"Whose?"

"The *Celeste*'s steward."

"Is it authenticated?"

"No. Why?"

"Then who's to say you didn't make it all up. If I was you, Michael, I'd forget it," said Sweeny, making for the door. "Try publishing and you'll be laughed to scorn."

Pausing by the door, Sweeny doffed his hat. "See you in New York, Michael."

★ ★ ★

The following evening, Colleen and a clean-shaven Callaghan were sitting at dinner together in the Hotel de Genes. He was ending his account, explaining that the Castello Portofino, situated at the tip of a lonely promontory, had been a military garrison ever since the Romans, only to be demilitarized five years ago and left deserted. Becker must have heard about the place after fleeing to Genoa to escape Bismarck's persecution of the Jesuits in Germany and had seen

627

its potential as an isolated indoctrination centre for his select band of young drug-induced assassins.

"They were all priests and novices who'd followed him from Berlin," Callaghan concluded. "From the very beginning, he used drugs to win them over, just like the Islamic Assassins."

"What about the *Celeste*?" asked Colleen. "Are you giving the story to Louis Jennings?"

"I've thought a lot about it," he replied. "Despite what Sweeny says, I think we could prove the diary's authenticity. But in the end, maybe it's best left as a mystery. We'll see what Jennings thinks. Otherwise the very fabric of Christianity might be undermined, because of one fanatic. Critics of religion — and I admit I was one of them — tend to judge God by the actions of those who claim to be believers. But thinking back to the castle, when I suddenly found myself defending the principles of the Sermon on the Mount, I now realize that God's existence is neither proved, nor disproved, by the actions of His followers, who are all human and subject to the same temptations. When one falls, then, as well as the so-called 'sinner', we also hold God guilty by association, to the point that some critics — and again I confess I was one of them — maintain that the very existence of sin is proof that there is no God. But to quote your Mr Turner: God did not create man to be a puppet. He gave him free will. To choose either good — or evil, as Becker did.

"The reason those poor kids back home go hungry is because of man's selfishness, not God's neglect. If one needs proof of God's existence, we have to look beyond man, to the wonder of Creation. The stars, the sun, moon, the very universe itself, revolving in an order, rather than disorder, is enough to make one realize there's a Creator behind it all." Callaghan's smile came from a renewed inner sense of conviction. "So, rather than allow the Church to be unfairly criticized because of the evil actions of one man, I think it's best to leave the *Celeste* well alone. Let her simply pass into history, and her mystery remain a mystery."

Colleen returned his smile, moved by his sentiments.

"But what about poor David and Oliver and the others still stuck in Gibraltar?"

"That shouldn't be too much of a problem," Callaghan replied. "When all's said and done, Flood's only got circumstantial evidence. And now we know that the threat against Desiah was only a bluff, David will be able to take the stand." He grinned mischievously. "I did consider sinking the vessel, but I don't think New York would appreciate having a hundred million dollars of its money lying at the bottom of Gibraltar harbour. Assuming David is awarded salvage, the cargo will continue on to Genoa, where Mr Spencer can arrange for the extra barrel to be taken to the consulate, and then inform New York."

"And when we ourselves get back there?"

"I'll take you up on the offer you made last night. But rather than sell your father's house, let's borrow against it, and sell mine instead. Together, we should raise enough to buy the newspaper back from the receiver." Callaghan looked thoughtful. "I keep remembering what Father Murray said about the United States one day becoming the leader of the English-speaking nations, and I agree with him. But there's so much to be done first — the continual fight against corruption in high places, like the Tweed Ring; the need to reconcile the North and South once again into one nation; and the constant struggle for a democracy in the face of the growing materialism created by the very rich. We can only assume the mantle of world-leader when all this is done, and we are truly 'united states'. It promises to be very exciting, and we can be a part of it, working together on our newspaper."

"And we can also help keep Sweeny, Cottone, and the Mafia out," Colleen added.

"Absolutely," Callaghan agreed. "Sweeny's gotten away with too much as it is."

He paused as a slim, dark-suited man approached the table and bowed. "Signor Callaghan?"

Callaghan nodded.

The man handed him a sealed envelope.

"A message, *signor*. From the American Consulate."

Callaghan opened it and read the brief note.

"What is it, Michael?"

"From Mr Spencer. His colleague in Florence has been to Fiesole. Apparently Father-General Beckx denies that the Society has a priest by the name of Karl Heinrich Becker."

Colleen frowned. "What do we make of that?"

Callaghan shrugged. "As far as I'm concerned, we should take it with a pinch of salt."

The dark suited man leant forward. "Is there any reply, *signor*?"

"No, thank you."

The man still hesitated, then asked, "I am sorry to trouble you, signor, but as I approached, I overheard you mention the name Sweeny. May I ask if you are acquainted with him?"

"We know of him," replied Callaghan.

"As the under-manager of the hotel, may I ask you whether you know his address, signor?" The man looked embarrassed. "I'm sure it must be an oversight, but Signor Sweeny left very early this morning without paying his account."

Colleen looked at Callaghan, a smile slowly spreading across her face. "What was that you were saying a second ago, Michael? About Sweeny having gotten away with too much?"

Epilogue

THE secret panelled door slid open and Father-General Beckx entered the Vatican.

Wearing his pure white robes, the Holy Father was at the far end of the *appartamenta*, seated on an ornate chair, on a raised dais. The Jesuit General slowly approached him, leaning heavily on his stick. The Pontiff held out his right hand, and lowering himself to his knees, Beckx reverently touched the tips of Pius's fingers, then kissed the papal ring. The Pope indicated a chair placed slightly to one side of the dais.

"How is your health, my friend?" The customary warmth was missing from Pius's voice.

"The mind is well, Holiness. The flesh less so. And the spirit is grieving that I was not able to fulfil your trust before the Act became law."

"God must have His purpose in allowing it, my friend," Plus said solemnly.

634

"I confess, despite much prayer, His reason remains obscure. According to the scriptures, man is told he is to be subject to sovereigns. But as Christ's sole appointed Vicar on Earth, my sovereignty is above all others. Were I to accept this usurper's conditions, then in the eyes of the world, I would be *his* subject, and, by implication, be acknowledging him as head of the Church."

"That is clearly not God's will, Holiness. Your mission must be to resist, and continue to refuse to leave the Vatican."

"Which it will be, my friend, up to the day when I am called to my eternal reward. But it would greatly encourage me to understand God's design. My only conclusion is that He is deliberately allowing us to go through the fire, so that we will emerge all the stronger to face the future challenges of the modern age. Already, with a common enemy to face, the process of conciliation has begun from within. For the first time in four hundred and fifty years, the great schism between ultramontane and Gallican is forgotten. They have put aside their claims for self-governing national churches, without reference to Rome, and join us in decrying this outrage against Holy Church. As a consequence, when Victor Emmanuel's soul is finally cast into the everlasting fire, the Church which emerges will be more united, and therefore all the more ready to assume its rightful position as the only true, universal Church of God."

"My spirit is already strengthened by your wise words, Holiness. It makes both of my crosses the easier to bear."

"*Both* crosses, my friend?"

"Yes, Holiness. The first was the unexplained withdrawal of a substantial sum promised by an American businessman currently on a cultural tour of Europe. The second was when my emissary to America, who was returning with a large contribution, went missing at sea. His vessel was discovered in mid-Atlantic with everyone on board missing, and no indication as to how they met their end. God alone knows what terrible fate the Evil One had waiting for them in the cold, grey Atlantic . . . " Beckx paused, unable to continue.

Pius leant forward in a gesture of compassion. "My friend, take strength in the fact that he is now receiving his reward. What was the name of the vessel?"

"The *Mary Celeste*, Holiness."

"*Maria Celeste*." Pius extended his arm and made the sign of the Cross. "And there is still no clue as to what happened?"

"None, Holiness. Only in Heaven is the answer known. On earth it will remain a mystery that will never be solved."

Historical Note

For over 120 years, the *Mary Celeste* has been one of the world's greatest sea mysteries, the subject of countless newspaper articles, books and TV documentaries, with theories ranging from giant squids, to UFOs, and the Bermuda Triangle.

Most of the myths surrounding the vessel can be attributed to a short story entitled, *J Habukuk Jephson's Statement*, published in Harper's Magazine, and written by a struggling twenty-five year old doctor named Arthur Conan Doyle, later to become famous as the creator of Sherlock Holmes. His first work of fiction, he deliberately misspelt her first name *Marie* — thus unintentionally giving her the name by which she is now more commonly known, even in public records. Among his story's many 'claims' was that 'the lifeboat was intact and slung upon the davits', a fact refuted by Gibraltar Consul Horatio Jones Sprague, in his report to Washington, dated 13th December 1872, in which he stated:

No ship's papers were found on board, except the log book, which has entries up to the 22nd or 23rd ultimo, nor were any boats found on board.

I began tackling the mystery in the circular book-lined room of the British Library. Here I discovered a book by Charles Edey Fay — an ex-vice president of the Atlantic Mutual Insurance, the *Celeste*'s insurers, still in business to this day — which turned out to be a mine of information. However, even Fay's book, as with all others on the subject, concentrates most of its attention on the *Celeste*, and gives very little about the *Dei Gratia*.

I therefore turned my attention to this ship, starting with the Maritime History Archive, Memorial University of Newfoundland. In response to my application for a copy of the *Gratia*'s crew list for 1872/73, I received the following reply:

Thank you for your letter of December 7, requesting information on the Dei Gratia. *We do not have the crew list or official log book for the vessel for 1872. I would suspect that it was not handed in to the Registrar General as it does not show on our index, and we had the locations of about 95% of existing crew lists.*

For the records relating to this particular voyage not to have been handed in, made me sense I was on to something. Deciding to find out all I could about the *Gratia*'s captain, David Morehouse, my next letter — to the Peabody Museum, Salem, Massachusetts — led me first to the Maritime Museum of the Atlantic, Halifax, Nova Scotia, and from there to the Volunteer Admiral Digby Historical Society — Digby (named after the Admiral) being the *Dei Gratia*'s port of registry. Here I struck gold in the person of Hilma Woods, the Society's Secretary, who not only informed me that a member of the Morehouse family, Inez Manzer Sypher Morehouse, had written a book entitled *330 years of Morehouse Genealogy, 1640 – 1970*, but also enclosed thirty photocopied pages on David Morehouse. Among them was a summary from an interview with Captain Morehouse's widow, published in the *Boston Sunday Post*, August 15, 1926, in which Mrs Morehouse had stated:

My husband knew Captain Briggs of the Mary Celeste well. In fact they were friends of many years. Now here is a strange coincidence that the Briggs family is evidently unaware of:

The Dei Gratia and the Mary Celeste were loading in New York at the same time. My husband frequently told me that on the night before the Mary Celeste sailed, he and Captain Briggs had a farewell dinner together at the old Astor House in New York. As both of their vessels were destined for Genoa, Italy, they parted with the friendly assurance that they would have another meal at that port.

The mystery now took on a new dimension. Before this, every article, book, documentary, had taken it for granted that the *Dei Gratia* had accidentally chanced on the *Mary Celeste* in mid-Atlantic. But now, the knowledge that the apparently deserted brig had drifted for nine days on one of the Atlantic's busiest sea-routes, without being discovered by any other vessel, then was chanced upon by the *Dei Gratia* — which did not leave until ten days after the *Celeste*, and whose captains had met at the Astor House the evening before the *Celeste* set sail — was, to put it mildly, rather coincidental.

My next step was to obtain copies of the Gibraltar Inquiry transcripts. On receipt, I found they contained only the replies of the witnesses, with very few commas or full stops to show where one sentence ended and the next began. Nor did they include the cross-questions asked by Solly Flood or Henry Pisani. The Inquiry scenes in this book — including especially Mr Flood's grilling, and the punctuation of the replies — are therefore based principally on the Admiralty advocate's suspicions and general temperament, as reported on in the newspapers of that time.

However, in reading the transcripts, my early suspicions were even further aroused by the fact that the *Gratia*, the heavier of the two vessels (transcripts, page 52) was able to make Gibraltar, yet Deveau in the lighter *Celeste* was forced 'to run up the Spanish coast, 30 miles after leaving Cape Cueta, or 40 miles that was after leaving Cueta at 6 a.m. in sight of land' (transcripts, page 10) despite the *Mary Celeste* keeping 'sight of the *Dei Gratia* until we arrived in the straits, when we lost sight of her' (page 20).

The Inquiry papers also revealed many other interesting facts:

1. That James Henry Winchester, major owner of the *Mary Celeste*, who sailed to Gibraltar to give evidence, stated under oath: 'I was in New York when the *Mary Celeste* sailed on her last voyage. I know what cargo she had on board. It consisted of 1701 barrels of alcohol, 1 barrel in dispute.' Asked about the sword discovered under Briggs's bed, he

replied: 'I do not know anything of the captain having a sword, nor of any sword being on board at all.'

2. That David Morehouse — without explanation — changed his mind and took the stand when the Inquiry resumed. Having stated under oath that the *Dei Gratia*'s cargo consisted of 'refined petrol, 1735 round barrels, and 1 in dispute', he did not volunteer, however, that he and Briggs knew one another, nor that they had dined together the night before the Celeste sailed.

3. Justice Sir James Cochrane, on being informed that the *Dei Gratia*, had left Gibraltar for Genoa with First Mate Deveau and the rest of the crew, while the Inquiry was still in progress, stated:

The conduct of the salvors in going away as they have done, has, in my opinion, been most reprehensible, and may probably influence the decision as to their claim for remuneration for their services; and it appears very strange why the captain of the Dei Gratia, *who knows little or nothing to help the investigation, should have remained here, whilst the first mate, and the crew who boarded the* Celeste *and brought her here, should have been allowed to go away as they have done.*

4. Deveau, when he returned to Gibraltar, did not endear himself to Sir James by revealing that the *Dei Gratia* had taken twenty-four days to sail to Genoa (a journey which took the *Mary Celeste*, when she was eventually released, only eleven days). Nor was Sir James pleased when Deveau informed the court:

I was obliged to leave one of the two men in hospital at Genoa, in consequence of his having strained or injured himself from over-exertion whilst bringing the Mary Celeste *to Gibraltar. His name is Charles Lund. He is still in hospital in Genoa.*

The fresh scrape marks on the bows, and the cut in the rail, were examined by John Austin, Surveyor of Shipping at Gibraltar, but never explained. Paras 24 and 47 of his Affidavit, refer to the 'sails split in a gale' and a 'length cut off with a knife' being used to cover the windows of the captain's cabin. Regarding the sword, Austin commented, in para 44:

I also observed in this cabin a sword in its scabbard which the marshal informed me he had noticed when he came on board for the purpose of arresting the vessel. It had not been affected by water, but, on drawing out the blade, it appeared to me as if it had been smeared with blood, and afterwards wiped.

The subsequent report of Dr J. Patron of Gibraltar, states that the sword blade, and 'some red-brown spots of wood, about half an inch in diameter with a dull aspect, which were separated with a chisel', were subjected to various tests '*according to present scientific knowledge*' and found to contain 'no blood'. (But what would present-day forensic tests have made of them? *Author*.)

The contents of the sea-chest marked 'Arian Martens' were never examined, only listed as part of the inventory of the *Mary Celeste*'s effects, made by the Vice-Admiralty Court.

On 5 February, the USS *Plymouth* under the command of Captain R. W. Shufeldt, arrived in Gibraltar on a routine visit. At the request of Consul Sprague, Shufeldt examined the *Mary Celeste*. The following day, 6 February, he submitted a written report to the consulate. The next day, 7 February, the USS *Plymouth* left Gibraltar. Sprague then submitted the report to the court. It included the following extract:

I am of the opinion that she (the Mary Celeste*) was abandoned by the master & crew in a moment of panic & for no sufficient reason. She may have strained in the gale through which she was passing & for the time leaked so much as to alarm the master, and it is possible that, at this moment, another vessel in* *sight, induced him (having his wife and child on board), to abandon thus hastily . . . Some day, I hope and expect to hear from her crew. If surviving, the master will regret his hasty action. But if we should never hear from them again, I shall nevertheless think they were lost in the boat in which both master & crew abandoned the* Mary Celeste.

As a result, on 14 March 1873, fully three months after reaching Gibraltar, Morehouse's claim was finally accepted, but rather than the usual one-half, he was awarded only £1,700 ($8,300), one-fifth of the value of ship and cargo, a percentage regarded by the insurance and shipping world at the time, as being totally incommensurate with such a hazardous salvage.

According to Maritime Registers, Deveau was allowed to leave Gibraltar before the award, rejoining the *Dei Gratia* as master and sailing to Sicily to pick up a return cargo of fruit for New York. On 13 May, on the journey home, the vessel called in at Gibraltar to pick up David

Morehouse, finally reaching New York on 19 June 1873.

As for the *Mary Celeste*, under a new master, Captain Blatchford, she was cleared from Gibraltar, with her original cargo, on 10 March, arriving Genoa on 21 March, where her hull was surveyed and found to be in perfect order. On 26 April, Consul O. M. Spencer wrote to Consul Sprague: 'There were landed 1701 barrels of alcohol. *The cargo came out in excellent condition.*' (Might it be that Mr Spencer was in fact acknowledging the safe receipt of the diamonds? *Author.*)

The *Celeste* was forced to remain in Genoa awaiting settlement, as a consequence of which, the charterers had to cancel her instructions to sail to Sicily for a cargo of fruit. She left Genoa on 26 June with a cargo for Boston, arriving there 1 September, and leaving 13 September, eventually reaching New York 19 September. Her subsequent career was an unhappy one. For the next thirteen years she went from owner to owner, seventeen in all, none succeeding in making her pay her way. Finally, her last owners deliberately wrecked the vessel on a reef off Haiti, in a vain attempt to make a false insurance claim. This escapade made her a total loss.

As for the *Dei Gratia*, she sank at her moorings in Cork Harbour, Ireland, in 1913. Her ribs and timbers were still showing as recently as 1947, but with the reclamation of land for an expansion of a dry dock, the vessel was finally buried out of sight.

Solly Flood never did succeed in returning permanently to London. He died in Gibraltar, on 13 May 1888, three months short of his 87th birthday.

★ ★ ★

Meanwhile, in Germany, at one o'clock on the afternoon of 13 July 1874 — seventeen months after the *Mary Celeste* Inquiry was closed — Count Bismarck was driving in an open carriage through the streets of Kissingen, when a man stepped out of the watching crowds, and fired a single pistol shot at the Chancellor from point-blank range. At that exact moment, Bismarck raised his

651

right hand to acknowledge the cheers of the people, thereby deflecting the fatal bullet.

Kullmann, the would-be assassin, was found to be a Roman Catholic. In defence of his action he claimed that Bismarck's Kulturkampf policy was threatening the very existence of his religion.

This gave Bismarck the ideal excuse to launch a furious attack on the Church of Rome. He returned to Berlin, to make a speech from the Reichstag, charging his enemies: 'You may try to disown the assassin, but nonetheless he clings to your coat-tails. Moreover, you will never be able to shake this murderer loose!'

He now increased his war on the Catholic Church. More bishops were thrown into prison, priests deprived of their parishes, until half the Catholic population in Germany had no spiritual leaders.

But his violent reaction created such a backlash of opinion he was forced to withdraw most of his anti-Catholic measures. Loath to admit defeat, he claimed he was giving up the struggle against 'Black International' (the Roman

Catholic Church) in order to concentrate on the rising threat of 'Red International' (the Socialist movement).

★ ★ ★

The citizens of Rome did not share the rest of the Catholic world's regard for Pope Pius IX (Pio Nono), who had kept them out of Italy for so long. When he died, on 7 February 1878, his tomb in San Lorenzo Fuore le Mure was not ready. When his body was finally moved there on its completion three years later, it was done at night for fear of demonstrations. But the people got to hear of it and turned out in their thousands, hurling bricks and stones at the coffin.

From then on, four succeeding popes — Leo XIII, Pius X, Benedict XV, and Pius XI — willed to remain as 'prisoners of the Vatican'. The latter, Pius XI — who, because of his Jesuit confessors, was rumoured to be a secret Jesuit — was appointed pope in 1922, the same year the Fascists marched on Rome. Seven years later, on 11 February 1929, the

Fascist leader, Benito Mussolini, signed the Lateran Agreement with a gold pen which Pius had just blessed.

This pact gave the Holy See complete sovereignty over a new Papal State, known as Vatican City, and a subvention of 750 million lire, plus the interest on 1,000 million lire of State Bonds, as a 'definite settlement of its financial relations with Italy in connection with the events of 1870'.

Pius called in the banker, Bernardino Nogara, an Italian Jew who had converted to Catholicism, to advise him. Nogara recommended that two-thirds of the lump sum settlement should be invested, with the remaining one-third ($30 million) converted into gold and deposited at Fort Knox, USA, where it still remains to this day, with a current value of over half a billion dollars.

★ ★ ★

Father-General Pierre Jean Beckx remained in Fiesole until 1883, when he finally retired because of ill-health. He was succeeded by Anthony M. Anderledy, a Swiss. Beckx returned to Rome, where he died in 1887. But the atmosphere in Rome remained so anti-Jesuit that the Society's temporary headquarters had to remain in Fiesole until 1895; and its General Congregation, three years earlier, in 1892, had to assemble at Loyola, Saint Ignatius' birthplace, in Spain.

★ ★ ★

The military fortress on the site of Castello Portofino was built by the Romans in about AD 400. It was added to by succeeding occupants, and extended considerably in the sixteenth century by a military engineer surnamed Olgiato. There were no roads to the promontory until 1876, four years after this story began — when one was built from Santa Margherita — so that even Napoleon, when he attacked it more than sixty years earlier, had to do so from the sea. The castle was demilitarized about 1867, some five to six years before the *Mary Celeste* affair, and remained unoccupied until after 1874 — the records disagree on the actual year of purchase — when it was bought as a private residence for £280 by Montague Yeats-Brown, the same British Consul who ordered Deveau to return to Gibraltar.

★ ★ ★

Louis Jennings, retired as editor of the *New York Times* in 1876. With his American wife, Madeline, daughter of David Henriques of New York, he returned to England, and became Conservative Member of Parliament for Stockport. He died at Elm Park Gardens, London, on 9 February 1893, aged fifty-six.

'Boss' Tweed was eventually brought to trial. He was found guilty of defrauding the City of New York. Sentenced to prison, he escaped to Europe, managed to reach Spain, but was caught and extradited. He died of pneumonia in Ludlow Street jail, New York, in April 1878, and was buried in white lambskin, 'the emblem of innocence'.

Mayor 'Elegant Oakey' Hall, having managed to stay in office to the end of his term, appeared in court four times, indicted on the same charges as Boss Tweed. He was finally acquitted on Christmas Eve 1873. He spent his remaining years as a newspaperman and attorney and, on 25 March 1898, was baptised into the Roman Catholic Church.

'Slippery Dick' Connolly remained abroad with a reputed $6 million. He spent his days wandering from one country to another, 'a lonely, melancholy man, shunned by everybody' (New York Times). He was tried and convicted in absentia, and he never returned to New York.

But Peter 'Brains' Sweeny did return, on 19 December 1876, having agreed to refund a mere $400,000 to the city in return for immunity from prosecution. The settlement was announced on 8 June 1877, and Sweeny made the payment from the estate of his late brother, James, leaving his own nest-egg untouched. The *New York Telegraph* stated that, by negotiating such a deal, Sweeny deserved to be called the Metternich, Talleyrand, and Pitt of New York. He resumed his worship at the Church of Saint Francis

Xavier, and it was Sweeny who, in 1898, proposed 'Elegant Oakey' into membership of the Roman Catholic Church. Sweeny died, a very wealthy man, at Lake Mahopac, New York, in 1911.

★ ★ ★

The records of the New York State Department of Justice (Organized Crime and Racketeering) confirm that Sicilian crime entered the USA, via New York, at about the same time Brains Sweeny returned home.

By the late 1880s it had spread into most major cities, but the word 'Mafia' did not appear until October 1890, when *The Times* of London used it in a report of a gangland war for control of the New Orleans waterfront, between the rival Sicilian families of Provenzano and Matranga. It was won by the Matranga family, with many corpses left on the streets of New Orleans, among them David Hennessey, a police chief who was probing energetically into the affair. That there was a connection between

658

the Mafia and New York's Tammany Hall, was claimed by Lieutenant Joe Petrosino, a tough New York cop and one of the Mafia's most bitter opponents. In one report — found in the Department of Justice archives — he states that once a *mafioso* arrived in the United States, he immediately joined a political gang, from which he received unlimited protection. 'Nothing we can do against so-and-so,' Petrosino was often heard to say, 'he's one of the Tammany Hall men'.

In 1909, Petrosino sailed to Palermo to check how many Sicilians were emigrating illegally. The Mafia were waiting for him, and on the instructions of Don Vito Cascioferro — Sicily's then *capomafia*, Petrosino was shot dead in the Piazza Marina, the very centre of Palermo.

However, the Mafia did not become a national threat until the 1920s. After considerable fighting with the Neapolitans, headed by Al Capone, the largest emergent family was the Castellamare, ruled by Don Salvatore Maranzano. Born in Castellamare del Golfo, Sicily, in 1868, he was college-educated, and also once studied at a seminary to become a priest. He arrived in New York in 1918. In 1931, he declared himself to be 'the boss of bosses', the supreme *Capo dei Capi*, ruling over an area stretching from New York, Buffalo, Boston and Chicago in the north; to Miami and New Orleans in the south; and Los Angeles and San Francisco in the west. He held his council meetings in a huge hall in the Bronx, festooned with religious pictures, and a crucifix over the platform. On 10 September 1931, on the orders of Salvatore 'Lucky' Luciano, four *mafiosi* — 'Bugsy' Seigel, Albert Anastasia, 'Red' Levine, and Thomas 'Three Finger Brown' Luccese — met Maranzano in his real-estate office on Park Avenue, and killed him with six knife wounds and four shots.

By the mid-1930s, the Mafia had become the largest, most powerful of the United States' syndicated crime networks. In most cities there was usually only one family in control. In New York there were five.

Investigations conducted by the various United States government agencies during the 1950s and 1960s, revealed the structure of the Mafia in the USA was very similar to its Sicilian prototype, and was now calling itself *Cosa Nostra*, meaning 'Our Affair'.

TO FIGHT THE WILD
Rod Ansell and Rachel Percy

Lost in uncharted Australian bush, Rod Ansell survived by hunting and trapping wild animals, improvising shelter and using all the bushman's skills he knew.

COROMANDEL
Pat Barr

India in the 1830s is a hot, uncomfortable place, where the East India Company still rules. Amelia and her new husband find themselves caught up in the animosities which seethe between the old order and the new.

THE SMALL PARTY
Lillian Beckwith

A frightening journey to safety begins for Ruth and her small party as their island is caught up in the dangers of armed insurrection.